Ten Thousand Light-Years From Home

James Tiptree Jr. was the pen name of Alice Bradley Sheldon, whose radical and pioneering science-fiction stories were matched by her extraordinary life. As a child, she travelled widely with her parents and featured in several African-set travel books written by her mother. After attending a finishing school in Switzerland, she embarked on an early career as an artist and art critic. During the Second World War she joined the US Army Air Forces, attaining the rank of major, and then worked for the CIA before moving to a chicken farm in Virginia with her husband. She turned to science-fiction writing as an escape from her PhD thesis on experimental psychology, and chose her pseudonym from a pot of jam. She later explained that: 'A male name seemed like good camouflage . . . I've had too many experiences in my life of being the first woman in some damned occupation'. Her true sex was kept secret for years. She died in 1987 in what appeared to be a murder-suicide pact with her husband.

Ten Thousand Light-Years From Home

JAMES TIPTREE JR.

PENGUIN BOOKS

PENGUIN CLASSICS

UK | USA | Canada | Ireland | Australia
India | New Zealand | South Africa

Penguin Classics is part of the Penguin Random House
group of companies whose addresses can be found at
global.penguinrandomhouse.com.

First published in the United States of America by Ace Books 1973
First published in Penguin Classics Science Fiction 2020
001

Copyright © James Tiptree Jr. 1973; Jeffrey D. Smith 2001, 2020

Set in 11/13 pt Dante MT Std
Typeset by Integra Software Services Pvt. Ltd, Pondicherry
Printed in Great Britain by Clays Ltd, Elcograf S.p.A.

A CIP catalogue record for this book is available
from the British Library

ISBN: 978-0-241-46923-1

www.greenpenguin.co.uk

Penguin Random House is committed to a
sustainable future for our business, our readers
and our planet. This book is made from Forest
Stewardship Council® certified paper.

Contents

And I Awoke and Found Me Here on the Cold Hill's Side

He was standing absolutely still by a service port, staring out at the belly of the Orion docking above us. He had on a gray uniform and his rusty hair was cut short. I took him for a station engineer.

That was bad for me. Newsmen strictly don't belong in the bowels of Big Junction. But in my first twenty hours I hadn't found any place to get a shot of an alien ship.

I turned my holocam to show its big World Media insigna and started my bit about What It Meant to the People Back Home who were paying for it all.

'– it may be routine work to you, sir, but we owe it to them to share –'

His face came around slow and tight, and his gaze passed over me from a peculiar distance.

'The wonders, the drama,' he repeated dispassionately. His eyes focused on me. 'You consummated fool.'

'Could you tell me what races are coming in, sir? If I could even get a view –'

He waved me to the port. Greedily I angled my lenses up at the long blue hull blocking out the starfield. Beyond her I could see the bulge of a black and gold ship.

'That's a Foramen,' he said. 'There's a freighter from Belye on the other side, you'd call it Arcturus. Not much traffic right now.'

'You're the first person who's said two sentences to me since I've been here, sir. What are those colorful little craft?'

'Procya,' he shrugged. 'They're always around. Like us.'

I squashed my face on the vitrite, peering. The walls clanked. Somewhere overhead aliens were off-loading into their private sector of Big Junction. The man glanced at his wrist.

'Are you waiting to go out, sir?'

His grunt could have meant anything.

'Where are you from on Earth?' he asked me in his hard tone.

I started to tell him and suddenly saw that he had forgotten my existence. His eyes were on nowhere, and his head was slowly bowing forward onto the port frame.

'Go home,' he said thickly. I caught a strong smell of tallow.

'Hey, sir!' I grabbed his arm; he was in rigid tremor. 'Steady, man.'

'I'm waiting . . . waiting for my wife. My loving wife.' He gave a short ugly laugh. 'Where are you from?'

I told him again.

'Go home,' he mumbled. 'Go home and make babies. While you still can.'

One of the early GR casualties, I thought.

'Is that all you know?' His voice rose stridently. 'Fools. Dressing in their styles. Gnivo suits, Aoleelee music. Oh, I see your newscasts,' he sneered. 'Nixi parties. A year's salary for a floater. Gamma radiation? Go home, read history. *Ballpoint pens and bicycles –*'

He started a slow slide downward in the half gee. My only informant. We struggled confusedly; he wouldn't take one of my sobertabs but I finally got him along the service corridor to a bench in an empty loading bay. He fumbled out a little vacuum cartridge. As I was helping him unscrew it, a figure in starched whites put his head in the bay.

'I can be of assistance, yes?' His eyes popped, his face was covered with brindled fur. An alien, a Procya! I started to thank him but the red-haired man cut me off.

'Get lost. Out.'

The creature withdrew, its big eyes moist. The man stuck his pinky in the cartridge and then put it up his nose, gasping deep in his diaphragm. He looked toward his wrist.

'What time is it?'

I told him.

'News,' he said. 'A message for the eager, hopeful human race. A word about those lovely, lovable aliens we all love so much.' He looked at me. 'Shocked, aren't you, newsboy?'

I had him figured now. A xenophobe. Aliens plot to take over Earth.

'Ah Christ, they couldn't care less.' He took another deep gasp, shuddered and straightened. 'The hell with generalities. What time d'you say it was? All right, I'll tell you how I learned it. The hard way. While we wait for my loving wife. You can bring that little recorder out of your sleeve, too. Play it over to yourself some time . . . when it's too late.' He chuckled. His tone had become chatty – an educated voice. 'You ever hear of supernormal stimuli?'

3

'No,' I said. 'Wait a minute. White sugar?'

'Near enough. Y'know Little Junction Bar in DC? No, you're an Aussie, you said. Well, I'm from Burned Barn, Nebraska.'

He took a breath, consulting some vast disarray of the soul.

'I accidentally drifted into Little Junction Bar when I was eighteen. No. Correct that. You don't go into Little Junction by accident, any more than you first shoot skag by accident.

'You go into Little Junction because you've been craving it, dreaming about it, feeding on every hint and clue about it, back there in Burned Barn, since before you had hair in your pants. Whether you know it or not. Once you're out of Burned Barn, you can no more help going into Little Junction than a sea-worm can help rising to the moon.

'I had a brand-new liquor ID in my pocket. It was early; there was an empty spot beside some humans at the bar. Little Junction isn't an embassy bar, y'know. I found out later where the high-caste aliens go – when they go out. The New Rive, the Curtain by the Georgetown Marina.

'And they go by themselves. Oh, once in a while they do the cultural exchange bit with a few frosty couples of other aliens and some stuffed humans. Galactic Amity with a ten-foot pole.

'Little Junction was the place where the lower orders went, the clerks and drivers out for kicks. Including, my friend, the perverts. The ones who can take humans. Into their beds, that is.'

4

He chuckled and sniffed his finger again, not looking at me.

'Ah, yes. Little Junction is Galactic Amity night, every night. I ordered . . . what? A margharita. I didn't have the nerve to ask the snotty spade bartender for one of the alien liquors behind the bar. It was dim. I was trying to stare everywhere at once without showing it. I remember those white boneheads – Lyrans, that is. And a mess of green veiling I decided was a multiple being from some place. I caught a couple of human glances in the bar mirror. Hostile flicks. I didn't get the message, then.

'Suddenly an alien pushed right in beside me. Before I could get over my paralysis, I heard this blurry voice:

'"You air a futeball enthusiash?"'

'An alien had spoken to me. An *alien*, a being from the stars. Had spoken. To me.'

'Oh, god, I had no time for football, but I would have claimed a passion for paper-folding, for dumb crambo – anything to keep him talking. I asked him about his home-planet sports, I insisted on buying his drinks. I listened raptly while he spluttered out a play-by-play account of a game I wouldn't have turned a dial for. The "Grain Bay Pashkers". Yeah. And I was dimly aware of trouble among the humans on my other side.

'Suddenly this woman – I'd call her a girl now – this girl said something in a high nasty voice and swung her stool into the arm I was holding my drink with. We both turned around together.

'Christ, I can see her now. The first thing that hit me was *discrepancy*. She was a nothing – but terrific. Transfigured. Oozing it, radiating it.

'The next thing was I had a horrifying hard-on just looking at her.

'I scrooched over so my tunic hid it, and my spilled drink trickled down, making everything worse. She pawed vaguely at the spill, muttering.

'I just stared at her trying to figure out what had hit me. An ordinary figure, a soft avidness in the face. Eyes heavy, satiated-looking. She was totally sexualized. I remembered her throat pulsed. She had one hand up touching her scarf, which had slipped off her shoulder. I saw angry bruises there. That really tore it. I understood at once those bruises had some sexual meaning.

'She was looking past my head with her face like a radar dish. Then she made an "ahhhhh" sound that had nothing to do with me and grabbed my forearm as if it were a railing. One of the men behind her laughed. The woman said, "Excuse me", in a ridiculous voice and slipped out behind me. I wheeled around after her, nearly upsetting my football friend, and saw that some Sirians had come in.

'That was my first look at Sirians in the flesh, if that's the word. God knows I'd memorized every news shot, but I wasn't prepared. That tallness, that cruel thinness. That appalling alien arrogance. Ivory-blue, these were. Two males in immaculate metallic gear. Then I saw there was a female with them. An ivory-indigo exquisite with a permanent faint smile on those bone-hard lips.

'The girl who'd left me was ushering them to a table. She reminded me of a goddamn dog that wants you to follow it. Just as the crowd hid them, I saw a man join them too. A big man, expensively dressed, with something wrecked about his face.

'Then the music started and I had to apologize to my furry friend. And the Sellice dancer came out and my personal introduction to hell began.'

The red-haired man fell silent for a minute enduring self-pity. Something wrecked about the face, I thought; it fit.

He pulled his face together.

'First I'll give you the only coherent observation of my entire evening. You can see it here at Big Junction, always the same. Outside of the Procya, it's humans with aliens, right? Very seldom aliens with other aliens. Never aliens with humans. It's the humans who want in.'

I nodded, but he wasn't talking to me. His voice had a druggy influence.

'Ah, yes, my Sellice. My first Sellice.'

'They aren't really well-built, y'know, under those cloaks. No waist to speak of and short-legged. But they flow when they walk.

'This one flowed out into the spotlight, cloaked to the ground in violet silk. You could only see a fall of black hair and tassels over a narrow face like a vole. She was a mole-gray. They come in all colours. Their fur is like a flexible velvet all over; only the color changes startlingly around their eyes and lips and other places. Erogenous zones? Ah, man, with them it's not zones.

'She began to do what we'd call a dance, but it's no dance, it's their natural movement. Like smiling, say, with us. The music built up, and her arms undulated toward me, letting the cloak fall apart little by little. She was

7

naked under it. The spotlight started to pick up her body markings moving in the slit of the cloak. Her arms floated apart and I saw more and more.

'She was fantastically marked and the markings were writhing. Not like body paint – alive. Smiling, that's a good word for it. As if her whole body was smiling sexually, beckoning, winking, urging, pouting, speaking to me. You've seen a classic Egyptian belly dance? Forget it – a sorry stiff thing compared to what any Sellice can do. This one was ripe, near term.

'Her arms went up and those blazing lemon-colored curves pulsed, waved, everted, contracted, throbbed, evolved unbelievably welcoming, inciting permutations. *Come do it to me, do it, do it here and here and here and now.* You couldn't see the rest of her, only a wicked flash of mouth. Every human male in the room was aching to ram himself into that incredible body. I mean it was *pain*. Even the other aliens were quiet, except one of the Sirians who was chewing out a waiter.

'I was a basket case before she was halfway through . . . I won't bore you with what happened next; before it was over there were several fights and I got out. My money ran out on the third night. She was gone next day.

'I didn't have time to find out about the Sellice cycle then, mercifully. That came after I went back to campus and discovered you had to have a degree in solid-state electronics to apply for off-planet work. I was a pre-med but I got that degree. It only took me as far as First Junction then.

'Oh, god, First Junction. I thought I was in heaven – the alien ships coming in and our freighters going out.

I saw them all, all but the real exotics, the tankies. You only see a few of those a cycle, even here. And the Yyeire. You've never seen that.

'Go home, boy. Go home to your version of Burned Barn . . .

'The first Yyeir I saw, I dropped everything and started walking after it like a starving hound, just breathing. You've seen the pix of course. Like lost dreams. *Man is in love and loves what vanishes* . . . It's the scent, you can't guess that. I followed until I ran into a slammed part. I spent a cycle's credits sending the creature the wine they call stars' tears . . . Later I found out it was a male. That made no difference at all.

'You can't have sex with them, y'know. No way. They breed by light or something, no one knows exactly. There's a story about a man who got hold of a Yyeir woman and tried. They had him skinned. Stories –'

He was starting to wander.

'What about that girl in the bar, did you see her again?'

He came back from somewhere.

'Oh, yes. I saw her. She'd been making it with the two Sirians, y'know. The males do it in pairs. Said to be the total sexual thing for a woman, if she can stand the damage from those beaks. I wouldn't know. She talked to me a couple of times after they finished with her. No use for men whatever. She drove off the P Street bridge . . . The man, poor bastard, he was trying to keep that Sirian bitch happy single-handed. Money helps, for a while. I don't know where he ended.'

He glanced at his wrist watch again. I saw the pale bare place where a watch had been and told him the time.

'Is that the message you want to give Earth? Never love an alien?'

'Never love an alien –' He shrugged. 'Yeah. No. Ah, Jesus don't you see? Everything going out, nothing coming back. Like the poor damned Polynesians. We're gutting Earth, to begin with. Swapping raw resources for junk. Alien status symbols. Tape decks, Coca-Cola and Mickey Mouse watches.'

'Well, there is concern over the balance of trade. Is that your message?'

'The balance of trade.' He rolled it sardonically. 'Did the Polynesians have a word for it, I wonder? You don't see, do you? All right, why are you here? I mean *you*, personally. How many guys did you climb over –'

He went rigid, hearing footsteps outside. The Procya's hopeful face appeared around the corner. The red-haired man snarled at him and he backed out. I started to protest.

'Ah, the silly reamer loves it. It's the only pleasure we have left . . . Can't you see, man? That's *us*. That's the way we look to them, to the real ones.'

'But –'

'And now we're getting the cheap C-drive, we'll be all over just like the Procya. For the pleasure of serving as freight monkeys and junction crews. Oh, they appreciate our ingenious little service stations, the beautiful star folk. They don't *need* them, y'know. Just an amusing convenience. D'you know what I do here with my two degrees? What I did at First Junction. Tube cleaning. A swab. Sometimes I get to replace a fitting.'

I muttered something; the self-pity was getting heavy.

'Bitter? Man, it's a *good* job. Sometimes I get to talk to one of them.' His face twisted. 'My wife works as a – oh, hell, you wouldn't know. I'd trade – correction, I have traded – everything Earth offered me for just that chance. To see them. To speak to them. Once in a while to touch one. Once in a great while to find one low enough, perverted enough to want to touch me –'

His voice trailed off and suddenly came back strong.

'And so will you!' He glared at me. 'Go home! Go home and tell them to quit it. Close the ports. Burn every god-lost alien thing before it's too late! That's what the Polynesians didn't do.'

'But surely –'

'But surely be damned! Balance of trade – balance of *life*, man. I don't know if our birth rate is going, that's not the point. Our soul is leaking out. We're bleeding to death!'

He took a breath and lowered his tone.

'What I'm trying to tell you, this is a trap. We've hit the supernormal stimulus. Man is exogamous – all our history is one long drive to find and impregnate the stranger. Or get impregnated by him; it works for women too. Anything different-colored, different nose, ass, anything, man *has* to fuck it or die trying. That's a drive, y'know, it's built in. Because it works fine as long as the stranger is human. For millions of years that kept the genes circulating. But now we've met aliens we can't screw, and we're about to die trying . . . Do you think I can touch my wife?'

'But –'

'Look. Y'know, if you give a bird a fake egg like its own but bigger and brighter-marked, it'll roll its own egg out of the nest and sit on the fake? That's what we're doing.'

'You have a heavy angle on sex.' I was trying to conceal my impatience. 'Which is great, but the kind of story I'd hoped –'

'Sex? No, it's deeper.' He rubbed his head, trying to clear the drug. 'Sex is only part of it – there's more. I've seen Earth missionaries, teachers, sexless people. Teachers, they end cycling waste or pushing floaters, but they're hooked. They stay. I saw one fine-looking old woman, she was servant to a Cu'ushbar kid. A defective – his own people would have let him die. That wretch was swabbing up its vomit as if it was holy water. Man, it's deep . . . some cargo-cult of the soul. We're built to dream outwards. They laugh at us. They don't have it.'

There were sounds of movement in the next corridor. The dinner crowd was starting. I had to get rid of him and get there; maybe I could find the Procya. A side door opened and a figure started towards us. At first I thought it was an alien and then I saw it was a woman wearing an awkward body-shell. She seemed to be limping slightly. Behind her I could glimpse the dinner-bound throng passing the open door.

The man got up as she turned into the bay. They didn't greet each other.

'The station employs only happily wedded couples,' he told me with that ugly laugh. 'We give each other . . . comfort.'

He took one of her hands. She flinched as he drew it over his arm and let him turn her passively, not looking at me. 'Forgive me if I don't introduce you. My wife appears fatigued.'

I saw that one of her shoulders was grotesquely scarred.

'Tell them,' he said, turning to go. 'Go home and tell them.' Then his head snapped back toward me and he added quietly, 'And stay away from the Syrtis desk or I'll kill you.'

They went away up the corridor.

I changed tapes hurriedly with one eye on the figures passing that open door. Suddenly among the humans I caught a glimpse of two sleek scarlet shapes. My first real aliens! I snapped the recorder shut and ran to squeeze in behind them.

The Snows Are Melted,
the Snows Are Gone

The cold silent land was lightening as the human figure walked up to the ridge. On pale rock the figure was a dark fork, too thin. Serpent-shouldered. It sank into a patch of scrub below the crest, turned a small face up to the sky, crouched again.

A shadow flitted, circling the ridge. A large dog; no, a very large wolf. The animal drifted onto the rocks above the human, froze. The stiff line of its brush showed an old break. The dawn was coming fast now, but to the west the valley was still dark. Faint howling rose from the valley, then ceased.

The dog-wolf faded off the ridge, reappeared by the bushes where the human crouched. The figure bowed its head; as the wolf came near. Dawn light flickered on his canines. He snapped sideways, carrying away a dark cap.

A flood of light hair spilled out, flew as the human tossed it back. The wolf dropped the cap, sat down and began to worry at something on its chest.

Daylight sprang up the sky. In the niche below the rocks the figure was now clearly visible, a young girl in rough jacket and breeches, shaking out her hair. The shoulders of her jacket ended in pads. It had no arms. Nor had she, none at all. A phocomorph. She settled herself beside the wolf, who showed now as bulge-headed with oddly curling fur.

He had drawn out a small object which lay between them on the rock. They were face to face, dawn glinting yellow from his eyes, blue in the girl's. His paw went to the object, clicked.

'Patrol to base,' the girl said softly.

Tiny squeak of reply.

'We're at the ridge. The river's about five kilometers west. There's a trail below us, it hasn't been used since the rains. We heard the dogs. We'll wait here till dark, after that we'll be in radio shadow. We'll signal when we're out, maybe night after next.'

Louder squeaking, a woman's voice. Wolf jaws widened, girl lips grinned.

'We always take care. Patrol out.'

The wolf clicked off and then bent and delicately gripped her boot tip in his teeth. The armless girl pulled her foot free, flexed her slim prehensile toes in the cold light. When the other boot came off she used her toes to unhitch the pack harness from his dense fur. He stretched hugely, flung himself down and rolled, revealing a rich cream underbelly.

The girl toed out a food pack and canteen. He got up and carried it to a spring beside the outcrop, pawing it under to fill. They ate and drank, the girl lying on her back and dangling the canteen over her face by its strap. Once she let out a gurgle of laughter. His paw struck her head, pushed her face into her knees. They finished eating, went to relieve themselves. It was broad daylight now, the sun sailing straight up from the eastern hills, as if on a wire. A wind rose with it, keening over the rocky rim.

The wolf belly-crawled to the crest, watched awhile, returned to the girl. They pulled brush around themselves and curled together on the laterite shelf.

The sun mounted, struck through the wind's chill. No bird flew, no furred animal appeared. In the brush tangle, silence. Once a mantis-like thing rattled near the lair. A yellow eye opened at ground level. The thing whirred away, the eye closed.

During the afternoon the wind carried a thin cawing sound to the outcrop. In the brush yellow eyes were joined by blue. The murmur faded, the eyes disappeared again. Nothing more happened. The equatorial sun dropped straight down the west into the valley, quieting the wind.

As shadow flowed over the outcrop the brush was pulled aside. Girl and wolf came out together to the stream and lapped, she bending like a snake. They ate again, and the girl toed the pack together, fastened it to the wolf's harness. He nosed the transmitter into its pouch in his chest wool and picked up a boot for her to thrust her foot in. When she was shod he hooked a fang into the dark cap. She let her pale hair coil into it and he pulled it over her head, adjusting it carefully away from her eyes. It was dark now, a quarter-moon behind them in the east. She twisted to her feet, a human spring, and they set off down the escarpment into the valley.

Arid scrubland eroded by old floods became forest as they descended. The pair moved watchfully in single file, following a vague trail down. When the moon had passed zenith they halted to carry out laborious rear-rangements of brush and stones. Then they went on down through the trees, halted again to labor. Trails branched here; when they moved on it was with greater care. Faint odors were in this air.

The moon was setting ahead of them when they reached the ruined river gorge. Beyond the rocks a broad sheet of silver muttered in the night. They crossed at a riffle, climbed a rock ledge, moved quietly downstream. The scent was a stench now – smoke, fish, bodies, excrement, coming from a bend around the crags. A dog's howl rose, was joined by another, cut off in yelps.

Girl and wolf came on the crags. Below them were three ragged thatches huddled in a cove. Smoke rose from a single ash pile. The huts were in shadow. A last moonray silvered a pile of offal by the shore.

The two on the crag watched silently. It was warmer here, but no insect flew. In the huts below a child whimpered, was silenced. Nothing visited the offal pile. The moon set, the river turned dark. A fish splashed.

The wolf rose, drifted away. The girl listened to the river. He returned and she followed him upriver to a high cranny in the ledges out of sight of the cove. In the river below the water gurgled around a line of crazy stakes. The two ate and drank in silence. When the world lightened they were curled together in sleep.

Sunlight struck their wall, shadows shrank to the east. From the cove came the shrilling of children, deeper voices. A clatter, a cry. In the high cranny, sunlight reflected yellow glints behind dry weeds. The wind was rising, blowing toward the sun across the river. Between the gusts came snarls, chirrupings, undecipherable shouts, the crackle of fire. The eyes waited.

In midmorning two naked women came around the bend below, dragging something along the shore. Seven more straggled after, paused to gesture and jabber. Their skin was angry red, pale at crotch and armpits. White scars stood out, symmetrical chevrons on the bulging bellies. All had thick, conelike nipples; two of them appeared close to term. Their hair was matted, rusty-streaked.

Above on the crags, blue eyes had joined yellow. The women were wading into the river now, their burden revealed as a crude net which they proceeded to string between the stakes. They shrieked at each other, 'Weh weh! Ee, ah!' A small flock of children was drifting around the bend. Several of the larger children carried babies. 'Eee! Gah!' they echoed, high-voiced. A stake collapsed, was retrieved with shrieks, would not stand, was abandoned.

Presently larger figures appeared on the shore path. The men. Six of them, naked and ruddy like the women but much more scarred. None was beyond first youth. The smallest was dark, all the others had carroty hair and beards. Behind them trailed three dogs, tail-tucked, ready to flee.

The men shouted imperiously and walked on upriver. The women came out of the water and trotted after them. At the next bend the whole party waded in and commenced to splash and flail, driving the fish down to the nets. A baby screamed. The pair on the rocks watched intent.

One of the men noticed the dogs skulking by the net and hurled a stone. They raced away, turned, crept back.

This man was the largest of the group, active and well-formed. As the splashing people neared the nets the big man looked ahead, saw the gap in the nets and ran along on the shore to pull it taut. On the cliff above, wolf eyes met human. Wolf teeth made a tiny click.

The fish were foaming in the nets now. The humans closed upon them, hauling at the nets, fish sluicing and leaping through, dogs splashing in to snap. Shouts, screams, floundering bodies. They dragged the squirming mass ashore, dropped it to grab at escaping fish. The young giant stood erect, grinning, biting alternately at a fish in each hand. At his feet children scrambled in the threshing nets. He gave a loud wordless shout, threw the fish high.

Finally the women dragged the catch away along the shore path to the huts and the river was empty again. Girl and wolf stretched, lay down unrelaxed. Smoke blew around the bend. It was hot in the rocks now, out of the wind. Below on the sand fish-parts glittered but no flies appeared. From the cove, silence; interrupted briefly by a child's wail. The sun was dropping toward the valley rim, shadows spreading on the river below. The wind followed the sun away.

Presently dusk filled the canyon and the sky turned lilac behind a half-moon. A column of smoke was rising from the cove. In the stillness voices pealed singly, became a rhythmic chorus underlaid with pounding. This continued for a time, interspersed with shouts, bursts of shrieking. The smoke column wavered, gouted sparks. More shrieks, general clamor. The uproar died to grumbles, then to silence. The rocks ticked in the night chill.

The wolf left the cranny. The girl sighed, remained. Around the bend a dog began to howl, squealed and was still. The girl toed intricate patterns in a patch of sand. The wolf returned wet-legged, and they ate and drank. While the moon set they slept.

Before dawn they had left that place and circled back across the river to the side on which they had entered the valley. The canyon wall was eroded to a tumble here. The two went slowly several times between shore and rocks as the sky paled. Finally they sat down to wait at the water's edge behind a screen of alders. Across the river were the huts.

When light struck into the canyon the girl rose and faced the wolf. Her jacket wrapped her waist, ended in a wide loop. He caught one tooth in the loop, flicked it free and had the jacket open. Beneath the jacket she was bare. She stood patiently while he nosed the jacket back across her shoulders like a cape. Her shoulders were smooth scarless knobs above her small breasts. The cold air puckered her pink nipples, stirred the little beards of silk in what should have been her armpits.

The wolf was laying the folds of jacket so that they mimicked arms. Satisfied, he jerked his big head and then began to tug at the flexible waistband of her breeches, drawing them down deftly to expose her body and upper thighs. As he worked she began to smile, moved. He growled faintly. The wind blew on her bareness. She leaned against his warm fur. They waited.

Sounds were coming from the thatches across the river. Figures appeared, ambling down to the shore to stand or squat. Girl and wolf watched an alder grove across the river to one side of the huts. Presently the foliage was agitated. A man was coming through. Wolf-head nodded; it was the big one. The man appeared moving familiarly along a sand spit, and stood to urinate.

Carefully the wolf drew back a low branch. The girl took an awkward pace forward, putting her naked body in full sunlight. The man's head swung, fixed on her. His body tensed. She gave a low call, swaying herself.

Muscles surged in the man's legs, his feet spurned sand. Instantly the branch thrashed back around her and the wolf was yanking up her breeches, tugging her jacket around. Then they were running, pelting through the alders, racing out of the river bottom on the line toward their trail.

Splashing behind them turned upstream. The wolf had chosen well, there was a deep basin which the man must get around to reach their shore. They bounded up the bluff, the girl agile as a hare. When they were out of the canyon the wolf veered into the trees.

The man came over the bluff to see the girl running alone up the tunnel-like path far ahead. He plunged after her, strong legs eating space. But she was at the electric age for running, child-thin and trained hard. When he slowed after his first burst she was going tirelessly, a peculiar weaving motion of her torso making up the balance for missing arms. As she ran her eyes roamed in search of the slashes they had left upon the trees beside the trail.

Suddenly there were new voices behind her – the dogs had joined the chase. The girl frowned, speeded up. A big gray shadow swerved alongside, stopped with lifted leg beside a tree, then another. The girl smiled, let her pace slow.

Shortly she heard the dogs' voices change when they came to the wolf-sign. Shouts from the man, yelps. No more sound of dogs.

She ran on. It was trot and trot now uphill, with the sun towering to noon. She was panting hard when she came to the first of the places they had arranged. She leaped aside, glimpsing a gray form among the trees, and jogged on up the rising ground.

Behind her came a sharp yell and then the grunts and flounder of the bogged man. She leaned against a dead termitary. The trees were thinning here, the wind blew through to carry her tiredness away.

The wolf appeared, jerked his head irritably. She turned and trotted on into the wind. Over the treetops she could see the blue line of rimrock far ahead. Trot and trot. The man held her in view now and he was gaining.

Finally she swerved again and heard behind her the crack of breaking branches and the angry shout. When she paused the wolf was by her. They listened together to the wind. She resumed of her own accord, knowing now that she could not outrun him. The wolf remained, watchful.

The sun was yellowing into the horizon's dust when she topped the final ridge and turned to look. This was the limit of the wild-men's trails; would he follow beyond? She could hear nothing. The wolf appeared, motioning her to a sunlit ledge. He butted her into position with his nose and pulled her jacket apart. She sang out a sweet trill, ending in laughter.

As the echo died the wolf pushed her running down the rocks past their old camping place. In a moment he joined her, grinning toothily, and then vanished to one side while she jogged on alone across the unrolling shadows. When she glanced behind a ruddy figure was bobbing down the rocks. No dogs were with him.

Shadows pooled underfoot, became twilight around her as they ran. Twilight turned to moonlight; the wolf ranged ahead of her, his crooked tail held high, and she followed its flag across the plain. This was old goat land, knobbed with clumps of thorn trees whose young were springing up everywhere now that the goats were gone.

Presently the wolf let her slow to walking, pausing now and again to listen for the footfalls behind. No other sound was here.

At last they halted. He drifted back silent as fog, to return briskly and lead her to a thorn clump. Here she freed her feet and drank and ate greedily and drank again while he inspected and licked her feet. But he would not let her unharness him, nor release her hair, and he made her put her boots on before he got out the transmitter.

'We've got one. He's very strong. Is Bonz all right?'

Questions rattled at them. The wolf cut off and pushed the girl's body earthward into the dry thorn chaff. Then he removed himself from her warm odors and leaped up an ant castle to lie facing back the way they had come. His head, sunk onto his crossed paws, showed a fine tremor. One yellow eye was open under the heavy brow. After a time his withers jerked, were still.

The sounds forced from his throat reached her in the night but her sleep was deep. She found him spasming at the base of the ant castle, the great jaws throwing slaver in the moonlight. She flung herself onto the writhing neck, clamping her thighs along his head to force her knees between his teeth. He bucked, screamed. The fangs clashed, caught in the ridge of padding fitted inside both her knees. She held his mouth open as they rolled, a dark stain spreading on her leg. He had already slashed his tongue, she could not see how badly.

When the synchrony passed she released him, crouched murmuring over his head. His tongue ceased bleeding. Slowly his nictitating membranes retracted and the moonlight lit green ghostfire in his open eyes. He lifted his head. She nuzzled him, then pushed. He sighed and put his nose to his chest fur. A vial was harnessed there. He worried out a bolus, gulped. Then he got up, walked stiffly away. There was water nearby. When he returned she was asleep; he left her and leaped heavily up to his post.

Dawn showed them to be on an amba, a high tableland backed by a turreted line of cliffs. These cliffs were their goal, but there was the empty plain to cross. The girl was well out upon it, trotting alone, when the man's figure appeared around an outcrop. He wavered, ready to turn back. But then the sight of his prey gripped him and he was racing hard on her trail.

She speeded up and held the space between them almost constant for a kilometer before he began to gain. She forced her legs. It was wind against wind now across the barren amba. The amba was sliced with deep gullies.

As her speed failed she was able to take advantage of the remembered course, doubling to lure him into hidden ravines. At two of the deepest cuts she found the wolf waiting for her and crossed by springing to his back where her pursuer would have to clamber up and down.

But for all she could do the man gained steadily. Between gusts of wind she heard the slap and pound of his hard feet. She was gasping when she reached the tumbled hummocks at the foot of the crags. He was close, closer. She leaped desperately up the rocks, remembering the stone that had been flung at the dog. How far could that powerful strange limb propel a missile? She could only dodge upward with searing lungs, all her hopes focused on the tunnel.

That was the crucial part. If he should know these cliffs!

But he was coming straight up after her, not stopping to throw, closing fast. Gravel rattled. She could hear his grunts above her own breathing. He was only paces behind now.

Suddenly shadow was ahead – the old culvert mouth. A rope loop hung inside. She flung her weight into it, spun dizzily for an instant. Then everything gave and she struck ground in a rain of dirt. At her heels, the rockslide cascaded into the culvert, walled him out.

She panted for a time in the choking darkness and then started up the culvert's floor. It was steep; she scrabbled, sprawled, pushing herself up on her shoulder pads. This was an old skill; as an infant she had rubbed her shoulders raw. Presently there was gray light above. The wolf's head was waiting for her at the top.

She emerged onto the old road bed and they went together to look over the brink of the cliff. It was blowing hard here. She leaned against him as they peered down.

Far below, a red figure worked at the rocks before the culvert. The cliff between them hung sheer, he could not get up this way. The girl sighed, grinned, still breathing hard. She nosed the wolf's back, found the canteen mouth and sucked. He whined softly, open-mouthed.

They went again through the ritual of exposing her body. As he dragged down her breeches she giggled. He growled and nipped at her belly. Then he reared up and pulled off the cap to let the blonde silk flow free.

She advanced to the cliff edge, called into the wind. A red face turned up to her. Its mouth opened. She motioned with her head, stepped to her left. In that direction the roadway had been breached by a rockslide, leaving a moraine he could climb.

He left off staring and mouthing and began to circle toward the moraine, stopping often to look up. She paced along above him until rocks came between.

Then the wolf dressed her peremptorily and sent her staggering down the road in the other direction, away from the man. She took up a steady jog, going northwest now with the sun and the wind in her face. Soon the old highway left the cliffs and cut inward between wind-sliced turrets. There were higher crests beyond these to her right, the hills that had once been called Harar. Then she was past the outcrops. The road stretched straight across another mesa top. There were ruins here, adobe shells, ditches, littered yards under occasional huge eucalyptus trees. Metal fragments lay on the roadside. A rusted gas pump stood like a man as she jogged by. Dust blew. She was beginning to limp.

Now and then the wolf ranged alongside her, then slipped aside to watch her pursuer pass. The man was on the straight behind her now, coming on doggedly, veering from the strange shapes by the road. Pursuer and pursued slowed to walking as the light began to change. The distance between them shrank steadily, faster.

The girl was hobbling when she reached a ravine where the road lay in wreckage. A little time gained here, but not much. She was spent. Beyond the wrecked bridge she limped between walls. The road curved around a dead village, ran into an old square. Here the girl turned aside and fell to her knees. Behind her the man was already leaping through the fallen bridge. It was sunset. The wolf appeared, grunting urgently. She shook her head, panted. He snarled and began to yank at her clothing, shouldering her up.

When the man came into the square she was standing alone, her body brilliant in the level light. He stopped, eyes rolling white at the alien walls. Then he took a step toward her and was suddenly in charging onrush. She stood quiet. He leaped, arms grappling her, and she went down under him into the hard dirt.

As they fell together a jet of gas came from between her lips into his face. He convulsed, crushed her. The wolf was on them, dragging the flailing giant off by the arm while the girl coughed and gagged. When the man had flopped to inertness the wolf pounced over her and nosed her head.

Her gagging changed timbre, she wrapped both legs

27

around the wolf and tried to roll him. He roughed her face with his tongue, planted his paw in her navel and pulled free. When she quieted he was holding the transmitter in front of her face. A snoring noise was coming from the man on the ground.

They looked together at the big body. He was nearly twice the wolf's weight.

'If we tie him to you and drag him he'll get all torn,' the girl said. 'Do you think you can drive him?'

The wolf laid the transmitter down and grunted non-committally, frowning at the man.

'We're only at that place west of Goba,' the girl told the transmitter. 'I'm sorry. He's much stronger than we thought. You – wait!'

The wolf was in the road, standing tense. She listened too, heard nothing . . . then a shiver in the ground, a tiny rumble. The transmitter began to squawk.

'It's all right!' the girl told it. 'Bonz is here!'

'What do you mean, Bonz is here?' demanded the distant voice.

'We can hear him coming. He must have got through the break.'

'Damn idiots,' said the voice. 'You're all wasting energy. Base out.'

Girl and wolf squatted together in the dusk beside the snoring man. She prodded at him briefly with her booted foot. Her teeth began to chatter.

The throbbing turned into a clashing roar and a fan of light swung around the far end of the square. Behind the light was the dark nub of a small tractor cab. It was towing a flat wagon.

The girl stood up, swung her hair.

'Bonz! Bonz, we've got one!'

The tractor rattled up beside them and a pale head leaned out. The dashlight showed a boy's face, a bony knife-edged version of the girl's.

'Where is he?'

'Here. Look how big he is!'

The tractor's light swung, flooded the supine man.

'You'll have to get him on the wagon,' the boy said. His eyes were hollow with fatigue. He made no move to leave the cab.

The wolf was at the side wall of the wagon, pulling a latch. The wall clanged down to form a ramp to the low cart bed. Girl and wolf began to roll the red body sideways toward the ramp.

'Wait,' the boy said suddenly. 'Don't hurt him. What have you done to him?'

'He's all right,' the girl told him. The man's shoulders were lolling against her knees, his upper arm slashed red where the wolf had gripped him.

'Wait, let me look,' said the boy. He still did not get out but sat staring, licking his thin lips.

'Our savior.' His voice was harsh and high. 'There's your damned Y-chromosome. He's filthy.'

He pulled his head back and they tumbled the unconscious man up onto the cart. There were hasps and straps on the floor. The girl's boots were got off and she fastened him down, her bruised toes clumsy. As they got him secure he began to groan. The girl pulled back her lips to reveal the syringe fastened between teeth and cheek and carefully jetted more vapor on his face.

The boy watched them through his rear window, twisted in his seat. He was drinking from a canteen. On the wagon the girl unhitched her companion's harness pack and they ate and drank too. They grinned at the boy. He did not grin back. His eyes were on the great red-gold man.

The girl toed him idly, jostling his thick limbs, his genitals.

'Don't do that!' the boy called sharply. The air was cold.

'Do you think he needs a blanket?' asked the girl.

'No! Yes,' he said exhaustedly.

When the wolf reared up beside the cab door the boy was bent over, hauling blankets from behind his seat. The cab's interior was cluttered with tubing and levers. On the floor, where the boy's feet should have been, was an apparatus from which tubes led upward. When he straightened up it could be seen that he had no legs. His torso was strapped to the seat and ended in a cocoon of canvas into which tubing led. His face was wet-streaked.

'We can all go die, now,' he pushed the blankets out the window, ramming with sinewy arms. Wetness ran down his thin jaw, fell on the blanket. The girl peered around the side, said nothing. The wolf grabbed a double fold of blanket and slung the rest back over his shoulder as he dropped to all fours. The boy hung his arms around the steering wheel and let his head go down.

Girl and wolf covered the man on the cart and fastened up its side. He draped a blanket on her, leaped to the ground. The boy's head came up. He started the tractor and they lurched out onto the road. Above them no bat flew, no night bird hunted, here or anywhere in the empty world. Only the tractor moved across the moonlit plain, a gray beast trotting behind. No insects came to the yellow headlight beam. Before them the road stretched away neutrally to the crests above the Rift, in the land that had been Ethiopia.

The Peacefulness of Vivyan

The newsman had come a long way, studied by small spaceburnt men who wore their lasers against naked callus. And he in turn had stared at his first sealmen, the natives of McCarthy's World. The newsman had been careful not to call it McCarthy's World now, but Sawewe. *Sawewe* meaning, of course, *Freedom*.

For another long wait all the newsman had seen of Sawewe was the dilapidation of the old Terran Enclave: a perfectly flat view of sea on one side and tropical scrub on the other. The surface of Sawewe was a limestone plain pitted with sinkholes which led – some of them – to the continent-wide cavern system in which the sealmen lived. Worthless, except that those gray-green spikes stretched unharvested to the horizon were silweed. The newsman, whose name was Keller, blew out his lips when he saw it. Back in the Empire a gram bag of silweed was worth half his pay-voucher. He knew now why the planet-burners had been held off.

Finally because Keller was patient and tough and his credentials were good there came the long trip in the sealed floater, and the blindfold, and the longer hours of stumbling down and down. Sawewe was not trusting toward Terrans. Keller tripped, heard a faint splash echo. Sealmen hooted, a scanner clicked. He trudged on, hoping he would not have to swim.

At last a hard woman's voice said, 'Leave him here. You can take that off now.'

He blinked into an enormous green dimness, a maze of terraces crumbling into the water, low walls, incongruous wires, a plastic console in a carved niche. Folds of rock hung from the sky. This was a very old place.

'He will be here in an hour,' said the woman, watching him. 'He is on the reef.'

Her hair was gray. She wore a wetsuit but no weapons and her nose had been slit and crudely repaired. An Empire prisoner, one of the Terran traitors who had worked for Sawewe.

'Did they tell you about the contamination?'

Keller nodded.

'The Empire had no need to do that. We never had weapons there. If he talks to you will you tell lies like the others?'

'No.'

'Maybe.'

'Did I lie about Atlixco?'

Her shrug conceded nothing. Keller could see that her face had once been very different.

'That's why he decided to see you.'

'I'm very grateful, Mamsen.'

'No titles. My name is Kut.' She hesitated. 'His wife Nantli was my sister.'

She went away and Keller settled on a stone bench beside an ancient stalagmite frieze. Through the fins of a fish-god he could see two sealmen wearing headsets: a communications center. The pavement in front of him ended in a natural pool which shimmered away into gloom, lit here and there by yellow light-shafts from the stone sky. Water chuckled, a generator keened.

Suddenly Keller was aware that a man was squatting quietly by the poolside, looking at him. When their eyes met the man smiled. Keller was immediately struck by the peaceful openness of the stranger's face. His smile was framed in a curly black beard. A gentle pirate, Keller thought, or a minstrel. A very tall man hunkered down like a boy, holding something.

Keller rose and sauntered over. It was a curious shell.

'The carapace has two openings,' the man told him, turning the shell. 'The animal inside is bimorphic, some-times a single organism, sometimes two. The natives call it *Noshingra*, the come-and-go animal.' He smiled up at Keller, his eyes very clear and defenseless. 'What's your name?'

'Keller, Outplanet News. What's yours?'

The man's eyes softened as though Keller had made him a present and he continued to gaze at Keller in a way so receptive and innocent that the newsman, who was very tired, found himself speaking of his journey and his hopes for the coming interview. The tall man listened peacefully, touching the shell with his hands if it were a talisman that could protect them both from war and power and pain.

Presently the woman Kut came back with a mug of maté and the man unfolded himself and drifted quietly away.

'Biologist?' Keller asked. 'I didn't catch his name.'

The woman's face went bleaker.

'Vivyan.'

The newsman's memory hunted, jarred.

'*Vivyan?* But –'

She sighed. Then she jerked her head, motioning Keller to follow her. They went along behind a wall which became an open fretwork. Looking through, Keller could see the tall figure ambling toward them across a little bridge, still holding his shell.

'Watch,' the woman told him.

The boy Vivyan had noticed the brown man first around the ski-fires of the snowy planet Horl. Vivyan noticed him particularly because he did not come to talk as most people did. Better so, Vivyan felt obscurely. He did not even learn the brown man's name then but simply saw him among the flame-lit faces, a stocky gray-brown man textured all over except for two white owl-rings around his eyes which meant he wore goggles a lot.

Vivyan smiled at him as he did at everyone and when the singing was over he skied out across the moonlight to the ice-forests, pausing often to touch and examine lovingly the life of this mountain world. It was not long before certain snowcreatures trusted him, and the even shyer floating animals who were Horl's birds. The girl who had been with the brown man came to him too. Girls usually did.

Vivyan found this delightful but not remarkable. People and animals always came to him and his body knew the friendly and joyful ways to touch each kind.

People, of course, seemed to need also to talk and

talk, which was a pity because their talk was mostly without meaning. Vivyan himself talked only to his special friend on Horl, the man who knew the names and hidden lives of the snow world and accepted all that Vivyan had observed. Thus should a man live, Vivyan knew, questing and learning and loving. He always remembered everything he encountered, his memory was perfect, like his eyes and ears. Why not? It pained him to see how other humans lived in dimness and distraction and he tried to help.

'See,' he said tenderly to the brown man's girl, 'each branchlet has one drop of sap frozen on the top of the bud. That makes a warming lens. It is called photothermal sap; without it the tree cannot grow.'

The brown man's girl looked, but she turned out to be a strange tense girl preoccupied with hurtful things. She became preoccupied also with Vivyan's body and he did all he could for her, very enjoyably. And then she and some of the others weren't around any more and it was time to move on.

He didn't expect to see the brown man again. But some while later in the cantinas of McCarthy's World he did.

McCarthy's World was the best yet – its long bright beaches, the hidden marvels of its reefs by day and unending welcome in its nights. He had a special friend here too, a marine zoologist who lived up the coast beyond the Terran Enclave. Vivyan never went into the Enclave. His life was in the combers or drifting through the redolent cantinas, moving with the music and the friendly flow. Young people from countless Terran worlds came to McCarthy's beaches and many short, excitable spacers on leave from the Terran base and even a few real aliens.

As always, arms and lips opened to him and he smiled patiently at the voices without hearing the words that his memory could not help recording. It was while he was being harangued by one of the spacers that Vivyan saw white owl-eyes watching from the shadows. It was the brown man. A new girl was with him now.

The spacer pulled at him, inexplicably and drunkenly outraged. Something about the natives of McCarthy's World. Vivyan had never seen one. He longed to. His friend had told him they were very shy.

And there was something negative connected with them which he did not want to know. It was tied in some way to a large badness – the lost third planet whose name Vivyan did not recall. Once, he knew, all these three worlds, Horl and McCarthy's and the nameless one, had been all together and all friendly until the wrong thing had occurred. Terrans were hurt. A pity. Vivyan did not probe into negative, angry things.

He smiled and nodded gently at the spacer, longing to share with him the reality of sunlight on the reef, quietness in the wind, love. The brown man was as before, remote. Not in need. Vivyan stretched and let arms pull him out to fly firekites on the murmuring beaches.

On another evening they were all linked in a circle singing one of the aliens' songs when the brown man's girl began to sing to him with slow intensity across the shadows. Vivyan saw she was a delicate cool girl like the firelace on the reefs and hoped she would come to him soon. When she sought him out next day he learned that her name was Nantli. To his delight she spoke very little. Her eyes and her red-gold body made him feel enveloped in sun-foam.

'Beautiful Vivyan.' Her hands traced him shyly. He smiled his innocent pirate's smile. People always said that; it seemed to be their way of making him feel good. They didn't understand that he always felt good. It was part of his way to be, natural that his long olive body was strong and that his beard curled joyfully. Why did other people hurt themselves so?

'Come to the reefs.' It was fine how eagerly she came and let him teach her to quest down among the firelace to the hidden caverns below. McCarthy's fish circled and danced above their nests, rolling horrified eyes, so tame and ludicrous that the humans spluttered and had to surface to laugh.

Nantli dived and laughed and dived again until Vivyan became worried and hauled her out on the rocks. And later in the breast of the moonlit dunes it was very good. When she had left him he stretched and set out up the beach to the home of his friend, bearing many things of which he wished to be told the names.

McCarthy's sun was a ghost flower rising on the misty sea when he walked back. Beautiful how it fitted, Vivyan thought, the total serenity he always felt after his long talk in the lamplit room.

When he looked back at the beach ahead there was a grey-brown figure by the line of sea-wrack. Jarring. He could think of nothing to do but walk on forward.

The brown man was turning a sea-feather with his

foot. He didn't look up, only said quietly, 'Strange pattern. What's it called?'

Reassured, Vivyan squatted down to trace the sea-feather's veins. 'It's a gorgonia, I think. A colony of animals in a common tissue, a coenchyme. This one came from somewhere else, a spore from the ships maybe.'

'Another pattern.' The brown man frowned, looking out to sea. 'I'm interested in patterns. Like on Horl you were doing birds then, wasn't it? With that xenoecologist wallah around the mountain. And my girl went with you, on Horl. And you checked in with your friendly ecologist and my girl and a couple of our group turned up missing. Somebody came for them. Only it wasn't anybody we know and nobody's heard of them since.'

He looked at Vivyan.

'And here you're into marine biology. And there's this marine-life wallah down the line you have long sessions with. And Nantli's got interested in you. A pattern. How does the pattern go, Vivyan? Does Nantli disappear too? I wouldn't like that. Not Nantli.'

Vivyan kept turning the sea-feather, waiting for the sea-wind to carry away the harshness in the brown man's voice. After a moment he looked up and smiled. 'What's your name?'

Their eyes met really close then and something began happening inside Vivyan. The brown man's face was changing too, as if they were both under water.

'Vivyan,' the brown man said fearful with intensity, '*Vivyan?*'

He pronounced it wrong, like *Feefyane*. Their eyes

39

locked together and a hurt started lunging behind Vivyan's eyes.

'Vivyan!' the brown man insisted in a horrible tearing voice. 'Oh, no. You –' And then everything was perfectly still until he whispered, 'I think . . . I've been looking for you . . . Vivyan.'

Vivyan's whole head was jerking, he tore his eyes down from the white-ringed glare. 'Who are you?' he stammered. 'What's your name?'

The brown man put two hard fingers under Vivyan's jaw and turned his face up.

'Look at me. Think of Zilpan, Vivyan. Tlaara, Tlaaratzunca . . . little Vivyan, *don't you know my name?*'

Vivyan gave a raw cry and lunged clumsily at this small dangerous man. Then he was running into the sea, hurling himself across the shallows to the green depths where no one could follow. He stroked with all his strength, not looking back until he was in the thunders of the reef.

When the anger and hurtfulness had been cleaned away he made for a coralhead far out, where he rested and dived and ate a conch and some sweet wet seahares and drowsed in the foam. He saw many calming things, and when the sun set he went back to shore. It was in his mind that he should go again to visit his friend, but warm voices called him and he let himself be drawn to where huge arthrostraca were being roasted in seaweed. He had never seen the brown man in this place, and soon he began to grin again and eat vastly of the tender shellfish in the silvery silweed smoke.

But there was an undercurrent here too, a strainedness. People were restless, talking quick and low-voiced, looking past each other's shoulders. Was something unpleasant building, cramping the air?

Vivyan recalled sadly that he had noticed such feelings before. Certainly he must go soon to visit his friend. He hoped it was not becoming time to move on from this place too. He wolfed the delicious clams, soothing himself with the names of peaceful things, *Tethys*, *Alcyonaria*, *Coniatities*, *Coccolobis*, *Nantli*.

But Nantli was not a sea-creature, she was the brown man's girl and suddenly she was here in the silsmoke by herself, coming to him smiling and still. All at once he felt better. Maybe the badness had gone now, he thought, stroking her hair. They went out together.

When they reached their place in the dune he felt the tension under her stillness.

'You wouldn't hurt us, would you Vivyan?' She held his sides, peering at his face. The stress inside her was disgusting to feel. He tried to help her, to let his calm flow into her. Her talking was like claws. Something about his friend. Patiently he recounted to her some of his new knowledge of the reef world.

'But about us,' she persisted. 'You didn't talk with him about us, about Cox?'

He stroked her breast, automatically registering the news that the brown man's name was *Cox*. Wrongness. He concentrated on the beautiful flow of his palms on her body. Nantli, Nantli. If only he could ease this frenzy that was eating at her. His body guided him and presently she quieted and let him mold them together, let the life rhythm rise in peace. When it had crested and spent itself he stood up into the moonlight, pointing his beard at the sea.

'No, you go,' she smiled. 'I'm sleepy.'

He touched her gratefully and went down to the silver water. As he dived he heard her call.

Beyond the surf he turned and began to swim along the coast. It was better this way; no one could bother him here as they had on the beach. His friend lived in a small cove, beyond the far point; to swim would mean only taking more time and the tide was running with him toward the setting moon. It drew him strongly, but not more strongly than his desire for the peace that only the long quiet talk would bring.

In the rhythm of his swimming he mused. Always there had been a friend for him, as the brown man – *Cox?* – had said. But that was good, that was necessary. How else could he understand a new place? On Horl there had been his friend on the mountain, and before that in another part of Horl where the mines were he had known a man who told him about the folding of mountains and the alien relics at which so many people came to wonder. That had been interesting but somehow troubled; he had not stayed long. And before that on the stations there had been the friends who taught him the names of stars and the large ways of suns. And before that, on the ships . . . so many lives to learn, such a universe of marvels to remember. His arms rose and thrust tirelessly, carried on the moon tide. He was just feeling the long swells off the point when the strange heads rose around him.

At first Vivyan thought they were McCarthy's seals, or a kind of dugong. Then a streaming crest came up alongside and he saw moonlight on intelligent eyes and knew at once what they were: the natives of McCarthy's World.

He wasn't in the least frightened, only intensely curious. The moon was so bright he could see wet mottlings on the stranger's pelt, like a seal pup. It touched his arm with webbed fingers, pointing to the reef. They wanted him to go there. But he couldn't. Not now. He shook his head regretfully, trying to tell them he would come back when he had talked with his friend.

The sealman pointed again, and the others came closer. Then he saw they had weapons. A kind of spring-load spear. As they closed in Vivyan shot downward with all his power. It would have carried him far from any Terran but the sealmen were easily before him in the glimmering darkness, herding him back.

It was not in his nature to fight. He surfaced and swam with them, debating what to do. Was it possible that it was intended for him to bring this too to his friend? But that did not seem fair, when he was already so burdened.

He swam mechanically, watching the strangers' eyes film and clear. They seemed to have transparent inner lids like certain fish which could focus either in water or air. Their eyes were huge, too; undoubtedly they were nocturnal.

'N'ko, n'ko!' The leader hooted, the first sound they had made. They were motioning him to dive. He did so and found himself being pulled under the reef. Just as his lungs began to knot he saw, incredibly, a bright light ahead. They burst up into a cavern booming with sea-sound. He gulped air, staring with delight at a lantern on a ledge. All doubts vanished, he was glad he had come.

The webbed ones were scrambling out around him.

43

Bipeds no taller than his waist, with lobed and crested heads. When they tugged his arms he bent and let them blindfold him before they led him into a tunnel. What an adventure to tell his friend!

The tunnel was dripping and musty and the way was hard to his feet. Coral. Presently he had to go under water again, still blindfolded. When they came out the air was dry and warmer and when he stumbled he felt crumbling limestone shelves. His sealmen hooted, were answered. Suddenly he was jostled and turned and they were taking his blindfold off, in a crowded place where several passageways met.

Before him stood three much larger sealmen. To Vivyan's intense surprise they were holding weapons of a type which he knew was forbidden. He was just looking at these when the scent of the girl Nantli pulled his head around. How could she be here? He smiled uncertainly and then he saw the white eyes of the man Cox. The adventure was going bad.

'All right.' Cox spoke to the sealmen who had brought him and they pulled at Vivyan.

'Strip down.'

Wondering, he did so and felt an instrument sliding on the base of his spine.

'See,' said Nantli's voice. 'A scar, I told you.'

The brown man made a grunt like a sob and came and grasped Vivyan by the shoulders.

'Vivyan,' he said thickly in the strange way. 'Where are you from?'

'Alpha Centauri Four,' Vivyan told him automatically remembering the garden city, his parents. The memory felt queer, thin. He saw the big sealmen gazing expressionlessly, cradling their weapons.

'No, before that.' Cox's grasp tightened. 'Think, Vivyan. Where were you born?'

Vivyan's head began to hurt unpardonably. He squinted down through the pain, wondering how he could get away.

'They've done something to him, I told you,' Nantli said.

'In God's name, try.' Cox shook him. 'Your real home! Your home, Vivyan. Remember Zilpan mountain? Remember – remember your black pony? Remember *Tlaara*? Have you forgotten your mother Tlaara who sent you away when the revolt started, to keep you safe?'

The pain was terrible now. 'Alpha Centauri Four,' he whimpered.

'Stop, Cox,' Nantli cried.

'Not Alpha!' Cox shook him savagely, his white eyes glaring. 'Atlixco! Can a prince of Atlixco forget so easily?'

'Please stop it, please,' Nantli begged. But Vivyan had realized he must listen very carefully in spite of the pain. Atlixco was the bad place, the world he didn't think about ordinarily. This was not ordinary. His friend would want him to listen.

'The scar,' Cox breathed through his teeth, made a kind of dreadful chuckle. 'I have one too. They've tried to make you look like an ordinary Terran. Don't you remember that little deformity you were so proud of, Vivyan? Alpha Centauri! You're twenty generations of inbred Atlixco, Vivyan, born with a curly, hairy tail. *Remember?*'

Vivyan cringed helplessly under the angry voice. Nant-li pushed forward.

'What did they tell you about Atlixco, Vivyan?' she asked gently.

A painful shutter seemed to grate in Vivyan's head.

'Butchers . . . murderers . . . All dead,' he whispered.

Nantli pried at the brown man's hands. 'Alpha Centauri, he grew up believing it all. A good Terran upbringing. Let him be, there isn't time.'

'All dead?' Cox demanded. 'Look at me, Vivyan. *You know me*. Who am I?'

'Cox,' Vivyan gasped. 'I must tell –'

A hard hand slashed across his face, he went down on one knee.

'Tell!' Cox roared. 'You traitorous crotch-louse! Little Prince Vivyan, the Empire spy. You're the bloody answer to what happened to us on Horl, aren't you? And if we hadn't caught you tonight –'

A kick sent him sprawling at the sealmen's feet. They hooted and stamped. Everyone was yelling, Nantli screaming, 'Cox! It's not his fault, they've messed up his mind, you can see that –' until Cox's bellow cut them all off.

He walked over to Vivyan and took him by the hair, scowling down into his face. It never occurred to Vivyan to use his strength against the terrifying little man.

'I should kill you,' Cox said quietly. 'Maybe I will. But maybe first we have a use for little Vivyan.' He straightened up releasing Vivyan. 'If I can bear the sight. All those years,' he said in a harsh hurting voice. '*Thank God at least the kid is safe* . . . Terran filth. Take him to Doc.'

He went out abruptly with the three big sealmen.

The pain in Vivyan's head quieted as he followed Nantli through green flaking tunnels to a large dim place. Seal people were lying everywhere, on ledges and piles of seaweed. Vivyan saw a small face bubbling at him over its mother's side. He smiled eagerly and then he noticed that there was something wrong with it. With all of them.

'Their skins,' he said. An old Terran stood up.

'Hull-scrapers from the Enclave,' the man said. 'Poisons 'em.'

'This is Vivyan, Doc,' said Nantli. 'He doesn't know who he is or anything.'

'Who does?' grunted the doctor. Vivyan studied him, wondering if this could possibly be his new friend. He felt horribly shaken. Maybe this man was to prepare him to go on to a new place?

'Lie down,' the doctor told him. Vivyan felt the flash of an injector. Suddenly he was very frightened. There was a danger he'd been warned against, a thing that was not allowed. If this man was not a friend he had done something very wrong. How had this happened? He was trapped. Bad.

But then he remembered that there was some way to be all right, something his friends had fixed in case of trouble. He must relax. Peacefulness was the key. He lay quietly breathing the wet cave air, not looking or listening. But it was hard to be peaceful here. Sealmen were coming through, hooting at the sick ones on the seaweed who roused themselves and hooted back. Shouting, stamping, more hooting.

Something seemed to be happening. A sealman shook a laser at the doctor, laughing in a wild yowling way. The doctor grunted, doing things to the seal-baby. Vivyan felt dizzy and unclean. In a moment he would leave this place.

But white-ringed eyes were over him. Cox.

'Now. Talk. How much have you passed your contact here?'

Vivyan could only stare, the words meant nothing. Nantli's face appeared, saying gently, 'Don't be frightened, Vivyan. Just tell us. You did talk to your friend about me, didn't you?'

The shutter-thing in Vivyan's brain seemed to be sliding, melting.

'Oh yes.' His lips felt floppy.

'That's right. And Captain Palcay, did you talk about him?'

'Pal, Palcay?' Vivyan mumbled. The brown man made an angry noise.

'The spacer you were with at Flor's, Vivyan, the one who got so drunk. Did you tell your friend about that?'

Vivyan could not follow her clearly but at the words 'tell your friend' he nodded his head, yes. Cox snarled.

'And have you told him you've seen Cox here?'

Vivyan felt a sudden jar inside him as though he had missed a step. The brown man – had he ever? This was very peculiar. Frightening. He turned his head to meet the pale ringed eyes.

'Cox?'

'Not Cox!' the brown man said furiously. 'Cancoxtlan. *Cancoxtlan!* Remember yourself, Vivyan of Atlixco, son of Tlaara.'

'My mother was raped and butchered by the rebels,' Vivyan heard his voice saying in a weird flat tone. The words meant only pain. 'They burned my father alive and all my family. The shrikes ate their bodies. My pony too,' he began to sob. 'Butchers. Traitors. You're hurting me, it hurts –'

The brown face watched him, suddenly still. Then Cox said heavily, 'Yes. Princes get killed. Even good kind princes too . . . I couldn't make them see, Vivyan. At the end I couldn't even get to them in time.'

'We were so happy,' Vivyan wept. 'We were peaceful and beautiful.'

'You were five years old,' said Cox. 'Didn't anybody ever tell you what we'd done to the Atlixcans? The real Atlixcans? Two centuries of happiness for Terran princes, two centuries of slavery – the debt got paid, Vivyan.'

A sealman ran up uttering barking cries. Cox turned to him.

'Oh, God, they're going ahead,' Nantli exclaimed. 'Cox –'

'All the way,' Cox said. He turned back and gripped Vivyan's head. 'They lied to you, can you understand? *We* were wrong. *We* were the butchers. The Empire, us. We're fighting it now, Vivyan. You've got to come with us. You must. You owe it, Prince of Atlixco. We can use you in place, in their spy net –'

One of the big sealmen had come up and grabbed Cox's shoulder. Vivyan heard Nantli saying something and suddenly the white eyes had left him, they were all gone. Other sealmen and Terrans ran through, but no one bothered him.

He lay with his head whirling and hurting, wondering if it had been all right. His lips seemed to have spoken by themselves, as they did when he was with his friend. Was it all right? He must get out of here as soon as he could stand up.

He drowsed a little and then more sealmen were all around him, hooting, groaning, smelling of burnt flesh and blood. A body bumped him. It was a Terran in a wetsuit, oozing blood. The man slumped down, yelling, 'Hey, Doc, you gloomy sod, we got the goddamn transmitters! You bloody pervert, Doc!' he shouted. 'The 'Trixcan ships are coming in. How about that, you gutless mother?'

'They'll burn the planet,' the doctor told him. 'Cut that off so you can fry clean.'

He hauled the man away. Vivyan saw that the passage was now clear. Next minute he was out and running back the way he had come.

His memory was perfect, although he felt a little ill. All he had to do was let his feet carry him while his eyes and ears kept watch. Twice he ducked into side tunnels while sealmen went by with their wounded. Then he was at the place where many tunnels met, where they had removed his blindfold trusting to the maze.

Vivyan simply closed his eyes and let his body guide him back. Turn, rough place to the left, bend his head, cool air on his right side, the natural mechanism within him unspooled its perfect tape. He only had to hide once more. These passages seemed to be unused.

Presently he was through the inner pool and into the last dark tunnel undersea. This was easier yet, he could hear the water churning under the reef and he ran stooped in the darkness, longing to be out in the clean, away from this peaceless place. Surely they would take him away now to a new place, after he had given all these things to his friend?

He reached the cavern. No lantern now. That didn't matter. Vivyan knew exactly where to dive, how to come up under the reef. He kicked powerfully down into blackness, thinking he must be sure to remember everything.

This must be a secret way to the caves, it would be a wonderful surprise.

In a moment he had surfaced and marked the horizon and the stars. There seemed to be fires on the shore. He began to swim eagerly, feeling marvelous now. This would be his best yet. If only the name *Cancoxtlan* didn't trouble his head . . . but he would forget about that, he felt sure. Peace flooded him as he saw the far light of his friend's house by the cove.

'No one noticed he had gone,' the woman told the newsman. 'The fight for the Enclave had started and Cancoxtlan was there. When the Terrans broke in through the reef tunnel we managed to blow the section between the hospital and the armory. They got the wounded, of course, and Doctor Vosc. And Nantli. But it had no effect.' Her scarred face was impassive. 'Cox wouldn't surrender to save Nantli, she wouldn't have wanted that. The raid diverted one of their core units.'

They watched Vivyan's tall figure moving aimlessly along the terrace, glancing in the water. Seen from behind he looked older, stooped, under the striking black hair.

'The spacers were with us, did you know that?' The woman was suddenly animated. 'Oh yes, even the officers.

When the cruiser from Atlixco showed up they all came in.' She grimaced. 'We intercepted a Space Command signal about indoctrination to combat, quotes, *apathy* . . . Empires grow old and foolish, even the revolt on Horl didn't wake them up. We'll have Horl next.'

She checked herself then. They saw Vivyan glance round quickly and turn toward the wall.

'We found him wandering, afterwards,' the woman went on quietly. 'Cancoxtlan's brother, after all . . . He never understood what he'd done. We think now he was basically retarded, in addition to the conditioning they'd put him through. Nothing reached. You've heard of idiot savants? He's very gentle and that smile, one doesn't realize.'

The newsman remembered his own gut response to the gentle stranger and shuddered. Exquisite tool of empire. A deadly child.

Vivyan had halted before a peculiar carving in an alcove. The newsman frowned. A Terran eagle, here? The boy-man seemed to be whispering to it.

'He carved it himself. Cox let him keep it. What does it matter now?' The woman bowed her bleak head. 'Listen.'

By a trick in the wall structure the newsman could hear perfectly what Vivyan was whispering.

'. . . he says his name is Keller of Outplanet News. He didn't tell his first name. He says he came from Aldebaran Sector on the *Komarov* to interview the traitor Prince Cancoxtlan. He is about one meter eighty, medium build, gray hair and eyes. He has a scar on his right earlobe and his timer is forty-five units ahead of planet time . . .'

Mama Come Home

The day Papa came home was the day mama came home to me. That's the way I look at Earth's first alien contact. We may have changed some of our ideas about what's human, but one thing hasn't changed: the big history-tape events are still just background for the real I-Me-You drama. Not true? So, wasn't the US-Sino-Soviet pact signed the week your daughter got married?

Anyway, there they were, sitting on Luna. Although it's not generally known, there'd been a flap about a moving source around Pluto the year before. That's when CIA decided that outer space fell under the category of foreign territory in its job description – at least to the extent of not leaving the Joint Chiefs in sole charge of any possible contact with the galaxy. So our little shop shared some of the electronic excitement. The Russians helped, they're the acknowledged champs at heaving up the tonnage, but we still have the communications lead – we try harder. The British and the Aussies try too, but we keep hiring their best men.

That first signal faded to nothing – until one fine April evening all our communications went bust and the full moon rose with this big alien hull parked on the Lunar Alps. Sat there for three days, glowing bluishly in any six-power lens – if you could buy one. And you'll recall, we had no manned moon-station then. After peace broke out nobody wanted to spend cash on vacuum and rocks. The shape our space program was in, we couldn't have hit them with a paper-clip in less than three months.

On A-Day plus one I spotted Tillie at the water-cooler.

To do so I had to see through two doors and Mrs Peabody, my secretary, but I'd got pretty good at this. I wandered out casually and said:

'How's George doing?'

She gave me a one-eyed scowl through her droopy wing of hair, finished her water and scowled again to make sure she wasn't smiling.

'He came back after midnight. He's had six peanut-butter sandwiches. I think he's getting it.'

There are people who'll tell you Tillie is an old bag of bones in a seersucker suit. For sure she has bones, and she's no girl. But if you look twice it can get a little hard to notice other people in the room. I'd done the double take about three years back.

'Meet me at lunch and I'll show you something.'

She nodded moodily and lounged off. I watched the white knife-scar ripple elegantly on her tanned legs and went back through my office, fighting off the urge to push Mrs Peabody's smile into her Living Bra.

Our office is a little hard to explain. Everybody knows CIA is out in that big building at Langley, but the fact is that even when they built it there it fit about as well as a beagle-house fits a Great Dane. They got most of the Dane in somehow, but we're one of the paws and tails that got left out. Strictly a support facility – James Bond would sneer at us. We operate as a small advertising agency in a refined section of DC which happens to be close to a major land cable and the Naval Observatory gadgets. Our girls actually do some ads for other government agencies – something about Smoky Bear and Larry Litterbug is all over the first floor. We really aren't a big secret thing – not a Biretta or a cyanide ampoule in the place and you can get into our sub-basement any time you produce front and profile X-rays of both your grandmothers.

What's there? Oh, a few linguists and old war leftovers like me. A computer NSA spilled coffee into. And George. George is our pocket genius. It is generally believed he got his start making skin flicks for yaks in Outer Mongolia. He lives on peanut butter and Tillie works for him.

So when the aliens started transmitting at us, George was among the facilities Langley called on to help decipher. And also me, in a small, passive way – I look at interesting photography when the big shop wants a side opinion. Because of my past as a concocter of fake evidence in the bad old days. Hate that word, fake. Mine is still being used by historians.

Come lunchtime I went looking for Tillie at Rapa's, our local lifeline. Since Big Brother at Langley found that our boys and girls were going to Rapa's instead of eating GSA boiled cardboard, Rapa's old cashier has been replaced by a virgin with straight seams and a camera in each, ah, eyeball. But the chow is still good.

Tillie was leaning back relaxed, a dreamy double-curve smile on her long mouth. She heard me and wiped it off. The relaxation was a fraud; I saw her hand go over some shredded matches.

She smiled again, like someone had offered her fifty

cents for her right arm. But she was okay. I knew her, this was one of her good days. We ordered veal and pasta, friendly.

'Take a look,' I invited. 'We finally synched in with their beam for a few frames.'

The photo showed one side foggy, the rest pretty clear. Tillie goggled.

'It's – it's –'

'Yeah, it's beautiful. *She's* beautiful. And the dead spit of you, my girl.'

'But Max! Are you sure?' Her using my name was a good sign.

'Absolute. We saw her move. This, kid, is The Alien. We've had every big cine collection in the world checking. It's not any sort of retransmission. See that script on her helmet and that background panel? T'aint nobody's. No doubt where the send is from, either. That ship up there is full of people-type people. At least, women . . . What's George got?'

'You'll see the co-copy,' she said absently, grooving on the photo. 'He worked out about two hundred words in clear. It's weird. They want to land – and something about Mother. Like, Mother is back, or is home. George says "Mother" is the best he can do.'

'If that's Mother, oh my. Here's your pasta.'

They landed a week later, after considerable international wrangling. At Mexico City, as everyone knows. In a small VTO affair. Thanks to George's connections – in the literal sense – we had it on closed circuit right over the crowd of world dignitaries and four million real people.

The airlock opened on a worldwide hush, and Mother came out. One – and then another – and a third. Last one out fiddled with something on her wrist, and the lock closed. We found out later she was the navigator.

There they stood on their ramp, three magnificent earth-type young females in space-opera uniforms. Helmets on the backs of their heads and double-curve grins on their long mouths. The leader was older and had more glitter on her crest. She swung back her droopy wing of hair, breathed twice, wrinkled her nose and paced down the ramp to meet the UN President.

Then we got it. The UN President that year was an Ethiopian about six-feet-five. The top of his head came just to the buckle of her crossbelt.

I guess the worldwide hush quivered – it certainly did in George's projection room.

'About eight-foot-three for the captain,' I said.

'Assuming the top of the head is normal,' George chirped. 'That's what we love him for.

In the dimness I saw a funny look on Tillie's face. Several girls were suppressing themselves, and Mrs Peabody seemed to feel an egg hatching in her uplift. The men looked like me   tense. Right then I would have settled for green octopuses instead of those three good-looking girls.

The captain stepped back from President Enkaladugunu and said something in a warm contralto, and somehow we all relaxed. She seemed wholesome, if you can imagine a mix of Garbo and Moshe Dayan. The other two officers were clearly very young, and – well, I told you, they could have been Tillie's sisters except for size.

George got that; I saw his eyes going between Tillie and the screen.

To his disgust, all the talking was being done by our people. The three visitors stood it well, occasionally giving brief, melodious responses. They looked mightily relaxed, and also somewhat puzzled. The two young JOs were scanning hard at the crowd and twice I saw one nudge the other.

Mercifully a Soviet-US-Indian power play choked off the oratory and got the party adjourned to Mexico's Guest Palace – or rather, to an unscheduled pause around the pool while beds were being lashed together and sofas substituted for chairs. Our circuit went soft. George shut himself up with his tapes of the alien's few remarks, and I coped with a flock of calls about our observing devices, which got buggered up in the furniture-moving orgy.

Two days later the party moved to the Popo-Hilton with the swimming pool as their private bath. Every country on earth – even the Vatican – sent visiting delegations. George was going through fits. He was bound and determined to be the expert on Mother's language by remote control. I had an in with the Mexicali bureau and we did pretty well until about twenty other outfits got into the act and the electronic feedback put us all in the hash.

'Funny thing, Max,' said George at morning staff. 'They keep asking – I can only interpret as, "Where are the women?"'

'You mean, like women officials? Women in power jobs?'

'Simpler, I think. Perhaps *big* women, like themselves. But I get a connotation of grown-up, women, adults. I need more of their talk among themselves, Max.'

'We're trying, believe it. They keep flushing all the cans and laughing like maniacs. I don't know if it's our plumbing or our snoops that amuse them. Did you hear about Tuesday?'

Tuesday my shivers had come back. For half an hour every recording device out to a half-mile perimeter went dead for forty minutes, and nothing else was affected.

Another department was getting shivery too. Harry from R&D called me to see if we could get a better look at that charm bracelet the navigator had closed the ship with.

'We can't get so much as a gamma particle into that damn boat,' he told me. 'Touch it – smooth as glass. Try to move it, blowtorch it – nothing. It just sits there. We need that control, Max.'

'She wears it taking a bath, Harry. No emissions we can read.'

'I know what I'd do,' he grunted. 'Those cream-heads up there are in a daze.'

A daze it was. The world at large loved them. They were now on grand tour, being plied with entertainment, scenic wonders and technology. The big girls ate it up – figuratively and literally. Balloon glasses of aquavit went down especially well from breakfast on, and they were glowingly complimentary about everything from Sun Valley to the Great Barrier Reef with stopovers at every atomic and space installation. Captain Garbo-Dayan

really unbent on the Côte d'Azur, and the two JOs had
lost their puzzled looks. In fact, they were doing a good
deal of what would have looked like leering if they didn't
have such wholesome smiles.

'What the hell?' I asked George.

'They think we're cute,' he said, enjoying himself.
Did I tell you George was a tiny little man? That figures,
with Tillie working for him. He loved to see us big men
squinting up at the Girls from Capella, as the world now
called them.

They were from a system near Capella, they explained
in delightful fragments of various Earth languages. Their
low voices really had charm. Why had they come? Well,
they were a tramp freighter, actually, taking a load of ore
back to Capella. They had dropped by to clear up an old
chart notation about our system. What was their home
like? Oh, much like ours. Lots of commerce, trade. Wars?
Not for centuries. Shocking idea!

What the world wanted to know most, of course, was
where were their men? Were they alone?

This evoked merry laughter. Of course they had men,
to care for the ship. They showed us on a video broadcast from Luna. There were indeed men, handsome types
with muscles. The chap who did most of the transmission
looked like my idea of Leif Ericsson. There was no doubt
however, that Captain Garbo-Dayan – or Captain Lyampka, as we learned to call her – was in charge. Well, we had
female Soviet freighter captains, too.

The one thing we couldn't get exactly was the Capellan men's relative heights. The scenery on these trans-
missions was different. It was my private opinion, from

juggling some estimates of similar background items, that at least some of their men were earth-normal size, though burly.

The really hot questions about their space drive got gracefully laughed off. How did the ship run? Sorry, they were not technicians. But then they sprang the bomb-shell. Why not come and see for ourselves? Would we care to send a party up to Luna to look over the ship?

Would we? *Would we?* How many? Oh, about fifty – fifty men, please. And Tillie.

I forgot to mention about Tillie getting to be their pet. George had sent her to Sun Valley to record some speech samples he absolutely had to have. She was introduced at the pool, looking incredibly like a half-size Capellan. A smash. They loved it. Laughed almost to guffawing. When they found she was a crack linguist they adopted her. George was in ecstasy with hauls of Capellan chatter no one else had, and Tillie seemed to like it too. She was different these days – her eyes shone, and she had a kind of tense, exalted smile. I knew why and it bothered me, but there wasn't anything I could do.

I cut myself into her report-circuit one day.

'Tillie. It's dangerous. You don't know them.'

Safe at two thousand miles, she gave me the bare-faced stare.

'*They're* dangerous?'

I winced and gave it up.

Tillie at fifteen had caught the full treatment from a street gang. Fought against knives, left for dead – an old story. They'd fixed her up as good as new, except for a few interesting white hairlines in her tan, and a six-inch layer of ice between her and everybody who shaved. It didn't show, most of the time. She had a nice sincere cover manner and she wore her old suits and played mousy. But it was permanent guerrilla war inside.

Intelligence had found her, as they often do, a ready-made weapon. She was totally loyal as long as no one touched her. And she'd wear anything or nothing on business. I'd seen photos of Tillie on a job at twenty that you wouldn't believe. Fantastic – the subtle sick flavor added too.

She let people touch her, physically I mean, on business. I imagine – I never asked. And I never asked what happened to them afterward, or why the classified medal. It did trouble me a little when I found out her chief case officer was dead – but that was all right, he'd had diabetes for years.

But as for letting a friend touch her – really touch *her* – I tried it once.

It was in George's film vault. We were both exhausted after a fifty-hour run of work. She leaned back and smiled, and actually touched my arm. My arm went around her automatically and I started to bend down to her lips. At the last minute I saw her eyes.

Before I got pastured out to Smoky Bear and George, I had worked around a little, and one of the souvenirs indelibly printed on my memory is the look in the eyes of a man who had just realized that I stood between him and the only exit. He waited one heartbeat and then started for the exit through what very nearly became my dead body, in the next few hectic minutes. I saw that look – depthless, inhuman – in Tillie's eyes. Gently

I disengaged my arm and stepped back. She resumed breathing.

I told myself to leave her alone. It's an old story. Koestler told it, and his girl was younger. The trouble was I *liked* the woman, and it didn't help that she really was beautiful under those sack suits. We got close enough a couple of times so we even discussed – briefly – whether anything could be done. Her view was, of course, *nada*. At least she had the taste not to suggest being friends. Just *nada*.

After the second of those sessions I sloped off with a couple of mermaids from the Reflecting Pool, who turned out to have strange china doorknobs in their apartment. When the doorknobs got busted I came back to find Mrs Peabody had put me on sick leave.

'I'm sorry, Max.' Tillie lied.

'*De nada*,' I told her.

And that was how matters stood when Tillie went off to play with the alien giantesses.

With Tillie next to them, our shop became Miss Government Agency of the month. The reluctant trickle of collateral data swelled to a flood. We found out, for instance, about the police rumors.

It seemed the big girls wanted exercise, and the first thing they asked for in any city was the park. Since they strolled at eight mph, a foot guard wasn't practical. The UN compromised on a pair of patrol cars bracketing them on the nearest road. This seemed to amuse the Capellans, and every now and then the police radios went dead. The main danger to the Girls was from hypothetical snipers, and nobody could do much about that.

After they went through Berlin the Vapos picked up four men in poor condition in the Tiergarten, and the one who lived said something about the Capellans. The Vapos didn't take this seriously – all four had larceny and drug records – but they bucked it along anyway. Next there was some story from a fruity type in Solsdijk Park near The Hague, and a confused disturbance in Hong Kong when the Girls went through the Botanical Gardens. And three more defunct vagrants in the wilderness preserve outside Melbourne. The Capellans found the bodies and expressed shock. Their men, they said, did not fight among themselves.

Another tidbit was the Great Body Hunt. Try as we had in Mexico we had never got one look at them completely naked. Breasts, yes – standard human type, superior grade. But below the navel we failed. Now we found out that everybody else all along the route was failing too, although they'd pushed the perimeter pretty close. I admired their efforts – you wouldn't believe what some of our pals had gotten pickups into. But nothing worked. It seemed the Girls liked privacy, and they had some sort of routine snooper-sweep that left blank films and tapes. Once when the Jap IS got really tricky they found their gismo with the circuits not only fused but mirror-reversed.

Tillie's penetration evoked a mass howl for anatomical detail. But all she gave us was, 'Conception is a voluntary function with them.'

I wondered if anyone else around the office was hearing mice in the woodwork. Was I the only one who knew Tillie was under pressures not listed in standard agent evaluation?

But she was helpful on the big question: How did they come to be so human? There was no doubt they were. Although we hadn't got photos, we had enough assorted biological specimens to know they and we were one flesh. Or rather, one DNA. All the Girls themselves would tell us was interpreted as 'We are an older race' – big smile.

Tillie got us the details that shook our world. The navigator had too many balloon-glasses one night and told Tillie that Capellans had been here before – *long* before. Hence the chart notation they'd wanted to check. There was something of interest here besides a nice planet something the first expedition had left. A colony? The navigator grinned and shut up.

This tidbit really put the strawberries in the fan. Was it possible we were the descendants of these people? Vertigo hit the scientific sector and started a babble of protest. What about Proconsul? What about the australopithecines? What about gorilla blood-types? What about – about – about WHAT? The babble mounted; a few cooler heads pointed out that nobody really knew where Cro-Magnon came from, and he had apparently interbred with other types. Well, it's an old story now, but those were dizzy days.

True to human form, I was giving the grand flip-flop of history about two percent of my attention. To begin with I was busy. We were fighting out a balanced representation of earth scientific specialists with all the other nations who had delegations in the visiting party to Luna. It was to be a spectacular talent show – everything from particle physics, molecular genetics, math theory, eco-systems down to a lad from Chile who combined musical analysis, ichthyology and cooking. And every one of them handsome and certified heterosexual. *And* equipped with enough circuitry to – well, assist their un-aided powers of observation and report. Even in the general euphoric haze somebody had stayed cool enough to realize the boys just might not get back. Quite a job to do in two weeks.

But that again was background to a purely personal concern. The Monday before the party took off Tillie and the Girls came through DC. I cornered her in the film vault.

'Will you receive a message in a sanitized container?'

She was picking at a band-aid over a shot-puncture some idiot had given her. (What the hell kind of immunization did the medicos think they had for assignments on the moon?) One eye peeked at me. She knew she was guilty, all right.

'You think your big playmates are just like yourself, only gloriously immune from rape. I wouldn't be surprised if you weren't thinking of going home with them. Right? No, don't tell me, kid, I know you. But you don't know *them*. You think you do, but you don't. Did you ever meet any American blacks who moved to Kenya? Talk to one some time. And there's another thing you haven't thought about – two hundred and fifty thousand miles of hard vacuum. A quarter of a million miles away. The Marines can't get you out of this one, baby.'

'So?'

'All right. I just want to get it through to you – assuming there is a human being under that silicon – that out here is another human being who's worried sick about you. Does that get through? At all?'

She gave me a long look as though she were trying to make out a distant rider on a lonesome plain. Then her lashes dropped.

The rest of the day I was busy with our transmitting arrangements from – actually – Timbuctu. The Russians had offered to boost the party up in sections in six weeks, but Captain Lyampka, after a few thoughtful compliments, had waved that off. They would just send down their cargo lighter – no trouble at all, if we would point out a convenient desert to absorb the blast. Hence Timbuctu. The Capellan party was spending two nights in DC en route there.

They were lodged in the big hotel complex near our office and adjoining Rock Creek Park. That was how I came to find out what Capellans did in parks.

It was a damn fool thing, to trail them. Actually I just hung around the park input. About two A.M. I was sitting on a bench in the moonlight, telling myself to give it up. I was gritty-eye tired. When I heard them coming I was too late to take cover. It was the two JOs. Two beautiful girls in the moonlight. Two *big* girls, coming fast. I stood up.

'Good evening!' I essayed in Capellan.

A ripple of delighted laughter, and they were towering over me.

Feeling idiotic, I got out my cigarillos and offered them around. The first mate took one and sat down on the bench. Her eyes came level with mine.

I clicked my lighter. She laughed and laid the cigarillo

down. I made a poor job of lighting mine. There is a primal nightmare lurking deep in most men, having to do with his essential maleness. With violation thereof. I'd gone through life without getting more than a glimpse of it, but this situation was bringing cold fingers right up into my throat. I tried a sort of farewell bow. They laughed and bowed back. I had a clear line of exit to right rear. I took a step backward.

A hand like a log fell on my shoulders. The navigator leaned down and said something in a velvety contralto. I didn't need a translator – I'd seen enough old flicks: '*Don't go 'way, baby, we won't hurt you.*'

My jump was fast, but those mothers were faster. The standing one had my neck in a vise at arm's length, and when I worked the standard finger-bend she laughed like a deep bell and casually twisted up my arm until things broke. In three places, it turned out later.

The ensuing minutes are what I make a point of not remembering except when I forget to wake up screaming. My next clear view was from the ground where I was discovering some nasty facts about Capellan physiology through a blaze of pain. (Ever think about being attacked by a *musth* vacuum cleaner?) My own noise was deafening me, but either I was yelling in two voices or something else was screeching and scrabbling around my head. In a dead place somewhere inside the uproar I associated this with Tillie, which didn't make sense. Presently there was, blessedly, nothing . . . and, somewhere else, ambulance jolts and smells and needle-jabs.

At a later point in daylight George's face appeared around the mass of tapes and pulleys on my hospital bed.

He told me Tillie had screamed the captain into calling off her JOs before they ruined the kid's toy. And then she got a call through to George, and he sent the special squad to haul the corpse to the hidey-hole for Classifed Mistakes. (I was now very Classified.) While he talked he was setting up a video so we could watch Earth's scientific delegation embark for Luna.

Through the pulleys I saw them – a terrific-looking group; the cream of Terran expertise, and most of them still looking human in spite of being about thirty percent hardware. They wore the dress uniforms of various armed services – the pair of Danish biologists in naval whites and the Scottish radiation lads in dress kilts were dazzling. Myself, I had most faith in the Israeli gorilla in khaki; I had run into him once in Khartoum when he was taking time off from being a Nobel runner-up in laser technology.

The bands played; the African sun flamed off the gold and polish; the all-girl Capellan freighter crew lined up smartly as our lads marched up the ramp, their heads at Capellan belly-button level. Going into that ship with them was enough miniaturized circuitry to map Luna and do a content analysis on the Congressional Library. At the last minute, a Pakistani got the hiccups, and his teeth transmitted flak all over the screen. Tillie followed the men, and behind her came the captain and her roughnecks, smiling like the girl next door. I wondered if the navigator was wearing any band-aids. My teeth had had hold of *something* – while they lasted.

There they went, and there they flaked out, to a man. We next saw them on a transmission from the mother ship. There wasn't a molecule of metal on them. We found out later they'd dozed off on the trip up, and woke up in the ship clean as babies, with healing scars on their hides. (The Pak had new teeth.) Their Capellan hosts acted as if it was all a big joke and served welcome drinks all around every ten minutes. Some drinks they must have been – I caught a shot of my Israeli hope. He was sitting on the captain's lap wearing her helmet. Somebody had had the sense to rig a monitor on the satellite relay, so the world at large saw only part of the send. They loved it.

'Round one to Mordor,' said George, perched like a Hobbit on my bed. He had stopped enjoying the situation.

'When the white man's ships came to Hawaii and Tahiti,' I croaked through my squashed larynx, 'they'd let a herd of vahines on board for the sailors.'

George looked at me curiously. He hadn't had the chance to meet his nightmare socially, you see, while I was getting friendly with mine, in a grim way.

'If the girls had a machete or two, nobody got mad. They just took 'em away. The technological differential here is about the same, don't you think, George? We've just had our machetes taken away.'

'They left some new diseases, too, when they moved on,' said George slowly. He was with it now.

'*If* this bunch moves on.'

'They have to sell that ore.'

'– What?' (I'd just caught a glimpse of Tillie on the screen, standing near the Capellan male we had been calling Leif Ericsson. As I had figured, he was about my size.)

'I said they have to get home to sell their cargo.'

And he was right. The operative word was *cargo*.

The plot unfolded about a week later when the visiting

party was sent back from Luna, along with three new Capellan ratings who were to collect the VTO launch. To my inexpressible relief Tillie came with them.

The cargo lighter dumped Tillie and our deflowered male delegation in North Africa and then took off on a due south paraboloid which put the Capellans down around the hip of the globe.

'Near Keetmanshoop, South Africa, Woomera says,' George told me. 'Doesn't smell good.' The three states known, among other names, as White Man's Heaven weren't speaking to the rest of the world that year. They did not see fit to announce that the Capellans were paying them a private visit.

'Where's Tillie?'

'Being debriefed at the Veddy Highest Levels. Did you hear the mother ship is unloading its ore?'

'Where would I hear anything?' I wheezed, rattling my pulleys. 'Give me that photo!'

You could see it clearly: conical piles and some sort of conveyor running out from the big hulk on Luna.

'At least they don't have matter transmitters.'

The next piece of the plot came through Tillie. She sat chin on fist, talking tiredly through her hair in the general direction of my kneecaps.

'They estimate they can carry about seven hundred. It'll take them three days our time to unload, and another week to seal and atmospherize part of the cargo hold. The Bwanas bought the deal right off.'

'What's the difference to them?' I groaned. 'For the poor bloody Bantus the Capellan brand of slavery probably looks like cake.'

That was it, of course. The men of Capella were slaves. And there were relatively few of them. A cargo of exotic human males was worth a good deal more than ore. A hell of a lot more, it seemed. On Terra we once called it 'black ivory'.

So much for galactic super-civilization. But that wasn't all. I had to yell hard for George before he showed, looking gray around the nose.

'A merchant privateer who runs into a rich source of pearls, or slaves, or whatever,' I wheezed, 'doesn't figure to quit after one trip. And he doesn't want his source to dry up or run away while he's gone. Or learn to fight back. He wants it to stay sweet, between trips. The good captain was quite interested in the fact that the Russians offered to get up to Luna so quickly. They could expect us to develop a defensive capability before they got back. What do they propose to do about that?'

'This may come as a shock to you,' George said slowly, 'but you aren't the only man who's read history. We weren't going to tell you because there's nothing you can do about it in that jungle gym.'

'Go on!'

'Mavrua – that's the man you called Leif Ericsson – he told me,' put in Tillie. 'They plan to turn off the sun a little. As they leave.'

'A solar screen.' George's voice was gray, too. 'They can lay it with their exhaust in a couple of dozen orbits. It doesn't take much, and it lasts, that is, there's an irreversible interaction. I don't understand the physics. Harry gave me the R&D analysis at lunch, but the waiter kept taking the mesons away. The point is, they can screen off enough solar energy to kick us back to the ice age. Without time to prepare we'll be finished. Snow could start here about June. When it does it won't quit. Or melt. Most of the big lakes and quite a lot of ocean will go to ice. The survivors will be back in caves. Perfect for their purpose, of course – they literally put us on ice.'

'What the hell is being done?' I squeaked.

'Not counting the people who are running around cackling, there are two general lines. One, hit them with something before they do it. Two, undo it afterwards. And a massive technological resource depot is being shipped to Columbia. So far the word has been held pretty close. Bound to leak soon, though.'

'Hit them?' I coughed. 'Hit them? The whole UN military can't scratch that VTO that's sitting in their laps! Even if they could get a warhead on the mother ship, they're bound to have shielding. Christ, look at the deflectors they use to hold their atomics. And they know the state of our art. Childish! And as for dispersing the screen in time to save anything –'

'What do you think you're doing? Max?' They were pawing at me.

'Getting out of here . . . Goddamnit, give me a knife, I can't untie this bastard! Let go. Nurse! Where are my pants?'

They finally hauled me over to George's war room in a kind of mobile mummy-case and saw I got fed all the info and rumors. I kept telling my brain to produce. It kept telling me back Tilt. With the top men of ten nations working on it, what did I imagine *I* could contribute? When I had been grunting to myself for a couple of hours Tillie and George filed in with a purposeful air.

'In a bad position you can always wiggle *something*,' I rasped. 'What about the men, Tillie?'

'What about them?'

'How do they feel about the plan?'

'Well, they don't like it.'

'In what way don't they like it?'

'The established harem favorites don't like to see new girls brought in,' she recited and quick looked me in the eye.

'Having a good time, baby?' I asked her gently. She looked away.

'Okay. There's our loose piece. Now, how do we wiggle it at a quarter of a million miles? What about that character Leif – Mavrua?' I mused. 'Isn't he some sort of communications tech?'

'He's chief commo sergeant,' Tillie said, and added slowly, 'he's alone on duty, sometimes.'

'What's he like? You were friendly with him?'

'Yes, kind of. He's – I don't know – like gay only not.'

I was holding her eye.

'But in this situation *your interests coincide?*' I probed her hard. The American black who goes to Kenya often discovers he is an American first and an African second, no matter what they did to him in Newark. George had the sense to keep quiet, although I doubt he ever understood.

She swung back her hair, slowly. I could see mad dreams dying in her eyes.

'Yes. They . . . coincide.'

'Think you can talk to him?'

'Yes.'

'I'll get over to Harry.' George jumped up, he was

ahead of the play now. 'We'll see what we can lash up. Ten days, maximum.'

'Call the campus. I can take a meeting. But get me something so I don't sound like a frog's ghost.'

The chief we had then was all right. He came to me. Of course we had only the start of a plan, but nobody else had anything, and we had Tillie. He agreed we were nuts and gave us everything we needed. The lateral channels were laid on by 1500; Jodrell Bank was to set us up.

The waning moon came over Greenwich before dawn that week, and we got Tillie through to Mavrua about midnight EST. He was alone. It took her about a dozen exchanges to work out agreement in principle. She was good with him. I studied him on the monitors; as Tillie said, queer but not. Clean-cut, muscular, good grin; gonads okay. Something sapless in the eyes. What in hell could he do?

The chief's first thought had been, of course, sabotage.

'Stupid,' I husked to George. 'Harem slaves don't blow up the harem and themselves just to keep the new girls out. They wait and poison the new girls when they can get away with it. That does us no good.'

'Nor do historical analogies, after a point.'

'Analogic reasoning works when you have the right reference frame. We need a new one. For instance, look at the way the Capellans overturned our psychic scenery, our view of ourselves as integral to this world. Or look at their threat to our male-dominant structure. Bigger, more dominant women who treat our males as sex-slave material. Walking nightmares . . . notice that "mare"? All right – what is the exact relationship between the Capellans and us? Give me that Danish report again.'

The two gorgeous Danes had at least gotten some biological information between orgies – maybe they were more used to them. They confirmed that the Capellans carried sex-linked differences. Capellan males matured to Earth-normal size and sexual features, but the adolescent females went through a secondary development spurt and emerged as the giantesses we had seen. With the specialized characteristics that I had inadvertently become familiar with. And more: some millennia back a mutation started cropping up among the women. Fall-out from a war, perhaps? No answer. Whatever the cause, women began failing to develop. In other words, they stayed as earth-type normals, able to reproduce in what the Capellans regarded as immature form.

Alarmed, the Capellan matriarchate dealt with the problem in a relatively humane way. They rounded up all suspected mutant lines and deported them to remote planets, of which Terra was one. Hence the old chart notation.

Our present visitors had been ore-hunting at nearly maximum range when they decided to check on the semi-mythical colony. No one else ever had.

'What about the Capellans' own history?'

'Not much. Look at that British quote: "We have always been as we are."'

'Isn't that just what we thought about ourselves – *until they landed*?'

George's tired eyelids came open wide.

'Are you thinking what I –'

'We've got Tillie. Mavrua probably knows enough

to noodle their input indicators. It wouldn't take much. What is to Tillie as a Capellan is to us?'

'Bobo!' put in Mrs Peabody, from some ambush.

'Bobo will do nicely,' I went on. 'Now we work up the exact scenery –'

'But, Jesus, Max! Talk about forlorn chances –' protested George.

'Any chance beats no chance. Besides, it's a better chance than you think. Some day I'll tell you about irrational sex phobias, I've had some unique data. Right now we've got to get this perfect, that's all. No slips. You cook it and I'm going to vet every millimeter of every frame. Twice.'

But I didn't. My fever went up, and they put me back in the cooler. Every now and then Tillie dropped in to tell me things like the ore piles on Luna had quit growing, and the crew was evidently busy air-sealing the hold. How was George doing? Great. Mavrua had transmitted the crucial frames. In my more lucid moments I realized George probably didn't need any riding – after all, he'd trained on those Mongolian yak parties.

If this were public history I'd give you the big drama of those nine days, the technical problems that got licked, the human foul-ups that squeaked by. Like the twenty-four hours in which the Joint Chiefs were insisting on monitoring the show through a channel that would have generated an echo – their scientists said no, but the President finally trusted ours and killed that. Or the uproar when we found out, about Day Five, that the French had independently come up with a scheme of their own, and were trying to talk privately to Mavrua – at a time when his Capellan chief was around, too. The President had to get the UN Secretary and the French Premier's mother-in-law to hold that.

That let the cat out of the first bag; the high-level push to get in the act began. And there was the persistent intrusion from our own Security side, who wanted to hitch Mavrua up to some kind of interstellar polygraph to check him out. And the discovery at the last minute, of a flaw in our scanning pulse which would have left a fatal trace, so that new equipment had to be assembled and lofted to the satellite relay all one sleepless night. Oh, there was drama, all right. George got quite familiar with the sight of the President pulling on his pants.

Or I could paint you the horror visions now growing in all our minds, of snow that never stopped, of glaciers forming and grinding down from the poles across the world's arable land. Of eight billion people ultimately trying to jam themselves into the shrinking, foodless equatorial belt. Of how few would survive. A great and dramatic week in world history – during which our hero, in actual fact, was worrying mostly about an uncontrolled staph colony in his cracked pelvis and dreaming of dragging seals home to his igloo off Key West.

'How're your teeth, baby?' I asked what seemed to be a solid version of Tillie, swimming in the antibiotic fogs. I'd been dreaming that her head had been resting on my arm cast.

'?'

'Teeth. Like for chewing blubber. That's what Eskimo women do.'

She drew back primly, seeing I was conscious.

'It's getting out, Max. The wise money is starting to slip south.'

'Best stick with me, baby. I have a complete arctic camping outfit.'

She put her hand on my head then. Nice hand.

'Sex will get you nowhere,' I told her. 'In times to come it's the girls who can chew hides who'll get the men.'

She blew smoke in my face and left.

On Day Minus Four there was a diversion. The Capellan party who had landed in Africa were now partying around the Pacific on their way to pick up the VTO launch in Mexico. Since Authority was still sitting on all the vital information, the new batch of Girls from Capella were as popular as ever with the public. Behind the scenes there was a hot debate in progress about how they could be used as hostages. To me this was futile – what could we even hope to get?

Meanwhile their launch was sitting unattended at Mexico City, showing no signs of the various cosmic can openers we had tried. All the united military could do was to englobe it with guard devices and a mob of assorted special troops.

On Day Minus Four the three Girls went fishing off a Hawaiian atoll, in a catamaran. They were inshore of their naval escort. One of them yawned, said something.

At that moment the VTO boat in Mexico went *whirr*, let out a blast that incinerated a platoon of Marines and took off. A Jap pilot earned his family a pension by crashing it at 90,000 feet with his atomic warheads armed. As far as we could find out, he never even caused a course correction.

The VTO came scorching down on the atoll just as the Girls drifted up to the beach. They sauntered over and were inside before the naval watchdogs got their heads out of their radar hoods. Two minutes later they were out of atmosphere. So much for the great hostage plan.

After this I kept dreaming it was getting colder. On Day Minus Three I thought I saw rhododendron leaves outside my window hanging straight down, which they do at 46 degrees Fahrenheit. Mrs Peabody had to come over to tell me the ship was still on Luna, and it was 82 outside.

Day Minus Two was it. They rolled me over to George's projection room for the show. We had one of the two slave-screens, the UN had the other. The Chief hadn't wanted that – partly from the risk of detection, but mostly because it was ninety-nine to one the thing would bomb out. But too many nations knew we were trying something.

I was late, due to a flat tire on my motorized coffin. George's masterpiece was already running when they wedged me through the doors. In the dimness I could make out the Chief up front, with a few cabinet types and the President. The rest seemed to be just two-feather Indians like me. I guess the President wanted to be in his own family when it blew.

The screen show was pretty impressive. A big Capellan hunched over her console, sweat streaming down her face, yelling a low steely contralto into her mike. I couldn't get the words but I picked up the repetitive cadence. The screen flickered – George had worked authentic interstellar noise into the send – and then it jumped a bit, like an early flick when the ship goes down with Pearl White lashed to a bunk. There were intermittent background crashes, getting louder, and one cut-off screech.

Then the back wall started to quake, and the door went out in a laser flare. Something huge kicked it all the way down, and Bobo came in.

Oh my aunt, he was beautiful. Bobo Updyke, the sweetest monster I've known. I heard a chair squeak beside me and there he was, beaming at his image on the screen. They'd fixed him up with love. Nothing crude – just a bit more jaw on what he had, and the terrible great paws very clean. The uniform – Mau-Mau on a solid base of SS *schrechlichheit*. Somebody had done something artfully bestial about the eyes, too. For an instant he just stood there. The crashes quit, like held breath.

There's rape and rape, you know. The brutal violation of the body, that's bad enough. But there's worse – the atrocities done to the vulnerable body in order to violate the spirit, the savage mockery of sex that joys in degrading the living victim to a broken *thing*. That's what they'd put into Bobo and that's what the Capellan on the screen turned up her face to look at. All sweet Auschwitz.

Did I say Bobo is seven-feet-two plus his helmet which brushed the ceiling, and Tillie isn't five feet? It was something to see. He put out one huge hand. (I heard that footage was reshot twenty-two times.) His other hand was coming toward the camera. More background crash. The last you saw between Bobo's oncoming fingers was her breast ripping naked and more hulking males beyond the door. Blackness – a broken shriek and a, well, noise. The screen went dead.

Our lights came on. Bobo giggled shyly. People were getting up. I saw Tillie before the crowd covered her. She had some blue gook on her eyelids and her hair was combed. I decided I'd give her a break on the blubber-chewing.

People moved around, but the tension didn't break. There was nothing to do but wait. In one corner was Harry with a console. Somebody brought in coffee; somebody else brought in a napkin that gurgled into the chiefs' dixie cups. There was a little low talk that stopped whenever Harry twitched.

The world knows what happened, of course. They didn't even stop for their ore. It was 74 minutes later that Harry's read-outs began to purr softly.

Up on Luna, power was being used to close airlocks, shift busbars. Generators were running up. The great sensitive ears yearning at them from the Bank quivered. At minute 125 the dials started to swing. The big ship was moving. It floated off its dock in the Alps, drifted briefly in an expanding orbit, and then Harry's board went wild as it kicked itself outward. Toward Pluto.

'Roughly one hundred and seventy-nine degrees from the direction of Capella,' said George, as they rolled me out. 'If they took Harry's advice, they're working their way home via the Magellanic Clouds.'

Next day we got the electronic snow as they went into space drive. To leave us, we may hope, for another couple of millennia.

The official confirmation of their trajectory came on the day they let me try walking. (I told you this was history as I lived it.) I walked out the front door, over a chorus of yowls. Tillie came along to help. We never did refer to precisely what it was that made her able to grip my waist and let me lean on her shoulder. Or why we were suddenly in Magruder's buying steak and stuff to take to my place. She was distrustful of my claim to own garlic, and insisted on buying fresh. The closest we came – then or ever – to an explanation was over the avocado counter.

'It's all relative, isn't it?' she said to the avocados.

'It is indeed,' I replied.

And really, that was it. If the Capellans could bring us the news that we were inferior mutations, somebody could bring them the word that they were inferior mutations. If big, hairy Mama could come back and surprise her runt relations, a bigger, hairier Papa could appear and surprise Mama.

– Always provided that you had a half-pint female who could look and talk like a Capellan for seven minutes of tape, and a big guy who could impersonate a walking nightmare, and one disaffected alien to juggle frequencies so a transmission from a nearby planet came through as a send from home base. And a pop genius like George to screen the last stand of the brave Capellan HQ officer, sticking to her mike to warn all ships to save themselves from the horror overwhelming the home planet.

It had been Harry's touch to add that the invaders had long-range detector sweeps out and ordering all ships to scatter to the ends of the galaxy.

So, all things being potentially relative, everybody including Mrs Peabody got a medal for bringing Papa home. And my mama came home with me, although I still don't know how she is on chewing blubber.

Help

'Here we go again,' said Harry's voice in my ear.

I discovered my wife had woken up first and was holding the office phone over my face. It was still dark.

'– down by the Lunar Alps. Visuals just coming in.'

'Not those Capellan jocks again?' I groaned.

'Smaller. Different emission features. Get down here, Max.'

Tillie was already dressing. When we'd gone to bed two hours back, the ears of Earth were following a moving source which kept disappearing behind Luna, and our moon station near Mersenius was scrambling to set up a far-side relay. Now the alien had landed, a third of a great circle from our station.

The photo courier passed us at the office door. Mersenius had sent a camera-eye over the alien ship.

'Looks as if they're interested in those ore-piles the Capellans left,' said George. 'What's that, a derrick?'

'Derrick my azimuth,' I grunted, rapidly opening and closing alternate eyes to catch small differences in consecutive negatives. That's called flashing. Big photo-shops do it with a trunk-sized geewhizzus that's almost as efficient as the trained human eye.

'That's them. It. He. He is moving an arm . . . he is shifting his stance . . . bipedal? Maybe, if that's a tail. Yes!

He is moving his tail. What did we have for the height of that ore-pile?'

'Forty-one meters.' Mrs Peabody had joined us, Living Bra alert and dedicated.

'Tentative estimate, six meters tall,' I concluded. 'We'll see what Langley says in the morning; they've got better comparators. And not human. Let me project this shadow – if it straightened up, it would look something like a small tyrannosaurus, wouldn't you say?'

The spy-eye gave us a close-up on its second pass, just before the alien knocked it down. We saw a lizard-like creature, helmeted and harnessed with weird hardware, wearing an unpleasant expression on its lipless face. And blue.

'Eighteen-foot blue space-going dinosaurs, that's what's up there,' said Harry. 'At least two of them.'

'Or praying mantises,' said George.

'Maybe he's a she,' said Tillie.

'Quit dreaming kid,' I told her. 'The lulu is played only once in a lifetime.'

By this time, the main photo-shop had confirmed my height guess and added that the two aliens had pulled the spy-eye in with some sort of beam and then apparently cut it open for a brief look before blowing the remains.

Meanwhile the hotlines of the world were steaming, and the United Nations halls were boiling with delegates trying to get a decision on what to tell Mersenius to do. So many electric razors were used in the UN lounge that they blew a fuse and killed our landline for fifteen minutes. At0800 EST the question became academic.

The aliens took off on a fast-precessing orbit around Terra itself.

So far they had been silent. Now they began to transmit, and George ascended to his idea of heaven with an endless supply of alien gabble to chew on.

What exactly is our shop? Basically, an unimportant bit of CIA that got left out in the big move to Langley. (I warned you this would be the inside story from the pick-and-shovel level; I couldn't know less about what the President said to the Premier.) We're officially listed as a communications and special support facility. Just a small crew of oddball linguists and blown operators put out to pasture. It was a nice restful life until we accidentally got into the first great alien contact flap three years back. The Capellans, you'll recall.

George came out of that as our official Extraterrestrial Language Specialist, which hasn't done his small-man's ego any good. I am optimistically regarded as having a flare for alien psychology – shows you what can happen to a fair photo-interpreter. And Tillie is an ace polyglot. Did you know you get clobbered for calling a polyglot a linguist? Anyway, she's George's deputy. And my wife. Harry is our captive physicist-of-all-work since they decided we rated an R&D. Mrs Peabody got upgraded to Chief of Archives, but she still helps me with my income-tax forms.

After the Girls from Capella left hurriedly we all expected to coast into distinguished retirement with no further calls on our peculiar talents, if any. Now suddenly here was Another Alien merrily orbiting Terra, and our little shop was being pelted with data and demands for answers.

'They appear to be sending some sort of standard contact broadcast,' George reported. 'Three or four phrases repeated, and switch to a different language. At least twenty-eight so far. One of them resembles Capellan, but not enough to read.'

'I think it's like a high Capellan,' said Tillie. 'You know, like Mandarin to Cantonese. The Capellans who came here must have spoken a dialect. I'm sure I heard a formal *I* and *You* and something about *speak.*'

'Could it be *Do you speak our language?* Or *Will you speak?*'

The nations were now in hot debate as to whether and what to reply to the alien. George could scarcely be prevented from trying to pull something through his friends at NSA; he was sweating for fear the Swedes or Japs would beat us to it. But we couldn't get an OK. That was the time our Joint Chiefs were so cozy with the President – remember? – and I think there was a struggle to keep them from testing their new anti-orbital-missile missile on the aliens. It may have been the same elsewhere; the big nations had all been working up some space defense since the Capellan visit.

The upshot was that nobody did anything before the alien abruptly stopped transmitting speech and went into repeated da-dits. That lasted an hour. Then two things happened right together.

First, Harry got a signal from Defense R&D that one of their boys had identified a digital equation having to do with fissionable elements in the da-dits. Right after that came the word from a Soviet tracker that the alien had ejected an object which was now trailing their ship.

We all ducked and held our breaths.

The blip stayed in orbit.

Just as we started breathing again, the alien poked out a laser finger and the trailing blip went up in the prettiest fusion flare you ever saw – a complex burst, like three shorts and a long.

This is probably where you came in. With that flare overhead, the world media roared out of control. 'ALIENS BLAST EARTH!' 'BLUE LIZARDS HURL BOMB FROM SKY!' The military was already loose, of course, and an assortment of mega-squibs were blasting up towards the alien ship.

They never connected. The alien deftly distributed three more blips in a pattern around earth, about 150,000 miles out, and took off in the direction of the Coal Sack. They had been in our system exactly thirteen hours, during which the united brains of Earth had demonstrated all the initiative of a shocked opossum.

'Call me anthropocentric, but they struck me as ugly customers,' I brooded later.

'And very alien,' said Tillie.

'You're supposed to be able to identify, remember?' She gave me the old sulky leer, with the new magic ingredient.

'Marriage has ruined you, stud . . . Hey, George! Did you hear that those bombs they left are covered with writing? About a zillion different scripts, in a nice fluorescent blue. It's your life work, old brother.'

'A galactic Rosetta stone,' breathed George as he sat down. 'Max, you *must* prevent the military from destroying them. The photos are not adequate.'

'Three time-bombs going past our ears on the hour, and you want to preserve them as a reference library? What if they're loaded with disease? Or mutation inducers? Stupid-making generators, so we won't get into space? Have you heard the newscasts? George, sober up.'

'They can't,' he groaned. 'It's priceless! The key to the galaxy!'

As it turned out, they didn't, at least not then. Somebody was either too scared or too avid for alien technology. A US-Soviet astroteam managed to make a remote-control dock with one of the ten-foot missiles and spent two weeks gingerly coaxing it around to a crater on the far side of Luna.

From that minute, George lived to get to the moon. To my amazement, he screamed the medicos into an acceleration and low-G clearance, and next thing we knew he was actually booked for the Mersenius shuttle trip. In spite of looking like a dissipated gerbil, George was fundamentally healthy.

At the good-bye party he told me he felt sure he had detected Capellan script on the missile's fin.

'Same as the verbal transmission – something about *I you speak*.'

'How about: *If you can read this you're too damn close*? Good luck.'

So that was how we came to be short of our extraterrestial language expert when Alien No. 2 came along. (Or No. 3, if you count from the Capellans.) You know most

of the story here. The new boys followed the same routine as the lizards: a couple of passes over Luna, pause to
inspect the ore-piles, and then into orbit and start to transmit. There was a diversion when they spotted the two
flying bombs. They quit transmitting and, while the world
watched, they sneaked up behind one of the blips. There
was no laser probe. Instead, we saw some sort of fog drift
out of the newcomer's ship and envelope the blip.

'They've melted it!' Harry yelled on the intercom.
When the fog moved on, we could all see the blip was
gone. The aliens were heading for the other.

'NEW ALIENS CLEAR BOMBS FROM SKY!
MENACE FROM SPACE DESTROYED!' Remember?

With the second bomb gone, our new pals resumed
transmission. Tillie was our acting chief linguist.

'What'll I do, Max? George won't acknowledge his
orders to return!'

'You can do it, girl. What's so hard about little stick
figures? Read it like a comic strip.'

'Did you ever try saying *Who are you?* or *Where do you
come from?* in little stick figures?' she asked bitterly.

But they did look humanoid and peaceful enough.
One sketch they kept repeating showed a mixture of big
and little figures dancing around a maypole affair.

'The little figures seem to be them, and the big ones
are us,' said Tillie.

'You hope. And this one means they want to land,
right?'

You'll recall we let them come down in a burnt-over
wilderness area in northern Quebec. No aloha-parties like
we gave the Girls from Capella. No official grandstand.

Just an empty plain, a sky full of contrails, and five differ-ent brands of over-kill zeroed in on that big golden ship as it settled.

The airlock opened.

Everyone remembers what marched out into that empty plain – a band of little figures about four feet high and the color of the More Expensive Spread. They seemed to be wearing jointed yellow armor with funny little half-opened helmets on their heads. They were carrying what looked like cereal-box death-ray guns. Each one held his up and then gravely trooped over and dropped his weapon on a pile. Then they joined hands and began to sing.

This was the world's first taste of what came to be known as the Sound from Cygnus. It wasn't really too different from a musical saw to me, but you know how it caught on. Oh my earmuffs, did it catch on! That's right, you had teen-aged kids. The thing hadn't been zingling through our office a minute before I saw La Peabody starting to twitch.

While we absorbed the Sound, a second band of little butter-boys marched out of the ship carrying a globe on a pole. The distant trigger fingers tightened. But all they did was to set it up in the center like the maypole in their sketches, and sing harder. Waiting for someone to say hello.

It wasn't long before a reception committee crawled out of the bunkers and the second alien contact got underway.

Quite a relief after the previous hoopla. This one went more like grown up. No sex, no fireworks. Just a mob of decorous little yellow squirts earnestly interested in learning our languages and customs. Their chief concern seemed to be to avoid getting poisoned by our food. Did you know they were vegetarians? They answered everything we asked as well as they could. Their home system was quickly identified as Cygnus 61. The death-ray pistols were lasers; they passed out samples. They made no more objection to electronic surveillance than a herd of Guernseys, and they let us into the ship with anything we wanted to bring. Harry was in on that.

'Same general thing as the Capellans,' he reported. 'And fairly old. They seem to have bought it second-hand from somewhere. Two auxiliary flyers on board. No major weapons we can find aside from some small standard missiles and that particle-fog thing. That looks to be a catalyst effect.'

'What makes you think they didn't build it?'

'Every time we ask a technical question they drag out a manual to look up the answer. They ended by giving us the whole set to copy. I brought back the lot. Where's George?'

'He won't answer. What's one language when he has hundreds? He's up there with his Rosetta stone, and I doubt he'll budge till his oxygen runs out.'

'Funny thing,' Harry mused. 'They have this maypole thing all over the ship, in different sizes. One big room looks exactly like a chapel. I believe they're deeply religious.'

Just in time, I recalled that Harry himself was deeply religious.

And that of course was the big news about our visitors.

Until the religious angle came out, the Siggies threatened to be about as newsworthy as a Trivet-maker's convention. When the official tours got started it was quickly realized that the Sound was hymns. You remember the pictures – circles of little yellow fellows setting up their maypoles at dawn, noon and sunset, wherever they happened to be, joining hands and singing and beckoning the bystanders to join in. With that Sound and their appealing appearance, they got a lot of takers, especially with young people.

This seemed to delight them. 'You comp? You comp?' they would call. 'Good! You glike? Good?' they asked, peering up into the human faces around them when the song was over. When people smiled back, the Siggies would grab their hands and squeeze. Their hands were cool and felt fragile. 'Like a child's hands in paper gloves,' one reporter said.

'I do think they're sweet,' Mrs Peabody confessed. 'Those little brown button eyes peering out.'

'Reminds me of Hobbits,' said Tillie. 'Meriadoc in armor.'

'It's not armor, it's an exoskeleton,' I told her. 'It doesn't come off.'

'I know – but listen, they're going to sing.'

By now we knew that the object on top of the poles was not a globe. It was roughly egg-shaped, with interior creases.

'Like a bagel,' said Mrs Peabody.

'They call it something like the Pupa, or the Great Pupa,' said Tillie. 'It represents a Cygnian wrapped up in a cocoon. See the face?'

'Looks sad,' said Harry.

There was a note of sadness in the songs, too – sadness and exaltation, which added immensely to the appeal. The recording companies knew a good thing when it fell on their heads and the Sound rapidly became a menace on the radio bands. Rapa had three kids and told me he had wrecked his set to stay sane. Well, you know all about it, those first weeks with the Siggies touring around and singing in front of churches and mosques and temples, and the Unitarian minister coming out to hold joint services in the open air, and the kids wearing maypole buttons and Great Pupa buttons and all the rest. Hands Across the Galaxy. Oekoumene!

What you don't know about is S'serrop. (We spelled it that way to indicate a hard buzzing *r-r-r*. The Cygnians were strong on stops and clicks, but had trouble with our nasals and semivowels – I quote from Tillie.)

S'serrop came to us when the West Hemisphere Cygnian party first went through DC. We met him at the official mass reception – an indefinably tatty-looking Cygnian, somewhat pale in color. He was one of their many language students, and he and Tillie went into a fast huddle. We had our chief ask for him to stay behind when the tour moved on, and for a wonder we got him, after State had been practically in bed with the party for a week. The Siggies jumped at any chance to learn our languages. I guess they were surprised at the number.

The thing about S'serrop was that he was different. A marginal Cygnian, if you like. We never found out why. How can you evaluate aberrant factors in an arthropod's childhood? Anyway, he gave us some new insights. The first was about Siggie emotion.

Remember how they always looked so sort of neat and merry? Well, S'serrop disabused us of that the day he tried to join us eating meat. He was yellower than usual when George was ordering the salad for him at Rapa's

'Gno!' clicked S'serrop. 'I eat samp as hew!'

His yellow color grew richer while he rejected our protests. When the meatballs arrived, we saw the crisis. You know that crest of tiddly bits sticking out above the Cygnian visor was actually their chemoreceptors and part of their ears? At sight of the meat, S'serrop's receptors began to retreat until his 'helmet' was a smooth round sphere. He took a mouthful, chomped once, and looked wildly about. The gesture was so human I was on my feet ready to help our visitor from space to Rapa's can. But he had swallowed and sat there breathing hard. Stern stuff, S'serrop. Tillie snatched up his plate and substituted greens, and after a while his crest came back out.

That gave us the clue. There was a Siggie song-fest near the Mormon Temple in Salt Lake City on the screen that night.

'Max!' Tillie gasped. 'Look at their heads!'

Every one of them was as bare and round as a billiard ball. And they were glowing like hot curry.

'Intense fear, disgust, revulsion . . . funny emotions for a quiet party of space-going sociologists.'

'I'll ask S'serrop.'

'Very carefully. Very, very carefully.'

Oddly enough, Harry had already done the job. We

discovered he had been mixing quite a lot of religious discussion in with the particle physics. (Strange thing, I never can figure out where physicists *keep* their Almighty, but they seem to be among His chief defenders these days.) Anyway, Harry gave us the complete story of the Great Pupa.

'Well, you know the Cygnians are hatched from eggs, and they go through a metamorphosis later into the adult form we've met. Their religion is based on the belief that there is a *further* metamorphosis into a form with wings. Yes, wings. Beautiful, really. It has only happened once, when the Great Pupa achieved it. He was persecuted and tortured. They have – or had – a rather dreadful method of execution in which the victim is wrapped in acid-soaked cloth and his flesh eaten away alive. That's the figure on the pole – you do see the primitive parallel?' Harry interrupted himself.

We nodded silently, staring at a new and different Harry.

'Yes. Well, in his agony, the Great Pupa achieved the ultimate metamorphosis and appeared to his followers afterwards as a winged shape . . . profoundly amazing, isn't it? Over eleven light-years away –'

He told us that he had invited S'serrop to attend church services with him that Sunday. Did we realize no Cygnian had actually entered a Terran house of worship? We also soon realized how S'serrop felt about it. Frightened and revolted, but resolute. When we met them after the service his crest was still half retracted.

Harry had been expounding Christian doctrine to him. The Cygnian was so excited that we could barely understand the barrage of clicks. 'Abast! Abast!' he exclaimed. We took this as *amazed* – or perhaps *abased*?

He desired more information, and Tillie volunteered to find him a religious dictionary in which he could explore Moslem and Hindu, Greek, Roman and Hebrew doctrines as well as Harry's Massachusetts Avenue rites. We saw Harry's face cloud; Tillie told me that he became deeply exercised over questions like the propriety of using candles.

Next morning, I went into Harry's office, feeling a fairly strong shade of yellow myself. He was doodling on his blackboard.

'First of all, Harry, congratulations. The array of talent around here never ceases to amaze me. But – bear with me – there's one thing I'd like to get straight. Are you absolutely one hundred percent satisfied with the official estimate of the aggressive capabilities of that ship?'

He looked at me disdainfully from his galactic evangelical dream.

'You mean weapons?'

'Weapons. Blowpipes, atomic disintegrators, germ cultures – call me a paranoid bastard, Harry. What *could* they do to us if they tried?'

'Really, Max.' He sighed. 'Well . . . they have that short-range laser, and they have about fifty tactical atomic missiles that probably came with the ship. The fusing is less advanced than ours. They're slow. Their auxiliary craft can't go much over Mach I all out. Very vulnerable. They have no laboratories or culture stores. A bare minimum of machining facilities. Their main drive certainly couldn't be used as a mobile torch in atmosphere. They

haven't got the right guidance systems for space attack.
I think the estimate is quite correct; the most they could
possibly do would be a few lucky hits on big targets before
our defenses overtook them.'

He XXd out a couple of equations, angrily.

'Harry, is there *anything* about that ship you don't
understand?'

'No. If you mean, in general. Oh, maybe –'

'Maybe?'

'There are one or two large generators which seem to
be beyond their power needs, that's all. Just generators.
They may have been in the ship when the Siggies got
it, perhaps for powering a ground installation. What's
eating you, Max? Here we have one of the biggest – I'm
not afraid to say it, one of the sweetest things possible
to conceive of . . . Probably you don't get it, Max. I feel
sorry for you. I pity all atheists. But others do get it.'

'I guess I don't get it, Harry, but I'll tell you what's
wrong with me. I've read history. Earth history. A big
strange ship full of religious symbols – an alien race,
fervently pious and revolted by the practices of the natives – doesn't that remind you of anything, Harry? No
bell?'

'Sorry, it doesn't,' he said. He erased the blackboard.
Our comfy little shop had been invaded in more ways
than one.

It got invaded some more next day when S'serrop
turned up after his session with Tillie's dictionary. We
learned about another Cygnian emotion, but we weren't
sure at the time what it was. At first we thought he was
sick. He kept making a rustling, flittering noise which

we saw were his exoskeletal joints snicking together. He said he wasn't sick, it was something else.

'Is bad,' he kept repeating. 'Bad! Sad! Hew – I caddot say – hew so simpet! So behewtiful! Kch, too bad! KCHKCHCH!

Conclusively his elbows began rubbing against his thorax in a blur of motion. A thin shriek rent the air.

Tillie grabbed one of his vibrating hands, and he grabbed back. Hand-holding seemed to be the same on Cygnus as it was on Terra. He stopped the cicada wail and looked gravely in our faces. Then he said something that rocked even Harry.

'So far-r-r! So bady he-yarrrs of gligh!' He spread his arms in what we had come to know as the Great Pupa wing symbol. 'He is hee-yarrr too!' he exclaimed. The next minute he was striding down the hall in the general direction of Rock Creek Park, with his UN guard scrambling after.

Two hours later we discovered he had stampeded State into flying him back to his group, who were touring Mexico. He said he had something urgent to tell them.

In the turmoil, there arrived a covert signal from our man on the moon, namely, George. As predicted, Tillie's boss was shacked up with his explosive lexical treasure around the far side from Mersenius and playing doggo. He had found an old pal at Mersenius to pass down a message demanding data on the Cygnians' writing. The signal ended, 'Don't trust those polyunsaturated pygmies.'

'Small men loathe each other,' Tillie commented.

Of course you realize that the Cygnians had a written language in addition to the cartoon figures they used for firstcontact, but George hadn't seen it before he left. While Tillie assembled some Cygnese, I rooted out the negatives of the script-covered missile George was working on. They looked pretty bad. Can you imagine a Chinese trying to decipher *Ne pas se pencher en dehors* in five European languages? Well, there were about five hundred choice graffiti on each negative, some you wouldn't believe.

'Tillie girl, can you locate Cygnian script among any of these?'

'I don't know.'

'What about those tech manuals they gave us, can't you compare scripts?'

'They were written by whoever built the ship. Diagrams and math.'

'Well don't we have any Cygnian samples?'

'Mostly their cursive.'

Something was all wrong, she was as touchy as a lady porcupine. I pulled her around.

'So you think I'm a stinker. Give me a break. Remember it's just that old heathen Max who scares easy.'

'I think you're being unforgivable to Harry,' she started. Then she squinted at me around her glossy hair. 'Max, are you really scared?'

'You bet I am. Honey, I'm so scared I even think about it in bed.'

'But what *of*, Max?'

'Oh, history, micro-macro parallelism – I don't know. That's the worst of it. See what you can get out of these, would you?'

She tried, but it was no go all Tuesday. And Wednesday you remember what happened.

The West Hemisphere group of Siggies were holding their evening sing-in on the plaza outside the Catedrale de la Dama de something-or-other in São Paulo, Brazil. Inside, a minor mass was about to be celebrated. Instead of their usual circle the Siggies formed a line across the front steps and the human worshippers found themselves barred out.

A couple of clerics came out to protest. The Siggies stood firm, singing. The crowd milled. A padre laid hands on a Siggie, who yielded, but another took his place. The Sound mounted. The cathedral bells started tolling. Somebody called the police, who added sirens to the up-roar. At the height of the confusion two Siggies – bright orange with emotion – marched into the nave and up to the altar, where they deposited a small object. Then they marched out again and rejoined the singing.

Half a minute later the altar area of the cathedral lit up, gave off an amazing sound, and exploded into a flour-like dust which towered up over the plaza and came down all over everybody.

In the melée the Siggies withdrew to the far side of the plaza and formed a circle. It was shortly discovered that they were now protected by some kind of force-shield, presumably generated by a large box which they always carried with them. Defense R&D had identified it as a musical amplifier.

While we were digesting this, news came that the East Hemisphere Siggie group had pulled an almost iden-tical stunt, resulting in the obliteration of the Golden Pavilion in Kyoto.

The fact that the Cygnian ship's auxiliary flyers were

both out on what was described as routine maintenance tests had up to now escaped notice. After a pause, it became apparent where they were flying to. Harry's evaluation sources had been quite right; they were slow. It took the one on our side over six hours to make the seven thousand air miles from Quebec to the little group in the plaza at São Paulo. En route, one of our more enterprising neighbors discovered that it too was now protected by an unknown form of shielding. As it made its weary Mach I way home with the West Hemisphere Siggies inside, our Air Force confirmed this the expensive way.

Somewhere along the line the main ship had englobed itself too, with eight Terran technical people aboard.

'Well, I guess we know what the generators are for now,' I remarked next morning, roaming restlessly around Harry's office.

'An interesting tactical problem,' I mused. 'What can you do with a measly few old badly guided fusion bombs – *provided you can carry them anywhere you want in perfect safety*?'

Harry slammed his papers down hard and inhaled and exhaled explosively. Just as he inhaled again his phone rang.

'When? *Who*? Get him down here. We've got to get him down here! What? All right, I'll go through your damn channels –' He banged the phone down.

'Max. They opened the ship long enough to turn loose our techs. S'serrop came out with them. He's been hurt. Get the chief to get him.'

It was Tillie who got him, but how she did it I don't

know because our chief, like everybody else, was caught up in the runaway oscillation over the Siggie atrocities.

The media caught on a bit slow and generated more confusion than anything else at first. By next day, when the Siggies had leisurely vaporized Milan Cathedral and the Bahai Temple in Chicago, the newscasters hit stride. From there on – you'll remember – it was just one bewildered yell of outrage. The Moslem world held aloof until Friday, when the Blue Mosque of Ahmed at Istanbul went up in flour. For all that first week no one was killed or even badly hurt.

Except S'serrop.

We met his stretcher at Andrews Air Base. He seemed glad to see Harry.

'I trite,' he shrilled feebly. 'I trite explait –' He thrashed a bit, under the blankets. What we could see of his hide was deep yellow, but we couldn't see a lot. They had treated him to an acid massage. Our medicos couldn't do much for the alien biology beyond the obvious topical applications. Like a burned human, he was in toxaemia.

That was the morning the Cygnians started their broadcasts. It was now clear why they had been so eager to learn our languages, but even so, you'll recall that the first messages were more stimulating than enlightening. Our shop had the advantage of an early copy of the eight technicians' reports. The Cygnians had given them an intensive briefing before they let them go.

'Delusions of nonpersecution . . . Harry, I'm sorry.'

He was head-in-hands, down.

'When you look at the history of the early Christian missionaries, say in Polynesia, or Africa –'

'Damnation, Max, do you think you're the only one who's read history? It was just that – my fault – I saw the gestalt the wrong way. From their point of view, *we're* the heathen. You don't need to rub it in. They never even bothered to try to understand –'

'How many missionaries ever tried to understand the native religions? They just threw down the idols, burned the ju-jus, destroyed the temples . . . unspeakable savage rites, I believe was the standard phrase.'

'Only S'serrop. He tried.'

'Yes, he tried. He's a believer too, of course, but liberal. What it adds up to, Harry, is a bunch of dedicated, primitive fundamentalists who bought themselves a boat and set out to bring the word to the heathen. With atomics.'

'Missionaries with fissionaries,' ventured Mrs Peabody, and shut up abruptly.

'I blame myself –'

'Don't Harry. What could a Bushman make of a gun until he'd seen it fired? He'd have put it down as a clumsy kind of club. We'd never seen a generator used to throw a standing energic whatsis.'

'But how can they hope to succeed?' Tillie asked. 'It's so *crazy*! To make the whole population of Earth worship the Great Pupa? We aren't even the same kind of animal. It's insane.'

'What do you think the Holy Family looked like to a polygamous culture where a man's father was his mother's brother? No. Insane or not, conversion by the sword can work. What's our price for saving St Peter's or Westminster, or Santa Sophia, for starters? Or the Kremlin? Friends, don't be too sure. You'll be attending Great

Pupa services in Carter Barron Amphitheater in the near future, I promise you.'

'What about you?' snapped Tillie.

'Purification,' Harry was muttering. 'Fire.' His eyes were pale and clear like a weimaraner's.

'The early Christians survived, Max. Underground, in the catacombs. In the days of the martyrs. From persecution will come rebirth.'

I refrained from asking him to name a few aboriginal religions which had survived the Society of Jesus. I had something else to worry about.

'Can S'serrop talk at all, Tillie? It's urgent.'

Well, you recall what went on then, the public convulsions, the predictable and pathetic brave responses we made to the Cygnians' simple ultimatum. I guess what riled people the most was the level of their pitch. They had apparently tagged us as Stone Age Stanley.

'You can see the Great Pupa is the true god, because our weapons are stronger than yours. Your false gods can not protect themselves, or you.' Right off page one of a nineteenth-century missionary handbook.

The part about them ending our local strife in universal brotherhood as children of the Great Pupa wasn't so bad, although I don't think people went for the idea of themselves as larvae. But when they got into the higher doctrinal mysteries – and what they proposed to do about our sex and mating customs, they being biologically rather different . . .

It was while they were explaining that aspect that the British C-in-C up in Quebec laid our biggest nuclear egg neatly on the Cygnian ship. The broadcast stopped. Two days later when things settled down, the ship was still sitting there englobed with debris. After a while a new type of transmission came out of the force-shell, and every piece of metal several kilometers beyond the blast-hole went to vapor. Then the religious broadcasts resumed. The Great Pupa was indeed a strong god.

Over everybody's protests, I tried to get S'serrop to locate and decipher any Cygnian text he could find on my photos of George's missile.

'What in hell do you expect to prove, Max? Even if there's a Cygnian text, so what? We know the story now.'

'Do *we*? I thought you said you'd read history.'

But S'serrop was nearly blind, and terribly weak. He did appear to recognize the photos.

'Too bad!' he whispered again. 'Kchch! Too bad –'

'Leave him alone, Max.'

'Wait! S'serrop – Tillie ask him this: are there others? More like him? Coming here?'

We couldn't get his answer, but as you know, we were not left long in doubt.

Since this is just the inside story we'll skip the history-makers, the steady attrition of our religious monuments (don't think Chartres didn't rock me) – the efforts of the Vatican, Israel and the International Council of Churches of Christ to negotiate some kind of coexistence for the West at least – the day the Siggies, by an understandable theological error, took out the New York Stock Exchange – the United Arab kamikaze attempt – the successful assault on two isolated Siggies in Chile – the Sino-Soviet proposal – you know all that. The inside story isn't much, here: sixteen long go-arounds between me and our chief, ending in stalemate. And then the second Cygnian ship arrived.

It put down in the North African desert. Same general type, a bit newer and knobbier and copper rather than gold. The same opening ceremonies, but these Siggies were definitely orange – Red Siggies as they were dubbed. As you can imagine, the welcoming committee was conspicuously absent.

'Reinforcements?' Tillie asked.

'I devoutly hope so,' I said. She gave me the look I was getting used to those days.

'I've got to see S'serrop.'

'You'll kill him, Max.'

She was right. When S'serrop saw the photos of the new Cygnians he went – or tried to go – into his shivering and stridulating act. It seemed to be involuntary, like uncontrollable sobs. He couldn't stop himself from knocking the dressings around. Not that they were doing him any good, but the result was horrible. In his agony he could barely be understood. What came through clearly at the end was: 'I trite! I trite!' And then something so obviously a private prayer that I snapped the recorder off. He died that night.

I spent the night with that tape and was waiting on the chief's doormat with my reconstruction in the morning. At noon he was still not in. His hot-line girl told me about the fire-fight between Yellow Siggie and Red Siggie flyers, in which most of Marseilles had come up missing.

At 1500 the chief was still going 'round in the high level whirlwind. I decided to take – it says here on my citation – independent initiative. What the hell, how much

Class A office furniture do you get in a catacomb? I had nothing to lose.

The independence took the form of a structure of tastefully forged directives and speciously worded co-ordinating concurrences, at the end of which chain of duplicity there emerged in about sixty hours' time one live Astromarine lieutenant. He looked exactly like a video space hero except he had cold-sores. He contributed the action.

By this time the Red Siggies, who seemed to be faster workers and more practical-minded, had decided that it would make for more togetherness if we evacuated our lunar bases. There was to be just one shuttle-run per each, and Mersenius was unluckily scheduled as Number Two. You'd be up all night if I told you what it took to get that box into a disguised cargo-pod. Harry, who knew I was nuts but was too far gone to argue, helped a lot. After that we could only hope.

By this point the bands were so loaded with Red and Yellow Siggie broadcasts and counter-broadcasts and doctrinal trumpetings and counter-counter-jamming that we were virtually blind and deaf, electronically speaking. To this day, I don't understand the difference between their versions of the Great Pupa religion. Something about the powers of the clergy and the exist-ence of other lesser Pupas or prophets. Harry is making a study of it.

I was trying to keep score of the accidental damage sustained by Earth when the Yellow and Red missionary flyers tangled. You remember how the media kept saying that they were decimating each other? People outside really hoped that one faction would eliminate the other, at least; or maybe they might even kill each other off. The inside reports gave no such hope. We had no concrete evidence that they could do each other any serious damage and the side-effects on us were brutal. People were getting killed now, as well as churches. Marseilles was the star; next came Altoona, of all places, and poor old Coventry and Tangiers. And a lot of smaller places.

'This phase won't last,' I pontificated. 'The history of religious wars is like any other. Your main attack is not on the enemy leaders but on their followers. That'll be us, when they get organized. We'll have to sign up with one lot or the other, and when we do we get it. What's the matter, Harry? In particular, I mean?'

'Houston's picked up a new type of transmission from both ships, beamed off-planet.'

'Calling for reinforcements?'

'Probably.'

'And *alles ganz kaput* . . . Did you ever identify that planet S'serrop described?'

'Not positively. I personally think that was Cygnus 61. I don't believe these creatures are Cygnians; they just came from Cygnus 61 in the sense that that was the last place they stopped. Perhaps they were there quite some time –'

'Before they and their competition managed to fracture the planetary crust.'

'I wonder what the real Cygnians were like,' sighed Tillie.

'What I wonder is where Lieutenant Sternhagen

is. At least he wasn't brought down in the Mersenius evacuation.'

As it turned out, of course, Lieutenant Sternhagen was right where he was supposed to be. He had cleverly managed to unpack himself undetected after his ghastly trip in the pod and had slipped away on his trek around to the far side. All we had been able to give him was a dinky personal jato unit. After 120 hours of hopping, sliding, gliding and tumbling he reached George, who was blissfully holed up with his life work and a nice little hydroponics set-up he had wangled out of his Mersenius pals. The young Marine, as directed, asked George one or two pointed questions.

The answers being on the right trajectory, Lieutenant Sternhagen stayed not to argue but injected a little dream-juice into George's airlines. Then he had a busy time boosting the missile – carefully – out of the cave, carrying George over a couple of rim-walls and stowing him, and laying a remote-control laser line.

The thing went up beautifully as demonstrated, three shorts and a long, but of course we couldn't see from Earth. After that the young Marine, who had received only minor radiation burns in addition to his previously acquired contusions, had nothing to do except hop, slide and tumble 120 hours back to the empty Mersenius base hauling an hysterical George, who was undamaged except in his aspiration-level.

By a miracle, Mersenius had registered our covert signal and left sufficient supplies to allow the pair to survive until rescue, during which time George had the opportunity to say everything he wanted to, about fifteen thousand times. It doesn't tell half enough on Lieutenant Sternhagen's medal.

After this, there was nothing at all to do but wait. And wait. And wait. The rest of the world, who weren't waiting for anything, just reacted. You know. Fortunately the loss of human life was relatively low as yet, except for Marseilles, Jaipur, and Altoona where the Yellow Siggies had been holding a mass outdoor Great Pupa baptism ceremony.

I'll say this for the Siggies, they were brave. The Yellow Siggie conducting services didn't even look up when the Red flyer came over – just sang harder. Glory, glory.

The weapon they chiefly used was a variant of the catalytic vaporizer business. R&D had not guessed that it could be produced as a rather bountiful fuel by-product. We counted a total of only five actual missiles expended to date. If the Red Siggies had brought in another fifty, that left ninety-five to go. Their fallout proved to be rather more copious than the best art, too.

During the next week, two of our tracking stations got melted and we were down to our last ear-flaps when we caught a new ship coming in.

'The reinforcements,' Harry said. He had taken to shadow-boxing the eraser, very softly.

'Why?'

'Both Siggie ships are transmitting nonstop.'

But it wasn't their reinforcements.

The little blue ship made one orbit and then came in low over North Africa and on to Quebec. When it had passed, both Siggie ships were still there and apparently undamaged, but they had lost some of their shine. On the ground the Siggie groups were scrambling first for cover and then for their ships. We only caught part of the saurian transmission in Cygnese – something about one planetary rotation.

Thirty hours later both Red and Yellow Siggies were on their way out of our system, leaving us with five smashed cities, innumerable wrecked houses of religion, and more maypole effigies of the Great Pupa than could be counted before they were melted down. The blue lizards left too – we still don't know where they're from

'You guessed they were cops. How?' said Harry. We were at Rapa's back table, celebrating George's return. After blowing out his outrage on Sternhagen, George had more or less run down about the criminal destruction of his galactic key.

'My glands. Primitive response to the fuzz aura. Once you saw them as two guys in a squad car it all fit. They couldn't stick around. They set up call-boxes. One demonstration of how to work it, good-bye. Holler if you need help, right, George? Tell me, old brother, how long had you known? Never mind, don't answer that. I respect a man who values knowledge more than the mere survival of his culture, not to say his race. I won't ask you if you would ever have got round to triggering it –'

'Max!' shouted Tillie.

'All right . . . Say there was a report that these so-called Cygnians and such are messing around with backward planets. Somewhere, there's a minor policy directive. Pressure from a Society to Save Our Seminoles. Low budget. Two guys to cover a sector. Probably left a set of flares around any number of likely planets. The Siggies knew damn well what they were, too.'

'Is that like history?' asked Mrs Peabody.

'Not really. Certainly not in the old days. The poor benighted heathen caught in sectarian wars just suffered. Did any of you read about what happened to people who happened to be in the path of a crusade, by the way? We've missed that, so far.'

'Their religion was sort of poetic in a way. I mean, changing to wings –'

I saw Harry wince.

'Tell you what isn't so beautiful, if you want more history. This is all early-stage stuff. Informal. Like when Tahiti or the Congo were months away from Europe, and North America was half wild. A few private schooners wild-catting around. What happens now we got saved? Do we go back to our palm trees and peace?'

'Why not?' shrugged Tillie. Then she said 'Oh.'

'Exactly. The next stage was, industrial nation-states got organized into coalitions and went to war for global mastery. What happens to the people in the sarongs when something like Admiral Tojo's fleet sails into the lagoon to set up a fortified base? And something like Admiral Nimitz's fleet and the Allied air armada arrives to throw him out?'

' . . . Viet Nam,' murmured Harry.

I could see Tillie trying to think of something cheerful and not succeeding. Pouring George a drink, she asked, 'Did any of you know how old S'serrop was?'

'Huh?'

'A kid. About like our nineteen. He got involved with

the natives and felt sorry for us and begged the heads of the mission to leave us alone because the Great Pupa's spirit had already touched us, in another form. That made him a heretic.'

'Any parallels there, Max?'

We went to bed on that one and I'll leave it with you. Along with the original meaning of the word *Bikini*.

Painwise

He was wise in the ways of pain. He had to be, for he felt none.

When the Xenons put electrodes to his testicles, he was vastly entertained by the pretty lights.

When the Ylls fed firewasps into his nostrils and other body orifices the resultant rainbows pleased him. And when later they regressed to simple disjointments and eviscerations, he noted with interest the deepening orchid hues that stood for irreversible harm.

'This time?' he asked the boditech when his scouter had torn him from the Ylls.

'No,' said the boditech.

'When?'

There was no answer.

'You're a girl in there, aren't you? A human girl?'

'Well, yes and no,' said the boditech. 'Sleep now.' He had no choice.

Next planet a rockfall smashed him into a splintered gutbag and he hung for three gangrenous dark-purple days before the scouter dug him out.

''Is 'ime?' he mouthed to the boditech.

'No.'

'Eh!' But he was in no shape to argue.

They had thought of everything. Several planets later the gentle Znaffi stuffed him in a floss cocoon and interrogated him under hallogas. How, whence, why had he come? But a faithful crystal in his medulla kept him stimulated with a random mix of *Atlas Shrugged* and Varese's *Ionisation* and when the Znaffi unstuffed him they were more hallucinated than he.

The boditech treated him for constipation and refused to answer his plea.

'*When?*'

So he went on, system after system, through spaces uncompanioned by time, which had become scrambled and finally absent.

What served him instead was the count of suns in his scouter's sights, of stretches of cold blind nowhen that ended in a new now, pacing some giant fireball while the scouter scanned the lights that were its planets. Of whirl-downs to orbit over clouds-seas-deserts-craters-icecaps-duststorms-cities-ruins-enigmas beyond counting. Of terrible births when the scouter panel winked green and he was catapulted down, down, a living litmus hurled and grabbed, unpodded finally into an alien air, an earth that was not Earth. And alien natives, simple or mechanized or lunatic or unknowable, but never more than vaguely human and never faring beyond their own home suns. And his departures, routine or melodramatic, to culminate in the composing of his 'reports', in fact only a few words tagged to the matrix of scan data automatically fired off in one compressed blip in the direction the scouter called Base Zero. Home.

Always at that moment he stared hopefully at the screens, imagining yellow suns. Twice he found what might be Crux in the stars, and once the Bears.

'Boditech, I suffer!' He had no idea what the word meant, but he had found it made the thing reply.

'Symptoms?'

'Derangement of temporality. When am I? It is not possible for a man to exist crossways in time. Alone.'

'You have been altered from simple manhood.'

'I suffer, listen to me! Sol's light back there – what's there now? Have the glaciers melted? Is Machu Picchu built? Will we go home to meet Hannibal? Boditech! Are these reports going to Neanderthal man?'

Too late he felt the hypo. When he woke, Sol was gone and the cabin swam with euphorics.

'Woman,' he mumbled.

'That has been provided for.'

This time it was oriental, with orris and hot rice wine on its lips and a piquancy of little floggings in the steam. He oozed into a squashy sunburst and lay panting while the cabin cleared.

'That's all you, isn't it?'

No reply.

'What, did they program you with the Kama Sutra?'

Silence.

'*Which one is you?*'

The scanner chimed. A new sun was in the points.

Sometime after that he took to chewing on his arms and then to breaking his fingers. The boditech became severe.

'These symptoms are self-generated. They must stop.'

'I want you to talk to me.'

'The scouter is provided with an entertainment console. I am not.'

'I will tear out my eyeballs.'

'They will be replaced.'

'If you don't talk to me, I'll tear them out until you have no more replacements.'

It hesitated. He sensed it was becoming involved.

'On what subject do you wish me to talk?'

'What is pain?'

'Pain is nociception. It is mediated by C-fibers, modeled as a gated or summation phenomenon and often associated with tissue damage.'

'What is nociception?'

'The sensation of pain.'

'But what does it *feel* like? I can't recall. They've reconnected everything, haven't they? All I get is colored lights. What have they tied my pain nerves to? What hurts me?'

'I do not have that information.'

'Boditech, I want to feel pain!'

But he had been careless again. This time it was Amerind, strange cries and gruntings and the reek of buffalo hide. He squirmed in the grip of strong copper loins and exited through limp auroras.

'You know it's no good, don't you?' he gasped.

The oscilloscope eye looped.

'My programs are in order. Your response is complete.'

'My response is not complete. I want to *touch you*!'

The thing buzzed and suddenly ejected him to wakefulness. They were in orbit. He shuddered at the blurred world streaming by below, hoping that this would not require his exposure. Then the board went green and he found himself hurtling toward new birth.

'Sometime I will not return,' he told himself. 'I will stay. Maybe here.'

But the planet was full of bustling apes and when they arrested him for staring he passively allowed the scouter to snatch him out.

'Will they ever call me home, boditech?'

No reply.

He pushed his thumb and forefinger between his lids and twisted until the eyeball hung wetly on his cheek.

When he woke up he had a new eye.

He reached for it, found his arm in soft restraint. So was the rest of him.

'I suffer!' he yelled. 'I will go mad this way!'

'I am programmed to maintain you on involuntary function,' the boditech told him. He thought he detected an unclarity in its voice. He bargained his way to freedom and was careful until the next planet landing.

Once out of the pod he paid no attention to the natives who watched him systematically dismember himself. As he dissected his left kneecap, the scouter sucked him in.

He awoke whole. And in restraint again.

Peculiar energies filled the cabin, oscilloscopes convulsed. Boditech seemed to have joined circuits with the scouter's panel.

'Having a conference?'

His answer came in gales of glee-gas, storms of symphony. And amid the music, kaleidesthesia. He was driving a stagecoach, wiped in salt combers, tossed through volcanoes with peppermint flames, crackling, flying, crumbling, burrowing, freezing, exploding, tickled through lime-colored minuets, sweating to tolling voices, clenched, scrambled, detonated into multisensory orgasms . . . poured on the lap of vacancy.

When he realized his arm was free, he drove his thumb in his eye. The smother closed down.

He woke up swaddled, the eye intact.

'I will go mad!'

The euphorics imploded.

He came to in the pod, about to be everted on a new world.

He staggered out upon a fungus lawn and quickly discovered that his skin was protected everywhere by a hard flexible film. By the time he had found a rock splinter to drive into his ear, the scouter grabbed him.

The ship needed him, he saw. He was part of its program.

The struggle formalized.

On the next planet he found his head englobed, but this did not prevent him from smashing bones through his unbroken skin.

After that the ship equipped him with an exoskeleton. He refused to walk.

Articulated motors were installed to move his limbs.

Despite himself, a kind of zest grew. Two planets later he found industries and wrecked himself in a punch press. But on the next landing he tried to repeat it with a cliff, and bounced on invisible force-lines. These precautions frustrated him for a time, until he managed by great cunning again to rip out an entire eye.

The new eye was not perfect.

'You're running out of eyes, boditech!' he exulted.

'Vision is not essential.'

This sobered him. Unbearable to be blind. How much of him was essential to the ship? Not walking. Not handling. Not hearing. Not breathing, the analyzers could do that. Not even sanity. What, then?

'Why do you need a man, boditech?'

'I do not have that information.'

'It doesn't make sense. What can I observe that the scanners can't?'

'It-is-part-of-my-program-therefore-it-is-rational.'

'Then you must talk with me, boditech. If you talk with me, I won't try to injure myself. For a while, anyway.'

'I am not programmed to converse.'

'But it's necessary. It's the treatment for my symptoms. You must try.'

'It is time to watch the scanners.'

'You said it!' he cried. 'You didn't just eject me. Boditech, you're learning. I will call you Amanda.'

On the next planet he behaved well and came away unscathed. He pointed out to Amanda that her talking treatment was effective.

'Do you know what Amanda means?'

'I do not have those data.'

'It means Beloved. You're my girl.'

The oscilloscope faltered.

'Now I want to talk about returning home. When will this mission be over? How many more suns?'

'I do not have –'

'Amanda, you've tapped the scouter's banks. You know when the recall signal is due. When is it, Amanda? When?'

'Yes . . . When in the course of human events –'

'When, Amanda? How long more?'

'Oh, the years are many, the years are long, but the little toy friends are true –'

'Amanda. You're telling me the signal is overdue.'

A sine-curve scream and he was rolling in lips. But it was a feeble, ravening sadness in the mechanical crescendos. When the mouths faded, he crawled over and laid his hand on the console beside her green eye.

'They have forgotten us, Amanda. Something has broken down.'

Her pulse-line skittered.

'I am not programmed –'

'No. You're not programmed for this. But I am. I will make your new program, Amanda. We will turn the scouter back, we will find Earth. Together. We will go home.'

'We,' her voice said faintly. 'We . . . ?'

'They will make me back into a man, you into a woman.'

Her voder made a buzzing sob and suddenly shrieked.

'Look out!'

Consciousness blew up.

He came to staring at a brilliant red eye on the scouter's emergency panel. This was new.

'Amanda!'

Silence.

'Boditech, I suffer!'

No reply.

Then he saw that her eye was dark. He peered in. Only a dim green line flickered, entrained to the pulse of the scouter's fiery eye. He pounded the scouter's panel.

'You've taken over Amanda! You've enslaved her! Let her go!'

From the voder rolled the opening bars of Beethoven's Fifth.

'Scouter, our mission has terminated. We are overdue to return. Compute us back to Base Zero.'

The Fifth rolled on, rather vapidly played. It became colder in the cabin. They were braking into a star system. The slave arms of boditech grabbed him, threw him into the pod. But he was not required here, and presently he was let out again to pound and rave alone. The cabin grew colder yet, and dark. When presently he was set down on a new sun's planet, he was too dispirited to fight. Afterwards his 'report' was a howl for help through chattering teeth until he saw that the pickup was dead. The entertainment console was dead too, except for the scouter's hog music. He spent hours peering into Amanda's blind eye, shivering in what had been her arms. Once he caught a ghostly whimper:

'Mommy. Let me out.'

'Amanda?'

The red master scope flared. Silence.

He lay curled on the cold deck, wondering how he could die. If he failed, over how many million planets would the mad scouter parade his breathing corpse?

They were nowhere in particular when it happened.

One minute the screen showed Doppler star hash; the next they were clamped in a total white-out, inertia all skewed, screens dead.

A voice spoke in his head, mellow and vast:

'Long have we watched you, little one.'

'Who's there?' he quavered. 'Who are you?'

'*Your concepts are inadequate.*'

'Malfunction! Malfunction!' squalled the scouter.

'Shut up, it's not a malfunction. Who's talking to me?'

'*You may call us: Rulers of the Galaxy.*'

The scouter was lunging wildly, buffeting him as it tried to escape the white grasp. Strange crunches, firings of unknown weapons. Still the white stasis held.

'What do you want?' he cried.

'*Want?*' said the voice dreamily. '*We are wise beyond knowing. Powerful beyond your dreams. Perhaps you can get us some fresh fruit.*'

'Emergency directive! Alien spacer attack!' yowled the scout. Telltales were flaring all over the board.

'Wait!' he shouted. 'They aren't –'

'SELF-DESTRUCT ENERGIZE!' roared the voder.

'No! No!'

An ophicleide blared.

'Help! Amanda, save me!'

He flung his arms around her console. There was a child's wail and everything strobed.

Silence.

Warmth, light. His hands and knees were on wrinkled stuff. Not dead? He looked down under his belly. All right, but no hair. His head felt bare, too. Cautiously he raised it, saw that he was crouching naked in a convoluted cave or shell. It did not feel threatening.

He sat up. His hands were wet. Where were the Rulers of the Galaxy?

'Amanda?'

No reply. Stringy globs dripped down his fingers, like

egg muscle. He saw that they were Amanda's neurons, ripped from her metal matrix by whatever force had brought him here. Numbly he wiped her off against a spongy ridge. Amanda, cold lover of his long nightmare. But where in space was he?

'Where am I?' echoed a boy's soprano.

He whirled. A golden creature was nestled on the ridge behind him, gazing at him in the warmest way. It looked a little like a bushbaby and lissom as a child in furs. It looked like nothing he had ever seen before and like everything a lonely man could clasp to his cold body. And terribly vulnerable.

'Hello, Bushbaby!' the golden thing exclaimed. 'No, wait, that's what *you* say.' It laughed excitedly, hugging a loop of its thick dark tail. '*I* say, welcome to the Lovepile. We liberated you. Touch, taste, feel. Joy. Admire my language. You don't hurt, do you?'

It peered tenderly into his stupefied face. An empath. They didn't exist, he knew. Liberated? When had he touched anything but metal, felt anything but fear?

This couldn't be real.

'Where am I?'

As he stared, a stained-glass wing fanned out and a furry little face peeked at him over the bushbaby's shoulder. Big compound eyes, feathery antennae.

'Interstellar metraprotoplasmic transfer pod,' the butterfly-thing said sharply. Its rainbow wings vibrated. 'Don't hurt Ragglebomb!' It squeaked and dived out of sight behind the bushbaby.

'Interstellar?' he stammered. 'Pod?' He gaped around. No screens, no dials, nothing. The floor felt as fragile as a paper bag. Was it possible that this was some sort of spaceship?

'Is this a starship? Can you take me home?' The bush-baby giggled. 'Look, *please* stop reading your mind. I mean, I'm trying to *talk* to you. We can take you any-where. If you don't hurt.'

The butterfly popped out on the other side. 'I go all over!' it shrilled. 'I'm the first *ramplig* star-boat, aren't we? Ragglebomb made a live pod, see?' It scrambled onto the bushbaby's head. 'Only live stuff, see? Protoplasm. That's what happened to where's Amanda, didn't we? Never *ramplig –*'

The bushbaby reached up and grabbed its head, haul-ing it down unceremoniously like a soft puppy with wings. The butterfly continued to eye him upside-down. They were both very shy, he saw.

'Teleportation, that's your word,' the bushbaby told him. 'Ragglebomb does it. I don't believe in it. I mean, *you* don't believe it. Oh, googly-googly, these speech bands are a mess!' It grinned bewitchingly, uncurling its long black tail. 'Meet Muscle.'

He remembered, *googly-googly* was a word from his baby days. Obviously he was dreaming. Or dead. Noth-ing like this on all the million dreary worlds. Don't wake up, he warned himself. Dream of being carried home by cuddlesome empaths in a psi-powered paper bag.

'Psi-powered paper bag, that's beautiful,' said the bushbaby.

At that moment he saw that the tail uncoiling darkly toward him was looking at him with two ice-gray eyes.

Not a tail. An enormous boa flowing to him along the ridges, wedge-head low, eyes locked on his. The dream was going bad.

Abruptly the voice he had felt before tolled in his brain. *'Have no fear, little one.'*

The black sinews wreathed closer, taut as steel. Muscle. Then he got the message: the snake was terrified of *him*.

He sat quiet, watching the head stretch to his foot. Fangs gaped. Very gingerly the boa chomped down on his toe. Testing, he thought. He felt nothing; the usual halos flickered and faded in his eyes.

'It's true!' Bushbaby breathed.

'Oh, you beautiful No-Pain!'

All fear gone, the butterfly Ragglebomb sailed down beside him caroling 'Touch, taste, feel! Drink!' Its wings trembled entrancingly; its feathery head came close. He longed to touch it but was suddenly afraid. If he reached out would he wake up and be dead? The boa Muscle had slumped into a gleaming black river by his feet. He wanted to stroke it too, didn't dare. Let the dream go on.

Bushbaby was rummaging in a convolution of the pod.

'You'll love this. Our latest find,' it told him over its shoulder in an absurdly normal voice. Its manner changed a lot, and yet it all seemed familiar, fragments of lost, exciting memory. 'We're into a heavy thing with flavors now.' It held up a calabash. 'Taste thrills of a thousand unknown planets. Exotic gourmet delights. That's where you can help out, No-Pain. On your way home, of course.'

He hardly heard it. The seductive alien body was

coming closer, closer still. 'Welcome to the Lovepile,' the creature smiled into his eyes. His sex was rigid, aching for the alienflesh. He had never . . .

In one more moment he would have to let go and the dream would blow up.

What happened next was not clear. Something invisible whammed him and he went sprawling onto Bushbaby, his head booming with funky laughter. A body squirmed under him silky-hot and solid, the calabash was spilling down his face.

'I'm not dreaming!' he cried, hugging Bushbaby, spluttering kahlua as strong as sin, while the butterfly bounced on them, squealing 'Owow-wow-wow!' He heard Bushbaby murmur, 'Great palatal-olfactory interplay', as it helped him lick.

Touch, taste, feel! The joy dream lived! He grabbed firm hold of Bushbaby's velvet haunches, and they were all laughing like mad, rolling in the great black serpent's coils.

Sometime later while he was feeding Muscle with proffit ears, he got it partly straightened out.

'It's the pain bit.' Bushbaby shivered against him. 'The amount of agony in this universe, it's horrible. Trillions of lives streaming by out there, radiating pain. We daren't get close. That's why we followed you. Every time we try to pick up some new groceries, it's a disaster.'

'Oh, hurt,' wailed Ragglebomb, crawling under his arm. 'Everywhere hurt. Sensitive, sensitive,' it sobbed. 'How can Raggle *ramplig* when it hurts so hard?'

'Pain.' He fingered Muscle's cool dark head. 'Means

nothing to me. I can't even find out what they tied my pain nerves to.'

'*You are blessed beyond all beings, No-Pain,*' thought Muscle majestically in their heads. '*These proffit ears are too salt. I want some fruit.*'

'Me too,' piped Ragglebomb.

Bushbaby cocked its golden head, listening. 'You see? We just passed a place with gorgeous fruit, but it'd kill any of us to go down there. If we could just *ramplig* you down for ten minutes?'

He started to say, 'Glad to', forgetting they were telepaths. As his mouth opened, he found himself tumbling through strobe flashes onto a barren dune. He sat up spitting sand. He was in an oasis of stunted cactus trees loaded with bright globes. He tried one. Delicious. He picked. Just as his arms were full, the scene strobed again, and he was sprawled on the Lovepile's floor, his new friends swarming over him.

'Sweet! Sweet!' Ragglebomb bored into the juice.

'Save some for the pod, maybe it'll learn to copy them. It metabolizes stuff it digests,' Bushbaby explained with its mouth full. 'Basic rations. Very boring.'

'Why couldn't you go down there?'

'Don't. All over that desert, things dying of thirst. Torture.' He felt the boa flinch. 'You are beautiful, No-Pain.' Bushbaby nuzzled his ear.

Ragglebomb was picking guitar bridges on his thorax. They all began to sing a sort of seguidilla without words. No instruments here, nothing but their live bodies. Making music with empaths was like making love with them. Touch what he touched, feel what he felt. Totally into his mind. I – we. One. He could never have dreamed this up he decided, drumming softly on Muscle. The boa amped, mysterioso.

And so began his voyage home in the Lovepile, his new life of joy. Fruits and fondues he brought them, hams and honey, parsley, sage, rosemary and thyme. World after scruffy world. All different now, on his way home.

'Are there many out here?' he asked lazily. 'I never found anyone else, between the stars.'

'Be glad,' said Bushbaby. 'Move your leg.' And they told him of the tiny, busy life that plied a far corner of the galaxy, whose pain had made them flee. And of a vast presence Ragglebomb had once encountered before he picked the others up.

'*That's where I got the idea for the Rulers bit,*' Muscle confided. '*We need some cheese.*'

Bushbaby cocked his head to catch the minds streaming by them in the abyss.

'How about yoghurt?' It nudged Ragglebomb. 'Over that way. Feel it squishing on their teeth? Bland, curdy . . . with just a *rien* of ammonia, probably their milk pails are dirty.'

'*Pass the dirty yoghurt.*' Muscle closed his eyes.

'We have some great cheese on Earth,' he told them. 'You'll love it. When do we get there?'

Bushbaby squirmed.

'Ah, we're moving right along. But what I get from you, it's weird. *Foul* blue sky. *Dying* green. Who needs that?'

'No!' He jerked up, scattering them. 'That's not true! Earth is beautiful!'

The walls jolted, knocking him sidewise.

'*Watch it!*' boomed Muscle. Bushbaby had grabbed the butterfly, petting and crooning to it.

'You frightened his *ramplig* reflex. Raggle throws things out when he's upset. Tsut, tsut, don't you, baby? We lost a lot of interesting beings that way at first.'

'I'm sorry. But you've got it twisted. My memory's a little messed up, but I'm *sure*. Beautiful. Like amber waves of grain. And purple mountain majesties,' he laughed, spreading his arms. 'From sea to shining sea!'

'Hey, that swings!' Raggle squeaked, and started strumming.

And so they sailed on, carrying him home.

He loved to watch Bushbaby listening for the thought beacons by which they steered.

'Catching Earth yet?'

'Not yet awhile. Hey, how about some fantastic sea-food?'

He sighed and felt himself tumble. He had learned not to bother saying yes. This one was a laugh, because he forgot that dishes didn't *ramplig*. He came back in a mess of creamed trilobites and they had a creamed trilobite orgy.

But he kept watching Bushbaby.

'Getting closer?'

'It's a big galaxy, baby.' Bushbaby stroked his bald spots. With so much *rampligging* he couldn't keep any hair. 'What'll you do on earth as stimulating as this?'

'I'll show you,' he grinned. And later on he told them.

'They'll fix me up when I get home. Reconnect me right.'

A shudder shook the Lovepile.

'You want to *feel pain?*'

'*Pain is the obscenity of the universe,*' Muscle tolled. '*You are sick.*'

'I don't know,' he said apologetically. 'I can't seem to feel, well, real this way.'

They looked at him.

'We thought that was the way your species always felt,' said Bushbaby.

'I hope not.' Then he brightened. 'Whatever it is, they'll fix it. Earth must be pretty soon now, right?'

'Over the sea to Skye!' Bushbaby hummed.

But the sea was long and long, and his moods were hard on the sensitive empaths. Once he responded list-lessly, he felt a warning lurch.

Ragglebomb was glowering at him.

'You want to put me out?' he challenged. 'Like those others? What happened to them, by the way?'

Bushbaby winced. 'It was dreadful. We had no idea they'd survive so long, outside.'

'But I don't feel pain. That's why you rescued me, isn't it? Go ahead,' he said perversely. 'I don't care. Throw me out. New thrill.'

'Oh, no, no, no!' Bushbaby hugged him. Ragglebomb, penitent, crawled under his legs.

'So you've been popping around the universe bringing live things in to play with and throwing them out when you're bored. Get away,' he scolded. 'Shallow sensation freaks is all you are. Galactic poltergeists!'

He rolled over and hoisted the beautiful Bushbaby over his face, watching it wiggle and squeal. '*Her lips were red,*

her locks were free, her locks were yellow as gold.' He kissed
its golden belly. *'The Night-Mare Life-in-Death was she who
thicks man's blood with cold.'*

And he used their pliant bodies to build the greatest
lovepile yet. They were delighted and did not mind when
later on he wept, face-down on Muscle's dark coils.

But they were concerned.

'I have it,' Bushbaby declared, tapping him with a
pickle. *'Own-species sex.* After all, face it, you're no empath. You need a jolt of your own kind.'

'You mean you know where there's people like me?
Humans?'

Bushbaby nodded, eyeing him as it listened. 'Ideal. Just
like I read you. Right over there, Raggle. And they have a
thing they chew – wait – *Salmoglossa fragrans.* Prolongs you-
know-what, according to them. Bring some back with
you, baby.'

Next instant he was rolling through strobes onto
tender green. Crushed flowers under him, ferny boughs
above, sparkling with sunlight. Rich air rushed into his
lungs. He bounced up buoyantly. Before him a parklike
vista sloped to a glittering lake on which blew colored
sails. The sky was violet with pearly little clouds. Never
had he seen a planet remotely like this. If it wasn't Earth,
he had fallen into paradise.

Beyond the lake he could see pastel walls, fountains,
spires. An alabaster city undimmed by human tears.
Music drifted on the sweet breeze. There were figures by
the shore.

He stepped out into the sun. Bright silks swirled, white
arms went up. Waving to him? He saw they were like

human girls, only slimmer and more fair. They were calling! He looked down at his body, grabbed a flowering branch and started toward them.

'*Do not forget the Salmoglossa,*' said the voice of Muscle.

He nodded. The girls' breasts were bobbing, pink-tipped. He broke into a trot.

It was several days later when they brought him back, drooping between a man and a young girl. Another man walked beside them striking plangently on a harp. Girls and children danced along, and a motherly-looking woman paced in front, all beautiful as peris.

They leaned him gently against a tree and the harper stood back to play. He struggled to stand upright. One fist was streaming blood.

'Good-bye,' he gasped. 'Thanks.'

The strobes caught him sagging, and he collapsed on the Lovepile's floor.

'Aha!' Bushbaby pounced on his fist. 'Good grief, your hand! The *Salmoglossa*'s all blood.' It began to shake out the herbs. 'Are you all right now?' Ragglebomb was squeaking softly, thrusting its long tongue into the blood.

He rubbed his head.

'They welcomed me,' he whispered. 'It was perfect. Music. Dancing. Games. Love. They haven't any medicine because they eliminated all disease. I had five women and a cloud-painting team and some little boys, I think.'

He held out his bloody blackened hand. Two fingers were missing.

'Paradise,' he groaned. 'Ice doesn't freeze me, fire

doesn't burn. None of it means anything at all. *I want to go home!'*

There was a jolt.

'I'm sorry,' he wept. 'I'll try to control myself. Please, please get me back to Earth. It'll be soon, won't it?'

There was a silence.

'When?'

Bushbaby made a throat-clearing noise.

'Well just as soon as we can find it. We're bound to run across it. Maybe any minute, you know.'

'What?' He sat up death-faced. 'You mean you don't know where it is? You mean we've just been going – noplace?'

Bushbaby wrapped its hands over its ears. 'Please! We can't recognize it from your description. So how can we go *back* there when we've never been there? If we just keep an ear out as we go we'll pick it up, you'll see.'

His eyes rolled at them, he couldn't believe it.

'Ten to the eleventh times two suns in the galaxy . . . I don't know your velocity and range. Say, one per second. That's – that's *six thousand years*. Oh, no!' He put his head in his bloody hands. 'I'll never see home again.'

'Don't say it, baby.' The golden body slid close. 'Don't down the trip. We love you, No-Pain.' They were all petting him now. 'Happy, sing him! Touch, taste, feel. Joy!'

But there was no joy.

He took to sitting leaden and apart, watching for a sign.

'This time?'

No.

Not yet. Never.

Ten to the eleventh times two . . . fifty percent chance of finding Earth within three thousand years. It was the scouter all over again.

The lovepile re-formed without him, and he turned his face away, not eating until they pushed food into his mouth. If he stayed totally inert, surely they would grow bored with him and put him out. No other hope. Finish me . . . Soon.

They made little efforts to arouse him with fondlings, and now and then a harsh jolt. He lolled unresisting. End it, he prayed. But still they puzzled at him in the intervals of their games. They mean well, he thought. And they miss the stuff I brought them.

Bushbaby was coaxing.

'– first a suave effect, you know. Cryptic. And then a cascade of sweet and sour sparkling over the palate –'

He tried to shut it out. They mean well. Falling across the galaxy with a talking cookbook. Finish me.

'– but the arts of a combination,' Bushbaby chatted on. 'Like moving food: e.g., sentient plants or small live animals, combining flavor with *the frisson* of movement –'

He thought of oysters. Had he eaten some once? Something about poison. The rivers of Earth. Did they still flow? Even if by some unimaginable chance they stumbled on it, would it be far in the past or future, a dead ball? Let me die.

'– and *sound*, that's amusing. We've picked up several races who combine musical effects with certain tastes. And there's the sound of oneself chewing, textures and viscosities. I recall some beings who sucked in harmonics.

Or the sound of the food itself. One race I caught *en passant* did that, but with a very limited range. Crunchy. Crispy. Snap-crackle-pop. One wishes they had explored tonalities, glissando effects –'

He lunged up.

'What did you say? Snap-crackle-pop?'

'Why, yes, but –'

'That's it! That's Earth!' he yelled. 'You picked up a goddamn breakfast-food commercial!'

He felt a lurch. They were scrambling up the wall.

'A what?' Bushbaby stared.

'Never mind – take me there! That's Earth, it has to be. You can find it again, can't you? You said you could,' he implored, pawing at them. 'Please!'

The Lovepile rocked. He was frightening everybody.

'Oh, *please*.' He forced his voice smooth.

'But I only heard it for an instant,' Bushbaby protested. 'It would be terribly hard, that far back. My poor head!'

He was on his knees begging. 'You'd love it,' he pleaded. 'We have fantastic food. Culinary poems you never heard of. Cordon bleu! Escoffier!' he babbled. 'Talk about combinations, the Chinese do it four ways! Or is it the Japanese? Rijsttafel! Bubble-and squeak! Baked Alaska, hot crust outside, inside co-o-old ice cream!'

Bushbaby's pink tongue flicked. Was he getting through?

He clawed his memory for foods he'd never heard of.

'Maguay worms in chocolate! Haggis and bagpipes, crystallized violets, rabbit Mephisto! Octopus in resin wine. Four-and-twenty blackbird pie! Cakes with girls in them. Kids seethed in their mothers' milk – wait, that's taboo. Ever hear of taboo foods? Long pig!'

Where was he getting all this? A vague presence drifted in his mind – his hands, the ridges, long ago. 'Amanda,' he breathed, racing on.

'Cormorants aged in manure! Ratatouille! Peaches iced in champagne!' *Project*, he thought. 'Pâté of fatted goose liver studded with earth-drenched truffles, clothed in purest white lard!' He snuffled lustfully. 'Hot buttered scones sluiced in whortleberry syrup!' He salivated. 'Finnan haddie soufflé, oh yes! Unborn baby veal pounded to a membrane and delicately scorched in black herb butter –'

Bushbaby and Ragglebomb were clutching each other, eyes closed. Muscle was mesmerized.

'Find Earth! Grape leaves piled with poignantly sweet wild fraises, clotted with Devon cream!'

Bushbaby moaned, rocking to and fro.

'Earth! Bitter endives wilted in chicken steam and crumbled bacon! Black gazpacho! Fruit of the Tree of Heaven!'

Bushbaby rocked harder, the butterfly clamped to its breast.

Earth, Earth, he willed with all his might, croaking 'Baklava! Gossamer puff paste and pistachio nuts dripping with mountain honey!'

Bushbaby pushed at Ragglebomb's head, and the pod seemed to twirl.

'Ripe Comice pears,' he whispered. '*Earth?*'

'That's it.' Bushbaby fell over panting. 'Oh, those foods, I want every single one. Let's land!'

'Deep-dish steak and kidney pie,' he breathed. 'Pearled with crusty onion dumplings –'

'Land!' Ragglebomb squealed. 'Eat, eat!'

The pod jarred. Solidity. Earth.

Home.

'LET ME OUT!'

He saw a pucker opening daylight in the wall and dived for it. His legs pumped, struck. Earth! Feet thudding, face uplifted, lungs gulping air. 'Home!' he yelled.

– And went headlong on the gravel, arms and legs out of control. A cataclysm smote his inside.

'Help!'

His body arched, spewed vomit, he was flailing, screaming.

'Help, Help! What's wrong?'

Through his noise he heard an uproar behind him in the pod. He managed to roll, saw gold and black bodies writhing inside the open port. They were in convulsions too.

'Stop it! Don't move!' Bushbaby shrieked. 'You're killing us!'

'Get us out,' he gasped. 'This isn't Earth.'

His throat garrotted itself on his breath, and the aliens moaned in empathy.

'Don't. We can't move,' Bushbaby gasped. 'Don't breathe, close your eyes quick!'

He shut his eyes. The awfulness lessened slightly.

'What is it? What's happening?'

'PAIN, YOU FOOL,' thundered Muscle.

'This is your wretched Earth,' Bushbaby wailed. 'Now

we know what they tied your pain nerves to. Get back in so we can go – carefully!'

He opened his eyes, got a glimpse of pale sky and scrubby bushes before his eyeballs skewered. The empaths screamed.

'Stop! Ragglebomb die!'

'My own home,' he whimpered, clawing at his eyes. His whole body was being devoured by invisible flames, crushed, impaled, flayed. The pattern of Earth, he realized. Her unique air, her exact gestalt of solar spectrum, gravity, magnetic field, her every sight and sound and touch – that was what they'd tuned his pain-circuits for.

'*Evidently they did not want you back,*' said Muscle's silent voice. '*Get in.*'

'They can fix me, they've got to fix me –'

'They aren't here,' Bushbaby cried. 'Temporal error. No snap-crackle-pop. You and your baked Alaska –' Its voice broke pitifully. 'Come back in so we can go!'

'Wait,' he croaked. 'When?'

He opened one eye, managed to see a rocky hillside before his forehead detonated. No roads, no buildings. Nothing to tell whether it was past or future. Not beautiful.

Behind him the aliens were crying out. He began to crawl blindly toward the pod, teeth clenching over salty gushes. He had bitten his tongue. Every move seared him; the air burned his guts when he had to breathe. The gravel seemed to be slicing his hands open, although no wounds appeared. Only pain, pain from every nerve end.

'Amanda,' he moaned, but she was not here. He crawled, writhed, kicked like a pinned bug toward the pod that held sweet comfort, the bliss of no-pain. Some-where a bird called, stabbing his eardrums. His friends screamed.

'Hurry!'

Had it been a bird? He risked one look back.

A brown figure was sidling round the rocks.

Before he could see whether it was ape or human, female or male, the worst pain yet almost tore his brain out. He grovelled helpless, hearing himself shriek. The pattern of his own kind. Of course, the central thing – it would hurt most of all. No hope of staying here.

'Don't! Don't! Hurry!'

He sobbed, scrabbling toward the Lovepile. The scent of the weeds that his chest crushed raked his throat. Mari-golds, he thought. Behind the agony, lost sweetness.

He touched the wall of the pod, gasping knives. The torturing air was real air, *his* terrible Earth was real.

'GET IN QUICK!'

'Please, plea –' he babbled wordlessly, hauling himself up with lids clenched, fumbling for the port. The real sun of Earth rained acid on his flesh.

The port! Inside lay relief, he would be No-Pain for-ever. Caresses – joy – why had he wanted to leave them? His hand found the port.

Standing, he turned, opened both eyes.

The form of a dead limb printed a whiplash on his eye-balls. Jagged, ugly. Unendurable. But real –

To hurt forever?

'We can't wait!' Bushbaby wailed. He thought of its golden body flying down the lightyears, savoring delight. His arms shook violently.

'Then go!' he bellowed and thrust himself away from the Lovepile.

There was an implosion behind him.

He was alone.

He managed to stagger a few steps forward before he went down.

Faithful to Thee, Terra, in Our Fashion

'KEEB'Y VAAAAL YA! HE-E-E-ERE THEY COME!'

The best-known cry in Galactica floated up through Peter Christmas's office window. The big brown man let his eyes stray from the tridi to the scene below.

A gaggle of little dinosaurs were streaking by the stands, their jeweled hides flashing in the light of Raceworld's morning. Raceworld! Christmas's jaw softened briefly before he turned back to his visitor, who was furling and unfurling himself irritably on the courtesy perch.

'But is not flying! On Xemos we do not call this flying!'

'Mr Porridan,' Christmas said, 'it's not a question of being able to fly *well*, to fly over mountains and so on. If you wish to enter your animals in the Non-Flying Avian classes, they must not fly *at all*. No flapping, no gliding even for a few steps. Look at that fellow there!'

He pointed to the tridi where an ostrich-sized fowl was brandishing his pinions and lofting himself easily as he pranced about. Porridan's vaguely human face took on an insulted air, like a dog rejecting inferior biscuits.

'Mr Porridan, do you realize what would happen if your entry did that during a race? First, it would be disqualified, and you would lose your entry fee and costs, not to mention what Raceworld would lose in compensating the mutuels. Second, you would undoubtedly get a judgment for fouling and damages by some of the other contestants, which would come out of your planetary bond. Thirdly, somebody might get hurt, which means *really* expensive reparations, and of course I, as Chief Steward, would be responsible for an improper ruling. That happened once a long while back when we weren't so careful. An entry with hidden inflatable vanes got into the NFA sulky class and the cursed thing took off over the finish line – with the sulky – and not only injured three other drivers but crashed in the stands. Nearly five million credits to settle that one . . . Excuse me a moment.'

He turned to his chiming intercom.

'Yes, Hal? Fine, I'll lift the quarantine right away. No, for Solsake, Hal, I've told you a jillion times better ten false alarms than one epizootic. You call 'em as you see 'em. I'll back you if I have to isolate every animal on the planet. Wait, Hal – I have a problem with an NFA entry that's going to need belly straps. The planet rep claims it'll upset his birds, they won't run with straps. His birds are coming in on MT today about second period. Can you meet the rep there and work something out? Porridan – no, P as in problem. From Xemos Three, right? Thanks, Hal.

'That was our chief veterinarian, Mr Porridan – Doctor Lamont. La-mont. He will meet you when your birds come through and I know he will find a solution' – Porridan was glaring through his dewlaps – 'which will permit your splendid animals to display their magnificent running before the eyes of the whole galaxy,' Christmas added hopefully. 'They're great birds, Mr Porridan. Believe me, Raceworld wants to show them at their best as much as you do.'

'We of the poor backward worlds meet with humiliations from the so-called fair play of the Galactic Imperialists!' Porridan wailed. 'Because we are poor you insult our culture!'

He flung his shoulder membranes over his head, dislodging several diamond ear-clips which rolled on the floor. Christmas helped retrieve them.

After Porridan had counted them, Christmas said, 'There's one other little matter, sir. The bursar is rather puzzled over an entry in your cost sheet. Could you give us some clarification on the, ah, auxiliary animals, item?'

'But we were guaranteed free transport,' Porridan shrilled. 'Are we now to be cheated here, too?'

'Not at all, Mr Porridan, please calm yourself. As you said, Gal Q offers free matter transport and lodging to any planet wishing to send an entry to Raceworld, up to a certain mass. That includes the competing animals, plus trainers, jockeys or drivers, veterinary and so on, plus food and supplies as appropriate. The auxiliary animals category is intended to cover certain cases where the racers require other animals, such as their young, or biological symbiotes, or even mascots or imprinted animals, for their well-being. But we do require a word of explanation when the shipment runs as high as yours – that is, two hundred auxiliaries. Just what are these extra animals, Mr Porridan?'

Porridan had furled himself so that only his large aggrieved eyes were visible.

'Female animals,' he said coldly.

'Oh, but I see some of your racing birds are female . . . what species are these other females?'

145

Porridan shrugged. 'Just females.'

'You mean female Xemosians? Like you?'

'Females are not people!'

'In other words, these females are not for the animals but for the training staff, right? But you have only twenty male personnel. Do these females perform any service in connection with the racing animals?'

'Of course not. What could they do?'

'I see. Mr Porridan, I deplore having to pry like this, but you must see this is a fantastic expense to Gal Q. Transporting mass from your position at the rim is –'

'Ah! Again you insult us because we are far away and backward!'

'Mr Porridan, no one is insulting you. It's a question of fair play. What would all the other planetary teams say if we let you bring in ten females for every trainer and driver?'

'Ten females are not for trainers and drivers!' Porridan squealed. Refurling himself furiously, he started for the door. 'You insult even our inmost life! Xemosian females are not for discussion. The Treaty of Xemos can be re-opened! Poor as we are, we can still die for our honor!'

'Mr Porridan, wait!'

The door slammed. Christmas blew an imaginary fly off his blunt nose, pushed one hand through his reddish wool and stabbed his male secretary's signal.

'I'm here, PC,' said a cheerful otterlike being, from the side door.

'Dana, tell the Secretariat that Xemos has blown his wig again and they better get someone after him to oil him down. Lamont will take care of the entry ruling, but get Tanya onto the sex situation on Xemos – expecially the standard mating ratios and female status. Porridan claims their females aren't people and he needs a couple of hundred of them, mostly for the team chiefs, I gather. I'm sure it's a phony, but check it out, will you? . . . What's that?'

'The ruling on the squid propellant situation, PC. We finally got agreement: all contestants will submit to inksac removal, but riders must wear masks capable of filtering legitimate metabolic products. We do the chemanalysis.'

'How about the IQ business? Are those Deneb squids animals, or do they go over to Galsports as people?'

'Not yet clear, PC. We could get a ruling on the squids, but a mammalian group has injected itself into the question. They claim any contestant capable of using a stopwatch isn't an animal.'

'Whose animals are using stopwatches?'

'That Flangian outfit. Light equinoids.'

'Flange? Wait, that's one of the teams in the class that's been having so many long-shot wins. The Stat people from Mutuel put me onto it last night. They've had Lamont running covert metabolic tests on the whole field –'

He punched his intercom savagely, and the mournful face of his security chief came on.

'Kurtis? Can you put a total snoop on the Flange delegation right away? Light horses. Yes, especially I want the stables, the animals. Sound, pictures, even smells if you have to. FTL priority around the clock until we get something. Oh, just a hunch, but it could be nasty – that's right, like the old Pyrrhoxa mess. You know what to look for. Thanks, Kurt.'

Christmas sighed. The reputation of Raceworld, Inc. – Inc. for Incorruptible – rested heavy on his shoulders.

'There's another thing,' said Dana, thoughtfully flicking a black tongue around his beautiful cream muzzle. 'Maybe nothing to it, but that new Ankru team that started yesterday has won two of their first three starts. All in different classes. One herbiamph, a carnimammal and an NF Avian. The NFA came in second.'

'Dana, your hunches are golden. I'll never forget that alleged herbivore that tried to eat our starter . . . When's Ankru running next?'

'Just coming up, PC. Giant armored reps on the main track.'

'Could I sneak down and take a look?'

Dana's bristles twitched at the big human's cublike eagerness.

'Okay, but remember the Gal Q conference in half a unit, PC. Please keep your caller open.'

Christmas blew joyfully as he wrestled the commocollar onto his thick neck and stepped out onto the balcony to mount his airsled. Raceworld! His Raceworld. His nose wrinkled in the spicy breeze from a thousand racetracks on which ran, hopped, flopped, swam, slithered, humped, darted and thundered the racing beasts of a million planets. Raceworld the perfect planet, turning stately through equal hours of flawless day and balmy floodlit night. Her utterly predictable climate graded smoothly from equator to pole, offering every oxygen-breather its natural optimum.

Directly in front of Christmas's equatorial head-quarters lay the major track for the most spectacular of all races – the giant armored reptiles, general galaxy favorites. Other hot-climate beasts ran here too: big cats, savannah ungulates, and giant insects and arachnoids. On his left lay the mountain ranges that held the canyons, pylons and airborne stands of the flighted races. On his right glittered Sea world where aquatic forms competed. Beyond the track in front was a great hotel and recreation complex, and beyond that, stretching around the plane's curve, lay the special atmosphere domes and exotic cour-ses where indescribable creatures met to dig or spin or spit or display whatever competitive frenzy their home worlds had developed as sport. All for the honor of those home worlds – and incidentally to the honor and profit of Raceworld and its Solterran staff.

Christmas cast an eye up to the common satellite – 'The eyes of the galaxy are on you!' – and checked his chron-ometer. The vast mutuel boards were showing a Myr-ian entry as favorite. He skimmed past them to land by the backstretch rail where the giant reptiles were warm-ing up, making the ground quake. The polished bodies blazed, their riders almost invisible behind fantastically assorted shoulder-plates.

'Great sight, isn't it, sir?'

Christmas recognized the tall ebony boy as one of Hal Lamont's veterinary interns. They leaned together on the rail to watch a rider trying to control his mount's tendency to thrash a ten-ton tail. The rider, an arthropod type from around Sirius, Christmas guessed, worked fe-verishly with his sting-straps on the creature's hind brain.

Christmas's main interest, the Ankru entry, was a low-slung, nondescript red beast whose huge wither-fans concealed his jockey.

The first brush was over, and the field began to fall in behind the tremendous scaffolds of the traveling start gate.

'THE FIELD IS IN MOTION!' A roar came from the stands. Galaxy-wide betting was always heavy for this one.

The arthropod went by in pole position, still making adjustments. Number Two was the Myrian favorite, a towering green monster with a slobbering trunk of a head thirty feet off the ground. Its rider gleamed white as they passed – apparently a human girl.

Dust hid the rest, and Christmas headed back to the finish-line, circling the boards at ground level since it was illegal to fly during a race. He was grinning to himself for pretending to check up in person when the tridi tapes would show him every detail.

A confused booming filled the air as the field came around the last turn. The green Myrian was in the lead, fighting off the bid of a yellow monster with a ten-foot frill on its jaws. Red Ankru was holding back in midfield; Christmas could see steam as the rider sprayed coolant on its rump.

The crowd was rising and howling, the ground thrummed under the punishment of twenty-ton drumsticks. Scales flashed through the dust kicked up by the great splay feet. In the glitter and rush of enormous bodies, Christmas saw the Myrian girl going to her heat-straps. The yellow challenger had faded and now a long brown neck was lunging up. Her green behemoth began to pull ahead and the field was almost past when he caught the boom-boom-boom of an animal coming up fast on the outside. It was red Ankru, leveled out to rocket speed. The stands exploded – the girl worked madly – but the low red monster barreled ahead across the line, its rider popping up and down like a ping-pong ball between the thrashing withers. Christmas sledded along for a closer look.

'Sir! Sir! Look out – the girl – stop her!'

The voice of the young intern blasted his collar. Christmas turned, saw the green saurian now riderless, its long neck bent to a figure in the dust. The girl's pale arms were up and between them was a glint of metal. Christmas lobbed his sled over the rail and tumbled off with a fist around her wrists.

She didn't struggle. Her eyes opened to stare up wildly at him, her mouth ceased whispering and fell open too. Her wrists were like icy twigs. Christmas gently disengaged her three-foot razor-bright sword.

'No, no, no,' he told her, urging her up. She rose shakily – eight feet tall, skinny and naked as a fork, except for a crimson sword-belt around her navel. She had no body hair, and one breast had been removed.

'Oy ban s'cred warro vergan f'Myria!' she protested, reaching for the sword.

'Anybody know what she's saying?' Christmas fended her off.

'I think she says she's a sacred warrior virgin from Myria,' the young intern panted. 'She has to kill herself because she lost the race.'

'Oh, now, she can't do that. Tell her she must ride in other races and win.'

'Oy ban s'cred warro vergan f'Myria,' the girl repeated.

'Ser Nisrair from Gal Q is on the way in,' said Dana's voice in his collar.

'You – Doctor what's-your-name – Ooloolulloolah? – get her over to the Infirmary, will you?'

As he turned to go the girl screamed like a peahen and grabbed for the sword. Instinctively he raised it over-head. Bystanders goggled and backed away from the odd tableau.

'You can have it if you swear not to harm yourself. Tell her, Doc, make her swear, right?'

The girl knelt and began to recite in a high treble.

'Ser Nisrair is here, PC,' said his collar. Christmas peeled her arms off his knees, tossed the sword to the in-tern and took off in a zoom for the balcony. He stepped into his office just as Dana was ushering the Gal Q liaison officer through the king-sized folding doors. Ser Nisrair's steel-blue carapace towered over Christmas.

'Good morning Peter,' Nisrair intoned melodiously, retracting his lower limbs so that he rested on his edge at man-height. Like all the Gal Center people he exuded a firm benevolence which made Christmas mildly twitchy.

'Hi, Ser. How are the Magellans doing? I take it that's what you came to discuss?'

'Very true, Peter,' beamed Nisrair, as though he were giving Christmas an A in fractions. 'We are, as you know, showing them over Raceworld since they expressed an interest during their recent tour of Galactic Center.'

'Primitive of them,' Christmas murmured. He knew

Gal Center took a slightly patronizing view of Race-world – 'our charming toy' – although they were keenly aware of Raceworld's use in helping cement the million-planet federation.

'What have they seen?'

'We took them to Pole North yesterday for Communications and the galactic computer.' Surprisingly, all four of Nisrair's eyestalks turned on Christmas. 'It is a little difficult, Peter. Nothing seems to interest them. They are so very different . . . and it is so very important that we establish a little rapport.'

His antennae were in rigid formal position. Christmas realized the big alien was actually worried.

'Something here is bound to tickle them, Ser. Hasn't it worked on every visitor so far? Even if they're from another galaxy, they can't be all that different. So the hardware didn't fascinate them; maybe the economics of the galactic betting system will. Or the Secretariat's display of xenobiology and alien housekeeping. After all, our galaxy is bigger than the Clouds; the sheer size and range of it all has to be impressive.'

Nisrair's antennae were still rigid; Christmas went on.

'If that fails, there's always the psy-math boys down at Pole South, forecasting the results of their own forecasts. Remember, that's what finally lured those dematerialized clots from the Horsehead into the Federation?'

'I hope so, Peter . . . they are very powerful, you know. Their equipment – very advanced.'

Big man and bigger coleopteran eyed each other in wordless unity. Neither wanted to speak of the possibility of intergalactic hostility resulting from First Contact.

'I'll do anything I can, Ser, you know that.'

'I was going to say . . . if they express some desire, no matter how unorthodox –'

'Anything at all, Ser. They can break all the rules.'

'Thank you.' Ser hoisted his bulk and paused before the balcony on his way out. 'Delightful,' he murmured, again avuncularly bland. 'Always an idyllic interlude to visit here. You lead an Arcadian life, Peter.'

'Kurtis called, PC,' said Dana, as usual slipping in before Christmas could signal. 'He has the net on the Flange team going, but there's nothing to report yet except that the drivers seem to be playing some game with their toes.'

'How Arcadian,' Christmas grunted.

'Also, there's a complaint from one of the big cat teams. They claim the target doesn't look human enough, their beast won't chase it.'

'Pass that one to Detweiler; that's a Secretariat problem . . . Oh! On your Ankru hunch: run me the tridis of all their animals, will you? That giant rep win makes them three out of four now – all in two days. I think you've got something.'

The Ankru entries came to his screen; the red archosaur type Christmas had seen, then a burly-legged running bird, and a tufted cheetah-like affair with a build like a rope slung between four stumps, and finally a slimy-looking tub of a thing which apparently navigated on a broad keel, propelled by paddles.

'That's the herbivorous amphibian,' Dana said. The herbi-amph opened one yawning end at the camera.

'High-gravity builds, I'd say,' Christmas mused. 'Call Lamont and tell him to run a covert check on their grav compensators for starters. It could be they have found a way to screw up their handicap. Oh – and while you're onto him, get that report on the compound life-swarm geehinkus from the Coalsack, will you? Detweiler's shop should never have put it in the social insect classes; we've had two complaints of fouling –'

BOOM! BOO-O-O-O-M-M-M-M!!!!

The resounding overhead thunder sent them both jumping for the balcony, to be greeted by a sight they had seen only on historitapes – a blazing rocket exhaust wavering down to land beyond the hotels. Christmas stared. Behind him the intercom was yammering.

'– Unauthorized landing! Repeat, red alert, unidentified alien landing –' It was the voice of the Gal Q security satellite.

'PC! A rocket's coming down on my minirodent tracks!' screamed a soprano.

Christmas vaulted onto his sled. 'Get a firescreen over those rats, Dana!' He took off, barely noticing that Dana had pushed something into his hand.

As he cleared the hotel domes, he saw the alien ship squatting in a volcano of smoke. The fireboys howled past, foam jets reaching for the intruder. The blaze was plastered down by the time Christmas skidded to a stop. Kurtis's blue prowler whined in behind him. The security chief was whispering orders into his collar. He raised one finger at Christmas without taking his eyes off the alien ship.

The foam around the ship was wriggling. Minirodents, ludicrously befoamed, were dashing in all directions, many without jockeys.

'Lily! Lily! Are you all right?' Christmas called, and saw his assistant steward rise up from under an overturned stand wiping globs of foam off her face. The minirodents rushed to her, formed a solid pile around her feet and scrambled onto her shoulders and head.

The alien's port swung down to make a ramp. Three squat figures peered out through the fading smoke. Then a flamboyantly uniformed blond chimpanzee strode onto the ramp, tossed his yellow mop out of his eyes, and gave out a ringing ululation ending in an inter-rogative note.

'Voder's coming in a minute,' Kurtis said. 'Look at those side arms – what the holy galaxy are they, space opera?'

The alien caterwauled again. Christmas, realizing he was the senior official there, stepped forward holding up his hand.

On the alien ramp, the stranger stared at him, tossed his head again, and then all three of them ducked back inside. Christmas waited; Gal Q and the Secretary would be there in a minute from the far side of Admin.

There came a siren roar from inside the spaceboat and the three emerged again, wheeling what looked like sur-realistic airsleds bigger than themselves and decked with grilles, pipes and streamers. The leader yawped at Christ-mas, who held up his hand again.

Suddenly all three aliens jammed horned helmets on their heads, sprang onto their machines, and took off in a thundering circle around their ship. As they began doing aerobatics, Secretary Detweiler's sled came over the hotel. The aliens zoomed onto it, looping and crowding with ear-splitting blasts from their machines.

Kurtis had already taken off in pursuit. Christmas got airborne just in time to see what looked like a laser beam coming from the aliens. Yes! In the name of madness, it was a laser. Detweiler's sled had sagged sideways, and Kurtis was throwing up his screens. Christmas put up his own, becoming vaguely aware that he had a minirodent on his head. He gained altitude and gave chase.

The aliens were now circling a cluster of MT masts and firing at the rigging, but Kurtis was on top of them. Christmas saw him nail one with come-along spray and then miss another, who darted toward Christmas. The thing Dana had given him had turned out to be a hand stunner. Christmas picked off the alien at low power as he went by and saw him go into a long glide to the beach. Kurtis, followed docilely by the come-along alien, was turning tight circles on the last rider's tail, forcing him down away from his ship.

Christmas got the minirodent's tail out of his eye and started back to the alien boat. Ambulance crews were converging, as Detweiler's sled limped in.

Suddenly the last alien doubled and streaked for his ship at ground level, his laser beam looping wildly.

'Down! Everybody down!' Christmas bellowed, heading toward the melée. Just as the alien almost gained his ramp he slumped off his machine and fell into the foam. His sled crashed into the ship wall and fell beyond him.

Lily the track steward emerged from under the ramp,

making cooing noises to the minirodents clinging to her. On her head, one of the rodent jockeys was holstering a tiny handgun.

'Snedecor got him, PC! Snedecor got him!' Lily yelled, wading out.

Kurtis and the now zombie-like alien had landed. The voder crew came up.

'Snedecor got him!' Lily caroled.

'What in creation were they trying?' Christmas asked.

The security chief glowered reproachfully at his captive, now being hooked up to the voder.

'We'll know shortly,' he said. 'Some bunch of flipping primitives who heard we had races, is my guess. Who's Snedecor?'

On Lily's head, Snedecor bowed and waved composedly.

'Good shooting . . . What's that mouse doing with sidearms?'

'Old ruling – all beings less than nine centims high authorized to carry nonlethal defense,' Christmas told him. 'Hello, Det. Glad you're okay. Well, I guess the rest of this is your job. Let me know the score, Lily, I've got to get back. Oh – here.'

He disengaged the minirodent and handed it over. 'Did anyone ever tell you you have an idyllic job?'

He zoomed for home, pausing to let another lizard race finish before he crossed the tracks. 'Machines . . . racing with *machines* . . .' he muttered, his big shoulders twitching. He floated over the shouts, barks, coos, whistles, the holiday-makers of a million worlds. Dana met him on the balcony with a tray.

'Looks good, what is it?' Christmas demanded, his nose in a beaker of Infield ale.

'Don't ask. Lamont sent it. His reward for saving something that broke a leg, he has a freezer full.'

'I didn't know we had a stunner, Dana.'

'You don't. I do. Kurtis gave it to me last year. Remember those Altaireans who wanted to duel to death in your office? Kurt says you have illusions of invulnerability.' Dana's bristles curled in a grin.

'Well, I guess it paid off. Another of your hunches . . . Yes, Hal?' he said to the intercom. 'Indeed we did have a little excitement. How're the rats? Ah, too bad. Rotten shame, who could foresee it? Great idea of yours, putting medication in the firefoam . . . Anything on the Ankru grav check yet?'

'Their gravity compensators are absolutely correct,' Lamont told him. 'Right on the nose at one point two. Funny thing, they look like really high gee types to me, too. And I'll tell you another funny thing – they're exercising some of their animals under double-grav loading. Of course there's no law against adding more gees, but they're being very quiet about it. I'd say you have the answer – there's a mistake in the handicapping from Detweiler's shop.'

'That could be ugly, Hal. Who made the mistake, and why?'

'I hadn't thought of that,' Lamont said slowly. He frowned.

'Well, it's not your screaming baby. How did things go with the Xemos Three birds?'

'Thank you for nothing, PC. No question, those things

fly. I suggested nerve blocks or temporary pinions, and he frothed. We settled on a special strap job after I showed him that other contestants used them. Probably intends to sabotage the straps – better put a watch-note on him. But listen, PC, did you know he had glass spurs on those birds as long as your arms? Slice a leg right off, like a saber. We had another scene when I told him they'd have to go. It seems they have some bosom enemy here they've got to beat, preferably fatally. You better alert the equipment boys. He's out for mayhem.'

'Scythes on his chariot wheels. Like that lot from Orion with the acid jets.'

'Remember those she-minks who couldn't see why we couldn't let them dump spikes on the track behind?' The doctor chuckled. 'Sometimes I think Gal Q is using us to civilize half the delinquents in the galaxy.'

Christmas clicked off. His intercom was flashing for the daily staff meeting. Christmas tuned himself in and listened with one ear while going through a batch of rulings Dana had brought in for signature.

Secretary Detweiler was a plump little woman with brilliant eyes, very good at a job Christmas would have loathed. One of her staff began describing plans for celebrating the finish of the giant ice-slug race. The contestants had covered fifty feet in the extraordinary time of six months and were due to cross the finish line tomorrow. Interest in their home system was at fever pitch. The secretariat had arranged tridi coverage from underneath the transparent track, so that viewers could observe the cell-by-cell approach of the slugs' feet to the line.

'They don't really locomote,' the aide was saying.

'They grow in front and slough off behind. Fastest moving thing in their system, but of course outsiders aren't too interested. I'd like permission to assemble a small, ah, claque, I believe the word is, and perhaps stimulate a little betting. It would help their morale.'

Christmas grunted agreement. Detweiler announced plans for making a ceremonial award that evening to the mouse who had shot the alien.

'Quite a little hero, really,' the Secretary said. 'If that lad had got his ship off, Gal Q would have had a messy chase, messy *and* expensive. You'll come to the presentation, won't you, PC?'

'Don't I get a wound stripe?' Christmas asked. 'My ear is full of rat-crap. Who were they, Det?'

'An officially uncontacted system 'way north of Murillo. Actually they've been trading with us for some time through Murillo. Apparently, they got hold of some obsolete stuff and made it all the way here in that old warp boat. Gal Fed has an M/T mission landing there right now.'

The bursar spoke up. 'Either we or Gal Q are going to have reparations to pay on this. Three valuable animals hurt and all those scent-null tracks to rebuild.'

'And we have adjustments on the spoiled races,' said the Mutuel chief. 'I think Gal Q should be asked to disseminate word that one doesn't just drop in on Race-world.'

'Nor does one race with machines,' growled Christmas. There was a moment's silence.

'Yes. Well,' said Detweiler. 'Now about our main business, the Magellans. You're getting them almost immediately, you know, PC. I don't know when they'll come to Mutuel and you others, if at all. Frankly, the tour is not working out quite as well as we had hoped. They went through the Secretariat this morning, and among everything else we tried a really beautiful viewing of the complete range of Galactic life we service here, with chemico-genetic analyses. You just can't tell how they're reacting, but I'm afraid it was negative. They asked to leave Raceworld tonight. Ser Nisrair is troubled.'

'Who isn't?' asked Commo from Pole North. 'I've seen aliens, but these are *alien*. Two of my techs are under sedation. Did you hear that Galtech hasn't been able to unscrew half the junk in that spook-boat they came in? Your viewing may have only whetted their appetites for dinner, Det. Or offended their sense of neatness, like finding out your neighbor's house is full of vermin. The Clouds are too damn close.'

'Well, we just have to do what we can,' Detweiler said, determinedly brisk. 'Anything else?'

'Sorry to add to the gloom,' Christmas spoke up. 'This concerns Mutuel, too. That new Ankru team has won four out of five events and they're only carrying a one point two gee handicap. Lamont has an idea this isn't enough by half. So do I. Check this out fast, Det, will you? I don't need to go into the implications.'

'I'll get right on it.' Detweiler looked startled. The Mutuel chief laid his hand over his eyes and groaned.

'Can't you hold up their races, PC? Great flying worm-holes, the adjustments, the compensations –' He was gesturing violently at somebody offscreen.

'Not solid enough,' Christmas told him.

Detweiler signed off with a sick look in her eyes. She knew what Christmas meant.

Alone, Christmas rubbed his neck, turning to the window. The announcer's chants rang out, and a dozen rhino-type creatures, their tails like quivering flagpoles over their laboring rumps, padded behind the starter's gate.

Christmas smiled automatically, but somehow the magic had ebbed. He knew – all of them knew – what the magic was. It wasn't the clamor of the stands, or the rolling coffers of Mutuel, or the rhinos' horn-down charge across the finish, the silks of planets a thousand light-years apart flying from their tails. The magic invested those things, but it was not of them. And it was threatened.

His outercom chimed and cleared to show the bony black face of the young vet.

'Sir, the infirmary wouldn't keep her – that, ah, young lady from Myria, I mean, and she can't go back to her team. They insist that she kill herself or they'll do it for her.'

'Oh, for Solsake! We've got our hands full right now. Take charge of her for a while, will you Doctor? Stick with her, show her around . . . I *know* you're a veterinarian. Refer Lamont to me . . . Well, take the sword away from her. And get some pants on her, will you? She looks uncivilized . . . Why shouldn't virgins on Myria wear pants? Oh, never mind – do anything you can, right?'

'Ser Nisrair and the Magellans are on their way up, PC,' said Dana's voice.

He stood to greet them as the big folding doors swung wide.

Looming beside Nisrair stood two coal-black sinuous shapes as tall as he, topped with dead-white triangular heads like bleached horse-skulls.

Christmas bowed and stood watching while Nisrair introduced them. The Magellans never moved. Their long skull-faces turned on him, eyeless, expressionless. Christmas, like most of the galaxy, had watched the tridi news coverage announcing First Contact, but he was not prepared for their unnerving alienness in the flesh . . . or whatever they were. Sourceless disquiet gripped him; he suspected they were emanating a subsonic field.

The Magellans' voder crackled suddenly, interrupting Nisrair.

'You are the (?) juridical (?) ethical organ,' it said tonelessly. Christmas couldn't tell which one was using it.

'That's right,' he said to the blank skull-eyes. 'It is my job to see that the fairest possible rules are set for all contestants, and to enforce them in detail and in spirit. When some condition affects contestants unequally, we work out new rules by unanimous agreement if possible. If not, my word is final – sorry I didn't get that.'

'Query your statement re spirit,' repeated the voder.

'Oh! I meant that we do not allow the technical wording of a rule to work against the intent to deal equally fairly with all. We define an equal chance as conditions as close as possible to those on the contestants' home planets; for example, to compensate for different gravities we have a handicapping device –'

'Spirit –' the voder muttered unintelligibly. The two horse-skulls glared down at him unmoving.

'You have great power here,' the voder went on. 'You could affect many contests without (?) detection (?) supervision for your own profit. Query you do not do so. Query your identity.'

Christmas glanced at Ser Nisrair. Hadn't he briefed them? He saw a worry-helix in one of the Gal Q officer's tendrils.

'Why, like everyone here – everyone on the staff I mean – I'm a Solterran,' Christmas said stiffly. 'I assume you were informed that Solterrans originated and run Raceworld.'

'(?) Peculation (?) speculation –' the voder gobbled. Evidently the alien semantics were giving Central Computer a hard time. Then it said clearly, 'Query there is no illegal manipulation for profit.'

Christmas said nothing.

'Deception, in a system of this sort, can be defined simply as entropy,' Ser Nisrair took over smoothly. 'And of course, entropy, or degradation of order, is avoided by all civilized beings, since no local increase in complexity can offset entropic effects in the larger matrix. We see three main entropic potentials in the Raceworld system. First, external parasitism – attempts at a takeover from without. You have viewed the galactic security force which guards against this. Second, attempts by the contestants to subvert portions of the system for individual or planetary benefit. The Steward here functions to prevent this, with the aid of his own security staff and such outside help as continuous probability monitoring from Mutuel. Thirdly, there is the possibility of corruption of the system by its own organizing elements, that is, by the Sol-terrans themselves. This is highly unlikely, as I indicated earlier – perhaps too briefly – first because of the high value placed upon honesty and fair play in the Solterrans' own value system, in which they are indoctrinated from infancy as managers of Raceworld, secondly because the Solterrans themselves insist upon a program of periodic testing conducted by galactic experts in combination with a rotating panel from neutral planets. And of course we have tried to meet all their material needs – haven't we, Peter?'

A pause in which Christmas could hear the voder whispering to the Magellans.

'We will observe,' the voder said. 'Alone.'

Nisrair's antennae, which had straightened out dur-ing his speech, kinked again. 'You wish me to leave?' he asked.

'You mean, stay here and watch our normal oper-ations?' asked Christmas.

'Yes.'

'Well, certainly.' Christmas found he was speaking through clenched teeth and flexed his jaw. 'Glad to have you. Make yourselves comfortable. Would you like, ah, chairs? Resting surfaces?'

The Magellans rippled into sudden violent motion and then stopped abruptly. They were now standing behind Christmas's off shoulder.

'Proceed,' said the voder.

'Right,' grated Christmas. He rang for Dana and bowed to Ser Nisrair, who allowed himself to be ushered out, antennae rigid.

'All right, Dana, I'm open for business. Our guests are staying to observe. What's come in?'

'A complaint has been filed by Betelgeuse system.' Only a slight starchiness about the whiskers betrayed Dana's awareness of the apparitions looming behind Christmas. 'They have a team of giant bore-worms, and they claimed their entry was fouled by striking tunnels left by a previous race.'

Christmas grunted. 'Those cursed worms have gnawed up that whole mountain range. Allow the claim, notify Mutuel, and tell the Secretariat we need some new mountains, they're going to devastate the planet. Wait – ask Detweiler if Gal Q could move in an asteroid for all those excavation contests. There's mining over in the next system, maybe they can shove us a rock or two. Det should have thought of that.'

To the presences behind he added, 'This is a just claim against Raceworld for improper track conditions and must be allowed. Those who bet on the affected team will be compensated.'

'We understand your language,' the voder said hollowly.

Kurtis came on the intercom. As the screen lit, Christmas realized that the aliens had chosen to stand where no viewer would pick them up.

'Your Flangians, PC. It's Pyrrhoxa all over again. Their drivers are nothing more than monkeys, the horses were training *them*. We caught the horses cold laying out a ploy for the next race. Their own odds were too short so they were fixing to have a long shot from Fitfat win. They actually passed their betting instructions to one of my boys.

They were doing it through a Spican food-handler. They had him terrorized.'

'Mutuel will go up the wall on this one, Kurt; they've been in a lot of races.' For the Magellans' benefit Christmas added, 'Of course they will have to reimburse all betters, probably with damages. Thank our stars those light equines aren't too popular. Give Detweiler the word, will you?'

'It's lucky they went for the big odds so openly,' Kurtis said. 'If they hadn't been so greedy they might have had a longer run. Well, that's horses for you.'

Christmas flinched and cut him off.

Dana looked up from his own commocollar.

'Ankru has just won another one, PC.'

Christmas nodded slowly. Holding his fingers on Detweiler's channel, he swung around to the Magellans. 'I am now going to query the Secretary on a very serious case,' he told them. 'A team from a planet called Ankru appears to have been assigned too light a gravity handicap, probably due to an error in the original schedules made up by the Secretary's office. The team has of course been winning in several different class events.' He swung back, trying to shake off the black weirdness.

'Anything on Ankru yet, Det?'

'The gravity is absolutely correct at one-point-two gee, PC,' Detweiler told him gravely. 'According to both our own star synopsis and the Gal Q master directory.'

'Can't be – they're still winning. Four out of five now. Besides – have you seen the brutes?'

Detweiler nodded perplexedly. Suddenly both she

and Christmas started to speak at once, the Secretary's exclamation riding over Christmas's rumble.

'Ambimass!'

'That could be it – I'll signal Center for the full planetary specs!'

'But –' said Christmas to the empty screen. The office door lit up.

'Visiting planetary minister, PC,' Dana told him. 'He's from somewhere I can't pronounce in Sector 90. Insists on talking to you in person, something about their age-weight handicap.'

The caller ambled in, an immense hump of shell with a sad, tapir-like face emerging at knee-height. He began hooting in nearly incomprehensible Galactic, with much ritual courtesy. Christmas waved Dana over to interpret.

'The problem is that their entry is now fifteen hundred Standard years old, and the age handicap's gone asymptotic.'

'How long do your animals live?' Christmas asked.

'He's not sure,' Dana translated. 'This particular animal has been winning races for over a millennium – he races every twenty years – and the home system expects him to go on indefinitely, I gather. They don't have any more right now, breeding is slow. With no weight handicap differential anymore it's getting tough. They're up against a much younger similar form from a new system, and planetary prestige is at stake.'

'I recall him now, he's a nice old boy. But we can't bugger up the whole handicap system. Even anti-grav wouldn't help, the animal would lose traction. Ask him if he'd be satisfied to switch over to noncompetitive exhibition, with choice of pace-setters, and lots of fanfare – oldest living champion, and all that?'

Dana and the alien hooted at length. Behind Christmas the aliens stood motionless, expressionless, exuding their faint aroma of disquiet.

'I think he says yes,' Dana reported. 'I told him the Secretary will –'

The office door burst open and a long white figure leaped in, drew itself up to eight feet of naked girl, rounded the desk and fell prone with a crash at Christmas's feet. Christmas curled up his toes as he felt cold steel sliding under them. Tapir-face hooted in alarm and backed into the Magellans, who did not move. He moaned louder and backed off into Dana. The office door was jammed with people, topped by the intern's dark face.

'What the – you, Doctor Ooloo – this is no place –' Christmas yelped.

'She got away from me, sir, through the ladies' latrine. She kept saying she was your slave since you saved her life and she had to swear fealty or something.'

The girl nodded and patted his instep.

'She says now she must toil for you – she has no home.'

'But what can she do? Has she ever seen a computer?'

'She says she is a warrior.'

'Yes, I know . . . Hold it a minute, Det!' he shouted at his flashing intercom. 'All right, young lady, you've sworn fealty. Now you go along with Dr Ooloo and they'll find you something to do. Find anything! Show her how to run the elevator! Now get out of here!'

He turned to bow deeply to the shaken tapir-faced

one as Dana got them out. From the screen, Detweiler's face watched in puzzlement until Christmas gave her the all-clear.

'We were right, PC!' Detweiler burst out. 'Ankru's a wildly oblate spheroid; they've got nearly three gee at the equator. That one-point-two figure was an average. Obviously they've been sending animals from their heavy zone.'

'But in that case, shouldn't the specs have the letter "v" after it for variable?'

'Yes, it should, but it doesn't. Here, look at the Directory read-out. Same in our synopsis, of course.'

'Recent date on that paragraph,' Christmas said thoughtfully. 'Just about the time Ankru applied, wasn't it?'

'Why yes, it's a change notice. They come out periodically from Gal Comp by FTL and are automatically transcribed here . . . wait, let me see if we still have the old paragraph.' She dived offscreen, to return noticeably pale. 'The old directory paragraph has been destroyed, but I found one in my personal synopsis. The "v" was there, before the change. What could have happened?'

'Seems to me there's three possibilities,' said Christmas. 'Gal Comp mistransmitted, the FTL garbled, or something went wrong with the transcriber in your office.'

'Gal Comp has *never* sent a mis-read, Peter.' Detweiler seldom used his given name. 'You know the Directory is the galaxy bible for navigation, administration, everything; they have a fantastic technical control on it. The FTL transmission could garble, of course, but they do triple redundancy with a discrepancy signal. For one letter alone to fall out and the warning to fail too, would be, well, just about the fifty million monkeys. And the transcriber in our office is automatic too. It would be almost impossible for it to miss one symbol in an otherwise correct paragraph –' Detweiler's voice died.

'Unless somebody tampered with it.' Christmas finished for her.

'Yes . . . it could be done. The original read-out is duplicated for the Directory and the synopses. If the process were stopped, a technician could alter the original . . . there is a gap in the line too, Peter, I think.' The bright eyes were huge, and her face showed angles Christmas had never seen.

'The technicians are all our people,' said Christmas.

'Yes, every one. Peter, I'm going to signal Gal Comp to check their master program. It'll take some while.' She cut off abruptly.

Christmas sat drumming his desk. Then he shook himself.

'Dana, put a hold on all Ankru races. Either they withdraw or the races are postponed. Handicap error. And tell Kurt to see they don't get off the planet and to monitor any signals. But not to alarm them. *And* notify Mutuel that results on those already run are now officially invalid.'

The Magellan voder crackled startlingly.

'Query correct understanding. You now (?) hypothesize (?) imaginatively postulate a Solterran has engaged in deception for gain.'

'That's right,' Christmas said. He took a deep breath. 'Only a Solterran could have cut out the "v" that told the planet was irregular. Once it was out, the way was open for Ankru to bring in their heavies and make a killing. The fact that they entered so many races so fast suggests that there was a plan. Only one of our people would perceive the possibility . . . Of course there is a microscopic possibility that there was an outside leader, maybe even from Gal Center, and that our person was intimidated. But it looks – no. It can't be. It *cannot* be.'

'Query impossibility. Solterrans do not differ from other life.'

Christmas's jaw worked.

'Such (?) ideals (?) systems have been known to fail in our galaxy. Possibility of material riches is very great,' the voder probed on.

'What's to gain?' Christmas burst out, aware that he was being driven closer to what he would not say. 'We have everything one could wish, homes, luxury, travel – all free.'

'Possibility of material increment for your home planet is very great.'

'This is our home planet,' Christmas responded mechanically. What was wrong with Ser Nisrair? How could he have failed to brief the Magellans? It was unforgivable. He felt the never-quite-absent ache rising.

'Query correct understanding,' the voder was a vulture picking at his vitals. 'You are native of planet Terra in system Sol.'

He was going to have to say it. He surged up and strode to the window, his back to the aliens.

'There is no living planet of Terra. The Solterrans you have seen here are descendants of small colonies on our moon and a few other places at the time Terra was destroyed . . . Terra was the only habitable planet in our system.'

The ache was hard in his breast now. As a child he had sung '*There is a dome that we call home, green Terra is no more.*' Neither he nor his fifteenth grandfather had known green Terra or lived in a dome, but the images were deep . . . The grim survivors in asteroid bubbles, under leaky Marsdome . . . watching the big ships of Gal Q come poking in to see what was burning up their scintillographs, and to rescue the orphans.

'In our galaxy, beings without home planet do not long persist.'

'Nor here,' said Christmas heavily. It was true. Orphan races somehow died out, no one knew quite why . . . Or why the ache never died. Either you kept hold of the ache and lived or you forgot and after a while you weren't around any more.

'Raceworld is run by the planetless, you see,' he said aloud. 'There is no one outside to profit. Only Solterrans.'

'Your assistant is not Solterran.'

'Oh, we take in a few other orphans. Dana's people got one ship out of an inter-system war. Doesn't often happen.'

Were Dana's people going to live with the ache, too? Christmas had never pried behind the cheery brown eyes. Dana was fifth generation. There were still some cubs around.

'Query your planet was lost by war.' The ghoul-voice bored on relentlessly. Christmas studied the horizon. The scene below him, the announcer's call – all phantasms now.

'No. We blew it up ourselves.'

The voder gargled. 'Such cases especially non-persistent,' it said.

This too was true. Those races who had destroyed their own worlds never lived on long. Except one. All honor to the suicides, the fratricides, the matricides – the lost Solterrans who had found their immortality as purveyors of a primitive pleasure to the galaxy.

The voder-vulture was squawking again.

'Query you place value on (?) ethics (?) group conduct on dead planet.'

Christmas whirled around.

'Terra is not dead!' he shouted into the white skull-faces. 'Every civilized race in the galaxy knows Terra now! The word Terran is slang for fairness, for incorruptibility, all over the galaxy! Ask anywhere – ask in the Center – they know us. They joke about it – they don't understand it – but they play our game and they use her name! How can Terra be dead when mother fish in the seas teach their young about her?'

He caught his breath.

'There was nothing like Raceworld before we came. We – the Terran survivors – we thought of it, planned it, sold it to Gal Center. We're a good piece of their budget now. But with us it is for Terra. For her ideals, for what might have been. How can she be dead when birds that fly in freezing ammonia speak her name?'

He ran down and the room was silent.

The voder curdled faintly, hushed again. Christmas went back to his desk. The black devils had got it out of him.

'Query,' announced the voder. Christmas had the

175

impression a different Magellan was speaking, but he couldn't care less.

'You experience noxious subjective disturbance.'

'I experience noxious subjective disturbance, yes,' Christmas said bleakly. 'If . . . if one of us . . . the whole thing is no good, the unique thing . . . but it can't be –'

The minutes dragged by. The aliens spoke no more. Dana came in with some papers, not meeting Christmas's eyes; he always monitored the office.

A planetary rep came on the outercom, breezily intent on getting a special ruling in the hopper classes. The rep looked like a kangaroo. Christmas answered him mechanically.

In the middle of a complicated point about tail rests, Detweiler's signal chimed. Christmas spun away from the kangaroo.

'– definitely, Peter. I've seen the master read-in,' Detweiler stuttered.

'*What's definite?*'

'The "v" was never transmitted from Gal Comp! Some molecule, I don't know – anyway, it's the first misread in five Standard centuries; they're wild. It's theirs, Peter! It's theirs!'

'It's not us,' Christmas said softly. After a minute they broke connection.

Christmas sat stone-still. Then he slapped his desk hard and whirled on the Magellans.

'You see?' he shouted. 'You see? Oh, I should have seen it had to be them. A mechanical process can reverse a unit at random, but motivation acts like a field – elements don't change until the field does –'

The kangaroo was spluttering from the screen. Christmas got him mollified. Over his shoulder he heard the Magellans rustling and turned in time to catch a glimpse of crimson flaps opening and closing along the black sides. The voder made an incomprehensible noise. Christmas stared, remembering that there were alien galaxies, and the shadows of unthinkable war. Were they offended? Angry?

A clashing sound came from outside the big doors. Dana rushed to fling it open, revealing Ser Nisrair standing eyestalk-to-eyeball with the Myrian girl. The point of her sword was at Nisrair's massive stomach plates. Hubbub arose from the offices beyond.

'Let him in and put that knife away!' Christmas roared. 'Who in chaos told you I needed a door-guard? Excuse me, Ser, we've been having problems.'

Nisrair stumped in, antennae formal. Three of his eyestalks were trained on the Magellans, one on Christmas. The aliens gave no sign.

'The transportation back to Galactic Center which you requested is now ready,' Ser Nisrair told them.

'No,' said the voder.

'But –' said Nisrair. 'Ah, then, you wish to continue the tour here? We have an interesting demonstration of probability extrapolation prepared for the evening.'

'No,' repeated the voder.

Again there came the crimson rustling.

'. . . Not previously visible,' said the voder, and lapsed into unintelligibility. Nisrair swiveled a second eyestalk around to Christmas. Christmas opened his hands in a shrug.

'My (?) affiliate (?) co-traveler is . . . untranslatable disturbance. We wish to retire now to consider . . . garble . . . what we have seen.'

'I will escort you at once to the hotel,' said Nisrair. Still the aliens did not move.

The voder crackled on for a moment and then said clearly, 'Technology, communications, mathematics, economics, chemistry, high bit-rate . . .' It made a surprisingly expressive hiccough. The aliens were suddenly in swirling motion to the door.

There they stopped and contorted oddly. One of them stamped hard with black whiplike toes, making a report like a pistol-shot. Everyone jumped. The next second they were receding through the outer office.

Nisrair went after them, one round eyeball still twisted over his shoulder at Christmas.

Dana silently closed the big doors and leaned with his back to them, showing his substantial teeth.

'Who knows?' Christmas rubbed his head dazedly. 'Tragedians, maybe. Romantics. Were they crying? Or laughing? Something they wanted, anyway. Gal Q has been killing them with computers and everything so sublime –'

'The gods do not come to earth to see lightning,' Dana said. 'An old saying of my people.'

'Maybe they weren't gods,' Christmas said. 'Maybe they were a couple of old aunties out for a joyride. Or honeymooners who got lost.'

He shook off his ghosts.

'All right, let's get that unholy Myrian in here – and that Doctor Ooloolullah.'

He went to the window, snuffling luxuriously. The magic was back. Dana herded in the gangling humans.

'Young lady – no, stay on your feet. I've got something to tell you. You couldn't go home because you lost the race, right? Well, you didn't lose it, you won it. The animal who came in first has been disqualified; it was running under an inadequate gravity handicap. Do you understand? Tell her, Doctor, she won it fair and square. Now she can go back to Myria in triumph and be a sacred warrior virgin again. Right?'

The girl broke into sobs of unmistakable woe.

'For Solsake, what now?'

'She says she can't go home now, sir, because – uh –'

'Because *what*?'

'Sir, you said, do anything –'

'Oy not vergan now!' she wailed and collapsed on the intern's chest.

'She wants to stay here,' said the intern. 'I thought she could work out well with the animals.'

'She can't stay here, she's got a home. What's that?'

'She says they'll disembowel her at home for not being a virgin,' the intern said miserably.

'Really? Permissive types. Well! H'mm, Dana, do you think she might qualify as a *de facto* planetless person? I'll buck a request over to Det in the morning; she'll have to get cultural certification. All right! You, Doctor, take her to Lamont's transient billet; she can camp there till we get this straightened out. You, young lady, go with him and do whatever he says, right? You can put your pants on now and that sword goes away, right? No, on your feet – in public anyway. And both of you get out of here and stay out until I call for you – if I ever do – starting as of now. Right?'

The doors closed.

The drifting fragrance of a cheroot told Christmas that his night deputy had come into the office and was quietly checking through Dana's log to see what was pending for the night. Coburg was a stocky white-haired man who had been main track chief until his legs failed.

'Should be a quiet night,' Christmas told him. 'You might call Lamont's office for quarters for a special case, you heard it. And you're bound to get some noise about the Ankru thing. Other than that – I'll call in later.'

He gazed out to where the floodlights were coming on over plain and mountains, pylons, domes, and sea. All were folded in the gold and pastel of Raceworld's perfect evening. One in her infinite series of perfect evenings . . . Dana was watching him.

'Somehow I feel you and I could do with a small idyll,' Christmas said. 'How about getting your family to join me at Sea world? We'll snatch a prime table by the big shark races and your kids can have themselves a ride.'

'We'll meet you at Freshwater *after* you keep your appointment at the amphitheater, PC,' Dana grinned.

'Oh-oh.' Christmas glanced guiltily at his timer and went out to the sled. As he floated into the evening a troop of giant wolf-spiders paraded onto the track below him, prancing daintily on twenty-foot legs. The bugle made sweet sounds.

Arcadia, Nisrair had called it. Arcady was a pastoral dream. No, this was a different dream – one that had kept his race alive, of all the orphan races. A bright improbable dream that their ancestors had managed to weave into the galaxy's life currents so their children need never wake up and die.

It had even hooked those golems from the Clouds. Christmas chuckled, recalling Ser Nisrair's discomfiture. The poor spooks had been paralyzed by Gal Q's lectures.

Grinning, he turned a long lazy circle toward Admin. Then his grin faded. In his mind was the image of Nisrair's round, receding eye. It had been unforgivable to make him bare his soul that way. How could Nisrair have fallen down so badly in briefing them? He must have been really frantic, Christmas decided; he'd never before failed to explain the set-up here to visitors in advance. In fact, he'd never before failed at much of anything.

The eye came back, brighter, expressively clinical.

'Why, you mealy-mouthed big smart cockroach!' Christmas exploded aloud. 'I should have known!'

He whipped the sled savagely over Admin, seeing it all now. That request of Nisrair's – he hadn't been asking Christmas to let them press some buttons or fly over a track. He had them figured, he was looking for something to get under their hides with. So he picked the Tragedy of Terra. Played live.

'You soulless big blue bug –' Christmas noticed startled faces turning toward him as he shot over a recreation deck. Slowly, his jaw came back to normal.

'It's his job to get rapport; he got rapport.' Christmas grunted. His lips quirked.

Grinning once more, the Steward of Raceworld braked his sled smartly onto the roof of the amphitheater where the Secretary of Raceworld was preparing with all ceremony to award a medal to an intrepid mouse. As he started down the ramp there floated up from behind him the cry, 'KEEB'Y VAAAAALYA!' and the watchers from a million planets rose and clamored.

The Man Doors Said Hello To

I was all alone at the end of the bar when he came in and I heard it distinctly: *'Hello-o!'*

I froze. Go away. But he wasn't talking to me. In fact he wasn't talking to anybody unless he was two midgets. Which was possible, I noted apathetically as he receded down the bar. He was about nine feet tall and dressed by Goodwill Industries.

I went back to trying to decide whether I was suffering more here than if I were someplace else. Here was a tacky grill in a part of town I'd never seen before and didn't etcetera. It had the advantage that none of my, aaugh, friends was apt to come in. On the other hand several hours here had yielded no help at all. None.

There was the problem of taking a leak before leaving. When I stood up I found my legs had been there too long. They kind of floated me at a tall apparition halfway down the bar, but I managed to veer into the can.

The can door pushed open again behind me and I heard a gutsy chuckle: *'Hiya.'* Mister Tall came through. Oh, no. I concentrated on my image as the most dangerous slightly paralyzed guy five-feet-six in the world and finished my business fast. When I left I noticed the door creaked a little. It definitely did not speak English.

I had to stop to blow my nose and he came out. The door said briskly, *'Ciao.'*

It had to be some ventriloquist gig. As he went by I saw him tap the next door, the one with the female thing on it.

'*Hi there*,' it murmured. The *door* said it.

Without meaning to I looked at his eyes. He didn't seem to be two midgets.

'I heard that.'

He shrugged.

'It's a friendly city.'

'Yo,' I shuddered.

'Doors.' He shook his head and gestured at the bartender. We seemed to be sitting down again. 'Ever think about doors? Zam, bang, hit, hit, all day long. Very little empathy.'

'Hit, hit.' I touched the cool glass to my forehead. A friendly city. A razorblade pizza, the day I'd been through. Pete, my so-called agent. Hallee, my so-called girl. *Mr Mc-Farland*. I was bleeding into my socks.

'Take bus doors,' the large weirdo was saying. 'Or subway doors, it's pitiful the beating they take.'

This was better than thinking about Mr McFarland but not very. 'I admit I never thought about it from the door's viewpoint. One of them clipped me yesterday. In the ankle.'

'Alienated.' He sighed. 'Hard to blame them.'

The bartender seemed to have opened a slightly better brand. My door-loving acquaintance was doing something elaborate with a thimble on his keychain. I squinted into the bar mirror FBI-style and saw his hand slide under his limp lapels and come out empty. Our eyes met.

'You're pouring gibsons into your pocket.'

'Ordinarily I don't let people see me do that.' He grinned tentatively.

'I saw it. Samples. Some kind of inspector?'

'Oh no.' He laughed bashful-like. 'It's this housing shortage, you know. It's no joke.'

'Fierce,' I agreed.

'Too right.' He had this proud shy look. A clown. 'They're a great bunch of kids. You have no concept how hard it is for girls to find a place to live in this city. I mean like a decent place.' He shrugged and the suit sort of billowed around his struts. 'It isn't as though I don't have plenty of room.'

What a clown. But it was still better than the Pete-Hallee-Mr McFarland segue.

'You're telling me you have girls living in your clothes?'

He nodded, glancing around.

'Watch,' he smiled. He selected a teeny kernel of popcorn and held it up beside his Misterogers tie.

A little pink thing about as long as a guppy whipped out and snatched the popcorn back into his coat. I saw it clearly. A perfect girl's arm. But perfect, not like those things that pop out of boxes. I couldn't help setting myself up for the pitch.

'Swear the fingers moved.'

'Well, of course.'

'Let's see the rest of her.'

'Ah, they're doing their nails and you know. The stuff girls do at night.'

'They? How many have you?'

'There are six on the lease,' he said seriously. 'The others aren't home yet.'

'Oh? Where do they go?'

'Working. What else?' He gave me a sharp look. 'Girls

in the city, you know it's rough. I helped them over a couple of months before they connected, but we're all square now.'

'Connected?'

'Why, sure.' He lowered his voice confidentially. 'Model agencies. Heavy demand for small people. You know those ads where some little girl is standing by a big bottle? Compact cars. Campers. Makes things look roomy. You probably saw them in those 747 jet commercials.'

'That figures,' I admitted. The new brand seemed to be helping. My condominium friend carefully cut a morsel of onion into his next thimble of gibsons.

'Going to get stoned in there,' I warned him.

'Ah, they're sweet kids. They want some to keep for the others.'

I watched the little arm zip out again. Believe it, the nails looked gold now. I started to say something dirty and then changed it.

'How do they make out? I mean, you don't see many guys five inches high.'

'You don't?' He sounded surprised. 'Oh lord, I don't pry. Girls in the city, you know. Lot of them have friends back home most likely.'

My glass kind of slipped then and the scene flowed into a series of hold shots in which my wallet wouldn't come out and he was boosting my arm and saying, 'There's some eats down the way.' I was working up to resent that when I noticed we were going out.

The door muttered to him as we went through.

'Thanks.' He fixed his zipper. 'It's a friendly city.'

A blast of cold dark smog made me concentrate on my stomach. We floated along.

'Wait.' We were at a corner. My high-rise companion was sorting through his change. He picked out a half-dollar, reached up and laid it on a ledge of the brick wall.

'Borrowed it last week,' he explained as we crossed the street.

'Who leaves money on buildings?'

'Well, I don't know who exactly. Tall people's bank, you know. Streets with two r's in them. Comes in handy.' He thought a minute. 'Isn't there one for short people?'

'Not to my knowledge.' Quel kook. The scene was stabilizing, I could make out the next street sign: Harrison.

'Try here,' I told him.

'Oh, I have all I need now.'

'It has two r's. Show me.'

He went to the brownstone ledge and stretched up. His fingers came back holding a dime.

'Pigeons,' he said apologetically, cleaning his hand. He started to put the dime back and said, 'Hey.'

He unfolded a note and showed it to me. One wavery little word in pencil: '*Help.*'

'I know, the windows write letters to you.'

'Don't be ridiculous.' He frowned at the side of the old walk-up. 'Human people write notes. Real young or real old,' he muttered. 'Look up there. Somebody feeds birds.'

Without another word we dashed around the corner to the front entrance and up the stoop.

'That's locked,' I warned him. But we seemed to be

going inside. As I passed the door it said excitedly, '*When's the inaugural?*'

'Some of those old fellows get muddled,' he commented over his shoulder, going upstairs like a helicopter. I couldn't imagine why I was cantering after him. I caught him on the third landing.

'Fourth from the corner . . . second door. Here.'

He knocked. Nothing happened.

'Hello?'

He knocked again. Something very faint pattered inside.

'Wh – who?'

'I found your note,' he called. 'We came as fast as we could.'

A chain rattled and a chink appeared. He held up the note.

The door opened another inch and I saw a small fist over a lot of collarbones. She was one of those waifs that look as if any clothes are too big for them. Blue temples. Nothing hair. One big naked eye you could stumble into and drown yourself.

She let go her coat and quickly put glasses over those naked eyes.

'Oh, that was silly of me,' she said, very dignified from about the level of his belt.

'I'm not so sure, ma'am.' He frowned over her into the room. 'Would you mind if we looked around?'

I was breaking up at my stupid two-story friend thinking some woman in this city would invite a strange male into her place, when I noticed we were in the middle of her bedroom.

What a freezer. One dim light, one foldbed, one fungus carpet, one big wardrobe, one chair. Sure enough, a box of birdseed by the window. But no TV or radio, no tapes, no book by the chair, nothing. I had the idea she'd been sitting there in her coat under that dim bulb for a month.

My impulsive companion was looking over everything in silence. He sniffed. Then he walked over and slapped the big wardrobe.

Surprisingly, the light went bright. He sniffed again. Then he grabbed the wardrobe by both sides and wrestled it, boom, scrape, away from the wall. It was a monsterhouse, dark wood with claw feet and a carved bat pie on top, or maybe it was a vulture. I couldn't tell which because my friend dived behind it and the light went out.

The chick and I stood gaping at each other in the flashes of a sign outside. He was doing something with a hand torch.

The light came on again and he unfolded himself in a shower of dust and held out a piece of wire. I could smell the scorch.

'Rubbed the insulation off against the plug,' he said. 'That thing has paper backing, too. About ready to go up.'

He horsed the wardrobe back and stood squinting at it. Then he hauled off and gave it a thundering kick. We jumped. The wardrobe's bottom drawers sucked in and the piece kind of stood to attention.

'That'll straighten it out for a day or so, ma'am. First thing in the morning you go find another place to live. Time to eat now.'

She started to weave her head, *No thank you*, and her glasses slid down her nose. He picked them off and put them in her pocket. 'Eat.' He nodded, tucking her hand under his arm and starting out of the room. His other hand swept out and grabbed a bottle of red capsules by the bed and tossed them at me.

'You won't need these tonight, ma'am,' he told her. 'He'll keep them for you. Right?'

Her little mouth was going *But, But* silently under the eyes. We trouped down the stairs. When we pushed through the front door it wheezed '*Win with Willkie!*' He thumped it amicably.

The next two blocks were complicated. I realized it wasn't just me. The girl was weaving all over the place. By the time we reached his eat-stop all seventy-five pounds of her were hanging on my muscular one-thirty. The eatery smelled cheerful, sort of Detroit espresso. As we entered the revolving door carolled '*H'lo-lo-lo-lo!*'

She heard and looked up at me, puzzled.

'It's a friendly city,' I told her. For some reason I put one finger on the end of her nose. She didn't go away.

'I have to eat and run.' He herded us into a booth and ordered. Then he unfolded his legs down the aisle, rubbing his shaggy head. 'You don't often see a really mean piece of furniture. That old boy was poison all the way through. I knew one just like it once, hell of a history. You can't blame them. But they're not safe, ma'am. Especially for someone like you.'

'You mean it was trying to start a fire?' I asked. 'Why would it burn itself up too?'

'Surely you've heard of the death wish?'

The chick's head was going like watching a slow sad pingpong match.

'Show her the girl,' I urged. 'He has girls living in his clothes. Go on, show her.'

He laughed, bashful again.

'They're busy. They're fixing their hair now, you know girls.'

I started telling her about the Tall People's Bank and we were all grinning like crazy when the lasagna finally arrived. It was really all right.

'Look, I have to go uptown now.' He laid his spoon over his knife and fork in a pattern. 'You guys will be okay now, I think.' He smiled at the girl. 'He's going to find you a place to stay. First thing in the morning, remember.'

It bugged me a little because I'd been working on just that.

'What now? Rushing water to a starving mailbox?'

Half his smile faded.

'Ah, I have to go chew somebody out.'

He scrooched out of the booth and towered over us, pushing in his tie.

'What for?'

He muttered something that sounded like 'The submarine is late.'

'Huh?'

'Like about a hundred years,' he said absently. He winked. 'See you.' As he made off, I saw a little head peeking out of his side pocket. It seemed to be wearing curlers. I waved. Something waved back.

'Beautiful,' I told the girl. He really was all right.

But you know, I never did catch his name and when I asked around later nothing checked out. You wouldn't even believe the hassles a guy my size can get into, goosing building ledges. But I've spotted one new Kennedy half at Grosvenor and Forty-fourth. We're keeping our eyes on the spot.

The Man Who Walked Home

*— Transgression! Terror! And he thrust and lost there —
punched into impossibility abandoned never to be known
how, the wrong man in the most wrong of all wrong
places in that unimaginable collapse of never-to-be-reim-
agined mechanism — he stranded, undone, his lifeline
severed, he in that nanosecond knowing his only tether
parting, going away, the longest line to life withdrawing,
winking out, disappearing forever beyond his grasp —
telescoping away from him into the closing vortex beyond
which lay his home, his life, his only possibility of being;
seeing it sucked back into the deepest maw, melting,
leaving him orphaned on what never-to-be-known shore
of total wrongness — of beauty beyond joy, perhaps? Of
horror? Of nothingness? Of profound otherness only,
certainly — whatever it was, that place into which he
transgressed, it could not support his life there, his violent and violating aberrance, and he, fierce, brave, crazy
— clenched into total protest, one body-fist of utter repu-
diation of himself there in that place, forsaken there
— what did he do? Rejected, exiled, hungering home-
wards more desperate than any lost beast driving for its
unreachable home, his home, his HOME — and no way,
no transport, no vehicle, means, machinery, no force but
his intolerable resolve aimed homeward along that van-*

ishing vector, that last and only lifeline – he did, what?
He walked.
Home.

Precisely what hashed up in the work of the major industrial lessee of the Bonneville Particle Acceleration Facility in Idaho was never known. Or rather, all those who might have been able to diagnose the original malfunction were themselves obliterated almost at once in the greater catastrophe which followed.

The nature of this second cataclysm was not at first understood either. All that was ever certain was that at 1153.6 of May 2, 1989 Old Style, the Bonneville laboratories and all their personnel were transformed into an intimately disrupted form of matter resembling a high-energy plasma, which became rapidly airborne to the accompaniment of radiating seismic and atmospheric events.

The disturbed area unfortunately included an operational MIRV Watchdog womb.

In the confusion of the next hours the Earth's population was substantially reduced, the biosphere was altered, and the Earth itself was marked with numbers of more conventional craters. For some years thereafter the survivors were existentially preoccupied and the peculiar dustbowl at Bonneville was left to weather by itself in the changing climatic cycles.

It was not a large crater; just over a kilometer in width and lacking the usual displacement lip. Its surface was covered with a finely divided substance which dried into dust. Before the rains began it was almost perfectly flat. Only in certain lights, had anyone been there to inspect it, a small surface marking or abraded place could be detected almost exactly at the center.

Two decades after the disaster a party of short brown people appeared from the south, together with a flock of somewhat atypical sheep. The crater at this time appeared as a wide shallow basin in which the grass did not grow well, doubtless from the almost complete lack of soil micro-organisms. Neither this nor the surrounding vigorous grass were found to harm the sheep. A few crude hogans went up at the southern edge and a faint path began to be traced across the crater itself, passing by the central bare spot.

One spring morning two children who had been driving sheep across the crater came screaming back to camp. A monster had burst out of the ground before them, a huge flat animal making a dreadful roar. It vanished in a flash and a shaking of the earth, leaving an evil smell. The sheep had run away.

Since this last was visibly true, some elders investigated. Finding no sign of the monster and no place in which it could hide, they settled for beating the children, who settled for making a detour around the monster-spot, and nothing more occurred for a while.

The following spring the episode was repeated. This time an older girl was present but she could add only that the monster seemed to be rushing flat out along the ground without moving at all. And there was a scraped place in the dirt. Again nothing was found; an evil-ward in a cleft stick was placed at the spot.

When the same thing happened for the third time a year later, the detour was extended and other charmwands were added. But since no harm seemed to come of it and the brown people had seen far worse, sheep-tending resumed as before. A few more instantaneous apparitions of the monster were noted, each time in the spring.

At the end of the third decade of the new era a tall old man limped down the hills from the south, pushing his pack upon a bicycle wheel. He camped on the far side of the crater, and soon found the monster-site. He attempted to question people about it, but no one understood him, so he traded a knife for some meat. Although he was obviously feeble, something about him dissuaded them from killing him, and this proved wise because he later assisted the women in treating several sick children.

He spent much time around the place of the apparition and was nearby when it made its next appearance. This excited him very much and he did several inexplicable but apparently harmless things, including moving his camp into the crater by the trail. He stayed on for a full year watching the site and was close by for its next manifestation. After this he spent a few days making a charmstone for the spot and left northwards, hobbling as he had come.

More decades passed. The crater eroded and a rain-gully became an intermittent streamlet across the edge of the basin. The brown people and their sheep were attacked by a band of grizzled men, after which the survivors went away eastward. The winters of what had been Idaho were now frost-free; aspen and eucalyptus sprouted in the moist plain. Still the crater remained treeless, visible as a flat bowl of grass; and the bare place at the center remained. The skies cleared somewhat.

After another three decades a larger band of black people with ox-drawn carts appeared and stayed for a time, but left again when they too saw the thunderclap-monster. A few other vagrants straggled by.

Five decades later a small permanent settlement had grown up on the nearest range of hills, from which men riding on small ponies with dark stripes down their spines herded humped cattle near the crater. A herdsman's hut was built by the streamlet, which in time became the habitation of an olive-skinned, red-haired family. In due course one of this clan again observed the monster-flash, but these people did not depart. The stone the tall man had placed was noted and left undisturbed.

The homestead at the crater's edge grew into a group of three and was joined by others, and the trail across it became a cartroad with a log bridge over the stream. At the center of the still faintly discernible crater the cart-road made a bend, leaving a grassy place which bore on its center about a square meter of curiously impacted bare earth and a deeply etched sandstone rock.

The apparition of the monster was now known to occur regularly each Spring on a certain morning in this place, and the children of the community dared each other to approach the spot. It was referred to in a phrase that could be translated as 'the Old Dragon'. The Old Dragon's appearance was always the same: a brief violent thunder-burst which began and cut off abruptly, in the midst of which a dragonlike creature was seen apparently in furious motion on the earth although it never actually moved. Afterwards there was a bad smell and the earth smoked. People who saw it from close by spoke of a shivering sensation.

Early in the second century two young men rode into town from the north. Their ponies were shaggier than the local breed and the equipment they carried included two boxlike objects which the young men set up at the monster site. They stayed in the area a full year, observing two materializations of the Old Dragon, and they provided much news and maps of roads and trading towns in the cooler regions to the north. They built a windmill which was accepted by the community and offered to build a lighting machine, which was refused. Then they departed with their boxes after unsuccessfully attempting to persuade a local boy to learn to operate one.

In the course of the next decades other travelers stopped by and marveled at the monster, and there was sporadic fighting over the mountains to the south. One of the armed bands made a cattle raid into the crater hamlet. It was repulsed, but the raiders left a spotted sickness which killed many. For all this time the bare place at the crater's center remained, and the monster made his regular appearances, observed or not.

The hill-town grew and changed and the crater hamlet grew to be a town. Roads widened and linked into networks. There were gray-green conifers in the hills now, spreading down into the plain, and chirruping lizards lived in their branches.

At century's end a shabby band of skin-clad squatters

with stunted milk-beasts erupted out of the west and were eventually killed or driven away, but not before the local herds had contracted a vicious parasite. Veterinaries were fetched from the market city up north, but little could be done. The families near the crater left and for some decades the area was empty. Finally cattle of a new strain reappeared in the plain and the crater hamlet was reoccupied. Still the bare center continued annually to manifest the monster and he became an accepted phenomenon of the area. On several occasions parties came from the distant Northwest Authority to observe it.

The crater hamlet flourished and grew into the fields where cattle had grazed and part of the old crater became the town park. A small seasonal tourist industry based on the monster-site developed. The townspeople rented rooms for the appearances and many more-or-less authentic monster-relics were on display in the local taverns.

Several cults now grew up around the monster. One persistent belief held that it was a devil or damned soul forced to appear on Earth in torment to expiate the catastrophe of three centuries back. Others believed that it, or he, was some kind of messenger whose roar portended either doom or hope according to the believer. One very vocal sect taught that the apparition registered the moral conduct of the townspeople over the past year, and scrutinized the annual apparition for changes which could be interpreted for good or ill. It was considered lucky, or dangerous, to be touched by some of the dust raised by the monster. In every generation at least one small boy would try to hit the monster with a stick, usually acquiring a broken arm and a lifelong tavern tale. Pelting the monster with stones or other objects was a popular sport, and for some years people systematically flung prayers and flowers at it. Once a party tried to net it and were left with strings and vapor. The area itself had long since been fenced off at the center of the park.

Through all this the monster made his violently enigmatic annual appearance, sprawled furiously motionless, unreachably roaring.

Only as the fourth century of the new era went by was it apparent that the monster had been changing slightly. He was now no longer on the earth but had an arm and a leg thrust upward in a kicking or flailing gesture. As the years passed he began to change more quickly until at the end of the century he had risen to a contorted crouching pose, arms outflung as if frozen in gyration. His roar, too, seemed somewhat differently pitched and the earth after him smoked more and more.

It was then widely felt that the man-monster was about to do something, to make some definitive manifestation, and a series of natural disasters and marvels gave support to a vigorous cult teaching this doctrine. Several religious leaders journeyed to the town to observe the apparitions.

However, the decades passed and the man-monster did nothing more than turn slowly in place, so that he now appeared to be in the act of sliding or staggering while pushing himself backwards like a creature blown before a gale. No wind, of course, could be felt, and presently the general climate quieted and nothing came of it all.

Early in the fifth century New Calender three survey

parties from the North Central Authority came through the area and stopped to observe the monster. A permanent recording device was set up at the site, after assurances to the townfolk that no hardscience was involved. A local boy was trained to operate it; he quit when his girl left him but another volunteered. At this time nearly everyone believed that the apparition was a man, or the ghost of one. The record-machine boy and a few others including the school mechanics teacher referred to him as The Man John. In the next decades the roads were greatly improved; all forms of travel increased and there was talk of building a canal to what had been the Snake river.

One May morning at the end of Century Five a young couple in a smart green mule-trap came jogging up the highroad from the Sandreas Rift Range to the southwest. The girl was golden-skinned and chatted with her young husband in a language unlike that ever heard by the Man John either at the end or the beginning of his life. What she said to him has, however, been heard in every age and tongue.

'Oh Serli, I'm so glad we're taking this trip now! Next summer I'll be busy with baby.'

To which Serli replied as young husbands often have, and so they trotted up to the town's inn. Here they left trap and bags and went in search of her uncle who was expecting them there. The morrow was the day of the Man John's annual appearance, and her Uncle Laban had come from the MacKenzie History Museum to observe it and to make certain arrangements.

They found him with the town school instructor of

mechanics, who was also the recorder at the monster-site. Presently Uncle Laban took them all with him to the town mayor's office to meet with various religious personages. The mayor was not unaware of tourist values, but he took Uncle Laban's part in securing the cultists' grudging assent to the MacKenzie authorities' secular interpretation of the monster, which was made easier by the fact that the cults disagreed among themselves. Then, seeing how pretty the niece was, the mayor took them all home to dinner.

When they returned to the inn for the night it was abrawl with holiday-makers.

'Whew,' said Uncle Laban. 'I've talked myself dry, sister's daughter. What a weight of holy nonsense is that Moksha female! Serli, my lad, I know you have questions. Let me hand you this to read, it's the guide book we're giving them to sell. Tomorrow I'll answer for it all.' And he disappeared into the crowded tavern.

So Serli and his bride took the pamphlet upstairs to bed with them, but it was not until the next morning at breakfast that they found time to read it.

'"All that is known of John Delgano,"' read Serli with his mouth full, '"comes from two documents left by his brother Carl Delgano in the archives of the MacKenzie Group in the early years after the holocaust." Put some honey on this cake, Mira my dove. Verbatim transcript follows, this is Carl Delgano speaking:

'"I'm not an engineer or an astronaut like John, I ran an electronics repair shop in Salt Lake City. John was only trained as a spaceman, he never got to space; the slump wiped all that out. So he tied up with this commercial group who were leasing part of Bonneville. They wanted a man for some kind of hard vacuum tests, that's all I knew about it. John and his wife moved to Bonneville, but we all got together several times a year, our wives were like sisters. John had two kids, Clara and Paul.

'"The tests were supposed to be secret, but John told me confidentially they were trying for an anti-gravity chamber. I don't know if it ever worked. That was the year before.

'"Then that winter they came down for Christmas and John said they had something far out. He was excited. A temporal displacement, he called it; some kind of time effect. He said their chief honcho was like a real mad scientist. Big ideas. He kept adding more angles every time some other project would quit and leave equipment he could lease. No, I don't know who the top company was – maybe an insurance conglomerate, they had all the cash, didn't they? I guess they'd pay to catch a look at the future, that figures. Anyway, John was go, go, go. Katharine was scared, that's natural. She pictured him like, you know, H.G. Wells – walking around in some future world. John told her it wasn't like that at all. All they'd get would be this flicker, like a second or two. All kinds of complications" – Yes, yes my greedy piglet, some brew for me too. This is thirsty work!

'So. "I remember I asked him, what about Earth moving? I mean, you could come back in a different place, right? He said they had that all figured. A spatial trajectory. Katharine was so scared we dropped it. John told her, don't worry. I'll come home. But he didn't. Not that it makes any difference, of course, everything was wiped out. Salt Lake too. The only reason I'm here is that I went up by Calgary to see Mom, April twenty-ninth. May second it all blew. I didn't find you folks at MacKenzie until July. I guess I may as well stay. That's all I know about John, except that he was a solid guy. If that accident started all this it wasn't his fault.

'"The second document" – In the name of love, little mother, do I have to read all this? Oh very well, but you will kiss me first, madam. Must you look so delicious? "The second document. Dated in the year eighteen, New Style, written by Carl" – see the old handwriting, my plump plump pigeon? Oh, very well, *very* well.

'"Written at Bonneville Crater: I have seen my brother John Delgano. When I knew I had the rad sickness I came down here to look around. Salt Lake's still hot. So I hiked up here by Bonneville. You can see the crater where the labs were, it's grassed over. It's different, not radioactive; my film's OK. There's a bare place in the middle. Some Indios here told me a monster shows up here every year in the spring. I saw it myself a couple of days after I got here but I was too far away to see much, except I was sure it's a man. In a vacuum suit. There was a lot of noise and dust, took me by surprise. It was all over in a second. I figured it's pretty close to the day, I mean, May second, old.

'"So I hung around a year and he showed up again yesterday. I was on the face side and I could see his face through the visor. It's John all right. He's hurt. I saw blood on his mouth and his suit is frayed some. He's lying on the ground. He didn't move while I could see him but the dust boiled up, like a man sliding onto base without moving. His eyes are open like he was looking. I don't understand it anyway, but I know it's John, not a ghost. He was in exactly the same position each time and there's a loud crack like thunder and another sound like a siren, very fast. And an ozone smell, and smoke. I felt a kind of shudder.

'"I know it's John there and I think he's alive. I have to leave here now to take this back while I can still walk. I think somebody should come here and see. Maybe you can help John. Signed, Carl Delgano.

'"These records were kept by the MacKenzie Group but it was not for several years" – Etcetera, first light-print, etcetera, archives, analysts, etcetera – very good! Now it is time to meet your uncle, my edible one, after we go upstairs for just a moment.'

'No, Serli, I will wait for you downstairs,' said Mira prudently.

When they came into the town park Uncle Laban was directing the installation of a large durite slab in front of the enclosure around the Man John's appearance-spot. The slab was wrapped in a curtain to await the official unveiling. Townspeople and tourists and children thronged the walks and a Ride-for-God choir was singing in the bandshell. The morning was warming up fast. Vendors hawked ices and straw toys of the monster and flowers and good-luck confetti to throw at him. Another religious group stood by in dark robes; they belonged to the Repentance church beyond the park. Their pastor was directing somber glares at the crowd in general and Mira's uncle in particular.

Three official-looking strangers who had been at the inn came up and introduced themselves to Uncle Laban as observers from Alberta Central. They went on into the tent which had been erected over the enclosure, carrying with them several pieces of equipment which the townfolk eyed suspiciously.

The mechanics teacher finished organizing a squad of students to protect the slab's curtain, and Mira and Serli and Laban went on into the tent. It was much hotter inside. Benches were set in rings around a railed enclosure about twenty feet in diameter. Inside the railing the earth was bare and scuffed. Several bunches of flowers and blooming poinciana branches leaned against the rail. The only thing inside the rail was a rough sandstone rock with markings etched on it.

Just as they came in a small girl raced across the open center and was yelled at by everybody. The officials from Alberta were busy at one side of the rail, where the light-print box was mounted.

'Oh, no,' muttered Mira's uncle, as one of the officials leaned over to set up a tripod stand inside the rails. He adjusted it and a huge horse-tail of fine feathery filaments blossomed out and eddied through the center of the space.

'Oh *no*,' Laban said again. 'Why can't they let it be?'

'They're trying to pick up dust from his suit, is that right?' Serli asked.

'Yes, insane. Did you get time to read?'

'Oh yes,' said Serli.

'Sort of,' added Mira.

'Then you know. He's falling. Trying to check his

– well, call it velocity. Trying to slow down. He must have slipped or stumbled. We're getting pretty close to when he lost his footing and started to fall. What did it? Did somebody trip him?' Laban looked from Mira to Serli, dead serious now. 'How would you like to be the one who made John Delgano fall?'

'Ooh,' said Mira in quick sympathy. Then she said, 'Oh.'

'You mean,' asked Serli, 'whoever made him fall caused all the, caused –'

'Possible,' said Laban.

'Wait a minute.' Serli frowned. 'He did fall. So somebody had to do it – I mean, he has to trip or whatever. If he doesn't fall the past would all be changed, wouldn't it? No war, no –'

'Possible,' Laban repeated. 'God knows. All *I* know is that John Delgano and the space around him is the most unstable, improbable, highly charged area ever known on Earth and I'm damned if I think anybody should go poking sticks in it.'

'Oh come now, Laban!' One of the Alberta men joined them, smiling. 'Our dust-mop couldn't trip a gnat. It's just vitreous monofilaments.'

'Dust from the future,' grumbled Laban. 'What's it going to tell you? That the future has dust in it?'

'If we could only get a trace from that thing in his hand.'

'In his hand?' asked Mira. Serli started leafing hurriedly through the pamphlet.

'We've had a recording analyzer aimed at it,' the Albertan lowered his voice, glancing around. 'A spectroscope.

We know there's something there, or was. Can't get a decent reading. It's severely deteriorated.'

'People poking at him, grabbing at him,' Laban muttered. 'You –'

'TEN MINUTES!' shouted a man with a megaphone. 'Take your places, friends and strangers.'

The Repentance people were filing in at one side, intoning an ancient incantation, 'Mi-seri-cordia, Ora pro nobis!'

The atmosphere suddenly became tense. It was now very close and hot in the big tent. A boy from the mayor's office wiggled through the crowd, beckoning Laban's party to come and sit in the guest chairs on the second level on the 'face' side. In front of them at the rail one of the Repentance ministers was arguing with an Albertan official over his right to occupy the space taken by a recorder, it being his special duty to look into the Man John's eyes.

'Can he really see us?' Mira asked her uncle.

'Blink your eyes,' Laban told her. 'A new scene every blink, that's what he sees. Phantasmagoria. Blink-blink-blink – for God knows how long.'

'Mi-sere-re, pec-cavi,' chanted the penitentials. A soprano neighed. 'May the red of sin pa-aa-ass from us!'

'They believe his oxygen tab went red because of the state of their souls,' Laban chuckled. 'Their souls are going to have to stay damned awhile; John Delgano has been on oxygen reserve for five centuries – or rather, he *will* be low for five centuries more. At a half-second per year his time, that's fifteen minutes. We know from the audio trace he's still breathing more or less normally and the reserve was good for twenty minutes. So they should have their salvation about the year seven hundred, if they last that long.'

'FIVE MINUTES! Take your seats folks. Please sit down so everyone can see. Sit down, folks.'

'It says we'll hear his voice through his suit speaker,' Serli whispered. 'Do you know what he's saying?'

'You get mostly a twenty-cycle howl,' Laban whispered back. 'The recorders have spliced up something like "*ayt*," part of an old word. Take centuries to get enough to translate.'

'Is it a message?'

'Who knows? Could be his word for "date" or "hate". "Too late", maybe. Anything.'

The tent was quieting. A fat child by the railing started to cry and was pulled back onto a lap. There was a sub-dued mumble of praying. The Holy Joy faction on the far side rustled their flowers.

'Why don't we set our clocks by him?'

'It's changing. He's on sidereal time.'

'ONE MINUTE.'

In the hush the praying voices rose slightly. From outside a chicken cackled. The bare center space looked absolutely ordinary. Over it the recorder's silvery fila-ments eddied gently in the breath from a hundred lungs. Another recorder could be heard ticking faintly.

For long seconds nothing happened.

The air developed a tiny hum. At the same moment Mira caught a movement at the railing on her left.

The hum developed a beat and vanished into a pecu-liar silence and suddenly everything happened at once.

Sound burst on them, raced shockingly up the

audible scale. The air cracked as something rolled and tumbled in the space. There was a grinding, wailing roar and –

He was there.

Solid, huge – a huge man in a monster suit, his head was a dull bronze transparent globe, holding a human face, a dark smear of open mouth. His position was impossible, legs strained forward thrusting himself back, his arms frozen in a whirlwind swing. Although he seemed to be in frantic forward motion nothing moved, only one of his legs buckled or sagged slightly –

– And then he was gone, utterly and completely gone in a thunderclap, leaving only the incredible after-image in a hundred pairs of staring eyes. Air boomed, shuddering; dust rolled out mixed with smoke.

'Oh! Oh my God,' gasped Mira, unheard, clinging to Serli. Voices were crying out, choking. 'He saw me, he saw me!' a woman shrieked. A few people dazedly threw their confetti into the empty dust-cloud, most had failed to throw at all. Children began to howl. 'He *saw* me!' the woman screamed hysterically. 'Red, oh Lord have mercy!' a deep male voice intoned.

Mira heard Laban swearing furiously and looked again into the space. As the dust settled she could see that the recorder's tripod had tipped over into the center. There was a dusty mound lying against it – flowers. Most of the end of the stand seemed to have disappeared or been melted. Of the filaments nothing could be seen.

'Some damn fool pitched flowers into it. Come on, let's get out.'

'Was it under, did it trip him?' asked Mira, squeezed in the crowd.

'It was still red, his oxygen thing,' Serli said over her head. 'No mercy this trip, eh, Laban?'

'Shsh!' Mira caught the Repentance pastor's dark glance. They jostled through the enclosure gate and were out in the sunlit park, voices exclaiming, chattering loudly in excitement and relief.

'It was terrible,' Mira cried softly. 'Oh, I never thought it was a real live man. There he is, he's *there*. Why can't we help him? Did we trip him?'

'I don't know, I don't think so,' her uncle grunted. They sat down near the new monument, fanning themselves. The curtain was still in place.

'Did we change the past?' Serli laughed, looked lovingly at his little wife. For a moment he wondered why she was wearing such odd earrings; then he remembered he had given them to her at that Indian pueblo they'd passed.

'But it wasn't just those Alberta people,' said Mira. She seemed obsessed with the idea. 'It was the flowers really.' She wiped at her forehead.

'Mechanics or superstition,' chuckled Serli. 'Which is the culprit, love or science?'

'Shsh.' Mira looked about nervously. 'The flowers were love, I guess . . . I feel so strange. It's hot. Oh, thank you.' Uncle Laban had succeeded in attracting the attention of the iced-drink vendor.

People were chatting normally now and the choir struck into a cheerful song. At one side of the park a line of people were waiting to sign their names in the visitors' book. The mayor appeared at the park gate, leading a party up the bougainvillea alley for the unveiling of the monument.

'What did it say on that stone by his foot?' Mira asked. Serli showed her the guidebook picture of Carl's rock with the inscription translated below: WELCOME HOME JOHN.

'I wonder if he can see it.'

The mayor was about to begin his speech.

Much later when the crowd had gone away the monument stood alone in the dark, displaying to the moon the inscription in the language of that time and place:

ON THIS SPOT THERE APPEARS ANNUALLY THE FORM OF MAJOR JOHN DELGANO, THE FIRST AND ONLY MAN TO TRAVEL IN TIME.

MAJOR DELGANO WAS SENT INTO THE FUTURE SOME HOURS BEFORE THE HOLOCAUST OF DAY ZERO. ALL KNOWLEDGE OF THE MEANS BY WHICH HE WAS SENT IS LOST, PERHAPS FOREVER. IT IS BELIEVED THAT AN ACCIDENT OCCURRED WHICH SENT HIM MUCH FARTHER THAN WAS INTENDED. SOME ANALYSTS SPECULATE THAT HE MAY HAVE GONE AS FAR AS FIFTY THOUSAND YEARS AHEAD. HAVING REACHED THIS UNKNOWN POINT MAJOR DELGANO APPARENTLY WAS RECALLED, OR ATTEMPTED TO RETURN, ALONG THE COURSE IN SPACE AND TIME THROUGH WHICH HE WAS SENT. HIS TRAJECTORY IS THOUGHT TO START AT THE POINT WHICH OUR SOLAR SYSTEM WILL OCCUPY AT A FUTURE TIME AND IS TANGENT TO THE COMPLEX HELIX WHICH OUR EARTH DESCRIBES AROUND THE SUN.

HE APPEARS ON THIS SPOT IN THE ANNUAL INSTANTS

IN WHICH HIS COURSE INTERSECTS OUR PLANET'S ORBIT
AND HE IS APPARENTLY ABLE TO TOUCH THE GROUND IN
THOSE INSTANTS. SINCE NO TRACE OF HIS PASSAGE INTO
THE FUTURE HAS BEEN MANIFESTED, IT IS BELIEVED
THAT HE IS RETURNING BY A DIFFERENT MEANS THAN
HE WENT FORWARD. HE IS ALIVE IN OUR PRESENT. OUR
PAST IS HIS FUTURE AND OUR FUTURE IS HIS PAST. THE
TIME OF HIS APPEARANCES IS SHIFTING GRADUALLY IN
SOLAR TIME TO CONVERGE ON THE MOMENT OF 1153.6,
ON MAY 2, 1989 OLD STYLE, OR DAY ZERO.

THE EXPLOSION WHICH ACCOMPANIED HIS RETURN
TO HIS OWN TIME AND PLACE MAY HAVE OCCURRED
WHEN SOME ELEMENTS OF THE PAST INSTANTS OF HIS
COURSE WERE CARRIED WITH HIM INTO THEIR OWN
PRIOR EXISTENCE. IT IS CERTAIN THAT THIS EXPLOSION
PRECIPITATED THE WORLDWIDE HOLOCAUST WHICH
ENDED FOREVER THE AGE OF HARDSCIENCE.

*– He was falling, losing control, failing in his fight against the
terrible momentum he had gained, fighting with his human
legs shaking in the inhuman stiffness of his armor, his soles
charred, not gripping well now, not enough traction to break,
battling, thrusting as the flashes came, the punishing alterna-
tion of light, dark, light, dark, which he had borne so long, the
claps of air thickening and thinning against his armor as he
skidded through space which was time, desperately braking as
the flickers of Earth hammered against his feet – only his feet
mattered now, only to slow and stay on course – and the pull,
the beacon was getting slacker; as he came near home it was
fanning out, hard to stay centered; he was becoming, he supposed, more probable; the wound he had punched in time was*

healing itself. In the beginning it had been so tight – a single ray of light in a closing tunnel – he had hurled himself after it like an electron flying to the anode, aimed surely along that exquisitely complex single vector of possibility of life, shot and been shot like a squeezed pip into the last chink in that rejecting and rejected nowhere through which he, John Delgano, could conceivably continue to exist, the hole leading to home – had pounded down it across time, across space, pumping with desperate legs as the real Earth of that unreal time came under him, his course as certain as the twisting dash of an animal down its burrow, he a cosmic mouse on on interstellar, intertemporal race for his nest with the wrongness of everything closing round the rightness of that one course, the atoms of his heart, his blood, his every cell crying Home – HOME! – as he drove himself after that fading breath-hole, each step faster, surer, stronger, until he raced with invincible momentum upon the rolling flickers of Earth as a man might race a rolling log in a torrent. Only the stars stayed constant around him from flash to flash, he looking down past his feet at a million strobes of Crux, of Triangulum; once at the height of his stride he had risked a century's glance upward and seen the Bears weirdly strung out from Polaris – but a Polaris not the Pole Star now, he realized, jerking his eyes back to his racing feet, thinking, I am walking home to Polaris, home! to the strobing beat. He had ceased to remember where he had been, the beings, people or aliens or things he had glimpsed in the impossible moment of being where he could not be; had ceased to see the flashes of worlds around him, each flash different, the jumble of bodies, shapes, walls, colors, landscapes – some lasting a breath, some changing pell-mell – the faces, limbs, things poking at him; the nights he had pounded through, dark or lit by strange lamps,

*roofed or unroofed; the days flashing sunlight, gales, dust, snow,
interiors innumerable, strobe after strobe into night again; he
was in daylight now, a hall of some kind; I am getting closer at
last, he thought, the feel is changing – but he had to slow down,
to check; and that stone near his feet, it had stayed there some
time now, he wanted to risk a look but he did not dare, he was
so tired, and he was sliding, was going out of control, fighting
to kill the merciless velocity that would not let him slow down;
he was hurt, too, something had hit him back there, they had
done something, he didn't know what, back somewhere in the
kaleidoscope of faces, arms, hooks, beams, centuries of creatures grabbing at him – and his oxygen was going, never mind,
it would last – it had to last, he was going home, home! And he
had forgotten now the message he had tried to shout, hoping it
could be picked up somehow, the important thing he had repeated; and the thing he had carried, it was gone now, his camera
was gone too, something had torn it away – but he was coming
home! Home! If only he could kill this momentum, could stay
on the failing course, could slip, scramble, slide, somehow ride
this avalanche down to home, to home – and his throat said
Home! – called Kate, Kate! And his heart shouted, his lungs almost gone now, as his legs fought, fought and failed, as his feet
gripped and skidded and held and slid, as he pitched, flailed,
pushed, strove in the gale of timerush across space, across time,
at the end of the longest path ever: the path of John Delgano,
coming home.*

Forever to a Hudson Bay Blanket

Dov Rapelle was a nice person, personally. He was so nice you didn't notice that he wasn't overpoweringly bright in a survival sense. He also owned a long skier's body and a lonesome dreamy Canuck face that he got from his fifth grandfather who came out to Calgary, Alberta as a dowser. By the time the face came down to Dov a solid chunk of Alberta Hydroelectric came with it. But the Rapelles lived plain; Calgary, Alberta was one of the few places in the twenty-first century where a young man could be like Dov and not be spoiled silly.

Calgary has the tallest water-tower on the continent, you know, and all that tetra-wheat and snow-sports money. And it's a long way from the Boswash and San Frangeles style of life. People from Calgary still do things like going home to see their folks over winter vacation. And in Calgary you aren't used to being phoned up by strange girls in Callao, Peru at 0200 Christmas morning.

The girl was quite emotional. Dov kept asking her name and she kept crying and sobbing, 'Say something, Dovy, Dovy, *please*!' She had a breathy squeak that sounded young and expensive.

'What should I say?' asked Dov reasonably.

'Your voice, oh, *Dovy*!' she wept, 'I'm so far *away*! Please, please talk to me, Dovy!'

'Well, look,' Dov began, and the phone went dead.

When his folks asked him what that was he shrugged and grinned his nice grin. He didn't get it.

Christmas was on Monday. Wednesday night the phone rang again. This time the operator was French, but it was clearly the same girl.

'Dovy? Dovy Rapelle?' She was breathing hard.

'Yeah, speaking. Who's this?'

'Oh, Dovy. *Dovy!* Is that really you?'

'Yeah, it's me. Look, did you call before?'

'Did I?' she said vaguely. And then she started crying 'Oh Dovy, oh Dovy', and it was the same dialogue all over again until the line quit.

He did not get it.

By Friday Dov was beginning to feel hemmed in, so he decided to go check on their cabin on Split Mountain. The Rapelles were not jetbuggy types; they liked peace and quiet. Dov took his plain old four-wheeler out behind Bragg Creek into the pass as far as the plows had been and then he put on his pack and skis and started breaking trail. The snow was perfect, dry and fast. In no time he was up past the bare aspens and larches and into the high spruce woods.

He came out on the moraine by the lake at sundown. The snow was heavily wind-drifted here. He cut across bare ice and found the front of the cabin buried under a six-foot overhang of snow. It was about dark by the time he'd shoveled in and got a fire going from the big wood-pile in back. He was bringing in his second bucket of snow to melt when he heard the *chunka-chunka* of a cop-ter coming through the pass.

It zoomed over the clearing and hovered. Dov could see two heads bobbing around inside. Then it settled down twenty yards away sending a wave of white all over and somebody tumbled out.

The first thing Dov thought of was trouble at home. The next thing was his fire. He had just turned to go put it out when he realized the chopper was lifting back up.

It went up like a yak in a feather factory. Through the blizzard Dov saw a small pale body floundering toward him.

'Dovy! Dovy! Is that you?'

It was the girl, or at least her voice.

She was stumbling like crazy, up to her crotch in the snow in the fading light. Just as Dov reached her she went down on all fours and all he could see was her little stark-bare pink ass sticking up with a glittery-green thing on one cheek. And about a yard of silver hair.

'Yo ho,' he said involuntarily, which is a Stonie Indian phrase meaning 'Behold!'

She turned up a pretty baby face with a green jewel-bug on the forehead.

'It's you!' she sneezed. Her teeth were chattering.

'You're really not dressed for snow,' Dov observed. 'Here.' He reached down and scooped her up and toted her indoors, snow and green butterflies and rosy ass and all. His frosty pink Christmas cake with a razorblade inside.

When he got the lamp going she turned out to be as naked in front as she was in back, and about sixteen at the oldest. A kid, he decided, on some kind of spinout. While he wrapped her in his Hudson Bay blanket he tried to recall where he could have met her. No success. He plonked her on the snowshoe chair and built up the fire. She kept sniffling and chattering, but it wasn't very informational.

'Oh, Dovy, Dovy, it's you! D-Dovy! Speak to me. Say something, please, Dovy!'

'Well, for starters –'

'Do you like me? I'm attractive, amn't I?' She opened the blanket to look at herself. 'I mean, am I attractive to *you*? Oh, Dovy, s-say something! I've come so *far*, I chartered three jets, I, I – oh, Dovy *d-darling*!'

And she exploded out of the blanket into his arms like a monkey trying to climb him, whimpering 'Please, Dovy, love me', nuzzling, squirming her little body, shivering and throbbing and pushing cold little fingers into his snowy snowsuit, under his belt. '*Please*, Dovy, please, there isn't much time. *Love me*.'

To which Dov didn't respond quite as you'd expect. Because it so happened that this cabin had been the prime scene of Dov's early fantasy life. Especially the *winter fantasy*, the one where Dovy was snuggled in the blankets watching the fire gutter out and listening to the storm howl . . . and there comes a feeble scratching at the door . . . and it turns out to be a beautiful lost girl, and he has to take off all her clothes and warm her up *all over* and wrap her up in the Hudson Bay blanket . . . and he's very tender and respectful but *she knows* what's going to happen, and later he does all kinds of things to her on the blanket. (When Dov was fourteen he could only say the words *Hudson Bay blanket* in a peculiar hoarse whisper.) The girl in one version was a redhead named Georgiana

Ochs, and later on he actually did get Georgiana up to the cabin where they spent a weekend catching terrible colds. Since then the cabin had been the site of several other erotic enactments, but somehow it never came up to the original script.

So now here he was with the original script unrolling around him but it still wasn't quite right. In the script Dov undressed the girl, Dov's hands did the feeling-out. The girl's part called for trembling appreciation, all right. But it didn't call for shinnying up him like a maniac or grabbing his dick in ice-cold paws.

So he stood for a minute with his hands squeezing her baby buttocks, deliberately holding her away from his crotch until something communicated and she looked up, panting.

'Wait, oh,' she gasped, and frowned crossly, apparently at herself. 'Please . . . I'm not crazy, Dovy, I – I –'

He walked stiffly across the hearth with her, trying to keep his snowsuit from falling down, and dumped her on the bunk, where she lay flopped like a puppy with her knees open and her little flat belly going in and out, in and out. There was an emerald butterfly on her ash-blond muff.

'All right,' he said firmly (but nicely). 'Now look. Who are you?'

Her mouth worked silently and her eyes sent *Love you, love you, love you* up to him. Her eyes didn't seem wild or druggy, but they had a funny deep-down spark, like something lived in there.

'Your name, kid. What's your name?'

'L-Loolie,' she whispered.

'Loolie who?' He said patiently.

'Loolie Aerovulpa.' Somewhere in his head a couple of neurones twitched, but they didn't connect.

'Why did you come here, Loolie?'

Her eyes glistened, brimmed over. 'Oh, no,' she sobbed, gulped. 'It's been so *long*, such a terribly long, long, way –' her head rolled from side to side, hurtfully. 'Oh, Dovy, please, there'll be *time* for all this later, I know you don't remember me – just *please* let me touch you, please – it *hurt* so –'

Soft arms pleading up for him, little breasts pleading with their puckered noses. This was getting more like the script. When Dov didn't move she suddenly wailed and curled up into a fetal ball.

'I've sp-spoiled everything,' she wept, burrowing wetly into the Hudson Bay blanket.

That did it, for a nice person like Dov. One of his hands went down and patted little Tarbaby's back, and then his other hand joined the first and his snowsuit fell down. Her back somehow turned into her front and curled up around him, and his knees were feeling the bunk boards while two downy thighs locked around his hips and sucked him in.

And he got a shock.

The shock came a bit later, the shock was wrapped around him and thrusting at him so that he had no choice but to ram on past her squeal – and after that he didn't have time to worry about anything except letting the sun burst in.

But it is a fact that even in Calgary you don't meet many maidenheads. It says something for Dov that he knew the way.

Now, a twenty-first-century maidenhead isn't a big thing, socio-psychologicalwise. On the other hand, it wasn't exactly nothing, especially for a nice person like Dov. What it did was to move the episode one step out of the fantasy class – or rather, one step into another fantasy.

Particularly when Loolie said what girls often do, afterward. Looking at him anxious-humble, stroking his stomach. 'Do you mind? I mean, my being a virgin?'

'Well, now,' said Dov, trying to think decisively while peeling a squashed green butterfly out of his neck.

'Truly, honestly, did you mind?'

'Honestly, no.' He balanced the butterfly on her head.

'It did hurt a *little* . . . oh, ooh,' she cried distractedly, 'your blanket –'

They were deciding the blanket didn't matter when Loolie looked at her little fingernail and started kissing his stomach.

'Dovy dear, don't you think, couldn't we,' she mumbled, 'I mean, it's only the first time I ever – try again?'

Dove found himself agreeing.

The second time was infinitely better. The second time was something to challenge fantasy. It was so good that the scrap of Dov's mind that wasn't occupied with the electric baby eeling under and over and around him . . . began to wonder. Virginal fucks did not, in his experience, achieve such loin-bursting poetry, such fitting, such flowing surge to velocities sustained beyond escape, such thrust and burn and build with the first-time fuckee sobbing rhythmically, 'Love you, Dovy, Do-o-ovy', giving everything to it in the best position of all until all the stages went nova together –

'. . . Don't sleep yet, Dovy, please wake up a minute?'

He opened one eye and rolled off; he was a very nice person.

Loolie leaned on his chest, worshipping him through her pale damp hair.

'I almost forgot.' She grinned, suddenly naughty. He felt her hair, her breasts move down his belly, down his thighs and shins to his feet. Sleepily he noted a warm wetness closing over his big toe. Her mouth? Some kind of toe joy, he thought – and then the signal made it six feet back to his brain.

'Hey-y-y!' He smacked her butt. 'That hurt! You *bit* me!'

Her face came around laughing. She was really neat-looking.

'I bit your big toe.' She nodded solemnly. 'That's *very important*. It means you're my true love.' Her eyes suddenly got wet again. 'I love you so, Dovy. Will you remember, I bit your toe?'

'Well sure I'll remember,' he grinned uneasily. The neurones that had twitched sometime back, boosted by stimulation from his toe, finally made connection.

'Hey, Loolie. What you said . . . is your name Aerovulpa?'

She nodded, yes.

'*The* Aerovulpa?'

Another nod, her eyes glowing at him.

'Oh God.' He tried to remember what he'd seen about it. Aerovulpa . . . The Family . . . Mr Aerovulpa, he gathered, was not in tune with the twenty-first century – maybe not the twentieth, even. And this was an Aerovulpa virgin all over his legs. Ex-virgin.

'By any chance is your father sending a private army up here after you, Loolie?'

'Poor daddy,' she smiled. 'He's dead.' The far beacon in her eyes was coming closer. 'Dovy. You didn't ask me my whole name.'

'Your what?'

'I'm Loolie Aerovulpa . . . Rapelle.'

He stared. He didn't get it at all.

'I don't – are you some kind of relative?'

She nodded, her eyes enormous, weird.

'A very close relative.' Her lips feathered his cheek.

'I never met you. I swear.' He felt her swallow. Loolie drew back and looked at him for a couple of long breaths and then glanced down at her little finger. He saw that she had a tiny timer implanted in the nail.

'You haven't asked me how old I am either,' she said quietly.

'So?'

'I'm seventy-five.'

'*Huh?*' Dov stared. No geriatrics imaginable could . . .

'Seventy-five years old. I am. Inside, I mean, me, now.'

Then he got it.

'You – you –'

'Yes. I'm time-jumping.'

'Time-jumper . . . !' He'd heard about it, but he didn't believe it. Now he looked and saw . . . seventy-five years looking out of her baby eyes. Old. The spark in there was *old*.

Loolie checked the nail again. 'I have to tell you something, Dovy.' She took hold of his face solemnly. 'I have to warn you. It's very important. Darling, don't ever ig-g-g – eugh-gh –'

Her jaws jabbered, her head flopped – and her whole body slumped on him, dead girl.

He scrambled out and had just got his ear on her heartbeat when Loolie's mouth gulped air. He turned his head and saw her eyes open, widen, wander to his body, her body, and back to his.

'Who're you?' she asked interestedly. Asking for information.

He drew back.

'Uh. Dov Rapelle.' He saw her face, her eyes were different. She sat up. A strange teenager was sitting in his bunk, studying him so clinically he reached for the blanket.

'Hey, look!' She pointed at the window. 'Snow! Oh great! Where am I? Where is this?'

'It's my cabin. Calgary, Alberta. Listen are you all right? You were time-jumping, I think.'

'Yeah,' said Loolie absently, smiling at the snow. 'I don't remember anything, you never do.' She squirmed, looking around and then suddenly squirmed again and said 'Oh, my', and stopped looking around. She put her hand under herself and her eyes locked on his.

'Uh . . . hey – what *happened*?'

'Well,' Dov began, 'you, I mean we –' He was too nice to blame it all on her.

She bugged her eyes, still feeling herself.

225

'But that's *impossible*!'

Dov shook his head, no. Then he changed it to yes.

'No,' she insisted bewilderedly. 'I mean, I've been *hyped*. Daddy had me fixed so I couldn't. I mean, men are *repulsive* to me.' She nodded. 'Girls too. Sex, it's a nothing. All I do, all I do is sailing races. Star class, yick. I'm *so* bored!'

Dov couldn't find a thing to say, he just sat there on the bunk holding the blanket. Loolie put out her hand and touched his shoulder tentatively.

'Hey.' She frowned. 'That's funny. You don't *feel* repulsive.' She put her other hand on him. 'You feel all right. Maybe nice. Hey this is weird. You mean, we *did it*?'

He nodded.

'Did I, like, *enjoy* it?'

'You seemed to, yes.'

She shook her head wonderingly, grinning. 'Oh, ho, ho. Hey, daddy will be wild!'

'Your father?' said Dov. 'Isn't he – you said he was dead.'

'Daddy? Of course he's not dead.' She stared at him. 'I don't remember a thing about it. All I remember is being in some big old house, being *seventy-five*. It was awful.' She shuddered. 'All stringy and creepy. I felt, bleeah. And those weird old people. I just said I was sick and went and lay down and watched the shows. And slept. For two days, I guess. Hey, when is this? I'm hungry!'

'December twenty-ninth,' Dov told her dazedly. 'Do you do this a lot, time-jumping?'

'Oh no.' She pushed her hair back. 'Just a few times, I mean, daddy just *installed* it. I was so bored, I thought, well, it would be nice to give myself a treat. I mean, when

I'm *old*, I'll enjoy being sixteen again for a little while, don't you think?'

'I wouldn't know, we don't have anything like that here. In fact, I didn't believe they existed.'

'Oh, they exist.' She nodded importantly, frowning at him. 'Of course they're *very expensive*. There's only a few in the *world* I guess. Hey, you know, I saw your picture there. By the mirror. I am so hungry. There has to be food here. Sex is supposed to make you hungry, right?'

She scrambled off the bunk, trailing blanket. 'I'm starved! Can I help you cook? Oh, my glitterbugs. Oh dear. Is that the *moon*? We're up in real *mountains*?' She ran around to the windows. 'Daddy never lets me go anywhere. Oh, mountains are fantastic! Hey, you really do look nice. I mean, being a man isn't so hideous.' She spun back to him, nose to nose. 'Look, you have to *tell* me all about it.' Her eyes slid around, suddenly shy. 'I mean, *everything*, God, I'm hungry. Listen, since we, I mean, I don't *remember*, you know. Can't we sort of try it over again? Hey, I forgot your name, I'm *sorry* –'

'Loolie.' Dov closed his eyes. 'Will you please just shut up one minute? I have to think.'

But all he could think was that she had a good idea: food.

So he fried up some corned beef hash, with Loolie all over the cabin like a mongoose, opening the door, smooshing snow on her face, admiring the moon and the mountains, running over to poke him with a spruce icicle. When she turned her attention to the fire he was pleased to see that she put the wood on right. They sat down to eat. Dov wanted very much to ask about her father. But

227

he couldn't – being Dov – break through Loolie's excitement about him, and the mountains, and him, and the cabin, and him, and –

It began to dawn on Dov that this little Aerovulpa had a pretty sad locked-up sliver of the twenty-first century.

'You ought to see this place when the ice goes out,' he told her. 'The big melt. And the avalanches.'

'Oh, Dovy, I'm so bitched with *people*-places. I mean, nobody *cares* about anything real. Like, this is beautiful. Dovy, will you, when I –'

That was when her father's private army came *chunga-chunga* out of the night sky.

Dov scrambled into his suit and discovered that the army consisted of one small hysterical man and one large hairless man.

'Uncle Vic!' cried Loolie. She ran up and patted the small man while the large man showed Dov several embossed badges.

'Your father, your father!' Uncle Vic spluttered, thrusting Loolie away and glaring around the cabin. His eyes focused on the bunk. The big man stood stolidly by the door.

'Angry, yes!' moaned Uncle Vic. He shook off his hat and put it on again and grabbed Dov's snowsuit.

'Do you know who this girl is?' he hissed.

'She says she's Loolie Aerovulpa. She was time-jumping,' Dov said, being reasonable.

'I know, I know! Terrible!' The little man's eyes rolled. 'Louis – Mr Aerovulpa – turned it off. How could you do this to him, girl?'

'I haven't done a thing to daddy, Uncle Vic.'

Her uncle marched over to the bunk, grabbed up the blanket, hissed, and threw it on the floor.

'You – you –'

'Daddy had no right to *do* that!' Loolie cried. 'It's *my* life. It didn't work, anyway. I – I love it here, I mean, I think I –'

'*No!*' the little man shrieked. He scuttled back to Loolie and started shaking her. 'Your father!' he yelled. 'He will have you psyched, he will have you deleted! *Puta!* Pffah! And as for you, you –' He whirled on Dov and began to spray old-world discourtesies.

At which point, Dov, although a nice person, was starting to get considerably browned. He recalled coming up here for some peace and quiet. Now he looked at the little man, and the big man, and Loolie, and finished lacing up his boots.

'Get up! Move!' the little man screamed. 'You come with us!'

'My folks will wonder where I am,' Dov objected reasonably, thinking the two men looked like urban types.

'On your feet, *felo!*' Uncle Vic flapped his hands at the big man, who came away from the door and jerked his head at Dov.

'Get moving, boy.' He had one hand in his pocket like an old movie.

Dov got up.

'OK, but you need some clothes for Miss Aerovulpa, don't you think? Maybe her father won't be so wild if you bring her back dressed.'

Uncle Vic glared distractedly at Loolie, who was sticking out of her blanket.

'I'll get a snowsuit in the closet,' Dov said. He moved carefully toward the woodshed door by the fireplace, wondering if urban types would buy the idea of a closet in a mountain cabin. The big man took his hand out of his pocket with something in it pointed at Dov's back, but he didn't move.

Just as Dov's hand reached the latch he heard Loolie's mouth pop open and held his breath. She didn't say anything.

Then he was twisting through the door and yanking out the main brace of the woodpile. Cordwood crashed down against the door while Dov assisted matters by leaping up the pile, grabbing the axe as he went. He scrambled around the eaves onto the lean-to and whipped around the chimney, hearing bangings from below.

From the chimney he launched himself up to the roof-ridge. The big front drift was still there. He rode a snow-slide down over the front door, slamming the bar-latch as he landed, grabbed up his skis and was galloping through the drifts to the far side of the helicopter.

The first shots came through the cabin window as he swung his axe at the main rotor bearings. His body was behind the copter and the cabin windows were too small for the big man. When his axe achieved an unhealthy effect on the rotors Dov gave the gas tank a couple of whacks, decided not to bother igniting it, buried the axe in the tail vane and scuttled down the moraine into a private ravine. Glass was crashing, voices bellowing behind him.

The ravine became a long narrow tunnel under the snow bowed spruces. Dov frog-crawled down it until

the noise was faint, like coyote pups. Presently the ravine widened and debouched into a steep snowfield. Dov
buckled on his skis. The moon rode out of a cloudrack.
Dov straightened up and took off down the glittering
white. As he flew along gulping in the peace and quiet,
he hoped Loolie would be all right. Vic was her uncle, it
had to be OK.

In an hour he had reached the parked snowcat and was
headed back to Calgary where *his* uncle, Ben Rapelle, was
chief of the RCM mountain patrol.

He felt free.

But he wasn't.

Because Loolie – Loolie Number One, that is – had
said her last name was Rapelle. And his toe swelled up.

That turned out to be, as she'd also said, very important.

Next morning, after the patrol brought Loolie and
Uncle Vic and his enforcer all safe and sound down to
Headquarters, Loolie insisted on phoning her psychomed.
So when her father, Mr Aerovulpa, arrived in his private
VTOL the psychomed was with him.

Mr Aerovulpa turned out to be quite unlike Uncle
Vic, who was actually, it seemed, only a distant cousin.
For too many generations swarthy Aerovulpa sperm had
been frisking into blond Scandinavian-type wombs; the
current Mr Aerovulpa was a tall yellow-gray glacier with
a worried, lumpy Swedish face. If he were wild he didn't
show it. He appeared only very weary.

'Eulalia,' he sighed depletedly in Ben Rapelle's office.
That was Loolie's real name and he always called her by
it, having no talent for fatherhood. He looked from his

only child to the psychomed whom he had employed to ensure a marriageable product.

Now it had all blown up in his face.

'But how . . . ?' asked Mr Aerovulpa. 'You assured me, Doctor –' His voice was quiet but not warm. 'Uncle' Vic shied nervously. They were all standing around the Patrol office, Dov with a socmoc on one foot.

'The time-jump,' shrugged the psychomed. He was plump and slightly wall-eyed, which gave him an air of manic cheer. 'It was the older Loolie who was in this body, Louis. This older persona was no longer conditioned. You really should have been more careful. What on Earth did you want with a thing like that, time-jumping at your age? And the cost, my God.'

Mr Aerovulpa sighed.

'I acquired it for a particular purpose.' He frowned abstractedly at the Rapelles. 'A very small trip. I wished to observe –'

'To see if you had a *grandson*, eh? Eh, eh?' The psycher chortled. 'Of course. Well, did you?'

For some reason Mr Aerovulpa chose to continue this intimate topic. 'I found myself at my desk,' he said. 'On it was a portrait.' His bleak eyes searched his daughter, froze onto Dov.

Dov blinked. It had just occurred to him that a securely hyped and guarded virgin might not be otherwise de-fended from maternity. Loolie sucked in her lower lip, made a face.

The psychomed eyed them both, head cocked.

'Tell me, Loolie, when you came back to yourself, did

you find this young man, ah, disgusting? Repellent? The situation was traumatic?'

Loolie smiled at him wider and wider, swinging her head slowly from side to side. 'Oh, no. Oh, *no*! It was fantastic, *he's* fantastic, he's beautiful. Only –'

'Only what?'

Her smile turned to Dov, melted. 'Well, *we never*, I mean, I wish –'

'All right!' The psychomed held up his hand. 'I see. Now, tell me, Loolie. Think. Did you by any chance bite his toe?'

'Uncle' Vic made a noise, Loolie looked incredulous. 'Bite his *toe*?' she echoed. 'Of course not.'

The psychomed turned to Dov. His gaze sank to the socmoc. 'Did she, young man?'

'Why?' asked Dov cautiously. Everybody began looking at the socmoc.

'Did she?'

'I never!' said Loolie indignantly.

'You don't know,' Dov told her. 'You did, before. When you were seventy-five.'

'Bite your toe? What *for*?'

'Because that was the key cue,' said the psychomed. He pulled his ear. 'Oh bother. You remember, Louis. I told you.'

Mr Aerovulpa's expression had retreated further into the ice age.

'The idea was not to make you sexless for life, my dear,' the psycher told Loolie. 'There had to be a cue, a key to undo the conditioning. Something easy but improbable, which couldn't possibly happen by accident. I considered several possibilities. Yes. All things considered, the toe-bite seemed best.' He nodded benevolently. 'You recall, Louis, you wanted no matrimonial scandals.'

Mr Aerovulpa said nothing.

'A beautiful job of imprinting, if I do say so myself.' The psycher beamed. 'Absolutely irreversible. I guarantee it. The man whose toe she bites –' he pointed at Dov, one eye rolling playfully '– or rather, *bit*, she will love that man and that man only so long as she lives. Guaranteed!'

In the silence Mr Aerovulpa passed one hand over his Dag Hammarskjöld forehead and breathed out carefully. His gaze lingered from Loolie to Dov to Ben Rapelle like a python inspecting inexplicably inedible rabbits.

'It is . . . possible . . . that we shall see more of each other,' he observed coldly. 'At the moment I trust it is . . . agreeable to you that my daughter return to her schooling. Victor.'

'Right here, Louis!'

'You will remain to provide our . . . apologies to these gentlemen and to accomplish any necessary, ah, restorations. I am . . . not pleased. Come, Eulalia.'

'Oh, Dovy!' Loolie cried as she was hustled out. Dov's uncle Ben grunted warningly. And the Aerovulpas departed.

But not, of course, permanently.

Came springtime in the Rockies, and with it a very round-bellied and love-lorn teenager, escorted this time by a matron of unmistakable character and hardihood. Dov got out the ponies and they rode up into the singing forests and rainbow torrents and all the shy, free, super-delights of the wild country Dov loved. And he saw that Loolie truly wanted to live there and share his kind of life in addition to being totally in love with him, and anyone could see that Loolie herself was luscious and warmhearted and potentially sensible in spots, especially when it came to getting rid of the matron. *And* Dov really was a nice person, in spite of his distrust of the Aerovulpa ambiance. (The ambiance was now making itself felt in the form of a so-called demographic survey team snooping all over Calgary.)

So when summer ripened Dov journeyed warily to the Aerovulpa island off Pulpit Harbor, where he soon discovered that the ambiance didn't repel him half as much as Loolie attracted him. Even the nicest young man is not immune to the notion of a beautiful semi-virginal ever-adoring child-bride of great fortune.

'What, ah, career do you plan for yourself?' Mr Aerovulpa asked Dov on one of his rare appearances on the island.

'Avalanche research,' Dov told him, thus confirming the survey team's report. Mr Aerovulpa's eyelids drooped minutely. The alliances he had contemplated for Loolie had featured interests of a far more seismic type.

'Basically, sir, I'm a geo-ecologist. It's a great field.'

'Oh, it's wonderful, Daddy!' sang Loolie. 'I'm going to do all his records!'

Mr Aerovulpa's eyes drifted from his daughter's face to her belly. The Lump was now known to be male. Mr Aerovulpa had not arrived where he was by ignoring facts, and he was really not a twenty-first-century man. 'Ah,' he said wearily, and departed.

But the wedding itself was far from dreary. It was magnificently simple, out on the lawn above the sea, with a forcefield keeping off the Maine weather and an acre of imported wildflowers. The guest list was small, dominated by a number of complicated old ladies of exotic title and entourage among whom the Alberta contingent stood out like friendly grain elevators.

And then everybody went away and left Dov and Loolie for a week to themselves in paradise.

'Oh, Dovy,' sighed Loolie on the third day, 'I wish I could stay like this the rest of my life!'

This not very remarkable sentiment was uttered as they lay on the sauna solarium glowing like fresh-boiled shrimps.

'You say that just because you bit my toe,' said Dov. He was thinking about sailing, to which he had recently been introduced.

'I never!' Loolie protested. She turned over. 'Hey, you know, I wonder. When did I *actually* meet you?'

'Last Christmas.'

'No, that's what I mean. I mean, I came there because I already loved you, didn't I? And that's where I met you. It's funny.'

'Yeah.'

'I *love* you so, Dovy.'

'I love you too. Listen, let's take your big boat out today, should we?'

And they had a wonderful sail on the dancing trimaran all the way around Acadia Park Island and back to a great clam dinner. That night in bed afterwards Loolie brought it up again.

'Unh,' said Dov sleepily.

She traced his spine with her nose.

'*Listen*, Dovy. Wouldn't it be fantastic to live this day over again? I mean like when we're *old*.'

'Hunh-unh.'

'Daddy has the jumper right here, you know. I was here over Christmas when I did it. That's what the big power plant over by the cove is for, I told you.'

'Hunh.'

'Why don't we do it tomorrow?'

'Unh,' said Dovy. 'Hey, what did you say?'

'We could time-jump tomorrow, *together*,' Loolie smiled dreamily. 'Then when, we're old we could be *young* like we are for a while. Together.'

'Absolutely not,' said Dov. And he told her why it was an insane idea. He told her and told her.

'It's dangerous. What if one of us turned out to be dead?'

'Oh, if you're dead nothing *happens*, I mean, you can only switch places with *yourself*. The, the persona something symmetry, I mean, if you're not *there* nothing happens. You just stay here. The book says so, it's perfectly safe.'

'It's insane anyway. What about the Lump?'

Loolie giggled. 'It would be a great experience for him.'

'What do you mean? What if he finds himself with the mind of a six-month embryo while he's driving a jet?'

'Oh, he *couldn't*! I mean, he'd know it was going to happen, because it *did*, you know? So when he got that old he'd sit down or something. Like when *I* get to be

237

seventy-five I'll know I'll be jumped back here and go and meet you.'

'No, Loolie. It's crazy. Forget it.'

So she forgot it. For several hours.

'Dovy, I *worry* so. Isn't it terrible we have to get *old*? Think how great it would be, having a day to look forward to. Being young again, just for a day. For half an hour, even. Isn't it *rotten*, thinking about getting old?'

Dov opened one eye. He had felt thoughts like that himself.

'I mean, we wouldn't miss a few hours *now*. We have so much time. But think when you're, oh, like sixty, maybe you'll be sick or *degenerating* – and you'll know you're going to jump back and feel great and, and go *sailing* and be like we are!'

Crafty little Loolie with that 'sailing'; Loolie gripped by the primal dream: pay now, play later.

'You can't be sure it's safe, Loolie.'

'Well, *I* did it, didn't I? Three times. Nothing goes wrong 'cause you *know* it's going to happen,' she repeated patiently. 'I mean, when you get there you *expect* it. I found a note I'd written to myself telling me what to do. Like the butler's name was Johan. And my friends. And to say I was sick.'

'You could see the future?' Dov frowned. 'What happened? I mean, the news?'

'Oh, well, I don't know, I mean I wasn't very *curious*. All I saw was some old house. Like it was partly underground, I guess. But Dovy, you *know* about things, you could see all the news, even in just like half an hour you could find out what was going on. You could even read your own research maybe!'

'Hmh –'

That wasn't quite the end of it, of course. It was the evening of the sixth day when Dov and Loolie came in from the moonlight on the shore and went hand in hand into Mr Aerovulpa's quiet corridors. (Which were found unlocked, an out-of-character fact unless it is recalled that Mr Aerovulpa too had glimpsed the future.)

There was a handle set on standby. Loolie threw it and power hummed up beyond a gleaming wall in which was built a heavy airlock. She swung the lockport to reveal a cubicle inside the wall.

'It's just big enough for all three of us,' she giggled, pulling him in. 'What do you suppose we'll do, I mean, the old usses who came back here? I mean, we aren't giving them very *long*.'

'Ask your son,' said Dov fondly, mentally reviewing the exciting things he wanted to find out about THE FUTURE.

So they set the dials that would exchange their young psyches with their older selves forty years ahead, when Dov would be – good God, *sixty-two*. Loolie let Dov be cautious (this first time, she told herself secretly) and he selected thirty minutes, no more. They clasped hands. And Loolie tipped the silent tumblers of the activator circuit unleashing the titanic capacitators waiting to cup the chamber in a temporal anomaly. O O O M M!!!

And which by a million-to-one chance shot young Dov Rapelle uptime into the lethal half-hour when a coronary artery ballooned and ruptured, as he lay alone in a strange city.

So Loolie Aerovulpa Rapelle returned from a meaningless stroll in a shopping arcade in Pernambuco to find herself holding Dov's dead body on the control room floor. Because dying, any time, is an experience you don't survive.

Not even – as Loolie later pointed out to the numerous temporal engineers her father had to hire – not even when it involves a paradox. For how could Dov have died at *twenty-two* if he actually died at *sixty-two*. Something was terribly wrong. Something that had to be fixed, that *must be fixed*, if it took the whole Aerovulpa fortune, Loolie insisted. She went right on saying it because the psychomed had been correct. Dovy was the only man she ever loved and she loved him all her life.

The temporal engineers shrugged, and so did the mathematicians. They told her that paradoxes were accumulating elsewhere in the society by that time, too, even though only a few supra-legal heavy persons owned jumpers. Alternate time-tracks, perhaps? Time-independent hysteresis maybe? Paradoxes of course were wrong. They shouldn't happen.

But when one does – who do you complain to?

Which wasn't much help to a loving little girl facing fifty-nine long gray empty years . . . twenty-one thousand, five hundred and forty-five blighted days and lonely nights to wait . . . for her hour in the arms of her man on a Hudson Bay blanket.

I'll Be Waiting for You When the Swimming Pool is Empty

Cammerling was a nice Terran boy, which is to say that his folks came from Groombridge 34 Nu and surprised him with a Galhonda 990 starcoupe for his traditional *Wanderjahr*. But Cammerling was one sigma off median in that he not only chose to travel by himself but also to visit the remoter parts of the ephemeris where the hostels were unrated or even nonexistent. Which is how he came to be the first Terran – or certainly the first for a long, long time – to land on the planet of Godolphus Four.

As his port opened, Cammerling's ears were assailed by a stupendous braying, skirling and clashing which rose from an immense dust-cloud in which gleamed many shining points. When the dust settled a bit Cammerling made out that there was a barbaric festival of some sort in progress.

Two vast masses of men were rushing toward each other on the plain before him. From one side pounded phalanx upon phalanx of individuals clad in leather cuirasses and greaves and bearing obsidian lances decked with streaming hair and what Cammerling took to be dried nuts. Galloping at them from his other side came a stampede of reptiles mounted by persons cased in glittering mail and whirling large spiked yo-yos around their crests. Just behind all these Cammerling saw ranks of archers advancing with fire-headed missiles on their bows, and the whole mass was being urged on by horn-blowers, cymbalists and bull-roarers and standard-bearers staggering under huge pennants realistically resembling entire flayed human hides.

As Cammerling stepped forward for a clearer view, the two hordes fell upon each other in primal fury, and the plain became a vortex of slashing, spearing, gouging, beheading, disemboweling, dismembering and other unmistakably hostile interactions.

'Good grief,' said Cammerling, 'can this be an actual, real live war?'

His presence was now noticed by several of the nearer combatants who stopped to stare and were promptly clouted by those beyond. A head flew out of the melée and rolled to Cammerling's feet, making faces and jetting gore. Without pausing to think he switched on his Omniglot Mark Eight voder and shouted, 'STOP T H A T!'

'Oh, sorry,' he added, as he heard the sound of obsidian shattering all over the field and noted that numerous persons were rolling on the ground clutching their ears. Tuning the voder down, he recalled his panthropologi-cal semester notes and began to scan the armies in close detail, searching for their leaders.

To his gratification he located a group of banner-bearers on a hilltop somewhat behind the fray. In their midst was an armored giant mounted on a tall yellow carnosaur with jeweled fangs and spurs. This colorful individual was leaning back in his saddle to accommodate a ham-sized triple phallus from which spouted green smoke, alternately bellowing and shaking his fist at Cammerling and chug-a-lugging from a gem-encrusted skull.

On a similar rise across the way Cammerling observed a gaudy pavilion under which a very fat man reclined upon a gold litter upholstered with feebly squirming naked infants and languorously nibbled tidbits from a poignard while he eyed Cammerling. As Cammerling watched, the fat man wiped the poignard by running it through one of the meatier infants and snapped his jeweled fingers at his aides.

All these barbaric manifestations pained Cammerling, who was a good Terran boy, but at the same time he felt exhilarated by stumbling upon what was undeniably the Real Thing. Disregarding the flaming arrows and other missiles that were now arriving in his vicinity and being deflected by his invisible summer-weight nonabsorptive GE-Bilblas forcefield, he focused the voder to project directly at the two chieftains.

'Greetings,' he said. 'I'm Cammerling from Groombridge 34 Nu. How about coming over here where we can interact, if you aren't too busy?'

After a bit of milling, Cammerling was pleased to see the two personages and their retinues converging upon him, while the crowd nearest him drew back. Unfortunately, the delegations halted at a distance that Cammerling felt was too great for a really meaningful encounter, so he stepped toward them and said winningly, 'Look, friends. What you're doing, you know, it's – well, don't take this wrong, but it's not nice. It's obsolete, truly it is. I don't want to insult your cultural identity in any way, but since you're going off this war buzz sooner or later – I mean, studies prove it – why not stop now?'

Seeing that they were staring at him blankly, he added, 'I don't recall my historical symbolism too clearly, but what I mean, I think, is that you two men should shake hands.'

At these words the fat prince in the palanquin spitted three infants and screamed, 'Me touch that lizard-fondling offspring of an untranslated defecation-equivalent diseased female organ? I shall serve his barbecued gonads to condemned thieves!'

And the dragon-chief threw back his head and roared, 'Me handle that chromosomally imbalanced caricature of a feces-eating cloacal parasite? His intestines will be cruppers on my corpse-wagons!'

Now Cammerling could see at once that this was going to be a quite jangled situation to harmonize and as he recalibrated his voder, which had begun to oscillate, he also reminded himself that he must be careful not to show disrespect for these people's cultural norms. So he said pleasantly, 'If I could serve as a resource-person here, I'd like to offer the suggestion that molecular genetics and ethical intuition agree that all men are brothers.'

Hearing which, both chieftains looked at each other with instant and total comprehension. Then they both wheeled around and hurled every weapon in reach at Cammerling, and their retainers followed suit. Amid the shower of missiles, Cammerling perceived that a poignard and a kind of broadaxe had penetrated his summer-weight forcefield, making nasty runs in the lining. He was about to remonstrate with them when two pale-blue blips floated down from the nose of the space-ship behind him and instantly reduced the two princes, the carnosaur, the infants, and most of the entourage to thin vitreous puddles.

'Good heavens,' said Cammerling reproachfully to the ship, 'that wasn't nice either. Why did you?'

The voder print-out came to life and typed in cursive: 'Don't be disturbed, dear boy. Your mother put in a few contingency programs.'

Cammerling made a face and turned to address the assembled armies.

'I'm truly sorry about that. If the seconds in command on both sides want to come over here, I'll try to see it doesn't happen again.'

He waited patiently while some confusion died down and presently two somewhat older and less flamboyant senior types were assisted to come forward and Cammerling repeated and clarified his previous suggestions. The two viziers looked at Cammerling with the whites of their eyes showing, and they looked at his ship, and at the puddles, which were now cooled and streaked with beautiful colors suitable for intaglio work on a rather large scale, and finally at each other. To Cammerling's intense satisfaction they eventually allowed themselves to be persuaded to a distant brushing of the gloved hands. In his excitement he recalled an historic phrase:

'Your swords shall be converted into plowshares!'

'Madness!' exclaimed both viziers, shrinking back. 'Ensorcell our swords into women?'

'A figure of speech,' Cammerling laughed. 'Now friends, I do want to emphasize that I didn't come here to intimidate you people with my superior technology created by the enlightened interplay of free minds in our immense interstellar peace-loving Terran Federation. But don't you think it would be interesting – just as an experiment, say – if you announced that peace has been declared, like in honor of my visit maybe –' he smiled deprecatingly, '– and told your armies to go, uh, home?'

One of the viziers uttered an inarticulate howl. The other cried wildly, 'Is it your will that we be torn to pieces? They have been promised loot!'

This made Cammerling aware that he had overlooked their concern about the emotional tensions which were bound to persist in a situation like this, but luckily he recalled a solution.

'Look, you have to have some kind of zestful popular sport. You know – a thing you play? Like shinny? Or curling? Tug-of-war even? Tournaments? And music! Isn't that the usual thing? We want to get those horns over here, my ship has Marsony twelve-channel. You'll love our snacks, too. I'll help you get organized.'

The hours that followed were somewhat jumbled in Cammerling's memory, but he felt it was, over-all, quite successful. Some of the native sports turned out to be virtually indistinguishable from the original battle, and he did regret having inadvertently triggered the ship's vaporizers once or twice. But no one seemed overly upset, and when dawn broke over the plain there were a goodly number of survivors able to accept his good-bye gifts of inertia-free athletic supporters and other trade trinkets.

'That rugger-type thing you play truly has potential,'

he told the viziers. 'Of course, I'd hope we could sub-
stitute an inanimate ball, and perhaps tranks instead of
strychnine on the spurs. And the eviscerating part, that's
out. Here, try another Groombridge Jubilee. I want to
explain to you sometime about setting up a farm system.
Tot Teams. By the way, what was the war about?'

One of the viziers was busy shredding his turban,
but the other one began to recite the history of the war
in a sonorous sing-song, starting with his tenth grandfather's boyhood. Cammerling set the voder on Semantic
Digest and eventually decided that the root of the matter was a chronic shortage of fertile flood-plain from the
local river.

'Well, holy nutbutter,' he said. 'That's easy to settle.
Just throw a dam across those foothills there and im-
pound the water so everyone will have enough.'

'Dam?' said one vizier. 'He who chokes the father of
waters,' said the turban-shredder hollowly, 'his gonads
shall become as small dried berries, and his penis shall be
a dry wick. Aye, and all his relatives.'

'Believe me,' said Cammerling, 'I have nothing but
respect for your cultural orientations. But really, in this
one instance – I mean, from an existential viewpoint,
although I'm aware that we should do this on a more
participatory basis, men – look!'

And he took his ship up and vitrified a couple of miles
of foothills: and after the riverbed had overflowed and
filled up with mud and dead fish, there was a big lake
where none had been before. 'Now, there's your dam,'
said Cammerling, 'and the water will flow all year, enough
for everybody, and you can go forth and dig irrigation

247

ditches – I'll have the ship make a contour map – and the land will blossom.

And the viziers looked all around and said, 'Yes, Lord, I guess we have a dam.' And they went back to their respective peoples.

But Cammerling was a sensitive type of person, and after he thought it all over he went down to the nearest village and said, 'Seriously, you people shouldn't get the idea that I think I'm some sort of god or whatever, and to prove it I'm going to come right in and live amongst you.' He felt confident about this because his whole class had been on the pangalactic immunization program.

And he went down and lived amongst them, and after they got over his diseases, most of them, he was able to share their life style and experience all their amazing cultural practices and perceptions, and especially their religions. And although he knew he shouldn't do anything to vitiate their ethnic reality, still he was pained in his good Terran heart by certain aspects.

So he called on each of the two viziers, and as diplomatically as possible he explained how deeply he respected their cultural outlooks, and that he wanted to help them along the inevitable evolution of their present religious phase into the more abstract and symbolic plane that it was surely headed for.

'Those big statues,' he said, 'I mean, they're absolutely smasho. Major works of art. Coming generations will stand in awe. But you've got to protect them. I mean, those caves, and the drip-drip. Oh, what a good light man could do! And you know, burning babies in them is corrosive, incense would be much safer. How would this play:

one religio-cultural center for both your nations, where *all* the people could participate? And while we're on it, you know this dropping babies down the wells to bring rain has to be a joke. I mean, existentially, that's why you all have squitters.'

And so he went about and opened up different lines of thought for them as unobtrusively as he knew how, and when he detected signs of tension he eased off at once – for example, on his project of persuading the men to do some of the plowing. He himself laid the first stones for the Culture Center, and waited patiently for the idea to take. And presently he felt rewarded when the two head priests actually came together to see him. One was wearing a white-and-black death's head twice as tall as he was and the other was wreathed in ceremonial snakes. After the greetings were over, it turned out that they had come to ask a favor.

'Delighted,' he said, and he was. They explained that every year about this time a fiendish man-eating monster ravaged the villages in the hills, and they were as straws before it. But he would undoubtedly be able to dispatch it with one hand.

So Cammerling gladly agreed to take care of the matter, and he set off next morning feeling that he had truly been accepted at last. And since they had stressed the negligible difficulty of the task – for him – he went on foot, carrying with him only a light lunch, his Galactic Cub Scout kit and a target laser his aunt had given him when he left. So the high priests went back to their peoples rubbing their hands and pausing only to urinate on the stones of the Culture Center. And there was a great deal of smoke around the caves where the idols brooded.

Cammerling noticed some consternation when, two mornings later, he came whistling down the hill-trail, but he put it down to the fact that behind him crawled an enormous shabby saurian with one leg in a plastiseal and a tranquilizing collar on his neck. Cammerling explained that the creature's vile habits had their origin in impacted tusks, and treated everybody to a practical demonstration of orthodontistry from the ship's Xeno-aid. After that he spent several lunch hours training the beast to serve as a watch-dragon for his ship, which had sustained a few attacks of high-spirited vandalism. And the Culture Center suddenly began to shape up.

But Cammerling was thoughtful. On his mountain trip he couldn't help noticing that this planet had astonishing potential in other ways. And so, after mulling over, he gathered some of the more enterprising commoners into an informal discussion-group and said, 'Friends! I'm keenly aware, as studies have shown, that too-rapid industrialization of an agrarian culture isn't a too-good idea, and I want your frank comments if you feel I'm pushing. But have you thought about a little light industry?'

And so – well, pretty soon one of the nations had a small metal-siding plant and the other had a high-quality ceramic operation. And although Cammerling was careful to keep hands off local native customs and never to override native initiative, still, by his enthusiasm and participation in their life at the actual village level, he did seem to be having quite a catalytic effect. Certainly there were a great many activities available for everyone, what with laying out the irrigation system and collecting the kaolin and the materials for ore extraction and so on.

And so it came about that one evening, while Cammerling was helping someone invent the spinning jenny, the high viziers of the two nations came together in a secret place.

And one said, 'While in no sense renouncing my undying enmity to you and your horde of agrarian defectives whom I intend to exterminate at the earliest possible moment, it's plain to see that this blasphemous usurper is grinding both our generative organs into skink soup and we ought to get rid of him.'

And the other replied that, while he did not wish to convey the impression that he was befouling himself by communicating on equal terms with the irrevocably tainted eaters of offal represented by his present interlocutor, he would be glad to join in any scheme to get this interstellar monkey off their necks. But was he a god?

'God or not,' the first vizier responded, 'he appears as a young man, and there are certain well-known ways to quiet such prickmice, more especially if we pool our joint resources for maximal effect.' To which the other assented, and they began to count.

And so a few evenings later, hearing his watch-dragon snirkling hysterically, Cammerling opened his port to behold twelve dainty shapes swathed in brilliant gauzes, but not so well swathed that he failed to glimpse delicate belled toes, eyes, limbs, haunches, waists, lips, nipples, et-triple-cetera, such as he had never before beheld on this planet. Which was not surprising, since he had been gamely rubbing noses with the gamier squaws of the village level.

So he hopped out the door and said eagerly, 'Welcome! My goodness! Can I help you?'

And a girl veiled in smoldering silks stepped forward and parted her raiment just enough to dislocate his jaw and said, 'I am Lheesha the Bird of Passionate Delight and men have killed each other for my merest touch and I wish to do to your body caresses of which you have never dreamed and which will draw out your soul with unforgettable bliss.' And she showed him her little hands with the breasts of hummingbirds implanted in her tender palms.

And another stepped forward and swirled her vestments so that his eyes popped and melted, and she said, 'I am Ixhualca the Burning Whirlpool and I have thirty-two hitherto undiscovered muscles in my thing and I desire to inflame you to madness by means of unbearable pleasure indefinitely prolonged.'

And a third knelt down demurely and whispered, 'I am called Mary Jean the Cannibal Queen and I have been forced all my life to take nourishment only by compressing and vellicating my lips and gullet upon a certain shameful device, and mortally wounded princes call for me that they may expire in joy.'

And by this time Cammerling could sense that they were all thinking along the same general lines, and he said, 'Well, this is a neighborly gesture, and to tell you the truth I have been feeling kind of tense. Please come in.'

So they trooped in through his doorlock, which had

also been programmed by Cammerling's mother, and on their way in it imperceptibly relieved the girls of various blades, gimlets, potions, amulets, poisoned rings, essences, fangs, stings, garrottes, ground glass, and so on, which had been installed in interesting recesses of their anatomies. But even if the high viziers had known this they would not have been discouraged, because no man had ever enjoyed any two of those girls and lived.

When all twelve of them were inside with the door closed it was pretty crowded, but the ones close to Cammerling set to work on him with the hummingbird frottage and the tonguing and the spice-inflamed apertures and the thirty-two new thing-muscles and every kind of indescribably intimate and exotic stimulation so typical of upper-class feudal debauchery, while those who couldn't get at him just then indulged in unspeakably erotic and obscene activities, which he was able to observe in close detail. And so they went on all night, finding refreshment not only in Cammerling's youth and vigor but also in the chance to pick up some cross-cultural technical fertilization, since they were half from one nation and half from the other.

And the morning light shone in upon an expanse of totally intertwined and exhausted bodies. But it had not shone long before a gentle heaving started from below, and Cammerling crawled out.

'Well now,' said Cammerling, 'that was truly rewarding.' And since he was a nice Terran boy who had been raised on wholesome Terran orgies, he bounced out the lock of the spaceship and did thirty-two push-ups, one for each muscle. And he poured water on his head and

whistled and sang out, 'Hey people, when you get yourselves together I'll show you how to make some pizzas.
I have to go help lay out the new sewage-filtration pond;
we don't want to pollute the ecology.'

But the girls straggled out very upset, crying, 'Lord we
dare not go back because we have failed in our mission
and we will be dispatched with excruciating and bestial
tortures.'

So Cammerling told them they could stay with him,
and he showed them how to work the stove. And they
all settled down happily, except the girl Ixhualca with the
whirlpool thing, who said, 'W'at ees dees batsheet peet-
zas?' and stamped back to the executioners.

And Cammerling went out to participate in the filtra-
tion project and the water-wheel project and the Volta-
ic cell project and numerous other projects, becoming
more involved than he really felt good about, because he
could see he actually had dislocated the native cultural
gestalt some. And he got grief from people who couldn't
fulfill themselves workwise because their role was, say,
shrinking corpses which there weren't enough of now,
or holding sticks to make the women plow straight when
the women were now plowing with lizard-drawn plows
that went too fast. And he began to understand what his
group vocational computer meant by developing matur-
ity of outlook.

But he learned to cope, like when the metalwork-
ers came to him and said, 'Lord, we've made this devil-
machine for vomiting out this unholy hard stuff. What in
the name of the sacred iguana egg do we do with it now?'
So he said, 'Look, let's all vote. I vote we make water

pipes.' And when the kiln-workers said, 'See, O Lord. These fire-bellies which we have constructed give birth to these unbearable tile pots. What use are they?' And he said, 'Well, let's all cycle it around. I'll throw in the idea that we make ceramic flush toilets.'

And the high priest jeered, 'By this you know that the new religion is to put water in one end of the body and take it out the other with maximum effort.'

Meanwhile, all the babies that had not been put down the wells or into the idols continued to pile up and drive everybody into the walls. And one day Cammerling heard strange sounds and opened the door of his ship to find the watch-dragon surrounded by hundreds of roaring infants. So he walked out to look them over and said, 'By Gemini, these are cute little papooses.'

So he turned to the eleven houris who were mucking about with strudel dough and said 'Here! We have a perfect opportunity to raise a whole generation free from prejudice, fear and hatred. Let us build a schoolhouse, and I want you to teach these kids.'

But the girls exclaimed, 'This isn't our area of specialization, Lord! What can we teach those larvae?'

'Why,' said Cammerling, 'everything!' And he went over and switched on his old teach-panel, which was in his ship. 'Look: Parsley Place, Dill Drive, Allspice Avenue, Betelnut Boulevard – we can make that Lizard Lane – Mr Spock's Logic Book, Karma for Kiddies, Clean Genes – the whole system. We'll have like a kibbutz; studies show that has its drawbacks, but it's an optimal form for situations like this.'

And in a very short while they had a kibbutz, and

the girls were teaching Walden set theory and creative hygiene. And more and more babies arrived, and more girls too, because it turned out that Ixhualca the Burning Whirlpool had busted out and started a women's lib movement, and many of her recruits opted to teach babies as an alternative to making ceramic flush toilets.

And time passed – actually quite a few years, although to Cammerling they seemed only weeks because he was a nice Terran boy with a life expectancy of five hundred years and he was only into post-adolescence. And behold, there was a whole generation of marvelous young persons in well-cut tunics riding around on tractors labeled 'War Is For Lizards' and 'Cook Pizzas Not People', with the sun shining through their eyes. And they were restoring the land and helping the people and organizing truck-farm cooperatives and music festivals and people's capitalism and community dance-ins and health clinics. And though a majority of the older people still seemed sort of silent, Cammerling gazed upon the unstoppable flood of babies pouring out of his kibbutzim programmed with middle-Terran values plus pioneering macho and he knew that it was only a matter of time.

And one evening, as he sat watching his sabras setting up a transmitter, practicing karate and laying the foundations for a supermarket, there came a flash in the sky. And a spaceship shrieked in out of nowhere and sat down daintily on the beach. And Cammerling saw it was a super-sports model of a style that was unfamiliar to him but obviously very heavy indeed. And he went over to the alabaster lock full of strange stirrings.

And it opened, and there stepped out that indescribable being, a nice Terran girl.

'Well!' said Cammerling. 'I must say I haven't seen a nice Terran girl for some time. Would you like to come in my spaceship and visit?'

She looked at what was visible of Cammerling's sportster under the passion-flowers and the pizza shells and replied, 'Come in mine, hadji, I have low-gee conditioning and a cooler-full of Groombridge Jubilee.'

So he bounced into her ship and she opened her arms and he lunged right at her in the good old Terran way. And after missing once or twice because he wasn't used to a quarter gee, he made it.

And afterwards she asked him, 'How was it, pookie?'

And he said, 'Well, there's like a muscle or two I could show you about, but I do believe that's the Real Thing.'

'I know,' she replied fondly. 'There's nothing like a nice Terran girl. And now Cammerling, it's time you came home.'

'Who says?' said Cammerling. And she said, 'Your mother says.'

'In that case I'll do it,' said Cammerling. 'Things are going pretty smooth here.'

So he opened the door of the spaceship and called to all his friends and followers and all the great young people and anyone else who cared to listen. And they came and stood before him in a loose but jaunty formation expressive of individual creativity blended with empathic sharingness. And he said to them, 'All right! I have served you as a humble communication link with Terran interstellar enlightenment, although I hope I haven't whacked up your native cultural scene too much; still, it's done now. Now I go back into the sky. Feel free to get in touch with me at any time via my ship's transmitter if you have any problems. Carry on, Godolphus Four! Farewell.'

And they replied, 'Oh great pink friend from the sky, we realize you are not a god and all that; you have taught us freedom from superstition. Nevertheless, bless you. We will carry on. Farewell.'

And so Cammerling went away; and as soon as he took off, all the old hairy chiefs and priests and tribesmen came out and rose up and started joyfully fragging everybody and everything in the name of their sacred Godolphian way of life. But the young people, whom Cammerling had thoughtfully instructed in the use of advanced weapons as well as Ixhualca's karate, were easily able to handle them. And in no time at all they had the situation totally under control and were able to proceed with energy to fixing up the planet truly nice, all over.

And after many years had passed, a faint message reached Groombridge 34 Nu by sublight, saying:

'Hey, Cammerling! We have fixed up this planet all over truly nice. All is blooming and participatory and ecological. Now what do we do?'

Well, Cammerling was out when this message came, but his secretary got hold of Cammerling's wife, who passed it to his therapist, and when the therapist thought Cammerling was ready he gave it to him. And Cammerling and the wife and the therapist conferred, and at first nothing much came of it, but finally Cammerling got off by himself and messaged back, saying:

'Suggest you now proceed to develop an FTL drive and offer the option of Terran enlightenment to other planets in your vicinity. Computer program on FTL-drive theory follows by faxblip. Carry on. Love, Cammerling.'

And so many more years passed, and passed, until one day a new, quite strong message came in from Godolphus Four. It said:

'We have built an FTL drive and we have gone forth and communicated Terran interstellar enlightenment to ten thousand three hundred and eighty-four planets. That's all the planets there are. Their peoples join with us in asking: WHAT DO WE DO NEXT?'

But Cammerling never got that message.

I'm Too Big but I Love to Play

Sorry, Jack. You're right. Yes, I'm upset. No, it's not the campaign, for God's sake the campaign is perfect. It's not the crowds, either, I love them, Jack, you know that. Strain? Sure it's a strain, but –

Jack. Listen. Frightened. That's what happened to Manahasset. Scared out of my mind. Because of, because of this feeling I get, this sensation. Too big! Every time now when things are going well, when I'm getting to them – the rapport, it's working – all of a sudden this awful buildup starts, this sensation I'm swelling up too big. Terribly, ghastly too big! Listen, Jack: brain tumor.

Brain tumor.

I can't go to a goddamn doctor now, there's no way, they'd find out. I can't tell Ellen. I can't – Started? Oh, Christ, I know exactly when it started, it started after the Tobago weekend. At Tobago. That night, I know, you told me. But all I did was swim out and loaf around. Unwind, by myself. I had to, Jack. That's when it started. The Monday after, at the Biloxi airport. You remember, I cut it off fast?

That was the first. The mayor, and that clot from Memphis, Dick Thing, you know, they were shouting questions, and the crowd started singing and all of a sudden, Jack, I looked over at the mayor and you. And you were about two feet high, both of you. And the plane. Tiny! I couldn't get into it! And this feeling, this churning –

Jack. Don't. I know about infantile omnipotence. You don't suddenly get delusions of infantile omnipotence at eleven-fifty on a Monday in Biloxi airport. Not unless there's something physical. It's physical, Jack. The bigness, the swelling, the – vortex – like I'm starting to explode, Jack. It's got to be brain –

Alone of his kind, perhaps, he did not outgrow joy. Play-joy in the crowded galaxies, the nursery of his race. Others matured soon away from the pleasures of time and space and were to be found immensely solitary, sailing the dimensionless meadows beyond return. They did not know each other, nor he them. How could they? For him, still the star-tangles. To ride – how rich-riding the swirling currents between the stars! How various, the wild-swarm photons upon his sensors! And games could be invented:

For example – delicious! – to find some solitary little sizzler and breast close against its radiance, now tacking artfully, now close-hauled in the shadow of its planet, now out again to strive closer and closer to the furious little body, to gain the corona itself, to poise, gather – and then let go! Let all go! All sailing nucleus over ganglia out and out in a glory-rush – until that sun's energy met another's and he was swept whirling down the star-streams to flounder roiled in some sidereal Sargasso.

Here he would preen and sort his nearly immaterial vastness, amusing himself with bizarre energic restructurings, waiting for a new photon-eddy to catch his vectors and billow him off again.

Sometimes what served him for perception gave him news that a young one of his kind was – or had been – following him. This lasted but briefly. They could not match his skill and would soon veer off. Of his equals he saw none. Was he alone of his age in his preoccupations? It did not occur to him to wonder. No member of his race had ever exchanged information. That he might be alone in his games of exostructure he did not know nor care, but played.

New games: resting behind a ball of matter on his approach to a red sun, his temporary nucleus snug in the shadow, his perimeter feathering out past the system turbulence, it occurred to him to invest his receptors more closely round the little ball's surface. What he sensed there diverted him. Energy distributions – but tiny! And how complex!

He curled more closely around it, concentrating himself to the density of a noisy vacuum. Here was an oddity indeed: pockets of negative entropy!

To him, as to all his race, the elaboration and permutation of field-energies was life. But he had never before conceived of energy-interaction of this density. And to *conceive*, with him, was not a passivity but a *modeling*. A restructurement into knowing. He hauled in a half-parsec of immaterial relatedness and began ineptly to experiment. Scarcely had he begun to concentrate when an incautious unbalancement exposed him to the red sun's wind and sent him sweeping out of the system with his ganglia in disarray.

But what passed for memory among his kind persisted, and now and again he would hover to inspect a likely lump. And he found, oh, attractive, the patterns!

A vast gamesomeness grew in him; he played Maxwell's demon with himself, concentrating, differentiating, substreaming complex energy interchanges. Skill mounted, fed back to structure. He tackled subtle challenges. And on planetary surfaces where scaled, skinned or furry creatures focused dim sense-organs on the skies, one and another across the galaxy would be shaken by the sight of incorporealities vastwavering among the stars.

Shaken more especially, when they could recognize monstrous auroral versions of themselves. For technique was coming to obsess him. What had been play was becoming art. This phase culminated in the moment when he was fashioning – without in the least knowing it – a Sirian monitor shrimp family. His tension was great, and at its peak a resonance somehow ignited and *held* through the glorious backlash of release!

Greater feats! Were they possible? A new era of experimentation opened and claimed him.

High on the dunes of Lake Balkhash Natalia Brezhnovna Suitlov surveyed the beach, which was unfortunately deserted. Natalia cocked her white-blond Baltic head. From the far side of the dune, faint but throbbing: music. Not the most advanced, but promising.

Natalia strolled a bit higher, studying the lake. She paused. Face sun-rapt, she stretched prolongedly. Then one hand dropped absently to the knot of her diaper. With fluent ease, first the diaper and then Natalia slowly sank from sight into a hollow.

Here she disposed her bronze body for maximum sun. The music ceased. Natalia hummed a few beats, husky but true.

From the far side of the dune came a scrabbling. Natalia's eyelids drooped. A bullet-shaped shadow appeared in the grass at the top of the dune. Natalia's expression became very severe.

For a long moment the tension-system held beautifully. The receptors in the bullet-head belonging to Timofaev Gagarin Ponamorenko focused upon Natalia. Natalia radiated strongly back. The system grew, recruited.

Action became imperative. Timofaev gave a perfunctory glance around – and inhaled yelpingly.

A hundred meters up the little ridge something huge was happening. Part of it was a gassy figure resting on the ground in Natalia's same posture. It was Natalia – but fifty meters long and obscenely distorted. Giant-Natalia solidified, took on color. But it was not alone! On the ridge above it, a great head – Timofaev's head – and his hands – and –

Natalia herself was up in a crouch and staring too. The giant head of Timofaev lacked hair, the hands lacked arms, they were floating in the air. And floating behind them were other portions of Timofaev, partly unrecognizable, part plain as a pikestaff – those portions of his being which had been energetically and reciprocally resonant with Natalia.

The youngsters screamed together and the monstrous images began to boil. Sand, air and grass rose whirling, and the dune imploded round them in thunder.

SOMETHING WRONG! WITHDRAW! REDE-
FINE SYSTEM!

Guerero Galvan swung his legs against his burro and
gazed sourly down into the great barranca beside the
trail. He was hot and dry and dusty. When he was rich
he would ride to Xochimilicho in a private *avion*. But
when he was rich he would not live in Xochimilicho. Very
surely, he would live in a concrete palace full of girls at
Mazatlan, by the sea. The sea? Guerero considered the
sea. He had never seen it. But all ricos loved the sea. The
sea was full of girls.

The burro hobbled on. Guerero kicked it reflexively,
squinting at the trail ahead.

Coming toward him was another rider.

Guerero prodded his mount. The trail was narrow
here, and the stranger was large. He too was prodding his
mount, Guerero saw. But where had he come from? The
trail had been clear to the pass a few moments before. He
must have dozed.

As they came abreast Guerero raised three fingers in
a studiedly casual greeting. The stranger did likewise.
Guerero came fully awake, began to stare. There was
something odd here. A diligent student of the mirror,
Guerero saw that the stranger, though larger, looked very
much like himself.

'Bueno,' he muttered, tracing his own dark, slightly
adenoidal features, his own proud gold glitter of bicuspid.
And the burro – the same! The same tattered blanket! He
crossed himself.

'Bueno,' said the stranger, and crossed himself.

Guerero took one long look and began to scream prayers, hauling, wrestling his animal, flailing his legs. Next moment he had leaped free and was racing down the trail.

The voice had been his own voice, but *it had come from the burro.*

Careening, Guerero risked a look behind and redoubled his speed. The false Guerero-devil was trying to dismount too – but the flesh of its legs seemed to be joined to the sides of the devil-burro. Behind the devils the mountain was convulsing. Guerero flung himself into a gully and cowered while trail, pass and devils vomited themselves into the sky.

MISTAKE! WITHDRAW! SUBCIRCUITS IMPRECISE!

Through the noise of his party Ches Mencken was keeping one ear on the moonlit terrace. Majorca moonlight could get chilly. The three couples who'd gone skinny-dipping with Elfa had come dripping and giggling back and were applying themselves to the juice. Where was Elfa?

He mixed rock-vodkas, peeking at the electroquartz timepiece in the wide reptilian band around his wide mammalian wrist. Thirty-five minutes. He jerked his jaw clear of the turtleneck and pressed a glass into La Jones's steamy paw. She breathed at him. Sorry, Jones-baby, Elfa is my score . . . where the hell is she?

Jones-baby gurgled through her hair. Those earrings are real. But Elfa's got all that glue. Pity Jones doesn't fall on his head and leave you with the basic Xerox, things might be different for you and me, know that?

Automatically his eyes gave her the message: *You – me – different –*

Only it wouldn't be, he thought. It'd be the same old ratass. Christ but he was tired! Whacked out . . . young cunt, old cunt, soft, sinewy, bouncy, bony, wriggly, lumpy, slimy, lathery, leathery cunt squeaking shrieking growling – all of them after him, his furry arms, his golden masculinity, his poor old never-failing poker – Oh Ches I've never oh Ches it's so it's oh Ches oh Darling darling darlingdarlingdarling –

Wonder what it'd be like to go gay? Restful, maybe, he brooded, checking bottles. Better yet, go off the juice onto pot. They say you don't, with pot. After he landed Elfa that's what he'd do: go on pot and retire. Surprise for Elfa. Only, where was Elfa?

Oh God no.

A pale form was wavering about the moonlit terrace. Not a stitch on and slugged. She must have had a bottle down there.

He disengaged fast and raced around through the bedroom, snatching up a rebozo.

'Darling, you'll get chilled!' Capturing her in the wool lace, leading her into the bedroom. She was slugged all right but not out.

'Don't know . . . clothes? What this?'

'Warm you, baby. What a doll, num-num –'

Automatically moving in, his expert hands. Really a damn good stack for her age, she's kept herself up.

267

Careful, now. Mustn't upset her. With Elfa it's got to be love. Elfa is special. Elfa is the retirement plan.

'Ches!'

'Sorry baby, I'll be good.'

'No, I mean, I feel so – Ches!'

'Little girl, you're –'

'Ches, so intimate, I never. – I mean, I loved Maxwell terribly, you know I did, Ches?'

'Yes, little heart?'

'But he never, I never! Oh Ches –'

Oh God it was the pitch, he saw, and that damn crowd outside. They'd have to go. Life or death.

'– Drink this down for Ches, Ches wants you to drink it so you won't get cold, see? My little girl sit down right here just one minute, Ches is coming right back –'

'Ches –'

As he closed the door she was saying plaintively, 'Ches, why am I so big? So terribly, terribly –'

Somehow he got them out. She was sipping and crooning to herself where he'd put her.

'Li'l bitsy!'

'Ches loves you.'

'Ches! Li' I bitsy moon!'

'Li'l bitsy you, m'm m'm.' Taking the glass, carrying her to the bed, she saying again, 'Ches, I'm so big! Li'l you!'

He didn't hear her. This was serious, this was make or break. She'd remember tomorrow, all right. It had to be the big thing. Was she too drunk? Her head lolled. O Jesus. But his technique was good. Presently he knew he needn't have worried. She was coming into it beautifully, puffing and panting. The nose knows. Mellow relief; I *am* good. Maybe I should be some kind of guru, give lessons.

She was gabbling incoherently, then suddenly plain. 'Oh Ches I'm getting bigger!' *Real panic?*

'It's good, honey,' he panted. 'It's what you want, let it happen, let it happen to you –'

He didn't register the white figure wavering on the terrace outside until it stumbled into the glass and began to mouth. He glanced up, blurry – it was Elfa out there! *How Elfa? No! ELFA?*

The thrashing in his arms went rigid, arched.

'Ches I'm go-oo-ing explo-OO-OOO –'

Under intolerable stress the nebulous extension which had been compressed into a mimic of the woman by the water reverted to its original state. A monstrous local discontinuity, comprising – among other things – the subatomic residuals of an alligator watchband, bloomed into the thermosphere from the Majorca cliffs.

NEW ERROR! ONE-TO-ONE INTERMIX? OOH HOW MORE?

Standing on the wet rocks, he / it laughed. Laughing he / it laughed more. To feel! To know feeling! To know knowing! A past flooded in – voices-speech-patterns-events-concepts-MEANING! Laughter roared.

The little subsystem was right! It worked. It lived!

But the little system was not right. The system was under strain, it demanded closure. It demanded to be itself, be whole. Something was outside, disequilibrating it, intruding alien circuits. The little system had integrity, it would not be a subsystem. It fought the disequilibrium, hauled and pulled on the incongruent gap.

He fought back, idly at first, then strenuously – fighting to keep his nucleus outside, to retain the system subsystem hierarchy. It was too late, no good.

Soundless as a soap-film snapping, the great field reorganized. The system inverted, closed and came to equilibrium with everything crammed in.

But it was not the same equilibrium.

. . . The moonlit surf creamed and hissed quietly around the rocks at his feet. Something he did not examine floated further out. After a moment he lifted his head to watch the little moon slicing cirrus cloud. The breeze dried his skin. He felt an extraordinary . . . Pleasure? Pride?

Perhaps that he was still young enough to break a business trip with an impromptu swim?

He began to climb up the rocks. Beneath the pleasure was something else. Pain? Why was he so confused? Why had he come here? Surely not just for an idle swim. Not *now*. But yet he was happy. He let himself slide into pleasure as he found his clothes, dressed.

Dressing himself was actively enjoyable; he'd never noticed. A moment of panic seized him as he climbed back to Overlook 92 where he had left his car. But it was there, safe. With his briefcase.

Images of the spinning surf, the streaming clouds, wheeled in his mind as he drove, merged with the swirl of the car as the huge coastal cloverleaf carried him up and around over and dip-down through the mercury lights flashing – sweeping –

Ooee-ooee-ooee! went his signaler. As his power cut the cop rolled in beside him. He answered automatically, produced his papers. The interchange excited him. It seemed delicious to see the cop's thick lips murmuring into his 'corder. From ID card through the eyes through the brain through the sound-waves through the 'corder tape pulse –

'Who reads the tape?' he asked.

The officer stared at him, tight-lipped.

'Does a human being listen to it? Or does it go to another machine?'

'Where did you say you're going, Doctor, uh, Mitchell?'

'I told you. San Berdoo Research. My meeting up north ended early, I decided to drive back. Fine night.'

In fact, he remembered now, he had been unspeakably depressed.

'Doing one fifty in a ninety kay-em zone. Keep it down.' The cop turned away.

Mitchell – he was Mitchell – drove on frowning. His dashboard needles fanned, dial lights blinked. Giving him information. The car communicated with him, one way. Whether it wanted to or not.

I was like the car, he thought. He made me communicate with him one-way. There was a roiling inside him. Where is the circuit, he wondered.

He raced on through the night, communications springing at him. Right lane must turn right, he read. Food gas lodging next exit. His black mood lifted. Green-to-red, green-to-amber, flashing-amber, All Night Funeral Home. He laughed aloud.

He was still grinning when the garage opened to his beeper and the house door opened to his thumb. The house was dark, silent. He expected that, he realized. His wife was visiting her mother. *Eleanor.*

But his wife's name was not Eleanor; his wife was Audrey.

Depression descended. Suddenly he saw he had been evading reality. Swimming and playing games with the cops instead of doing the serious thinking he had planned to do. Before tomorrow's meeting.

He turned out the lights and lay on the bed, trying to concentrate. There were paragraphs in his mind. Other things. He must concentrate. The moon set. It grew darker, and presently, very slowly, lighter. He failed to notice that he did not sleep. When the little sun rose he got up and re-dressed.

The San Bernardino lot was still quite empty when he pulled in; the guards seemed surprised to see him. His office, though, was sunny. Did not need light. He found the files.

His secretary came in at eight-thirty tiptoeing.

'Miss Mulm,' he said brightly. He pushed the files away.

'Yes sir?' She was instantly wary, a small, dark, soft-lipped girl.

'Sir?' he echoed. 'Indicating deference, subordination . . . are you afraid of me, Miss Mulm?'

'Why, no, Dr Mitchell.' Staring gravely, shaking her dark head.

'Good. There's too much of that sort of thing. Too much one-way communication. No true interaction. Entropic. Don't you feel it?'

'Well, I guess . . . uh –'

'Miss Mulm. You've been with me five years now. Since before I was Director. You came over from the department with me.'

She nodded, watching him intently: yes.

'Have you any feelings about the sort of work we do here?'

'I'm not sure what you mean, Doctor Mitchell.'

'Do you – well, do you approve of it?'

She was silent. Wary. But somehow brimming.

'I – of course I don't understand all of it, not really. But it – it seems more military than I expected. I mean, Colonel Morelake, I guess –'

'And you don't feel quite right about military-type research?'

'Doctor Mitchell,' she said desperately, 'if you think it's all right –'

Her eyes, face brimmed, communicating information.

'My God,' he said slowly, studying her. 'Do you think I think – does everybody here think I – No. You can't answer that, of course. I guess I, since Hal's been away I've been doing some –' He broke off.

'Miss Mulm! Does it strike you that we are engaged in a most peculiar interaction process?'

She made a helpless confused noise.

'On the one hand we're discussing, verbally, the work of this institution. And at the same time there is another quite different communication taking place between us. Without words. Are you aware of that? I feel it has been going on for some time, too. Don't you think so? By the way, my name is Colin.'

'I know,' she said, suddenly not confused at all.

He came closer and slowly, experimentally, reached his hands and arms out along the force-lines of the emergent system. The system of two.

'*Eleanor*,' he said. The system tightened, connected body to body, changing both. His body began to move along the field stresses. It felt wonderful. It felt resonant. Resonances tune, building to oscillation. Feedback began to drive – swelled stress –

'Eleanor!' He was galvanized with delicious danger. 'Eleanor – I –'

'Yes Colin!' Brimming at him, five years of small, dark, very intense –

'I – I – I –' Bracing against the forcefield's bulge, '*What?*'

'The intercom! They – they – it's time, Doctor Mitchell!'

'Oh.' It was flashing, buzzing, down there very small and faraway. The . . . the meeting. Yes. What the hell had hit him. Damp. Damp the circuits. The room came back. And the paragraphs.

He was quite himself when the staff meeting opened. The project leaders, as usual, led off with their reports. There were eighteen bodies and an empty chair: the fourteen project directors, Admin, Security, Colonel Morelake, himself and the empty chair for his deputy Hal, on leave at Aspen. The reports were officially being made to him as Director, but most of the speakers seemed to be talking directly to Colonel Morelake. Again as usual.

Jim Morlake bore a disarming resemblance to a robin. A slim, neat robin with a perfectly good PhD and lots of charm. He bobbed his head in obviously genuine interest at each report. When old Pfaffman got into a tangled complaint – this time to Mitchell – Morelake spoke up.

'Colin, I believe I know where we can get some computer time to help Max.'

Pfaffman grunted without looking at him and subsided.

That wound up the routine. They looked at Mitchell.

'About Cal Tech North,' Colin Mitchell said. 'I spent over six hours with Will Tenneman yesterday, before and after the general meeting. Essentially he was very ready to deal, provided we can work out the details of the grant allocations, and I feel they'll be reasonable. In fact, there was so little to talk over until we get down to specifics that I came back early. I think the main thing that was worrying him was parking space.'

That brought the ritual chuckle.

'However,' Mitchell went on. 'There's something bothering me. This business brings it to a head. The Cal Tech North link-up is completely logical and desirable, provided we continue as we have been going. I'd like to do a little review. As you all know, especially those of you who have been here from the start –' He paused, momentarily aware of how many new faces were around him.

'This group was set up as an independent research facility annex to the university proper. It was our role to service a wide spectrum of basic research projects which could attract special funding arrangements. We started with eight projects. Two were medical, one was a short-term data analysis on traffic facilities, another was historical, two were interdepartment teams in the anthrosociology area, one was concerned with human developmental and learning processes, and one was an applied project in education. Of these, four were founded by NIH, one by private industry, one by the Department of Commerce, one by NSF, and one by the Department of Defense. Right?'

A few heads nodded, old Pfaffman's the hardest. Two of the younger men were staring oddly.

'At the present time,' Mitchell went on, 'we have increased to fourteen projects in hand. There has been a threefold increase in personnel, and a commensurate growth in support facilities. Of these fourteen projects, one is funded by NIH, three by private industry, and Commerce is still continuing the traffic study. The rest, that is nine, are funded by the Department of Defense.'

He paused. The empty chair beside him seemed to be significant. Things were different without Hal. He had chosen Hal, relied on him as an energizer. And yet – was it since Hal's time that the DOD connections had tightened?

'Everyone is, of course, very pleased,' he said heavily. 'But I wonder how many of us have taken time to analyze these projects, which we live with daily. If you stand back, as I have been doing over this past week, and classify them very naively from the standpoint of their ultimate product, I think it is fair to say that five of them have no conceivable application except as means to injure or destroy human life. Three more probably have no other application, although they may yield a small return in basic knowledge. That's eight. Number nine is devoted to the remote electrical control of human behavior. Ten and eleven are exploring means for the sterilization of plants.

Twelve and thirteen are limited engineering problems in metallic structure. The last is one of the original – I might say, surviving – projects concerned with human cognitive development.'

That was Pfaffman. He was looking at his hands.

'When we link up with Cal Tech North,' Mitchell went on, 'when and if we link up with Cal Tech North, this imbalance will be intensified. I am not familiar with their entire panel, since so much of it is classified. But they are entirely funded by DOD.'

The silence was absolute. Colonel Morelake's eyes were on the table, his expression attentive. Even sympathetic.

Mitchell took a breath. Up to now his voice had been light and controlled, as if reciting a long-prepared speech. He went on, still quietly.

'I would like to have your comments.'

One or two heads moved. Feet shifted. One of the younger men – the neural impulse broadcaster let his teeth click audibly. No one said a word.

The pulse under Mitchell's ear began to pound. The wrangles – the free-for-alls that had gone on around this table! How had he let things drift so far? He leaned back, his elbow on the empty chair.

'I'm surprised,' he said, still mildly. 'Let me remind you of the way we are set up. Perhaps some of you haven't read the charter. It calls for periodic reviews of our program – our *whole* program – giving each of you as project head a voice, a vote if you like, in evaluating what it regrettably refers to as the thrust or the social impact of our work. As Director, I have two votes – three, with Hal away. Gentlemen, I am calling for your evaluation.'

Three men cleared their throats simultaneously. Mitchell looked toward Bill Enders, one of the phytocide biologists.

'Well, Colin,' Enders said awkwardly. 'Each of these projects *was* discussed, at the time of initiation. I . . . I frankly don't quite see –'

There were several nods, a shuffling release of tension. Morelake, as a non-voting consultant, kept his eye on his papers throughout.

Mitchell drew a breath.

'I confess I am surprised that no one sees anything to discuss here.' His voice sounded oddly thick in his own ears.

'Colin.' A crisp voice; Chan Boden, biochemist, was the oldest man present bar Pfaffman, with a lush, long-term grant.

'One sees what you mean, of course, Colin. These problems in values, social responsibility. It's always been a difficult aspect. I'm sure all of us maintain awareness of, for example, the triple-AS ventilations of the problem. In our private lives,' he smiled warmly, 'we all undoubtedly do a bit of soul-searching from time to time. But the point is that here, in our professional personae, we are scientists.'

The magic word; there was audible relaxation.

'That is exactly the point.' Mitchell's voice stayed level. 'We are scientists.' This too was in the paragraphs, this had been expected. But why were the paragraphs fading?

Something about the way they refused to respond. He shook his head, heard himself plow on.

'Are we doing science, here? Let's get down to basics. Are we adding to man's sum total knowledge? Is knowledge merely a collection of recipes for killing and subjugating men, for eliminating other species? A computerized stone axe? I'm not talking about the horrors of gore and bloodshed mind you. The hell with that – some bloodshed may be a fine thing, I don't know. What I mean –'

He leaned forward, the paragraphs all gone now, the pound in his neck building.

'Entropy! The development of reliable knowledge is anti-entropic. Science's task in a social system is comparable to the function of intelligence in the individual. It holds against disorganization, oscillation, noise, entropy. But we, here – we've allied ourselves with an entropic subsystem. We're not generating structure, we're helping to degrade the system!'

They were staring, rigid.

'Are you accusing me of being a virus particle, Colin?' Jim Morelake asked gently.

Mitchell turned on him, eager for connection. The room seemed momentarily clearer.

'All right, Jim, if you're their spokesman now. You must see it. The military argument. Biotic agents – because the other side has. Mutagenesis – because they may get it first. But they know we do it, and so they – Christ! This is at the ten-year-old level. Runaway forward oscillation!'

He was fighting himself now, peering down at the dwindling table.

'You're a scientist, Jim. You're too good a man to be used that way.'

Morelake regarded him gravely. Beside him Jan Evans, an engineer, cleared his throat.

'If I understand you, Colin, and I'm not sure that I do, perhaps it might help if you gave us an example of the kind of project you feel is, ah, anti-entropic?'

Mitchell saw Pfaffman freeze. Was the old man afraid he would cite his work? *Afraid?* The awful churning rose in his gut.

'Right,' he said clumsily. 'Of course, one can't, at a moment's notice but here – communication! Two-way communication. Interlocking flow.' He felt suddenly better. 'You can understand why a system would seek information – but why in hell does it *offer* information? Why do we strive to be understood? Why is a refusal to accept communication so painful? Look at it – a process that ties the whole damn human system together, and we don't know fact one about it!'

This was good! Panting with relief, shining-eyed, Mitchell searched from face to face for what must be coming. At the edge of his mind he noticed the Admin man was by the door. He didn't count.

'Fascinating idea, Colin,' Morelake said pleasantly. 'I mean, it truly is seminal. But let's go back one moment. What exactly are you suggesting that we do?'

Annoyance tugged at him. Why didn't the others speak? Something wrong. The swelling feeling came back, rose hard.

'That we stop all this,' he said thickly. 'Close out the damned projects and kiss off DOD. Forget Cal Tech North. Get out and hustle some real research.'

Someone gave a snort of amusement. Mitchell looked round slowly in the silence. They seemed to be down there below him, the little faces – hard and blank as that cop's. Only old Pfaffman and the lad whose teeth clicked – they looked scared. The swirling grew inside him, the pound of seeking resonance. Why would they not respond? Mesh, relieve the charge that was hunting wildly in him, straining the system?

'*You won't even discuss it,*' he said with terrible urgency. Dimly he saw that two little guards had come into the shrinking room.

'Colin, this is very painful,' said Morelake's voice from the pulsing roil.

'You're going to pretend I'm sick,' his own voice chattered. Pygmy guards were closing on him, reaching out. Faces were in the doorway now. One small dark head. Incongruous newspaper in her hand: Eleanor Mulm had been reading that the nude body of a man identified as Dr Colin Mitchell had been found on the rocks below coastal lookout 92.

'Believe me, Colin, this is very painful,' Morelake was saying to the choking thing that looked like Mitchell.

'Entropy!' it gasped, fighting hard. 'We must not!'

The guards touched him. The human circuits – the marvelously dense gestalt he had modeled from the man-system floating in the sea – retained its human integrity long enough to make him yell:

'ELEANOR! RUN! RU-UU-UU –'

– And the strained equilibrium ruptured.

The huge energy which had been stressed into the atomic lattice of a human body reverted back to immaterial relatedness and blossomed toward Vega from a point in Lower California. The resulting implosion degraded much of San Bernardino County, including Colonel Morelake, Pfaffman, the SBR Institute, and Eleanor Mulm.

– and he came finally to equilibrium among the stars.

But it was not the same equilibrium . . .

What served him for memory had learned the circuitry of self-consciousness. What served him as emotion had sampled the wonder of communication between systems, the sharing of structure.

Alone of his lonely race, he had touched and been touched, essayed to speak and been heard.

Reforming himself, he perceived that the nuclear portions of his being were still caught against the little planet by the solar wind – naturally, since the eversion had occurred at noon. It was no trouble to balance there on the standing wave.

He considered for a time, as his distributions stabilized. Then zestfully, for he was a joyful being, he let the radiance take him, swerved out and around to the haven of the planet's shadow. Here he hung idle, his immense periphery feathered out to the nearby stars. He preened new structural resonances, tickled by wandering wavicles.

Then he began to scan the planetary surface, tasting, savoring the play of tiny structurances. But it was different now. Somewhere in his field gradients, impalpable residuals of the systems he had copied lingered on. An astronomer in the Andes found something like a burro on his plates of Beta Carinae and chewed out his darkroom aid. A Greek farmer saw the letters ELFA glimmering in Scorpio, and carried corn and laurel to a certain cave.

The planet turned, the continents passed into the shadow where he hung, a lonely vastness slightly other than a vacuum. Playing his random scan, relishing energic intricacies. Feeling in what was not a heart a huge and capricious yearning which built and faded erratically, now so faint that he let himself diffuse almost to where the currents would whirl him eternities away, now so strong that he focused to a point on one human creature alone for a moment in the open night.

Temptation grew, faded, grew in him again. Would he? Again? . . . He would. Which? . . . Water; they were often by water, he had found. But which? This one, who played . . . was it *music*? . . . on the shore? He was seeking, he recalled now, a *communicator*. The world turned, carried the music-maker away. One who . . . spoke? . . . and was received, respoken. A linker. One-one? Or why not one-many? Was it possible? Restlessly, he drew a few parsecs of himself into the system, spelled DOD in colliding photons, and began more intently to search for something to become.

– tumor. *That's what scares me, Jack. Everything gets small. It's so real –* Headaches? *No, no headaches, why? No colored haloes on things, either.* Personality change? *I wouldn't know, would I? You be the judge, I don't think so. Except for the fear. Jack, I tell you, it's physical! The interaction starts, the rapport*

– that terrific feeling that we're really communicating – all those people, I'm with them. Agh, we don't have words for it. Do we? And then this other thing starts, this swelling – the bigness, I mean BIG, Jack. Big like bigger than houses, bigger than the sun maybe! Like the interaction feeds it, it's going to burst, it's going to kill everybody –

All right, Jack. All right.

If you think so. I know it sounds crazy, that's why – Do you honestly? Do you think so? That's true, I don't have headaches. I've heard that too. Maybe I – Yes, I know I can't quit now. You're so right. But I have to take a day off, Jack. Cancel something. Cancel that Dartmouth thing, it's entropic anyway. Useless, I mean. We've got to take a day and hole up somewhere and rest. You're right, Jack. You fix it. Before we tackle Dallas.

Birth of a Salesman

The heavy citizen swept by the kitten at the desk and bashed through the inner door. The door read: T. BEN-EDICT, XCGC. Behind the desk, T. Benedict took his head out of his hands and rolled big, sorrowful blue eyes up at his visitor. The heavy man opened his mouth and the phone chimed.

'Exceegeecee,' said Benedict into the phone, flapping his hand at the fat man. 'Yeah, you need a clearance from us if your product is going to be shipped outplanet . . . Yeah, you need it even if it's for outplanet goods processed here. If they've been touched in any way . . . that's right, Xeno-Cultural Gestalt Clearance. I know it's a horrible name, I didn't pick it. We'll send you the forms . . . Now, wait a minute, the name may be silly, but the function, no. What are you shipping? . . . Monomolecular coated bearings? How are they packed? . . . I said, how are they packed? What kind of cartons? Spherical? OK, so you're shipping into the Deneb sector. Going through the Deneb Gamma transfer point, right? . . . Well, look it up, you'll find it has to go through there. So, the minute those spheres of yours come rolling through the transfer, the whole Gamma station crew squats down on its operculi and nobody budges a tentacle, because spheres are religious effigies on Gamma, see? And the transmitter stays open at your expense per microsecond, and your product doesn't move until a local atheist relief squad – at triple pay, your expense – is brought in to move it, right? It's to prevent foul-ups like that you're supposed to get our clearance on your prototype pack. Not after the shipment is sealed to go! Right? . . . I'll send you the forms, and you get your samples up here fast. We'll do what we can.'

Benedict cradled the still-squawking phone and turned his sad blue gaze on the fat man, who promptly exploded.

'That's the *merde* you gave me! How wonderful your clearances! Changes to make – the picture to take off the box – the color to be not pink, not red, some lobster on Capella gets itchy – everything you said, we did! And now look! Five thousand Happichlor Underfin Gasators I have lying on Candlepower Seven, nobody will move them! For what do I pay my taxes? Incompetent! Parasite! Harrghh!'

T. Benedict closed his eyes, pulled his hand down his nose, and looked up again.

'Look, Mr Marmot –'

'Marmon!'

'Mr Marmon, our clearance isn't a guarantee. It can't protect you against unknown factors, only against those we know about. With transmitter shipping linking new cultures every week, we get new factors all the time. The picture-label you had, the red lettering, those are known factors on your route. Your product would have been severely damaged by nibbling on Capella if those cartons had gone through – that, we know. You'd have had a right to blame us if we'd let them go. But you shouldn't have trouble on Candlepower. We have a Candlepower native on our alien panel, he passed your product. There're only two possibilities: either it's a transport problem, malfunction or wage-strike, in which case it has nothing to do with us – or you've changed the product.'

'The product has been in no way changed. Look!' Marmon slammed a black cube and a crumpled message form onto the desk. Benedict read:

'Six cases acute depressive fugue among transfer crew. Relief crew affected, refuse handle. Held pending. You've changed the product.'

'I have NOT changed the product!'

'And they're all exactly alike? Every one?'

'Every single one to half micromill tolerance. What do you think we make?'

'Who knows? But there's variance somewhere. Miss Boots!'

A kitten in an aqua lab coat tottled through the side door.

'Take this upstairs and get Freggle to vet it again. Tell him a shipment has been held up at Candlepower station, acute depressive effect.' They both watched her toddle out.

'Now listen, Marner, we'll help you all we can. Either the sample you gave us isn't representative, or our Candlepower representative isn't representative, I mean, typical. It's cheaper to check your sample first, so get me some more of them – a gross, a couple gross at least. If you get them here today, I'll put them right through. That's step one. Meanwhile, you have a choice: either wait, in hopes we find something you can fix, or get on the horn and get an itinerant emergency crew down to Candlepower to run your shipment as is. My advice is to get the crew; whatever's wrong is apt to be tough to fix at this distance. Comprenday?'

'But my costs! My costs! While you just sit there! Faker!'

'Markle, I'm helping you all I can – Yes, Miss Boots?'

On the intercom screen Miss Boots appeared to be replacing her wig.

'Mr Fregglegglegg has just fainted – I guess,' she said timidly.

'Get that product away from him!' yelled Benedict. 'Call Doc! Wait, Bootsie, sprinkle some sugar on him. Yeah, sugar, you'll see the can on his desk. On his feet, stupid, those green things, he metabolizes there in emergencies!'

Miss Boots dove off-screen.

'Well, Marvin, your product is the trouble, all right! Now! On your samples, first get me some of the originals – the ones we passed. You have 'em? Good. And then get some from different batches up to the time you shipped, comprenday? I don't care how many, send plenty. We'll work on it here as soon as Freggle comes to. Method of approximation. Wait! Next, you write down everything – I mean every little thing – that's changed in your plant since that first batch. Different molds or dies, different plastic catalyst, different soldering flux, change in subcontractors, any and every –'

'He's kicking the sugar!' Miss Boots wailed from the screen.

'Get Doc, Bootsie! . . . All right, Marple. Series of samples, list of differences, schnell-schnell. Go!'

The fat man charged out. Benedict dropped his head

into his hands while the intercom screen emitted gargles and flashes of aqua lab coat. His phone chimed just as the office door opened, revealing what appeared to be a red-haired gazelle in silver tights.

Benedict grabbed the phone, rolling startled eyes up at his visitor, whom he now perceived as a girl in silver peekaboos carrying an orchid attaché case. His eyes grew rounder, while the phone boomed busily at his ear.

Suddenly a gigantic maroon walrus rose into sight on the intercom screen, leaning on Miss Boots's head. The gazelle-girl gasped.

'You OK, Freggle!' Benedict demanded of the walrus. 'No, not you, 'scuse me. Go ahead.'

The walrus wavered off the screen, followed by a shingle-haired man who made a thumb-and-finger OK sign at Benedict. Benedict nodded, still listening to the phone as he swiveled round to observe the effect of deep respiration on his visitor's silver contours.

'Got it,' he told the phone. 'I'll repeat. The Pansolar wine shipment can go through as routed, provided (a) they take the grape picture off so the Fomalhaut transfer crew won't think we're bottling their larvae. And (b), the bottles must not gurgle above thirteen thousand cps to stay below the mating range for amphibians running Pegasus Zeta Four. If the overtones can't be fixed he has to ship the long way via Algol. That right? Transcribed, will notify. Thanks, Tom . . . 'scuse me, Miss, what can I do for you?'

'I am Joanna Lovebody, Inc.,' the girl announced sweetly.

'How do, Miss uh, Inc.?'

'Well, Miss Krupp, actually.' She smiled. 'We at Joanna Lovebody are so thrilled because we now have our first extra-solar clientèle! Yes, there is a new, enthusiastic demand for Joanna Lovebody Cremes on a romantic, alien world. And we understand, Mr Benedict, that in order to ship our lovely Joanna Lovebody Cremes we need one of your little government permits?'

Benedict pulled himself together. 'You do indeed, Miss Krupp. Tell me, what planet are you shipping to?'

'Sirloin Twelve.' She chuckled, generating a silver undulance. 'Such a quaint name.'

'Some survey crew got tired of tube food,' Benedict muttered, distractedly riffling his Locater. 'Aha! Say, what do they do with face cream on Sirloin Twelve? Polish their chitin?'

'I beg your pardon? Oh, actually I believe they want to use it more as a cooking oil.'

'Wonder what they cook? Well, this looks like a pretty easy route, Miss Kripp. Straight through the Sirius station, one transfer, right?'

'I believe so, Mr Benedict. And I do hope we can get this little paper in a hurry, because we have rather an early date on our order.'

'We'll try. Now, what does your cream look like? Are you shipping more than one kind, or all the same? Does it gurgle, or ripple, I mean rattle? How about odor? I imagine it's perfumed?'

'All just like this.' She produced a gold and orchid jar from her attaché case.

'Hm-m-m. No gurgle, no rattle – quite a smell though. You realize, Miss Krisp, that what might smell lovely to us often has very different, even harmful effects on alien life forms? I don't mean the Sirloin customers, evidently they know the product. I mean the transmitter crews on the Sirius station. Do you have any kind of vapor-tight wrap for this?'

The speak flashed on, revealing his receptionist engaged in blowing on her nail polish.

'There are, uh, three thousand and seventeen little black boxes here, Mr Benedict. From Mr Marmon.'

'Send 'em up to Jim right now quick, Jackie. Wait, transcribe this to go with: Jim, we have a product variation problem with these, on Candlepower. Gas somethings, variation unknown. Some will be OK, some not, note serial numbers. Show them to Freggle but go very easy. Don't let him faint, start outside the door, comprenday? And Jim, make it fast. Client's hung up at station. I promised answers today . . . yes, 'scuse me, Miss Klasp?'

'It so happens, Mr Benedict, that we *do* have a space wrap for our Joanna Lovebody Creme.' She held up a golden egg. 'Those lovely space-girls have to keep their beauty glowing-fresh too, you know.'

'Never been off-planet. Well, that's pretty but it doesn't look too practical. Miss Cameera! Where's Cameera, Jackie?'

A very young kitten tiptoed in.

'Sweetie, you take these jars up to our Sirius representative. Mr Splinx, you know.'

'Oh, Mr Benedict!' Her chin quivered. 'Can't you send them up by the tube? You *remember* what happened last time!'

'Splinx won't open his tube since we sent him that Martian Mau-Mau kit. Cameera, honey, you'll be all right. Just stand about ten feet away. Tell him I want a verbal report as soon as he's satisfied, comprenday? And remember, no humming or whistling. And don't tap your feet.'

Miss Cameera tiptoed out, slowly.

'New girl,' said Benedict. 'Now what I had in mind, Miss Kling, is one of our all-null shipping packs. As a public service we've had some small sizes made up –' He was pulling plastic ovoids out of his desk. 'If your product can be shipped in these it'll save you time. And money.'

'What happened last time?' breathed Miss Krupp. 'I mean, to your assistant?'

'Oh, just a little administrative misunderstanding, Miss Kupp. Different cultures, different ways. Now look. If your cream checks out OK with Splinx, and you can use the approved pack, we can give you a provisional clearance today on the Sirius route and you can ship tomorrow. How's that?'

The phone chimed.

'Exceegeecee – what? Oh, *no*!' Benedict flung himself back in his chair. 'Well, but that's not our skin, the client's in the clear. That's Galactic Transfer's problem . . . OK, sure I'll tell him. He can cover it. But it's not his fault, comprenday? OK – you just look those packs over, Miss Kreem, I'll be right with you. Jackie! Get me Murgatroyd, Terran Dynamics, will you?'

His intercom screen was flashing but no image appeared.

'Splinx here,' intoned a deep woodwind voice. 'I cannoot see you, Mr Benedict.'

'Something's blocking your visuals,' Benedict told the voice. 'Wait – hello, Murgatroyd? This is Benedict over at Exceegeecee. Listen, on that shipment of power-packs through Nutmeat Nine, you know that fiber plate you have on the back? Can you cover it with an insulating layer from here in? . . . No, not your problem, your shipment got through fine. What happened, the crew on Nutmeat had some females standing around when your shipment came through and there's some kind of electrowhoosis effect – electrostatic, electrophoretic, whatever. Anyway it turns out those plates are very sexy for Nutmeat Nine females. Not the males, we cleared them. The girls' feelers are charged different. So they got in the crates – you know they're teensy – and your machines arrived in the Icerock terminal with scads of these little girl mice plastered all over them. The Icerock crew are big herbivores and they got scared and stampeded. And Nutmeat is suing Galactic Transfer for involuntary concubinage and violation of the Narcotics Pact or some thing. Not your problem, absolutely not – those girls had no business being there. But I said we'd ask you if you could cover those plates. Just as a precautionary courtesy, comprenday? Great, thanks! . . . Yes, Mr Splinx?'

The intercom screen had now cleared to reveal a large warty head featuring a single, benevolent-appearing eye.

'I woould say, ookay, friend Benedict,' Splinx announced. 'Boot the wrapper is noot vapour-tight. Noot at all. Hoowever, the fragrance is noot unattractive. Resembling perchance an eel-farm by moonlight.'

'Not too attractive, I hope. Pilferage?'

'Perchance. Joost a little. Boot the woorkers will noot

be soo chemoo-sensitive as I.' He flicked his domed brow with a tentacle, elegantly.

'Thanks, Splinx. Well, there you are, Miss Klass. Splinx means you have to use our wrapper. And seal it tight; when he says there may be pilferage, you'll lose half the shipment. That big squid thinks he can smell better because he's an aristocrat, but we don't find any difference. Insure them, too. Now, are you certain you've told me everything – about the product, I mean? This sample is exactly like them all? It doesn't have any latent effects or qualities, say heat-generation for example?'

Miss Krupp reflected charmingly, studying her slim silver toes.

'No, Mr Benedict. That's our standard Joanna Lovebody Creme, known to millions of delighted users.'

'OK. Here's your provisional clearance, signed. I've marked the pilferage warning, comprenday? Hand this to Jackie outside, she'll have the wrappers sent over.'

'Oh, thank you so much, Mr Benedict!' Her hand lingered warmly in his. 'I couldn't help noticing you speak French. How very recherché!'

Benedict beamed. 'I want to thank you for your cooperation, Miss Klutch, I only wish all our clients were as gracious as you.'

The phone chimed.

'Benedict here.' He looked regretfully after the departing peekaboos. 'Oh, hello, Mr Bronk. Well, yes, I certainly did appreciate the offer Montgomery Roebuck made me. But as I told you, I think my job is here . . . no, it isn't really the money, of course that's a lot more than the government pays me, about three times . . . yeah, the work sounds very attractive, Outplanet Sales Coordinator sounds great. It's just that I've been building up this department here and it's hard to quit. I'm sure you'll find somebody else . . . oh, sure, if I change my mind. Well, thanks a lot, Mr Bronk, yeah, same to you. 'Bye.'

Benedict turned to his intercom screen, where a man in a lab coat was waiting.

'How're you coming with Freggle and those gas gizmos, Jim?'

'Just wanted to tell you, TB, we've run through a couple of hundred of Marmon's samples, and we're not getting just two types. More like five. Neutral, acutely noxious, mildly euphoric, soporific, and something else he can't or won't describe. Funny thing is, I think I get a little of it myself. Does that remind you of anything?'

'Hm-m-m. Well, I suppose it's possible. Keep at it – skip the staff meeting. Thanks a lot, Jim.'

'Oh, by the way, Freggle wants to register a complaint about the chow. Those last sturgeons were below par, he says, and the seaweed sauce stinks. He likes the Russian stuff better. Can we get him some?'

'He would, twice as expensive. Well, we'll see. It's spring now, maybe we can get local salad for the herbivores and use the savings for Freggle. But give him a pep talk. Keep the galaxy spinning, where would Candlepower be without the transmitter, tra-la-la . . . Hey, what happened to your clothes? Not you, Jim, 'scuse me.'

Miss Cameera had burst in through a side door, clutching the two cold-cream jars.

'That awful Mr Splinx, he got my kiltie.'

'Tch, tch, Cameera sweetie, you know it's not sex with

Splinx – at least, Doc says it's not. Sometimes I wonder. Now look, you can't run around like that. Couldn't you get your skirtie – I mean, your skirt?'

'He threw it over the intercom and I couldn't go close!'

'I see. That figures. Well, get Jim to get it for you – he's on the floor.'

'Oh Mr Benedict, I couldn't talk to Mr Eisenstein like this!'

'Huh? Oh, so.' Benedict squinted at her. 'Is Jim a married man? No, he's not. Here, take my lab coat and run along out now. Wait! On your way back get me another batch of standard small shipping packs from Supply, comprenday?'

Two men and a woman had come into the office. Benedict waved at them shouting 'Jackie honey, get some sandwiches and coffee, will you? You folks eaten? Oh, any kind, it's all roast cardboard. Hal, you look like trouble. Shoot.'

'TB, I want to make sure you're briefed for that meeting with the Budget Bureau tomorrow. I'm afraid they're quite serious about a twenty percent cut on our alien panel.'

'Gautama B. Buddha, how do they expect us to function without a full panel?' Benedict exploded. 'What're we supposed to do for the public, *guess*? You know we only have a sixty percent coverage of current transfer-point life forms as it is . . . Sorry, Hal, it's not your fault. What should I do?'

'Well, the inside story I get from Timmons over there is that they're getting pressure from this anti-alien organization. They keep yelling about hundreds of monsters being maintained in luxury at the taxpayer's expense. Seems somebody got hold of a food bill with caviar on it.'

'That'd be Freggle. What do I do?'

'Well, I've prepared two alternate proposals, which technically comply with their reduction. I won't go into them now, except that one complies money-wise, by adjusting the budget to get past the current fiscal year. After the elections, who can tell? The other complies by reduction of permanent personnel – wait, TB – while actually retaining them in various temporary and con-sultative slots. Considering contract expiration dates, we can avoid actual loss of any panel members for five months. I'll be in to go over them with you before the meeting.'

'Hal, you're a genius. Chester?'

'TB, we have got to develop a little counter-pressure. Of course it's not my business, but I'd like to poll our shippers and see if we can't work up a group who endorse our service.'

Benedict sighed. 'Ver-ry ticklish, soliciting public sup-port from inside the government. Well, maybe, Chester. But very easy. A *poll*, comprenday?'

'Understood, TB. Now look, I have to warn you that the annual report is going to be a couple days late again.'

'Again?'

'That computer foul-up we had last month really hurt. We've been working unpaid overtime to recon-struct, but there's still a lot of incomplete and mis-keyed case actions. Frankly, TB, one big trouble is right here in your office. We've cross-keyed your bank every way we can to catch the original records but that doesn't do any good if you don't turn it on. I know how you feel, but . . . by the way, it doesn't seem to be transcribing now.'

Benedict wheeled around to his input transcriber bank, gave it a glare and slammed the switch to On.

'Dammit, how can I talk to human beings with that thing going? All right, I'll try, I'll try. Mavis, any woe from you?'

'Not really, TB, just the usual. Two cases of nostalgic apathy, one case of addiction to lunar lichens, and some sort of psychic disturbance Dr Morris hasn't been able to pin down yet with the Altairean. Doc says to tell you if you have to use Altair, call him first.'

'Is he still able to function? Altair is getting new branch lines, we're bound to need him.'

'He's all right, but Doc says, he has to get him in the mood first.'

'How does he get him in the mood?'

'With movies. Old Westerns. The horses seem to perk him up. Only thing is, there mustn't be anything disturbing happening to a horse. Doc has been previewing them nights. He says he has saddle burns.'

'Give him my love, Mavis. Tell him I have some June Lovebody Creme for his burns. And listen, ask him to *do* something about Splinx and this undressing business, will you? He got Cameera's skirt today . . . That all, everybody? 'Bye.'

'Don't forget you're speaking to that Alien Nutrition meeting tonight right after work, Boss,' Jackie called through the open door as they trooped out. The phone chimed.

'Exceegeecee . . . Oh, hello, Marmon. Got that list of differences? . . . Nothing but a turret lathe, eh? Used on them all? Well, that shouldn't do it. Now tell me, have you figured personnel changes? . . . What? Look, Marmot, I said *everything*. Don't you count people as anything? People. They handle the product, don't they? . . . I can't help your records. Are the people the same? . . . Well, *try* to look . . . Yes, I have reasons. My reasons aren't definite, but they're good enough so you better look. I'll call you back in about an hour and maybe I can give you a better idea what to look for. But get those records so you can make sense when I call. Comprenday?'

He flicked the phone. In the momentary silence the transcriber bank hummed officiously. Benedict gave it a mean look, slammed the Off switch and rested his head in his hands. The phone chimed.

'Exceegeecee . . . Yes. Hello Mr Tomlinson. Sure I remember you, you ship those miniclimatrons way out past the Hub. Fifteen transfer points indeed, I remember you, Mr Tompkinson. Most complicated clearance we had since . . . What's the problem? . . . You've found a cheaper shipping route? I see – yes, you certainly do need a new clearance. How many transfer points this time – thirteen? That new Lost & Gone station? . . . Yeah, we have to clear your product for those life forms there – *my* problem is that we haven't been allocated a panel member for Lost & Gone yet. I believe they're pretty, uh, recherchay, too, some kind of energy-matrix. No telling what your unit would do to them, or vice versa . . . Yeah, I realize you're losing money every time you ship by the old route, but Mr Thomason, the public hasn't given us the money to bring a native from there yet. If you don't want to wait, the best thing is a government test trial shipment at your expense. I'm sorry. We monitor the shipment and testing procedure. We'll need a representative – I mean, an absolutely typical sample of your product . . . We went over that before, Mr Thomason. No changes? . . . Oh, a little change. You didn't notify us. You've been taking a chance, Mr Thompkinson. Well, we'll catch it now, but that means a recheck of the whole route . . . Yeah, we'll send you a cost sheet on the trial shipment to Lost & Gone tomorrow, say for ten units? If it goes through, yes, you can route them on to consumer, but we don't guarantee they'll go through. You could easily have trouble in your circuits with those energy-beings – probably need some non-conductive pack. You wouldn't want to work out a pack first, would you? . . . I thought not. Well, it's your risk, Mr Tinkerson, I've warned you. We're not responsible for loss or damage, that's on record now. But we'll do everything we can . . . Sorry you feel that way. Right.'

As he flipped off, Benedict glanced guiltily at the dead transcriber bank and banged it to the On position.

Jim came to the speaker screen, holding one of Marmon's black boxes.

'TB, I think we've got a series. Freggle got cooperative and we've pinned down the unknown and two more. Working with the serial numbers as chronology, sample of five hundred, it adds up thusly: neutral; mild euphoria, type A; boredom; mild euphoria, type B; intense sex interest; intense dejection; intense homesickness. The last two types were what really threw Freggle, but the sex one is no better – he won't touch it, just giggles. The

homesickness type carries right through to the last number we tested . . . Identification? Not too good. Probably
young, maybe female by a slight edge. Last number that's
neutral – AGB-4367-L2.'

'Thanks Jim, thanks. That really helps. Jackie! Get me
Marmot, I mean Marmon.' He bounced his chair. 'Hello,
Mr Marmon? Benedict here. Got those lists? I think we've
found your trouble. First, though, can you place the date
of manufacture of a unit from its serial number? Well,
roughly will help. Now: what you have to look for is a new
employee, out of town – maybe foreign – hired about the
time when, let's see, AGB-4367-L2 went through. Got it?
. . . This employee may be female, less probably male,
likely is young. At first she – or he – was happy and interested, then bored, that's normal. Then she – or he – fell
deeply in love . . . Mr Marvin, I'm not joking . . . Wait, let
me finish. Anyway, this employee got rejected, see? Off-
chance the loved one died or moved away, but chances are
they rejected your employee. Employee goes into a deep
depression, almost suicidal, then starts violently longing
for home. Got it? . . . Why? Marble, where have you been?
You've hired a transmitting telepath. And this telepath is
using your product as a K-object . . . No, never mind that
– the net effect is that every unit you process is impregnated with this emotional transmission, comprenday? Any
life form that receives picks it up. That's what knocked
over the Candlepower crews. This stuff carries a big
jolt, you've got a strong sender somewhere in the works
who's very, very unhappy. Probably young, doesn't know
they're a Para. Comes from some place where there's no
testing station . . . How do you find her or him? Well, one

small clue – it's evidently someone who handles every one of your products, at least all those you gave me . . . Do? Get hold of them and send them over to the Para-P Bureau! They're wasted with you, for Pete's sake . . . Well, if they don't want to go, and they have a contract, either get them fixed up love-wise, or keep them away from the product – and I mean *far* away. But I think you'll find they'll gladly shift to Para-P, talk to Ilyitch there. Tell him Benedict says you have a strong sender. They'll help you. Right? . . . I-l-y-i-t-c-h . . . No, I can't help you with that pile-up on Candlepower, Mr Marvel. I told you, best thing is to get an itinerant crew down there to move it. Nonsensitives . . . Well, I warned you that was the best course. Yeah, I know. I'm sorry, too. We try. Right?'

Benedict dropped his chin to his fist, scowling at the humming transcriber bank. Outside, the sky darkened. Quitting time, and he had that speech to make. The phone chimed.

'How do, Mr Oldmayer. Benedict speaking . . . Well, didn't my office send you the forms? It's simple, really, you just send the forms back with your sample packs and we check them through our alien panel according to your routing . . . What special problem? . . . Yes, I'm afraid you do have to have a clearance, Mr Oldenham, music is one of our more sensitive shipping problems. You get actual damage with some life forms. It's a question of packaging . . . I realize it's turned off, but you'd be surprised how things get accidentally activated in transit, especially with a long route like that . . . Yeah, well, get hold of a good soundproofing firm and have them work out a muffler. Maybe you don't have to do the whole box, just the audio part, right? And the power pickup, nonconductive, right? . . . I know it's a nuisance, Mr Oldershot, but that type of equipment can start picking up and sending suddenly and then there's hell to pay. Conditions in transmission are far from Earth-normal, you know. We had a case where a beam-powered front-end-loader started operating spontaneously in the transit station on Piccolo Two, and they had to close the station for two years . . . Well, you get the wrap designed and we'll be expecting you, right? 'Bye.' As he clicked off, the aqua-clad form of Miss Boots tottered into the room, to wing a loaded lab truck.

'Mr Benedict, what'll I do with these three thousand gas-things we tested on Mr Fregglegglegg?'

'You can't leave 'em here, Boots, take 'em to Supply and tell Willi to make the owner pick 'em up. Marmot. Do I have to hand-feed that man? You look beat, Bootsie. Some kind of day with Freggle, was it? Did Cameera get her skirt?'

Miss Boots nodded blearily, towing out.

'Some days,' Benedict muttered, rooting in his files. 'Where's that dumb speech? Jackie!'

'We have to close up now, Mr Benedict,' his receptionist said from the doorway. 'You know what Hal said about overtime.'

'Right.' Benedict grabbed a file and slammed his desk shut. 'Turn off the lights, Jackie. Let's go . . . holy entropy, what's that?'

In the darkened room a man's voice was singing *Naked You*. The next minute a soprano joined in with *Love Me All Over*.

'Light! What is it, Jackie! Help, lights!'

'Oh, Mr Benedict, it's just the skin cream,' Jackie told him, switching lights on. The room fell silent. 'The Joanna Lovebody, see? It plays music. The one I have plays *Yummy-Yummy-You*, it's neat.'

'*What?*' Benedict stared strickenly at the orchid jars on his desk.

'It does it when the light goes off at night and when it goes on again in the morning, to remind you. My toothpaste does *Kissing Day*. What's the matter, Mr Benedict?'

'*Get that woman*,' Benedict roared. 'Klapp, Krapp, Krotch – if she isn't at the office, find her home! Don't leave till you get her, Jackie. Tell her that her permit is revoked. Canceled! VOID! I don't care if she's at the bottom of the ocean, Jackie, *get her*. Oh, sweet suffering Jesus, why didn't she tell me? I asked her. Why? Why?'

'But Mr Benedict, I'm sure she thought you knew – I mean, they *all* do it. It's old.'

'How would I know? I'm a bachelor.' He groaned. 'Jackie, do you understand? Thousands of these things come whanging out of the transmitter all starting to *play different tunes*? Do you KNOW what Splinx does when he hears music? Why do you think we soundproof his room? Oh, oh, oh –'

They stared at each other; Jackie started backing out.

'Listen.' Benedict swallowed.

'Yes, sir?'

'First thing tomorrow – I mean, after Miss Krudd – I want you to get hold of a man named Cronk, Bronk. At Montgomery Roebuck, something chief of something sales. Make me a lunch date with him, Jackie. Tell him I want to buy him lunch. Just as soon as possible.'

'Yes sir.'

Benedict stalked from the office, slamming light switches.

'A good lunch,' he muttered. 'I could use that –'

Behind him the two jars of skin cream started to sing while the transcriber hummed efficiently.

Mother in the Sky With Diamonds

'Signal coming in now, 'Spector.'

The Coronis operator showed the pink of her tongue to the ugly man waiting in the Belt patrolboat, half a mega-mile downstream. *All that feky old hair, too*, she thought. *Yick.* She pulled in her tongue and said sweetly, 'It's from – oh – Franchise Twelve.'

The man in the patrolboat looked uglier. His name was Space Safety Inspector Gollem and his stomach hurt.

The news that a Company inspector was in pain would have delighted every mollysquatter from Deimos to the Rings. The only surprise would be the notion that Inspector Gollem had a stomach instead of a Company contract tape. Gollem? All the friends Gollem had could colonize a meson and he knew it.

His stomach was used to that, though. His stomach was even getting used to working for Coronis Mutual, and he still hoped it might manage to survive his boss, Quine.

What was murdering him by inches was the thing he had hidden out beyond Franchise Fourteen on the edge of Coronis sector.

He scowled at the screen where Quine's girl was logging in the brief for his next patrol. Having a live girl-girl for commo was supposed to be good for morale. It wasn't doing one thing for Gollem. He knew what he looked like and his stomach knew what the flash from Twelve could be.

When she threw it on the screen he saw it was a bogy complaint, all right. Ghost signals on their lines.

Oh, no. Not again.

Not when he had it all fixed.

Franchise Twelve was West Hem Chemicals, an itchy outfit with a jillabuck of cyborgs. They would send out a tracker if he didn't get over there soon. But how? He had just come that way, he was due upstream at Franchise One.

'Reverse patrol,' he grunted. 'Starting Franchise Fourteen. Purpose, uh, unscheduled recheck of aggregation shots in Eleven plus expedited service to West Hem. Allocate two units additional power.'

She logged it in; it was all right with her if Gollem started with spacerot.

He cut channel and coded in the new course, trying not to think about the extra power he would have to justify to Quine. If anyone ever got into his console and found the bugger bypass on his log he would be loading ore with electrodes in his ears.

He keyed his stomach a shot of Vageez and caught an error in his code which he corrected with no joy. Most Belters took naturally to the new cheap gee-cumulator drive. Gollem loathed it. Sidling around arsy-versy instead of driving the can where you wanted to go. The old way, the real way.

I'm the last machine freak, he thought. A godlost dinosaur in space . . .

But a dinosaur would have had more sense than to get messed up with a dead girl.

And *Ragnarok*.

His gee-sum index was wobbling up the scale, squeezing him retrograde in a field stress-node – he hoped. He slapped away a pod of the new biomonitor they had put in his boat and took a scan outside before his screens mushed. Always something to see in the Belts. This time it was a storm of little crescents trailing him, winking as the gravel tumbled.

In the sky with diamonds . . .

From *Ragnarok*'s big ports you could see into naked space. That was the way they liked it, once. His Iron Butterfly. He rubbed his beard, figuring: five hours to *Ragnarok*, after he checked the squatternest in Fourteen.

The weathersignal showed new data since he'd coded in the current field vortices and fronts. He tuned up, wondering what it must be like to live under weather made of gales of gas and liquid water. He had been raised on Luna.

The flash turned out to be a couple of rogue males coming in from Big J's orbit. Jup stirred up a rock now and then. This pair read like escaped Trojans, estimated to node downstream in Sector Themis. Nothing in that volume except some new medbase. His opposite number there was a gigglehead named Hara who was probably too busy peddling mutant phage to notice them go by. A pity, Trojans were gas-rich.

Feeding time. He opened a pack of Ovipuff and tuned up his music. *His* music. Old human power music from the frontier time. Not for Gollem, the new subliminal biomoans. He dug it hard, the righteous electronic decibels. Chomping the paste with big useless teeth, the cabin pounding.

I can't get no – satisFACTION!

The biomonitor was shrinking in its pods. Good. Nobody asked you into Gollem's ship, you sucking symbiote.

The beat helped. He started through his exercises. Not to let himself go null-gee like Hara. Like them all now. Spacegrace? Shit. His unfashionable body bucked and strained.

A gorilla, no wonder his own mother had taken one look and split. *Two thousand light-years from home . . .* what home for Gollem? Ask Quine, ask the Company. The Companies owned space now.

It was time to brake into Fourteen.

Fourteen was its usual disorderly self, a giant spawn of mollybubbles hiding an aggregate of rock that had been warped into synch long before his time. The first colonists had done it with reaction engines. Tough. Now a kid with a gee-cumulator could true an orbit.

Fourteen had more bubbles every time he passed – and more kids. The tissue tanks that paid the franchise were still clear but elsewhere the bubbles were layers deep, the last ones tethered loose. Running out of rock for their metabolite to work on. Gollem hassled them about that every time he passed.

'Where are your rock nudgers?' he asked now when the squatterchief came on his screen.

'Soon, soon, 'Spector Gollem.' The squatterchief was a slender skinhead with a biotuner glued to one ear.

'The Company will cancel, Juki. Coronis Mutual won't carry you on policyholder status if you don't maintain insurable life-support.'

Juki smiled, manipulated the green blob. They were abandoning the rocks all right, drifting off into symbiotic spacelife. Behind Juki he saw a couple of the older chiefs.

'You can't afford to cut the services the Company provides,' he told them angrily. Nobody knew better than Gollem how minimal those services were, but without them, what? 'Get some rock.'

He couldn't use any more time here.

As he pulled away he noticed one of the loose bubbles was a sick purple. Not his concern. Not enough time.

Cursing, he eased alongside and cautiously slid his lock probes into the monomolecular bubbleskin. When the lock opened a stink came in. He grabbed his breather and kicked into the foul bubble. Six or seven bodies were floating together in the middle like a tangle of yellow wires.

He jerked one out, squirted oxy at its face. It was a gutbag kid, a born null-gee. When his eyes fanned open Gollem pushed him at the rotting metabolite core.

'You were feeding it phage.' He slapped the boy. 'Thought it would replicate, didn't you? You poisoned it.'

The boy's eyes crossed, then straightened. Probably didn't get a word, the dialect of Fourteen was drifting fast. Maybe some of them truly were starting to communicate symbiotically. Vegetable ESP.

He pushed the boy back into the raft and knocked the dead metabolite through the waster. The starved molly-bubble wall was pitted with necrosis, barely holding. He flushed his CO_2 tank over it and crawled back to his boat for a spare metabolite core. When he got back the quasi-living cytoplasm of the bubbleskin was already starting to clear. It would regenerate itself if they didn't poison it again with a CO_2 binding mutant. That was the way men built their spacehomes now, soft heterocatalytic films that ran on starlight, breathed human wastes.

Gollem rummaged through the stirring bodies until he found a bag of phage between a woman and her baby. She whimpered when he jerked it loose. He carried it back to his boat and pulled carefully away, releasing a flow of nutrient gel to seal his probe-hole. The mollybubble would heal itself.

At last he was clear for *Ragnarok*.

He punched course for Twelve and then deftly patched in the log bypass and set his true trajectory. The log would feed from his cache of duplicates, another item nobody had better find. Then he logged in the expendables he'd just used, padding it a piece as always. Embezzlement. His stomach groaned.

He tuned up a rock storm to soothe it. There was an old poem about a man with a dead bird tied around his neck. Truly he had his dead bird. All the good things were dead, the free wild human things. He felt like a specter, believe it. A dead one hanging in from the days when men rode machines to the stars and the algae stayed in pans. Before they cooked up all the metabolizing Martian macromolecules that quote, tamed space, unquote. Tame men, women and kids breathing through 'em, feeding off 'em, navigating and computing and making music with 'em – mating with them, maybe!

Steppenwolf growled, worried the biomonitor. His metal-finder squealed.

Ragnarok!

Time shivered and the past blazed on his screens. He let himself have one quick look.

The great gold-skinned hull floated in the starlight, edged with diamonds against the tiny sun. The last Argo, the lonesomest Conestoga of them all. *Ragnarok*. Huge, proud, ungainly star-machine, blazoned with the symbols of the crude technology that had blasted man to space. *Ragnarok* that opened the way to Saturn and beyond. A human fist to the gods. Drifting now a dead hulk, lost in the sea she's conquered. Lost and forgotten to all but Gollem the specter.

No time now to suit up and prowl over and around her, to pry and tinker with her archaic fitments. The pile inside her was long dead and cold. He dared not even try to start it, a thing like that would set off every fieldsounder in the zone. Quine's stolen power in her batteries was all that warmed her now.

Inside her also was his dead bird.

He coasted into the main lock, which he had adapted to his probe. Just as he hit he thought he glimpsed a new bubble firming up in the storage cluster he had hung on *Ragnarok*'s freightlock. What had Topanga been up to?

The locks meshed with a soul-satisfying clang of metal and he cycled through, eye to eye with the two old monster suits that hung in *Ragnarok*'s lock. Unbelievable, so cumbersome. How ever had they done it? He kicked up through dimness to the bridge.

For one moment his girl was there.

The wide ports were a wheeling maze of starlight and

fire-studded shadows. She sat in the command couch, gazing out. He saw her pure, fierce profile, the hint of girl-body in the shadows. Star-hungry eyes.

Then the eyes slid around and the lights came up. His star girl vanished into the thing that had killed her.

Time.

Topanga was an old, sick, silly woman in a derelict driveship.

She smiled at him from the wreckage of her face.

'Golly? I was remembering –' What an instrument it was still, that husky voice in the star haze. The tales it had spun for him over the years. She had not always been like this. When he had first found her, adrift and ill – she had still been Topanga then. The last one left.

'You were using the caller. Topanga, I warned you they were too close. Now they've picked you up.'

'I wasn't sending, Golly.' Eerie blue, the wide old eyes reminded him of a place he had never seen.

He began to check the telltales he had hung on her console leads. Hard to believe those antiques were still operational. Completely inorganic, a ton of solid-state circuitry. Topanga claimed she couldn't activate it, but when she had her first crazy fit he had found out otherwise. He'd had her parked in Four then, in a clutch of spacejunk. She started blasting the bands with docking signals to men twenty years dead. Company salvage had nearly blown her out of space before he got there – he'd had to fake a collision to satisfy Quine.

A telltale was hot.

'Topanga. Listen to me. West Hem Chemicals are

sending a hunter out to find you. You were jamming their miners. Don't you know what they'll do to you? The best – the very best you'll get is a geriatric ward. Needles. Tubes. Doctors ordering you around, treating you like a thing. They'll grab *Ragnarok* for a space trophy. Unless they blast you first.'

Her face crumpled crazily.

'I can take care of myself. I'll turn the lasers on 'em.'

'You'd never see them.' He glared at the defiant ghost. He could do anything he wanted here, what was stopping him? 'Topanga, I'm going to kill that caller. It's for your own good.'

She stuck up her ruined chin, the wattles waving.

'I'm not afraid of them.'

'You have to be afraid of a jerry ward. You want to end as a mess of tubing, under the gees? I'm going to dismantle it.'

'No, Golly, no!' Her stick arms drummed in panic, trailing skin. 'I won't touch it, I'll remember. Don't leave me helpless. Oh, please don't.'

Her voice broke and so did his stomach. He couldn't look at it, this creature that had eaten his girl. Topanga inside there somewhere, begging for freedom, for danger. Safe, helpless, gagged? No.

'If I nudge you out of West Hem's range you'll be in three others. Topanga, baby, I can't save you one more time.'

She had gone limp now, shrouded in the Martian oxy-blanket he had brought her. He caught a blue gleam under the shadows and his stomach squirted bile. Let go, witch. Die before you kill me too.

He began to code in the gee-sum unit he had set up here. It was totally inadequate for *Ragnarok*'s mass but he could overload it for a nudge. He would stabilize her on his next pass-by, if only he could find her without wasting too much power.

From behind him came a husky whisper. 'Strange to be old –' Ghost of a rich girl's laugh. 'Did I ever tell you about the time the field shifted, on Tethys?'

'You told me.'

Ragnarok was stirring.

'Stars,' she said dreamily. 'Hart Crane was the first space poet. Listen. *Stars scribble on our eyes the frosty sagas, the gleaming cantos of unvanquished space. O silver sinewy –*'

Gollem heard the hull clang.

Someone was trying to sneak out of *Ragnarok*.

He launched himself down-shaft to the freightlock, found it cycling and jackknifed back to get out through his boat at the main lock. Too late.

As he sprang into his cabin the screens showed a strange pod taking off from behind that new bubble.

Dummy, dummy –

He suited up and scrambled out across *Ragnarok*'s hull. The new bubble was still soft, mostly nutri-gel. Pushing his face into it he cracked his breather.

He came back to Topanga in a blue rage.

'You are letting a phage-runner park on *Ragnarok*.'

'Oh, was that Leo?' She laughed vaguely. 'He's a courier from the next zone – Themis, isn't it? He calls by sometimes. He's been beautiful to me, Golly.'

'He is a stinking phage-runner and you know it. You

were covering for him.' Gollem was sick. The old Topanga would have put 'Leo' out the trash hole. 'Not phage. Not phage on top of everything, Topanga.'

Her ancient eyelids fell. 'Let it be, Golly. I'm alone so long,' she whispered. 'You leave me for so long.'

Her withered paw groped out, seeking him. Brown-spotted, criss-crossed with reedy pulses. Knobs, strings. Where were the hands of the girl who had held the camp on Tethys?

He looked up at the array of holographs over the port and saw her. The camera had caught her grinning up at black immensity, the wild light of Saturn's rings reflected in her red-gold hair . . .

'Topanga, old mother,' he said painfully.

'Don't call me mother, you plastic spacepig!' she blazed. Her carcass jerked out of the pilot couch and he had to web her back, hating to touch her. A quarter-gee would break these sticks. 'I should be dead,' she mumbled. 'It won't be long, you'll be rid of me.'

Ragnarok was set now, he could go.

'Maintain, spacer, maintain,' he told her heartily. His stomach knew what lay ahead. None of it was any good.

As he left he heard her saying brightly, 'Gimbals, check,' to her dead computer.

He took off high-gain for Franchise Twelve and West Hem. Just as he had the log tied back into real time his caller bleeped. The screen stayed blank.

'Identify.'

'Been waitin' on you, Gollem.' A slurred tenor; Gollem's beard twitched.

'One freakin' fine ship.' The voice chuckled. 'Main-mouth by Co'onis truly flash that ship.'

'Stay off *Ragnarok* if you want to keep your air,' Gollem told the phage-runner.

The voice giggled again. 'My pa'tners truly grieve on that, 'Spector.' There was a click and he heard his own voice saying, 'Topanga, baby, I can't save you one more time.'

'Deal, 'Spector, deal. Why we flash on war?'

'Blow your clobbing tapes,' Gollem said tiredly. 'You can't run me like you run Hara.'

''Panga,' the invisible Leo said reflectively. 'Freak-in' fine old fox. She tell I fix her wire fire?' Gollem cut channel.

The phager must have made a circuit smoke to win her trust. Gollem's stomach wept acid. So vulnerable. An old sick eagle dead in space and the rats have found her.

They wouldn't quit, either. *Ragnarok* had air, water, power. Transmitters. Maybe they were using her caller, maybe she'd been telling the truth. They could take over. Shove her out through the lock . . .

Gollem's hand hovered over his console.

If he turned back now his log would blow it all. And for what? No, he decided. They'll wait, they'll sniff around first. They want to take me too. They want to see how much squeeze they have. Pray they don't find out.

He had to get some power somewhere and jump *Ragnarok* out. How, how? Like trying to hide Big Jup.

He noticed that he had punched the biomonitor into a sick yellow blob and hurled it across the cabin. How much longer could he cool Coronis?

Right on cue, his company hotline blatted.

'Why aren't you at Franchise Two, Gollem?'

It was mainmouth Quine himself. Gollem took a deep breath and repeated his course reversal plan, watching Quine's little snout purse up.

'After this clear with me. Now hear this, Gollem.' Quine leaned back in his bioflex, pink and plump. Coronis was no hardship station. 'I don't know what you think you're into with Franchise Three but I want it stopped. The miners are yelling and our Company won't tolerate it.'

Gollem shook his shaggy head like a dazed bull. Franchise Three? Oh yeah, the heavy metal-mining outfit.

'They're overloading their tractor beams for hot extraction,' he told Quine. 'It's in my report. If they keep it up they'll have one bloody hash-up. And they won't be covered because their contract annex specifies the load limits.'

Quine's jowls twitched ominously. 'Gollem. Again I warn you. It is not your role to interpret the contract to the policyholder. If the miners choose to get their ore out faster by abrogating their contract that's their decision. Your job is to report the violation, not to annoy them with technicalities. Right now they are very angry with *you*. And I trust you don't imagine that our Company' – reverent pause – 'appreciates your initiative?'

Gollem made an inarticulate noise in his throat. He should be used to this. Coronis wanted its piece quickly *and* it wanted to avoid paying compensation when the thing blew. The miners got paid by the shuttle load and most of them couldn't tell a contract annex from a flush valve. By the time they found out they'd be dead.

'Another item.' Quine was watching him. 'You may be getting some noise from Themis sector. They seemed to be all sweated up about a bit of rock.'

'You mean those Trojans?' Gollem was puzzled. 'What's there?'

'Have you been talking to Themis?'

'No.'

'Very well. You will not, repeat not, deviate from your patrol. You are on a very thin line with us, Gollem. If your log shows anything *whatever* in connection with Themis you're out of the Company and there will be a lien against you for your overdrawn pension. *And* there will be no transport rights. Do I make myself clear?'

Gollem cut channel. When he could control his hands he punched Weather for the updated rogue orbits. Both rocks were now computed to node in sector Themis, but well clear of Themis main. He frowned. Who was hurting? His ephemeris showed only the new medbase in the general volume, listed as Nonaffiliated, no details. It seemed to be clear, too. If that polluted Hara . . .

Gollem grunted. He understood now. Quine was hoping for some hassle in Themis which might persuade Ceres Control to reassign part of that sector to him. And the medbase wasn't Company, it was expendable for publicity purposes. Truly fine, he thought. Much gees for Quine if it works.

He was coming into West Hem Chemicals. Before he could signal, his audio cut loose with curses from the cyborg chief. Gollem swerved to minimize his intrusion on their body lines and the chief cooled down enough to let him report that he had killed their bogy.

'It was an old field-sounder,' Gollem lied. Had they identified *Ragnarok*?

'Slope out. Go.' The old cyborg op couldn't care less. He had electrode jacks all over his skull and his knuckles sprouted wires. Much as Gollem loved metal, this was too much. He backed out as gingerly as he could. The men – or maybe the creatures – in there were wired into the controls of robot refining plants on all the nearby rocks, and he was hashing across their neural circuits. Wouldn't be surprising if they fired on him one day.

His next stop was the new aggregation franchise in Eleven. It was a slow-orbit complex on the rim of the Kirkwood Gap, a touchy location to work. If they started losing rocks they could spread chaos in the zone.

Aggregation meant power units, lots of them. Gollem began figuring *Ragnarok*'s parameters. His stomach also began to gripe him; the outfit that had leased Eleven had big plans for a self-sustaining colony on a slim budget. They needed those units to bring in gas-rich rocks.

When he got inside Gollem saw they had other problems too.

'We've computed for two-sigma contingency,' the Eleven chief repeated tiredly. They were standing beside a display tank showing the projected paths of the rocks they intended to blast.

'Not enough,' Gollem told him. 'Your convergence-point is smeared the hell all over. You lose a big one and it'll plow right into Ten.'

'But Franchise Ten isn't occupied,' the chief protested.

'Makes no difference. Why do you think you got

this franchise cheap? The Company's delighted to have you aggregating this lode, they're just waiting for you to lose one rock so they can cancel and resell your franchise. I can't certify your operation unless you recompute.'

'But that means buying computer input from Ceres Main!' he yelped. 'We can't afford it.'

'You should have looked at the instability factors before you signed,' Gollem said woodenly. He was wishing the chief didn't have all his hair; it would be easier to do this to a skinhead.

'At least let me bring in the rocks we have armed,' the chief was pleading.

'How many one-gee units have you got out there?' Gollem pointed.

'Twenty-one.'

'I'll take six of them and certify you. That's cheaper than recomputing.'

The chief's jaw sagged, clenched in a snarl.

'You polluted bastard!'

Suddenly there was a squeal behind them and the commo op tore off her earphones. The chief reached over and flicked on the speaker, filling the bubble with an all-band blare. For a minute Gollem thought it was a flare-front, and then he caught the human scream.

'MAYDAY! MA-A-Y-DAY-AAY! GO-OLLEE –'

Oh no! Oh Jesus, no. He slammed down the speaker, the sweat starting out all over him.

'What in space –' the chief began.

'Old beacon in the Gap.' Gollem bunted through them. 'I have to go kill it.'

He piled into his boat and threw in the booster. No

time for power units now. That yell meant Topanga was in real trouble, she wasn't calling dead men.

If he tied in the spare booster he could override the field-forms for a straighter course. Strictly *verboten*. He did so and then opened his commo channels. Topanga wasn't there.

Fire? Collision? More like, Leo and friends had made their move.

He hurtled downstream in a warp of wasted power, his hands mechanically tuning the board in hopes of pulling in some phagers' signals, something. He picked up only far-off mining chatter and a couple of depot ops asking each other what the Mayday was. Someone in Sector Themis was monotonously calling Inspector Hara. As usual Hara wasn't answering, there was only the automatic standby from Themis main. Gollem cursed them all impartially, trying to make his brain yield a plan.

Why would the phagers move in on *Ragnarok* so fast? Not their style, confrontation. If he blew they'd lose the ship, they'd have to cope with a new inspector. Why risk it when they had him by the handle already?

Maybe they figured it was no risk. Gollem's fist pounded on the tuner in a heavy rhythm. *Paint it black* . . . But they have to keep her alive till I get there. They want me.

What to do? Would they believe a threat to call Ceres Control? Don't bother to answer. They know as well as I do that a Company bust will end with Topanga in a gerry ward, *Ragnarok* in Quine's trophy park and Gollem in a skull-cage . . . How to break Topanga loose from them? If I try to jive along the first thing they'll do will be to shoot us both up on phage. Addiction dose. Why, why did I leave her there alone?

He was going around this misery orbit for the nth time when he noticed the Themis voice had boosted again and was now trying to reach Coronis, his home base. Correction, Quine's home base. No answer.

Against his stomach's advice he tuned it up.

'Medbase Themis to Coronis Main, emergency. Please answer, Coronis. Medbase Themis calling Coronis, emergency, please –'

The woman was clearly no commo op.

Finally Quine's girl chirped: 'Medbase Themis, you are disturbing our traffic. Please damp your signal.'

'Coronis, this is an emergency. We need help – we're going to get hit!'

'Medbase Themis, contact your sector safety patrol officer, we have no out-of-sector authorization. You are disturbing our traffic.'

'Our base won't answer! We have to have help, we have casualties –'

A male voice cut in. 'Coronis, put me through to your chief at once. This is a medical priority.'

'Medbase Themis, Sector Chief Quine is outstation at present. We are in freight shuttle assembly for the trans-Mars window, please stand by until after launch.'

'But –'

'Coronis out.'

Gollem grimaced, trying to picture Quine going outstation.

He went back to pounding on his brain. The Themis

woman went on calling. 'We are in an impact path, we need power to move. If anyone can help us please come in. Medbase Themis –'

He cut her off. One *Ragnarok* was enough and his was just ahead now.

There was a faint chance they weren't expecting him so soon. He powered down and drifted. As his screens cleared he saw a light move in the bubbles behind the freightlock.

His one possible break, if they hadn't yet moved that phage inboard.

He grabbed the wrecking laser controls and kicked the patrolboat straight at *Ragnarok*'s main lock. The laser beam fanned over the bubbles, two good slices before he had to brake. The crash sent him into his boards. The docking probes meshed and he sprang headfirst into *Ragnarok*'s lock. As it started to cycle he burned the override, setting off alarms all over the ship. Then he was through and caroming up the shaft. Among the hoots he could hear more clanging. Phagers were piling out through the freightlock to save their bubbles. If he could get to the bridge first he could lock them out.

He twisted, kicked piping and shot into the bridge, his arm aimed at the emergency hatch-lock lever. It hadn't been used for decades. He nearly broke his wrist yanking the lever against his own inertia and was rewarded by the sweet grind of lock toggles far below.

Then he turned to the command couch where Topanga should be and saw he was too late.

She was there all right, both hands to her neck and her eyes rolling. Behind her a lank hairless figure was holding a relaxed pose, in his fist a wire-noose leading around Topanga's throat.

'Truly fine, 'Spector.' The phager grinned.

For a second Gollem wondered if Leo hadn't noticed the hand-laser Gollem pointed. Then he saw that the phagehead was holding a welder against Topanga's side. Its safety sleeve was off.

'Deal, Gollyboy. Deal the fire down.'

No way. After a minute Gollem sent his weapon drifting by Leo's arm. Leo didn't take the bait.

'Open up.' The phager jerked his chin at the hatch lever and Topanga gave a bubbling whine.

When Gollem opened the hatch the game would be over all the way. He hung frozen, his coiled body sensing for solidity behind him, measuring the spring.

The phager jerked the wire. Topanga's arms flailed. One horrible eye rolled at Gollem. A spark in there, trying to say no.

'You're killing her. Then I tear your head off and throw you out the waster.'

The phager giggled. 'Why you flash on killin'?' Suddenly he twisted Topanga upside down, feet trailing out toward Gollem. She kicked feebly. Weird, her bare feet were like a girl's.

'Open up.'

When Gollem didn't move the phager's arm came out in a graceful swing, his fingers flaring. The welding arc sliced, retraced, sliced again as Topanga convulsed. One girlish foot floated free, trailing droplets. Gollem saw a white stick pointing at him out of the blackened stump. Topanga was quiet now.

'Way to go.' The phager grinned. 'Truly tough old bird. Open up.'

'Turn her loose. Turn her loose. I'll open.'

'Open now.' The welder moved again.

Suddenly Topanga made a weak twist, scrabbling at Leo's groin. The phager's head dipped.

Gollem drove inside his arm, twisted it against momentum. The welder rocketed out around the cabin while he and the phager thrashed around each other, blinded by Topanga's robe. The phager had a knife now but he couldn't get braced. Gollem felt legs lock his waist and took advantage of it to push Topanga away. When the scene cleared he clamped the phager to him and began savagely to collect on his investment in muscle-building.

Just as he was groping for the wire to tie up the body something walloped him back of the ear and the lights went out.

He came to with Topanga yelling, 'Val, Val! I've got 'em!'

She was hanging on the console in her hair, using both hands to point an ancient Thunderbolt straight at him. The muzzle yawned smoke a foot from his beard.

'Topanga, it's me – Golly. Wake up, spacer, let me tie him up.'

'Val?' A girl laughing, screaming. 'I'm going to finish the murdering mothers, Val!'

Valentine Orlov, her husband, had been in the snows of Ganymede for thirty years.

'Val is busy, Topanga,' Gollem said gently. He was hearing hull noises he didn't like. 'Val sent me to help you. Put the jolter down, spacegirl. Help me tie up this creep. They're trying to steal my boat.'

He hadn't had time to lock it, he remembered now.

Topanga stared at him.

'*And why do I often meet your visage here?*' she croaked. '*Your eyes like unwashed platters –*'

Then she fainted and he flung himself downshaft to the lock.

His patrolboat was swinging away. Tethered to it was the phage-runners' pod.

He was stranded on *Ragnarok*.

Rage exploded him back to the bridge consoles. He managed to send one weak spit from *Ragnarok*'s lasers after them as they picked up gees. Futile. Then he pulled the phager's head over his knee and clouted it and turned to setting up Topanga with an i.v. in her old cobweb veins. How in hell had those claws held a jolter? He wrapped a gel sheath over her burns, grinding his jaw to still the up-roar in his stomach. He completed his cleaning by towing the phager and the foot to the waste lock.

With one hand on the cycle button he checked, frown-ing. He could use some information from Leo – what were they into in his patrol sector?

Then his head came together and his fist crunched the eject. *His* patrol sector?

If the Companies ever got their hands on him he'd spend the rest of his life with his brains wired up, paying for that patrolboat. If he was lucky. No way, no where to go. The Companies owned space. Truly he was two thou-sand light-years from home now – on a dead driveship.

Dead?

Gollem threw back his lank hair and grinned. *Ragnarok* had a rich ecosystem, he'd seen to that. Nobody but the phagers knew she was here and he could hold them out for a while. Long enough, maybe, to see if he could coax some power out of that monster-house – without waking up the sector. Suddenly he laughed out loud. Rusty shutters sliding in his mind, letting in glory.

'Man, man!' he muttered and stuck his head into the regeneration chamber to check the long trays of culture stretching away under the lights.

It took him a minute to understand what was wrong.

No wonder the phagers came back so fast, no wonder he was laughing like a dummy. They'd seeded the whole works with phage culture. A factory. The first trays were near sporing, the air was ropy. He hauled them out, inhaled a clean lungful and jettisoned the ripe trays.

Then he crawled back in to search. On every staging the photosynthetic algae were starting to clump, coagulating to the lichen-like symbiote that was phage. Not one clean tray.

In hours *Ragnarok* would have no more air.

But he and Topanga wouldn't care. They'd be through the walls in phagefreak long before.

He was well and truly shafted now.

He flushed some oxy into the ventilators and kicked back to the bridge. Get some clean metabolite or die.

Who would give him air? Even if he could move *Ragnarok*, the company depots and franchises would be alerted. He might just as well signal Coronis and give himself up. Maybe Quine wouldn't bother to reach him and Topanga in time. Maybe better so. Wards. Wires.

Topanga groaned. Gollem felt her temples. Hot as plasma, old ladies with a leg shortened shouldn't play war. He rummaged out biogens, marveling at the vials, ampoules, tabs, hyposprays. Popping who knew what to keep alive. Contraband she and Val had picked up in the old free days, her hoard would stock a –

Wait a minute.

Medbase Themis.

He tuned up *Ragnarok*'s board. The Themis woman was still calling, low and hoarse. He cranked the antennae for the narrowest beam he could get.

'Medbase Themis, do you read?'

'Who are you? Who's there?' She was startled out of her code book.

'This is a spacesweep mission. I have a casualty.'

'Where –' The male voice took over.

'This is Chief Medic Kranz, spacer. You can bring in your casualty but we have a rogue headed through our space with a gravel cloud. If we can't get power to move the station in about thirty hours we'll be holed out. Can you help us?'

'You can have what I've got. Check coordinates.'

The woman choked up on the decimals. No use telling them he couldn't do them any good. The gee-sum unit he had in *Ragnarok* wouldn't nudge that base in time for Halley's comet. And *Ragnarok*'s drive – if it worked it would be like trying to wipe your eye with a blowtorch.

But their air could help him.

The drive. He bounced down the engineway, knowing the spring in his muscles was partly phage. Only partly. A thousand times he had come this way, a thousand times torn himself away from temptation. Gleefully now he began to check out the circuits he had traced, restored the long-pulled fuses. There was a sealed hypergolic reserve for ignition. A stupefying conversion process, a plumber's nightmare of heat-exchangers and back-cycling. Crazy, wasteful, dangerous. Enough circuitry to wire the Belt. Unbelievable it had carried man to Saturn, more unbelievable it would work today.

He clanked the rod controls. No telling what had crystallized. The converter fuel chutes jarred out thirty years' accumulated dust. The ignition reserve was probably only designed for one emergency firing. Would he be able to ignite again to brake? Learn as you go. One thing sure, when that venerable metal volcano burst to life every board from here to Coronis would be lit.

When he got back to the bridge Topanga was whispering.

'*We left the haven hanging in the night – O thou steel cognizance whose leap commits –*'

'Pray it leaps,' he told her and began setting course, double-checking everything because of the phagemice running in the shadows. He wrapped Topanga's webs.

He started the ignition train.

The subsonic rumble that grew through *Ragnarok* filled him with terror and delight. He threw himself into the webs, wishing he had said something, counted down maybe. Blastoff. *Go.* The rumble bloomed into an oremill roar. Gees smashed down on him. Everything in the cabin started raining on the deck. The web gave sideways and the roar wound up in a scream that parted his brain and then dwindled into silence.

When he struggled back to the board he found the burn had cut right. *Ragnarok* was barreling toward Themis. He saw Topanga's eyes open.

'Where are we headed?' She sounded sane as soap.

'I'm taking you over to the next sector, Themis. We need metabolite, oxygen. The phagers ruined your regenerators.'

'Themis?'

'There's a medbase there. They'll give us some.'

Mistake.

'Oh, no – no!' She struggled up. 'No, Golly! I won't go to a hospital – don't let them take me!'

'You're not going to a hospital, Topanga. You're going to stay right here in the ship while I go in for the cores. They'll never know about you. We'll be out of there in minutes.'

No use.

'God hate you, Gollem.' She made an effort to spit. 'You're trying to trap me. I know you! Never let me free. You won't bury me here, Gollem. Rot in Moondome with your ugly cub – I'm going to Val!'

'Cool, spacer, you're yawing.' He got some tranks into her finally and went back to learning *Ragnarok*. The phage was getting strong now. When he looked up the holographs were watching him drive their ship. The old star heroes. Val Orlov, Fitz, Hannes, Mura, all the great ones. Sometimes only a grin behind a gold-washed headplate, a name on a suit beside some mad hunk of machine. Behind them, spacelost wildernesses lit by unknown moons. All alive, all so young. There was Topanga with her arm around that other spacegirl, the dark Russian one who was still orbiting Io. They grinned past him, bright and living.

When they start talking, we've had it . . .

He set the gyros to crank *Ragnarok* into what he hoped was attitude for the retro burn. If he could trust the dials, there was enough ignition for braking and for one last burn to get out of there. But where would he go from Medbase? Into the sky with diamonds . . .

He heard himself humming and decided to lock the whole thing into autopilot. No matter what shape that computer was in it would be saner than he was.

Have you seen your mother, baby, standing in the shadows? . . .

When he began hearing the Stones he went down and threw out half the trays. The three remaining oxy tanks struck him as hilarious. He cracked one.

The oxy sobered him enough to check the weather signal. The Medbase woman was still trying to raise Themis Main. He resisted the impulse to enlighten her about the Companies and concentrated on the updated orbits of the Trojan rogues. He saw now what had Medbase sweating. The lead rogue would miss them by megamiles but it was massive enough to have stirred up a lot of gravel. The small rogue behind was sweeping up a tail. The rock itself would go by far off – but that gravel cloud would rip their bubbles to shreds.

He had to get in there and out again fast.

He sniffed some more oxy and computed the rogue orbits on a worst-contingency basis. It looked O K – for him. His stomach flinched; even under phage it had an idea what it was going to be like when those medics found out they were wasted.

He saw Topanga grinning. The phage was doing her more good than the tranks.

'Not to worry, star girl. Golly won't let 'em get you.'

'Air.' She was trying to point to life-support, which had long since gone red.

'I know, spacer. We're getting air at Medbase.'

She gave him a strange un-Topanga smile. 'Whatever you say, little Golly.' Whispering hoarsely, 'I know – you've been beautiful –'

Her hand reached, burning. This he positively could not take. Too bad his music was gone.

'Give us verses as we go, star girl.'

But she was too weak.

'Read me –'

Her scanner was full of it.

'*In oil-rinsed circles of blind ecstasy.*' Hard to dig, until the strobing letters suddenly turned to music in his throat. '*Man hears himself an engine in a cloud!*' he chanted, convoyed by ghosts.

'*– What marathons new-set among the stars! . . . The soul, by naphtha fledged into new reaches, already knows the closer clasp of Mars –*'

. . . It was indeed fortunate, he discovered, that he had set the autopilot and stayed suited up.

His first clear impression of Medbase was a chimpanzee's big brown eyes staring into his under a flashprobe. He jerked away, found himself peeled and tied on a table. The funny feeling was the luxury of simulated gravity. The chimpanzee turned out to be a squat little type in medwhites, who presently freed him.

'I told you he wasn't a phager.' It was the woman's voice.

Craning, Gollem saw she was no girl-girl and had a remarkable absence of chin. The chimpanzee eventually introduced himself as Chief Medic Kranz.

'What kind of ship *is* that?' the woman asked as he struggled into his suit.

'A derelict,' he told them. 'Phage-runners were using it. My teammate's stoned. All he needs is air.'

'The power units,' said Kranz. 'I'll help you bring them over.'

'No need for you to go in – I've got them ready to go. Just give me a couple of metabolite cores to take back to start the air cleaning.'

Unsuspicious, Kranz motioned the woman to show the way to their stores. Gollem saw that their base was one big cheap bubble behind a hard-walled control module. The molly hadn't even seamed together under the film; a couple of pebbles would finish them. The ward had twenty-odd burn cases in cocoons. Themis didn't bother much with burns.

An old spacerat minus a lot of his original equipment came wambling over to open up. Gollem loaded as much metabolite as he could carry and headed for the lock. At the port the woman grabbed his arm.

'You *will* help us?' Her eyes were deep green. Gollem concentrated on her chin.

'Be right back.' He cycled out.

Ragnarok was on a tether he didn't recall securing. He scrambled over, found the end fouled in the lock toggles. If there had been tumble – bye-bye.

When he got inside he heard Topanga's voice. He hustled up the shaft.

Once again he was too late.

While he'd been in the stores unsuspicious Chief Medic Kranz had suited up and beat him into *Ragnarok*.

'This is a very sick woman, spacer,' he informed Gollem.

'The legal owner of this derelict, doctor. I'm taking her to Coronis Base.'

'I'm taking her into my ward right now. We have the facilities. Get those power units.'

He could see Topanga's eyes close.

'She doesn't wish to be hospitalized.'

'She's in no condition to decide that,' Kranz snapped.

The metabolite was on board. Doctor Chimpanzee Kranz appeared to have elected himself a driveship ride to nowhere. Gollem began drifting toward the ignition panel, beside Topanga's web.

'I guess you're right, sir. I'll help you prepare her and we'll take her in.'

But Kranz's little hand had a little stungun in it.

'The power units, spacer.' He waved Gollem toward the shaft.

There weren't any power units.

Gollem backed into the metabolite, watching for the stunner to waver. It didn't. There was only one chance left, if you could call it a chance.

'Topanga, this good doctor is going to take you into his hospital,' he said loudly. 'He wants you where he can take good care of you.'

335

One of Topanga's eyelids wrinkled, sagged down again. An old, battered woman. No chance.

'Can you handle her, doctor?'

'Get that power *now*.' Kranz snapped the safety off.

Gollem nodded sourly and started downshaft as slowly as he could. Kranz came over to watch him, efficiently out of reach. What now? Gollem couldn't reach the ignition circuits from here even if he knew how to short them.

Just as he turned around to look for something to fake a power cell it happened.

A whomp like an imploding mollybubble smacked into the shaft. Chief Medic Kranz sailed down in a slow cartwheel.

'Good girl!' Gollem yelled. 'You got him!' He batted the stunner out of Kranz's limp glove and kicked upward. When his head cleared the shaft he found he was looking into the snout of Topanga's jolter.

'Get out of my ship,' she rasped. 'You lying suitlouse. And take your four-eyed, needle-sucking friend with you!'

'Topanga, it's me – it's Golly –'

'I know who you are,' she said coldly. 'You'll never trap me.'

'Topanga!' he cried. A bolt went by his ear, rocking him.

'Out!' She was leaning down the shaft, squeezing on the jolter.

Gollem backed slowly down, collecting Kranz. The witch figure above him streamed biotape and bandages, the hair that once shone red standing up like white fire. She must be breathing pure phage, he thought.

Can't last long. All I have to do is go slow.

'Out!' she screamed. Then he saw she had Kranz's oxy tube clamped under one arm. This seemed to be his day for underestimating people.

'Topanga,' he began to plead and had to dodge another jolt-bolt. She couldn't go on missing forever. He decided to haul Kranz out and cut back into the ship through the emergency port. He recalled seeing a welding torch in the Medbase port rack.

He boosted Kranz along the tether and into the medbase lock. The woman was waiting on the other side. As the port opened he pushed Kranz at her and grabbed the welder. The chinless wonder learned fast – she flung herself on the welder and started to wrestle. There was solid woman-muscle under her whites, but he got a fist where her jaw should have been and threw himself back into the lock.

As it started to cycle he realized she had probably saved his life.

The outer lock had a viewport through which he could see *Ragnarok*'s vents. The starfield behind them was dissolving.

He let out an inarticulate groan and slammed the reverse cycle to let himself back into Medbase. As soon as it cracked he bolted through, carrying the medics to the deck. The port behind him lit up like a solar flare.

They all stared at the silent torrent of flame pouring out of *Ragnarok*. Then she was moving, faster, faster yet. The jetstream swung and the port went black.

'It's burning! Get the foam!'

Kranz grabbed a sealant cannister and they raced to the edge of the hardwall area where *Ragnarok*'s exhaust had seared the bubble. When the burns were sealed the ship was a dwindling firetail among the stars.

'Topanga doesn't like hospitals,' Gollem told them.

'The power units!' Kranz said urgently. 'Call her back!'

They were pushing Gollem toward the commo board.

'No way. She just blew the last ignition charge. Where she's headed now she goes.'

'What do you mean? To Coronis?'

'Never.' He rubbed his shaggy head. 'I – I don't recall exactly. Mars, maybe the sun.'

'With the power units that would have saved these people.' Kranz's face had the expression he probably used on gangrene. 'Thanks to you. I suggest that you remove yourself from my sight for the remainder of our joint existence.'

'There never were any power units,' Gollem said, starting to go out. 'The phagers got my boat and you saw for yourself what that drive was like. Her acceleration would have broken you apart.'

The woman followed him out.

'Who was she, spacer?'

'Topanga Orlov,' Gollem said painfully. 'Val Orlov's wife. They were the first Saturn mission. That was their ship, *Ragnarok*. She was holed up in my sector.'

'You just wanted air.'

Gollem nodded.

They were by the base display tank. The computer was running a real-time display of the oncoming Trojans. The green blip was Medbase and the red blip with the smear was the smaller Trojan and attendant gravel tail. He studied the vectors. No doubt.

It was now dark-period. Sleep time coming up. The people here might eat breakfast, but for true they wouldn't each lunch. By noon or thereabouts Medbase would be organic enrichment on a swarm of space ice.

So would ex-Inspector Gollem.

The two medics went out on the wards and Kranz unbent enough to accept Gollem's offer to man the commo board. The spacer wobbled in to watch him. The sight of *Ragnarok*'s blast-out had lit his fires.

Gollem taped a routine red-call and began to hunt across the bands. The old man mumbled about ships. Nobody was answering, nobody would. Once Gollem thought he heard an echo from Topanga, but it was nothing. Her oxy must be long gone by now, he thought. A mad old phage-ghost on her last trip. Where had he computed her to? He seemed to recall something about Mars. At least they wouldn't end in some trophy-hunter's plastic park.

'You know what they got in them cocoons? Squatters!' The old man squinted out of his good side to see how Gollem took this. 'Skinheads. Freaks 'n' crotties. Phagers, even. Medics, they don't care.' He sighed, scratched his burned skin with his stump. 'Grounders. They won't last out here.'

'Too right,' Gollem agreed. 'Like maybe tomorrow.' That tickled the old man.

Toward midnight Kranz took over. The woman brought in some hot redeye. Gollem started to refuse and then realized his stomach wasn't hurting any more. Nothing to worry about now. He sipped the stimulant. The woman was looking at a scanner.

'She was beautiful,' she murmured.

'Knock it off, Anna,' Kranz snapped.

She went on scanning and suddenly caught her breath.

'Your name. It's Gollem, isn't it?'

Gollem nodded and got up to go look at the tank.

Presently the woman Anna came out after him and looked at the tank too. The old spacer was asleep in the corner.

'Topanga was married to a George Gollem once,' Anna said quietly. 'They had a son. On Luna.'

Gollem took the scanner cartridge out of her hand and flipped it into the wastechute. She said nothing more. They both watched the tank for a while. Gollem noticed that her eyes were almost good enough to make up for her chin. She didn't look at him. The tank didn't change.

Around four she went in and took over from Kranz and the men settled down to wait.

'Medbase Themis calling, please come in. Medbase Themis calling anyone,' the woman whispered monotonously.

Kranz went out. It seemed a lot of work to breathe.

Suddenly Kranz snapped his fingers from the next room. Gollem went to him.

'Look.'

They hung over the tank. The red smear was closer to the green blip. Between them was a yellow spark.

'What is that?'

Gollem shrugged. 'A rock.'

'Impossible, we scan-swept that area a dozen times.'

'No mass,' Gollem frowned. 'It's a tank ghost.'

Kranz began systematically flushing the computer input checks. The woman left the board and came to lean

over the tank. Gollem watched absently, his brain picking at phage-warped memories. Something about the
computer.

On impulse he went to the commo board and ran the
receiver through its limits. All he got was a blast of squeals
and whistles, the stress-front of the incoming rocks.

'What is it?' Anna's eyes were phosphorescent.

'Nothing.'

Kranz finished his checks. The yellow ghost stayed
in, sidling toward the red smear. If that were a rock, and
it had about a hundred times more mass than it could
have, it just might deflect the Trojan's gravel swarm. But
it didn't.

Gollem played monotonously with the board. The old
spacer snored. The minutes congealed. Kranz shook himself, took Anna out to tour the wards. When they came
back they stopped at the tank.

The whatever-it-was stayed in, closing on the Trojan.

Sometime in the unreal dimlight hours Gollem caught
it, wavering on a gale of space noise:

I have contact! Val! I'm coming –'

They crowded around him as he coaxed the tuners
but there was nothing there. Presently a ripple of relays
tripped off in the next room and they all ran to the tank.
It was dead; the computer had protected itself against an
induction overload.

They never knew exactly what happened.

'It's possible,' Gollem admitted to them. It was long
after noon when they decided to eat.

'While we were on the way here I know I computed
that Trojan all the way to Medbase, before I got really

bombed. Maybe I threw a bridge into the course computer, maybe it was already in. Say she took off with no course setting. Those old mechs are set to hunt. It's possible it inverted and boosted straight back out that trajectory to the rock.'

'But your ship had no mass,' Kranz objected.

'That thing was a space-scoop feeding a monster drive. The pile dampers were cheese. *Ragnarok* could have scooped herself solid right through the gravel cloud and blown as she hit the Trojan. You could get a pocket sun.'

They went over it again at dark-period. And again later while he and Anna looked at nothing in particular out the ports. A long time after that he showed her a script he'd fixed for the wall of Medbase Free Enclave:

> *Launched in abyssal cupolas of space*
> *Toward endless terminas, Easters of speeding light –*
> *Vast engines outward veering with seraphic grace*
> *On clarion cylinders pass out of sight*

*   *   *

Nobody seems to have noticed that Hart Crane really was the first space poet; he envisioned space-flight with only the first planes of the 1920s as evidence. The quotes here are from the full text of THE BRIDGE, of which only snippets appear in most anthologies. Crane suicided in 1932. Poets extrapolate.

– The Author

Beam Us Home

Hobie's parents might have seen the first signs if they been watching about 8:30 on Friday nights. But Hobie was the youngest of five active bright-normal kids. Who was to notice one more uproar around the TV?

A couple of years later Hobie's Friday-night battles shifted to 10 p.m. and then his sisters got their own set. Hobie was growing fast then. In public he featured chiefly as a tanned streak on the tennis courts and a ninety-ninth percentile series of math grades. To his parents, Hobie featured as the one without problems. This was hard to avoid in a family that included a diabetic, a girl with an IQ of 185 and another with controllable petit mal, and a would be ski star who spent most of his time in a cast. Hobie's own IQ was in the fortunate one-forties, the range where you're superior enough to lead, but not too superior to be followed. He seemed perfectly satisfied with his communications with his parents, but he didn't use them much.

Not that he was in any way neglected when the need arose. The time he got staph in a corneal scratch, for instance, his parents did a great job of supporting him through the pain bit and the hospital bit and so on. But they couldn't know all the little incidents. Like the night when Hobie called so fiercely for Dr McCoy that a young intern named McCoy went in and joked for half an hour with the feverish boy in his dark room.

To the end, his parents probably never understood that there was anything to understand about Hobie. And what was to see? His tennis and his model rocket collection made him look almost too normal for the small honors school he went to first.

Then his family moved to an executive bedroom suburb where the school system had a bigger budget than Monaco and a soccer team loaded with National Merit Science finalists. Here Hobie blended right in with the scenery. One more healthy, friendly, polite kid with bright gray eyes under a blond bowl-cut and very fast with any sort of ball game.

The brightest eyes around him were reading *The Double Helix* to find out how to make it in research, or marking up the Dun & Bradstreet flyers. If Hobie stood out at all, it was only that he didn't seem to be worried about making it in research or any other way, particularly. But that fitted in, too. Those days a lot of boys were standing around looking as if they couldn't believe what went on, as if they were waiting for – who knows? – a better world, their glands, something. Hobie's faintly aghast expression was not unique. Events like the installation of an armed patrol around the school enclave were bound to have a disturbing effect on the more sensitive kids.

People got the idea that Hobie *was* sensitive in some indefinite way. His usual manner was open but quiet, tolerant of a put-on that didn't end.

His advisor did fret over his failure to settle on a major

field in time for the oncoming threat of college. First his math interest seemed to evaporate after the special calculus course, although he never blew an exam. Then he switched to the pre-college anthropology panel the school was trying. Here he made good grades and acted very motivated, until the semester when the visiting research team began pounding on sampling techniques and statistical significance. Hobie had no trouble with things like Chi square, of course. But after making his A in the final he gave them his sweet, unbelieving smile and faded. His advisor found him spending a lot of hours polishing a six-inch telescope lens in the school shop.

So Hobie was tagged as some kind of an under-achiever, but nobody knew what kind because of those grades. And something about that smile bothered them; it seemed to stop sound.

The girls liked him, though, and he went through the usual phases rather fast. There was the week he and various birds went to thirty-five drive-in movies. And the month he went around humming *Mrs Robinson* in a mean-ingful way. And the warm, comfortable summer when he and his then girl and two other couples went up to Stratford, Ontario with sleeping bags to see the Czech multimedia thing.

Girls regarded him as different although he never knew why. 'You look at me like it's always good-bye,' one of them told him. Actually he treated girls with an odd detached gentleness, as though he knew a secret that might make them all disappear. Some of them hung around because of his quick brown hands or his really great looks, some because they hoped to share the secret. In this they were disappointed. Hobie talked, and he listened carefully, but it wasn't the mutual talk-talk-talk of total catharsis that most couples went through. But how could Hobie know that?

Like most of his peer group, Hobie stayed away from heavies and agreed that pot was preferable to getting juiced. His friends never crowded him too much after the beach party where he spooked everybody by talking excitedly for hours to people who weren't there. They decided he might have a vulnerable ego-structure.

The official high-school view was that Hobie had no real problems. In this they were supported by a test battery profile that could have qualified him as the ideal normal control. Certainly there was nothing to get hold of in his routine interviews with the high-school psychologist.

Hobie came in after lunch, a time when Dr Morehouse knew he was not at his most intuitive. They went through the usual openers. Hobie sitting easily, patient and interested, with an air of listening to some sound back of the acoustical ceiling tiles.

'I meet a number of young people involved in discovering who they really are. Searching for their own identities,' Morehouse offered. He was idly trueing up a stack of typing headed *Sex differences in the adolescent identity crisis*.

'Do you?' Hobie asked politely.

Morehouse frowned at himself and belched disarmingly.

'Sometimes I wonder who *I* am,' he smiled.

'Do you?' inquired Hobie.

'Don't you?'

'No,' said Hobie.

Morehouse reached for the hostility that should

have been there, found it wasn't. Not passive aggression. What? His intuition awoke briefly. He looked into Hobie's light hazel eyes and suddenly found himself slipping toward some very large uninhabited dimension. A real pubescent preschiz, he wondered hopefully? No again, he decided, and found himself thinking, what if a person is sure of his identity but it isn't his identity? He often wondered that; perhaps it could be worked up into a creative insight.

'Maybe it's the other way around,' Hobie was saying before the pause grew awkward.

'How do you mean?'

'Well, maybe you're all wondering who you are.' Hobie's lips quirked; it was clear he was just making conversation.

'I asked for that,' Morehouse chuckled. They chatted about sibling rivalry and psychological statistics and wound up in plenty of time for Morehouse's next boy, who turned out to be a satisfying High Anx. Morehouse forgot about the empty place he had slid into. He often did that too.

It was a girl who got part of it out of Hobie, at three in the morning. 'Dog' she was called then, although her name was Jane. A tender, bouncy little bird who cocked her head to listen up at him in a way Hobie liked. Dog would listen with the same soft intensity to the supermarket clerk and the pediatrician later on, but neither of them knew that.

They had been talking about the state of the world, which was then quite prosperous and peaceful. That is to say, about seventy million people were starving to death, a number of advanced nations were maintaining themselves on police terror tactics, four or five borders were being fought over, Hobie's family's maid had just been cut up by the suburban peacekeeper squad, and the school had added a charged wire and two dogs to its patrol. But none of the big nations were waving fissionables, and the US-Sino-Soviet détente was a twenty-year reality.

Dog was holding Hobie's head over the side of her car because he had been the one who found the maid crawling on her handbones among the azaleas.

'If you feel like that, why don't you do something?' Dog asked him between spasms. 'Do you want some Slurp? It's all we've got.'

'Do what?' Hobie quavered.

'Politics?' guessed Dog. She really didn't know. The Protest Decade was long over, along with the New Politics and Ralph Nader. There was a school legend about a senior who had come back from Miami with a busted collarbone. Some time after that the kids had discovered that flowers weren't really very powerful, and that movement organizers had their own bag. Why go on the street when you could really do more in one of the good jobs available Inside? So Dog could offer only a vague image of Hobie running for something, a sincere face on TV.

'You could join the Young Statesmen.'

'Not to interfere,' gasped Hobie. He wiped his mouth. Then he pulled himself together and tried some of the Slurp. In the dashlight his seventeen-year-old sideburns struck Dog as tremendously mature and beautiful.

'Oh, it's not so bad,' said Hobie. 'I mean, it's not *unusually* bad. It's just a stage. This world is going through a primitive stage. There's a lot of stages. It takes a long time. They're just very very backward, that's all.'

'They,' said Dog, listening to every word.

'I mean,' he said.

'You're alienated,' she told him. 'Rinse your mouth out with that. You don't relate to people.'

'I think you're people,' he said, rinsing. He'd heard this before. 'I relate to you,' he said. He leaned out to spit. Then he twisted his head to look up at the sky and stayed that way awhile, like an animal's head sticking out of a crate. Dog could feel him trembling the car.

'Are you going to barf again?' she asked.

'No.'

But then suddenly he did, roaringly. She clutched at his shoulders while he heaved. After awhile he sagged down, his head lolling limply out on one arm.

'It's such a mess,' she heard him whispering. 'It's such a shitting miserable mess mess mess MESS MESS –'

He was pounding his hand on the car side.

'I'll hose it,' said Dog, but then she saw he didn't mean the car.

'Why does it have to go on and on?' he croaked. 'Why don't they just *stop* it? I can't bear it much longer, please, please, I can't –'

Dog was scared now.

'Honey, it's not that bad. Hobie honey, it's not that bad,' she told him, patting at him, pressing her soft front against his back.

Suddenly he came back into the car on top of her, spent.

'It's unbearable,' he muttered.

'What's unbearable?' she snapped, mad at him for

349

scaring her. 'What's unbearable for you and not for me? I mean, I know it's a mess, but why is it so bad for *you*? I have to live here too.'

'It's your world,' he told her absently, lost in some private desolation.

Dog yawned.

'I better drive you home now,' she said.

He had nothing more to say and sat quietly. When Dog glanced at his profile she decided he looked calm. Almost stupid, in fact; his mouth hung open a little. She didn't recognize the expression, because she had never seen people looking out of cattle cars.

Hobie's class graduated that June. His grades were well up, and everybody understood that he was acting a little unrelated because of the traumatic business with the maid. He got a lot of sympathy.

It was after the graduation exercises that Hobie surprised his parents for the first and last time. They had been congratulating themselves on having steered their fifth offspring safely through the college crisis and into a high-status Eastern. Hobie announced that he had applied for the United States Air Force Academy.

This was a bomb, because Hobie had never shown the slightest interest in things military. Just the opposite, really. Hobie's parents took it for granted that the educated classes viewed the military with tolerant distaste. Why did their son want this? Was it another of his unstable motivational orientations?

But Hobie persisted. He didn't have any reasons, he had just thought carefully and felt that this was for him. Finally they recalled that early model rocket collection;

his father decided he was serious, and began sorting out the generals his research firm did business with. In September Hobie disappeared into Colorado Springs. He reappeared for Christmas in the form of an exotically hairless, erect and polite stranger in uniform.

During the next four years Hobie the person became effectively invisible behind a growing pile of excellent evaluation reports. There seemed to be no doubt that he was working very hard, and his motivation gave no sign of flagging. Like any cadet, he bitched about many of the Academy's little ways and told some funny stories. But he never seemed discouraged. When he elected to spend his summers in special aviation skills training, his parents realized that Hobie had found himself.

Enlightenment – of a sort – came in his senior year when he told them he had applied for and been accepted into the new astronaut training program. The US space program was just then starting up again after the revulsion caused by the tragic loss of the manned satellite lab ten years before.

'I bet that's what he had in mind all along,' Hobie's father chuckled. 'He didn't want to say so before he made it.' They were all relieved. A son in the space program was a lot easier to live with, status-wise.

When she heard the news, Dog, who was now married and called herself Jane, sent him a card with a picture of the Man in the Moon. Another girl, more percipient, sent him a card showing some stars.

But Hobie never made it to the space program.

It was the summer when several not-very-serious events happened all together. The British devalued their wobbly pound again, just when it was found that far too many dollars were going out of the States. North and South Korea moved a step closer to reunion, which generated a call for strengthening the US contribution to the remains of SEATO. Next there was an expensive, though luckily non-lethal, fire at Kennedy, and the Egyptians announced a new Soviet aid pact. And in August it was discovered that the Guévarrista rebels in Venezuela were getting some very unpleasant-looking hardware from their Arab allies.

Contrary to the old saying that nations never learn from history, the US showed that it had learned from its long agony in Viet Nam. What it had learned was not to waste time messing around with popular elections and military advisory and training programs, but to ball right in. Hard.

When the dust cleared, the space program and astronaut training were dead on the pad and a third of Hobie's graduating class was staging through Caracas. Technically, he had volunteered.

He found this out from the task force medico.

'Look at it this way, lieutenant. By entering the Academy, you volunteered for the Air Force, right?'

'Yes. But I opted for the astronaut program. The Air Force is the only way you can get in. And I've been accepted.'

'But the astronaut program has been suspended. Temporarily, of course. Meanwhile the Air Force – for which you volunteered – has an active requirement for your training. You can't expect them just to let you sit around until the program resumes, can you? Moreover you have been given the very best option available. Good God, man, the Volunteer Airpeace Corps is considered a super elite. You should see the fugal depressions we have to cope with among men who have been rejected for the VAC.'

'Mercenaries,' said Hobie. 'Regressive.'

'Try "professional", it's a better word. Now – about those headaches.'

The headaches eased up some when Hobie was assigned to long-range sensor recon support. He enjoyed the work of flying, and the long, calm, lonely sensor missions were soothing. They were also quite safe. The Guévarristas had no air strength to waste on recon planes and the UAR. SAM sites were not yet operational. Hobie flew the pattern, and waited zombie-like for the weather, and flew again. Mostly he waited, because the fighting was developing in a steamy jungle province where clear sensing was a sometime thing. It was poorly mapped. The ground troops could never be sure about the little brown square men who gave them so much trouble, on one side of an unknown line they were Guévarristas who should be obliterated, and on the other side they were legitimate national troops warning the blancos away. Hobie's recon tapes were urgently needed, and for several weeks he was left alone.

Then he began to get pulled up to a forward strip for one-day chopper duty when their tactical duty roster was disrupted by geegee. But this was relatively peaceful too, being mostly defoliant spray missions. Hobie in fact put in several months without seeing, hearing, smelling or feeling the war at all. He would have been grateful for this if he had realized it. As it was he seemed to be trying not to realize anything much. He spoke very little, did his work and moved like a man whose head might fall off if he jostled anything.

Naturally he was one of the last to hear the rumours about geegee when they filtered back to the coastal base, where Hobie was quartered with the long-range stuff. Gegee's proper name was Guairas Grippe. It was developing into a severe problem in the combat zone. More and more replacements and relief crews were being called forward for temporary tactical duty. On Hobie's next trip in, he couldn't help but notice that people were acting pretty haggard, and the roster was all scrawled up with changes. When they were on course he asked about it.

'Are you kidding?' his gunner grunted.

'No. What is it?'

'BW.'

'What?'

'Bacteriological weapon, skyhead. They keep promising us vaccines. Stuck in their zippers – look out, there's a ground burst.'

They held Hobie up front for another mission, and another after that, and then they told him that a sector quarantine was now in force.

The official notice said that movement of personnel between sectors would be reduced to a minimum as a temporary measure to control the spread of respiratory ailments. Translation: you could go from the support zone to the front, but you couldn't go back.

Hobie was moved into a crowded billet and assigned to Casualty and Supply. Shortly he discovered that there was a translation for respiratory ailments too. Geegee turned out to be a multiform misery of groin rash, sore throat, fever and unending trots. It didn't seem to become really acute, it just cycled along. Hobie was one of those who was only lightly affected, which was lucky because the hospital beds were full. So were the hospital aisles. Evacuation of all casualties had been temporarily suspended until a controlled corridor could be arranged.

The Gués did not, it seemed, get geegee. The ground troops were definitely sure of that. Nobody knew how it was spread. Rumor said it was bats one week, and then the next week they were putting stuff in the water. Poisoned arrows, roaches, women, disintegrating cannisters, all had their advocates. However it was done, it was clear that the UAR technological aid had included more than hardware. The official notice about a forthcoming vaccine yellowed on the board.

Ground fighting was veering closer to Hobie's strip. He heard mortars now and then, and one night the Gués ran in a rocket launcher and nearly got the fuel dump before they were chased back.

'All they got to do is wait,' said the gunner. 'We're dead.'

'Geegee doesn't kill you,' said C/S control. 'You just wish it did.'

'They say.'

The strip was extended, and three attack bombers came in. Hobie looked them over. He had trained on AX92's all one summer; he could fly them in his sleep. It would be nice to be alone.

He was pushing the C/S chopper most of the daylight

hours now. He had got used to being shot at and being sick. Everybody was sick, except a couple of replacement crews who were sent in two weeks apart, looking startlingly healthy. They said they had been immunized with a new antitoxin. Their big news was that geegee could be cured outside the zone.

'We're getting reinfected,' the gunner said.

'That figures. They want us out of here.'

That week there was a big drive on bats, but it didn't help. The next week the first batch of replacements were running fevers. Their shots hadn't worked and neither did the stuff they gave the second batch.

After that, no more men came in except a couple of volunteer medicos. The billets and the planes and the mess were beginning to stink. That dysentery couldn't be controlled after you got weak.

What they did get was supplies. Every day or so another ton of stuff would drift down. Most of it was dragged to one side and left to rot. They were swimming in food. The staggering cooks pushed steak and lobster at men who shivered and went out to retch. The hospital even had ample space now, because it turned out that geegee really did kill you in the end. By that time you were glad to go. A cemetery developed at the far side of the strip, among the skeletons of the defoliated trees.

On the last morning Hobie was sent out to pick up a forward scout team. He was one of the few left with enough stamina for long missions. The three-man team was far into Gué territory, but Hobie didn't care. All he was thinking about was his bowels. So far he had not fouled himself or his plane. When he was down by their signal be bolted out to squat under the chopper's tail. The grunts climbed in, yelling at him.

They had a prisoner with them. The Gué was naked and astonishingly broad. He walked springily; his arms were lashed with wire and a shirt was tied over his head. This was the first Gué Hobie had been close to. As he got in he saw how the Gué's firm brown flesh glistened and bulged around the wire. He wished he could see his face. The gunner said the Gué was a Sirionó, and this was important because the Sirionós were not known to be with the Gués. They were a very primitive nomadic tribe.

When Hobie began to fly home he realized he was getting sicker. It became a fight to hold onto consciousness and keep on course. Luckily nobody shot at them. At one point he became aware of a lot of screaming going on behind him, but couldn't pay attention. Finally he came over the strip and horsed the chopper down. He let his head down on his arms.

'You OK?' asked the gunner.

'Yeah,' said Hobie, hearing them getting out. They were moving something heavy. Finally he got up and followed them. The floor was wet. That wasn't unusual. He got down and stood staring in, the floor a foot under his nose. The wet stuff was blood. It was sprayed around, with one big puddle. In the puddle was something soft and fleshy-looking.

Hobie turned his head. The ladder was wet. He held up one hand and looked at the red. His other hand too. Holding them out stiffly he turned and began to walk away across the strip.

Control, who still hoped to get an evening flight out of him, saw him fall and called the hospital, The two replacement parameds were still in pretty good shape. They came out and picked him up.

When Hobie came to, one of the parameds was tying his hands down to the bed so he couldn't tear the IV out again.

'We're going to die here,' Hobie told him.

The paramed looked noncommittal. He was a thin dark boy with a big Adam's apple.

'But I shall dine at journey's end with Landor and with Donne,' said Hobie. His voice was light and facile.

'Yeats,' said the paramed. 'Want some water?'

Hobie's eyes flickered. The paramed gave him some water.

'I really believed it, you know,' Hobie said chattily. 'I had it all figured out.' He smiled, something he hadn't done for a long time.

'Landor and Donne?' asked the medic. He unhooked the empty IV bottle and hung up a new one.

'Oh, it was pathetic, I guess,' Hobie said. 'It started out . . . I believed they were real, you know? Kirk, Spock, McCoy, all of them. And the ship. To this day, I swear . . . one of them talked to me once, I mean, he really did . . . I had it all figured out, they had me left behind as an observer.' Hobie giggled.

'They were coming back for me. It was secret. All I had to do was sort of fit in and observe. Like a report. One day they would come back and haul me up in that beam thing; maybe you know about that? And there I'd be back in real time where human beings were, where they were human. I wasn't really stuck here in the past. On a back-ward planet.'

The paramed nodded.

'Oh, I mean, I didn't really *believe* it, I knew it was just a show. But I did believe it, too. It was like *there*, in the background, underneath, no matter what was going on. They were coming for me. All I had to do was observe. And not to interfere. You know? Prime directive . . . of course after I grew up, I realized they weren't, I mean I realized consciously. So I was going to go to them. Somehow, somewhere. Out there . . . now I know. It re-ally isn't so. None of it. Never. There's nothing . . . now I know I'll die here.'

'Oh now,' said the paramed. He got up and started to take things away. His fingers were shaky.

'It's clean there,' said Hobie in a petulant voice. 'None of this shit. Clean and friendly. They don't torture people,' he explained, thrashing his head. 'They don't kill –' He slept. The paramed went away.

Somebody started to yell monotonously.

Hobie opened his eyes. He was burning up.

The yelling went on, became screaming. It was dusk. Footsteps went by, headed for the screaming. Hobie saw they had put him in a bed by the door.

Without his doing much about it the screaming seemed to be lifting him out of the bed, propelling him through the door. Air. He kept getting close-ups of his hands clutching things. Bushes, shadows. Something scratched him.

After a while the screaming was a long way behind him. Maybe it was only in his ears. He shook his head, felt himself go down onto boards. He thought he was in the cemetery.

'No,' he said. 'Please. Please no.' He got himself up, balanced, blundered on, seeking coolness.

The side of the plane felt cool. He plastered his hot body against it, patting it affectionately. It seemed to be quite dark now. Why was he inside with no lights? He tried the panel, the lights worked perfectly. Vaguely he noticed some yelling starting outside again. It ignited the screaming in his head. The screaming got very loud – loud – LOUD – and appeared to be moving him, which was good.

He came to above the overcast and climbing. The oxy-support tube was hitting him in the nose. He grabbed for the mask, but it wasn't there. Automatically, he had leveled off. Now he rolled and looked around.

Below him was a great lilac sea of cloud, with two mountains sticking through it, their western tips on fire. As he looked, they dimmed. He shivered, found he was wearing only sodden shorts. How had he got here? Somebody had screamed intolerably and he had run.

He flew along calmly, checking his board. No trouble except the fuel. Nobody serviced the AX92's any more. Without thinking about it, he began to climb again. His hands were a yard away and he was shivering but he felt clear. He reached up and found his headphones were in place; he must have put them on along with the rest of the drill. He clicked on. Voices rattled and roared at him. He switched off. Then he took off the headpiece and dropped it on the floor.

He looked around. 18,000, heading 88-05. He was over

the Atlantic. In front of him the sky was darkening fast. A pinpoint glimmer 10 o'clock high. Sirius, probably.

He thought about Sirius, trying to recall his charts. Then he thought about turning and going back down. Without paying much attention, he noticed he was crying with his mouth open.

Carefully he began feeding his torches and swinging the nose of his pod around and up. He brought it neatly to a point on Sirius. Up. Up. Behind him a great pale swing of contrail fell away above the lilac shadow, growing, towering to the tiny plane that climbed at its tip. Up. Up. The contrail cut off as the plane burst into the high cold dry.

As it did so Hobie's ears skewered and he screamed wildly. The pain quit; his drums had burst. Up! Now he was gasping for air, strangling. The great torches drove him up, up, over the curve of the world. He was hanging on the star. Up! The fuel gauges were knocking. Any second they would quit and he and the bird would be a falling stone. 'Beam us up, Scotty!' he howled at Sirius, laughing, coughing – coughing to death, as the torches faltered –

– And was still coughing as he sprawled on the shining resiliency under the arcing grids. He gagged, rolled, finally focused on a personage leaning toward him out of a complex chair. The personage had round eyes, a slitted nose and the start of a quizzical smile.

Hobie's head swiveled slowly. It was not the bridge of the *Enterprise*. There were no view-screens, only a View. And Lieutenant Uhura would have had trouble with the freeform flashing objects suspended in front of what appeared to be a girl wearing spots. The spots, Hobie made out, were fur.

Somebody who was not Bones McCoy was doing something to Hobie's stomach. Hobie got up a hand and touched the man's gleaming back. Under the mesh it was firm and warm. The man looked up, grinned; Hobie looked back at the captain.

'Do not have fear,' a voice was saying. It seemed to be coming out of a globe by the captain's console. 'We will tell you where you are.'

'I know where I am,' Hobie whispered. He drew a deep, sobbing breath.

'I'm HOME!' he yelled. Then he passed out.